I0772193

To Walk into the Sands

Sands of Nanterac
Book 1

To Walk into the Sands

D. Lambert

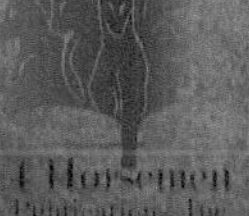
4 Horsemen
Publications, Inc.

To Walk into the Sands
Copyright © 2025 D. Lambert. All rights reserved.

4 Horsemen
Publications, Inc.

Published By: 4 Horsemen Publications, Inc.

4 Horsemen Publications, Inc.
PO Box 417
Sylva, NC 28779
4horsemenpublications.com
info@4horsemenpublications.com

Cover & Illustration by CD Corrigan
Typesetting by Autumn Skye
Edited by Joseph Mistretta

All rights to the work within are reserved to the author and publisher. No part of this publication may be reproduced, stored in a retrieval system, or transmitted in any form or by any means, electronic, mechanical, photocopying, recording, scanning, or otherwise, except as permitted under Section 107 or 108 of the 1976 International Copyright Act, without prior written permission except in brief quotations embodied in critical articles and reviews. Please contact either the Publisher or Author to gain permission.

All characters, organizations, and events portrayed in this novel are either products of the author's imagination or are used fictitiously. No generative artificial intelligence was used in the creation of this book or its cover.

All brands, quotes, and cited work respectfully belongs to the original rights holders and bear no affiliation to the authors or publisher.

Library of Congress Control Number: 2024952330

Paperback ISBN-13: 979-8-8232-0800-0
Hardcover ISBN-13: 979-8-8232-0801-7
Audiobook ISBN-13: 979-8-8232-0803-1
Ebook ISBN-13: 979-8-8232-0802-4

To Garrett. It's your fault for
filling my head with ideas!

CONTENTS

Part 1

CHAPTER 1

The drumbeat thundered through the sandstone streets, cleaving the air and piercing through Askaran's bones. People stopped in the red canopy shadows, assessing the rhythm.

In Askaran's mind, the demon sharpened its attention, identifying the signal instantly—*Danger.* An intruder in their territory. A chance for, perhaps, a bit of freedom.

The early-morning workers pulled their shawls low and retreated into the nearest buildings, no one checking which home they entered. It did not matter when the alarm sounded.

"A demon?" a light voice asked. At eight years old, the young seer holding Askaran's hand had not yet lost her wide-eyed curiosity. Her dark eyes stared up at him like a newborn ranna calf's, unafraid. "You need to go, Askaran."

"Get inside," he told her, leading her to the nearest door. After knocking on the post, the hide door flap pulled wide, and one of the baker families welcomed the seer. Askaran received a nod of understanding and respect from the father of the family.

"I'll meet you at the Sandstone Gate when you're done," the seer told Askaran. "Then we can go outside. We must go outside today."

The door fell shut, lashed against the wind, the sand, and the drums' warning.

"Never occurs to you that it might kill me," Askaran muttered. "Maybe you know it won't." No one else was around to appreciate the irony of that hope. The streets stayed deserted under the beat of the drums.

He swapped his earlier meander for a run, aiming for the nearest gate as required to present himself. It was the Sandstone Gate.

Askaran was second to arrive at the gate; a hound shifter by the name of Maurn was already atop the parapets overlooking the Sandstone Gate. The younger shifter stared at the figure on the edge of the Last City's surrounding pasture, his muscles tense despite how still he stood, making his white ink tattoo prominent.

Askaran joined him there, his eyes handling the distance better.

"Tusked demon," Askaran said, seeing the four long tusks extending from the maned head of the demon on the horizon. The beast swung its barbed tail, catching the low sunlight in a warning glint.

Askaran's own demon growled. Askaran consciously suppressed his desire to do the same.

Maurn swallowed audibly. "Nice to have you join me," he said. Two more shifters arrived—Berro and Morton—and Maurn relaxed further. In addition to the wool shendyts around their waists, both new arrivals wore woven collars of leather extending down their chest to act as light armor. A hound demon tattoo in white ink looked at Askaran from Berro's arm and from the shadow of the Heart Hall tattoo on Morton's back. Somewhere buried in those depictions were the original scars that had made them into shifters.

"Tusked, eh?" Berro asked, his voice gravelly from too much pipe smoke. "Arrogant bastards and rightly so. Where's Yarr? We'll need more…"

Choran's arrival silenced Berro, and the three hound shifters gave the other veteran space to join Askaran at the viewpoint.

Unlike Askaran, Choran carried no weapons. A hint of gray streaked the shifter's plaited hairstyle, mirroring Askaran's own. The scar from the winged demon that had wounded him stretched from his left hip, across his stomach, and to the middle of his ribs. As thick as a finger, the line of white looked like a turbulent river cutting through the dark forest of pale vines and leaf tattoos. A dozen smaller scars, souvenirs from other demons, decorated his chest and legs, leaving little skin bare. True to tradition, he had a small winged demon hidden in the foliage, but it was hard to make out.

"Good to see you, Choran," Askaran said, his eyes going back to the tusked demon that had taken its first steps into the irrigated lands around the City. "Going to need you on this one."

Choran squinted into the distance and harrumphed upon seeing the monster. He took to unlacing his sandals, then removed his shendyt. Nearby, the other three shifters stripped as well.

Askaran did not join them, but he did place his sack down on the wall walk.

"If it's tusked," Choran said, "we'd do well to have the rest of the—" The bellow of the monster passed through the City, sounding like an entire herd of ranna with one voice. Dust kicked up behind the demon as it lumbered out of the sands and into the farmlands closer to the City.

For a blink, Askaran's demon surged to the front of his mind in objection, and he saw red. Askaran focused on thinking like an Ennead and forced aside the rising rage; the closer the tusked demon came, the more the City was at risk. He could not allow a demon to jump the walls. Only shifters could resist the blood of demons.

"We can't wait for the others," he declared. The others heeded him and quickly left the vantage point.

Soon, the five stood outside, the sand-iron gates sealed at their backs. Each of the others had left their clothing behind and stood naked, Askaran alone in his shendyt, sandals, and kukris. The grip of the weapons was all too familiar.

Runners gathered with the watchmen on the ramparts above, having been called in from their duties outside by the drums. They lifted flags and banged the bone shafts against the walls, chanting, as the shifters passed through the gates. The thumps of their beat matched the stomping steps of the approaching demon, one beat for each footprint in their toiled lands, one beat for every second it drew closer.

Berro and Morton, old enough to be filled with anticipation of the battle and young enough to catch the excitement, shot each other a glance and hurried to shift.

The shifters' bodies changed, their normal ebony skin hardening to crimson scales and black fur. The head of the hound demon had no fur or skin but was an exposed white skull with a long snout and razor teeth. At the neck, the hackles along the spine came in as bone-white, like teeth set on each vertebra. The eyes glowed red within their sockets, the hallmark of a demon.

The runners above cheered, the chant becoming the names of the two who had shown their demons.

With a bark, both hound shifters trotted forward, their shoulders brushing close to Askaran's hip.

Choran shrugged, then shifted. The winged demon weighed twice as much as the hounds and had more scales than fur. Petrified bone, thinly covered by scales, stretched around his head in a fan angled to defend the demon's neck. Similar plates covered all the joints from the broad shoulders to the individual links of the tail. Two mammoth tusks extended on either side of his head. The faint lines of vines and leaves could still be seen tracing up the legs and thick-scaled torso.

The crowd screamed his name in building thrill, their beat accelerating.

Snorting, the winged demon loped forward, leaving Askaran and Maurn for a moment behind.

Askaran felt Maurn's eyes on him. "You'll warn us before you shift, right?" Maurn shouted. He looked nervously at the runners above. Some had reached a frenzy, hammering the bones without rhythm, as if their energy could lend strength and fortune to those chosen to fight. A runner's greatest asset was their speed; every last one was young. *Naïve*, Askaran thought.

Maurn became more agitated as the voices above grew in strength, not inspired but intimidated. His fear was obvious in his trembling.

Askaran gripped his kukris, knowing the runners would not call his name unless something went very wrong. The familiar wood of the weapon handles fit his hand perfectly. Within his mind, he placed a foot against the cage he had built around the colossus demon soul and held it firmly. "I'll give my usual scream," he said aloud. Seeing the younger Ennead's eyebrows lift, he added, "Ask Choran about the last time I shifted. Let's go."

Maurn crouched, saying, "Shall I walk, so you can keep up?" By the time Askaran could answer, the hound shifter had taken the full form of his demon, and the young Enneads above swapped their chant to his name.

"Let's see who has to work to keep up," Askaran replied, sprinting off.

Maurn joined him, lines of white marking the tattoos on each of his legs even in shifted form.

They caught up with the others, forming a pack of four demons and a single Ennead with blades. Once close enough, the tusked demon gave a thunder of challenge, ducked its head, and charged. Its target was Askaran.

Kept in a corner of Askaran's mind, a colossus demon bellowed in answer. The pressure inside Askaran's skull intensified, the strength of the colossus demon stretching the bars of the mental cage containing it. In his ears, Askaran heard the roar of frustration.

The tusked demon was beneath him and would pay dearly for its arrogance in entering his territory.

He set his sights upon the encroaching demon and shoved against the cage in his mind, holding the door shut as his body rushed the enemy.

The pack split, leaving Askaran as the target. Seeing the blind eagerness of the enemy, Askaran skidded to a halt and let the others get ahead of him.

All demons existed to kill Enneads. Despite the substantial threat of the shifted demons surrounding it now, the tusked demon struggled to pull its attention off Askaran, slowing in conflicted indecision. When Choran and Maurn were within pouncing distance, the tusked demon finally acknowledged the greater threat, but the delay had allowed the other shifters to get behind it. In facing the winged demon shifter, the tusked beast opened itself to the two other hound demons, and to Askaran himself as he resumed his run.

Maurn ducked and bolted from the charging tusks, his scales too thin to resist the impact. Choran deflected the blow across one plated shoulder as Berro, followed on his heels by Morton, landed squarely on the tusked demon's back and bit down.

Their teeth were not long enough to cut through the plated scales, but the jaws crushed into muscle and bone. The tusked demon bucked, and both hound demons were tossed from their perches. Berro bounced off the barb of the tusked demon's tail in his fall.

Choran lunged in, his horns catching the tusked demon's neck and sinking into the softer scale of the underside. As the tusked demon lashed down with his hooves, battering Choran's plated throat, Askaran had his opportunity.

Skipping over the tail and up onto the back, Askaran slashed between scales with the thin edge of the kukris. He cut the tendons of the tail, dropping it flat into Berro's maw when the younger shifter bit down on it.

Black blood seeped from the wounds on the tail and along the spine.

Another flick of Askaran's blade mid-back collapsed the hind limbs, dumping the ruddy monster into the pasture. The monster bellowed and snapped at Choran as the winged demon skidded clear, but in extending its neck toward the shifter, it opened a gap in the spine at the top of its head above the thick mane. Askaran's kukri slid off the bone on either side—the gap was as thin as the blade itself—but it dug deep enough to sever the spine.

The creature gave a shudder and crumpled.

In Askaran's mind, the persistent press of his demon lessened. The threat was over. The colossus demon went back to the dark corner of Askaran's skull.

Askaran leaped from the tusked demon's back as the body, no longer maintained by the energy of the demon, crumbled to dust. Only bones, instantly sun-bleached, remained when the wind stirred loose the ashes of the body and dispersed them across the field.

The other shifters assembled, Morton limping on a broken limb from his fall. When the Ennead shifted back, he held his arm tenderly to his chest. His black skin now glistened with purple and red bruising.

Once the blood had dried and flaked from his kukris, Askaran sheathed them. Maurn checked Morton's arm and reported no external bleeding. They each took turns being examined, but no one had been cut. The blood of the demon itself had turned to ash. Satisfied they could all return to the City, they headed back.

"You ever think about shifting to scare them off? You know, so we don't have to get beaten up?" Maurn asked. He glanced at Morton's broken arm pointedly.

Askaran took a long look around him, suddenly struck by how much the company he was keeping had changed over the last few years. "Illum's blessing," he cursed, "when did I become the oldest here?"

Choran, picking at his teeth with a small twig of zahra grass as he sauntered nude at Askaran's side, answered, "When Joban walked into the sands last year, Askaran. You want me to answer that young idiot's question?"

He had never thought of himself as old, but seeing the younger men around him, some of them half his age, made Askaran sharply aware of his years. Askaran had been born the last child of the original shifters over three hundred years before. Now he was the last of that generation, his many cousins gone. Choran was closest to Askaran's age, but there was a century between them.

"You want that one going back to tell the others where to find us?" Askaran answered Maurn.

"Demons don't talk," Maurn replied like a child told a folktale he did not believe.

"Not with words, maybe," Choran pointed out. "But you wouldn't want them organizing another demon army, would you? Bring all those demons here under the leadership of a colossus demon or two?"

This time Maurn looked like a child who believed the monster under the bed had come to life. He stiffened his jaw, ready to declare he was not afraid of such mysteries in a voice that showed he was terrified.

"I heard stories of the demon armies from my mother," Askaran said, his eyes on the sparkling hues of the walls as they returned to the City. New mud and sand mixes patched the rotting wood around the gate, and the mural tiles along the walls had cracked or disappeared.

The carvings had been replaced by mosaics, panel by panel, and even those were chipped by time and sand. "We do not want to see that on Nanterac." He looked around once more, seeing the youth accompanying him. "Do not underestimate demons. They are not the mindless beasts we'd like them to be."

Ahead of them, the fluttering of the canopies died down as the heat of the day settled in. Sand-iron gates, decorated with glass and gold, gleamed in the dawn, their surface speckled by the passage of previous sandstorms. Now that the demon was ash and bones, the gate opened. The first out were the runners, bolting to their assigned markers with whoops of delight, their shendyts flapping against their legs. Some patted the shifters on the back or shoulder, but none touched Askaran.

With their belongings brought down, the shifters dressed while the farmers and herders slunk out. From the east gate, the herds of ranna were led out to graze, their shaven coats short.

Standing at the center of the gateway with the last three of the Last City's shifters behind her was the Youngest Seer, a sack slung over her shoulder. Yarr, the imposing man a head taller than even the other shifters, tilted his head toward Askaran over her. Askaran nodded to the other shifter to take custody of the seer. With a shrug, Yarr then took the three shifters with him, too late to contribute to the defenses. The monster was dead.

Askaran watched them disperse, counting in his head. Eight shifters. Himself, two winged, one tusked, the rest hounds. Each of the others was a grandchild of the first generation and less than two hundred years old. Despite limited resources forced upon the Enneads by the dry climate, shifters never wanted for anything, and each of the new generations had grown taller and broader than Askaran. Yarr had even been bold enough to seek a tusked demon to key himself to, something no other shifter dared repeat. The next generation, without a doubt, was stronger than their predecessors.

With gray hairs on his head, Askaran felt decidedly old as he presented himself to the little seer, who beamed up at him. "Now can we go?" she asked.

"You got a date today, Askaran?" Choran laughed. "What happened to our after-demon drink?"

The tradition was now almost a hundred years old; after a demon lay dead outside the City, Choran and Askaran went to the drinking house and got drunk on qileeo spirits. The practice reduced their aches from the shifting and, more importantly for Askaran, lulled the demon in his mind to sleep.

"This fine young lady has asked for my protection today."

"It *has* to be Askaran!" she said. The seer skipped up to his side and waited as he adjusted his sandals to wrap up his legs against the sand.

"Oh?" Askaran asked. "Why me?"

The seer shrugged under her jellabiya, one shoulder coming clear of the simple garment. She had recently been given a larger one but needed to grow into it, and was at risk of slipping on its long hem. As a desert seer, she wore no scarf or beads with the simple white garment. "Nihai is already out on a hunt. Cirtus is passing judgment today. Berro and Morton are heading north hunting. Yarr doesn't like me…"

"Doesn't like you?" Askaran asked. He glanced at Choran, who paused as well to listen. "He tell you that?"

"I think I scare him," the seer replied, her voice shy.

Choran grunted and finished adjusting his shendyt. "You?" he said. "The Youngest Desert Seer? Is the mighty tusked shifter scared you might beat him up?"

She smiled sadly up at Askaran, her eyes glassy. "Scared of what I might see," she said.

"Then he shouldn't do things he's worried a desert seer might see. You need not worry about that." He looked pointedly at Choran. "Choran can help the Eldest Seer sort that out. Those who obey the laws of the City have no reason to fear a seer. And you are too young to be having visions."

Askaran pulled his sand-cloak out of his bag and fastened it quickly. Once he had tossed his bag over a shoulder, he extended his hand, and the seer took it.

"I will see you tonight for the drink, Choran," he said. He would have to apologize later to whichever lover he had been assigned today. If he could not blind his mind overnight with alcohol, nightmares would haunt him. That would make for bad company.

"Take care of yourself," Choran called after them. "And her too!"

"I can take care of myself," the seer told Askaran. A moment later, she squeezed his hand. "But I'm glad you're here to help."

Although there were thirteen desert seers in the City, the value of each was emphasized. They lived short lives, often making it only into their thirties. He could not allow anything to happen to any desert seer while he was on duty.

Besides, the Youngest Seer had a joy that made him smile. After over three hundred years of duty, the happiness she brought made her more precious than the Heart Hall itself.

They called her a desert seer. At her birth, she had been "Youngest Seer." Growing up, she had moved from "Second Youngest" to "Third Youngest." As years passed and older seers surrendered to the early death of their kind, her name had changed. Now she was the Second Eldest Seer of the Enneads. She was given access to the Heart Hall and the secrets of the City. She was brought to meetings as an advisor, and the powers contained in her mind blossomed. The visions came in torrents.

The Eldest Seer did not tell her everything because he did not have to. She had seen the dirty basement of the City and knew of the poison of the waters it leaked into the dry lands.

After nearly a hundred days of absence, she stood atop a dune with the desert stretching all around. The Ennead City lay ahead, the bones of a freshly killed tusked demon standing like a fenced yard in the pastures. The army with the Second Eldest Seer had spent the night at the last of the oases and would soon pass into the watered grounds surrounding the City. The eight-day journey was coming to a close, something she knew would satisfy the Berintan archon following her. His army was tired and thirsty but ready to take the City. Then, with the Eldest Seer deposed, the Second Eldest Seer could seek out the portal beneath the City and break it. Whether the Enneads remained on Nanterac did not matter to her; she only cared that the fastening destroying two worlds was broken.

Her visions, powered by the hekau of her mind, had taken her to the Ennead homeland Terac, the jungle behind the portal stone, and the draining lakes there. For each drop of water that fell into this world providing for the City, less remained on Terac. Here, there were thousands of Ennead lives relying on the water. There, millions. The Eldest Seer seemed to think nothing of it, but the Second Eldest Seer understood the imbalance the Enneads and their presence on Nanterac had created. The portal had to be closed.

Unable to find sufficient support among the Enneads, her search for a solution had taken her across the desert without shifter escort, a great transgression. She had followed the sense of life, surprising herself when she located another people across the desert. These were Berintans, golden-skinned and brown-eyed, but otherwise Ennead-like. Their leader, Grand Archon Amadi, had heeded her pleas and sent an army back with her to free the City and, at any cost, close the portal. The Grand Archon's fiercest and strongest archon, Archon Farai, marched at the head of the army. With the Second Eldest Seer at his side, he and his forces remained unseen by the City's seers on their approach.

But as the Second Eldest Seer glimpsed the first hint of morning smoke from the City, new visions crept into her mind. Demonstrating powers the Second Eldest Seer had not known Berintans possessed, the Grand Archon had spoken to his general from afar. The plans were changing.

Archon Farai arrived at her side atop the dune, surrounded as usual by his ark members. Seeing him, she knew he had come immediately here with the new orders, expecting her to be aware of them through her hekau. The bright-skinned man loomed over her, his lizard skin armor and weapons glittering in the new light of the desert. Midday heat would render the dunes impassable to the army; they would have to be on the pasture circle by then, or the siege would have to wait for another day.

The seer saw the raid in her mind with perfect clarity, but the details were changing, modified by the Grand Archon's orders. The seer had allies within the City ready to make the attack swift and avoid bloodshed. The Ennead people did not know about the portal and could be spared. They were not warriors; they would not stand in the way of the army once the gates opened. Only the liars at the Heart Hall needed to be imprisoned. Then she could find her way into the underground of the City and seek out the...

Where she had seen herself lead the way through twisted tunnels, now the visions showed Archon Farai in her place. Opened gates were closed, and a barrage of invaders assaulted the sandstone walls of the City. The Enneads panicked, their warriors cut down. Blood spilled into the streets. There would be no sparing of the common people. A demon appeared by the gate, horns lowered in charge. The Berintans cut the monster down, only to see the scarred form change into that of an Ennead, one she knew was named Choran.

The seer opened her eyes, her sight blurred by tears. Glancing to her right, she found the archon at an easy stance overlooking the same dunes, but her psychic energy perverted the view, and now she saw him coated in blood. He held an Ennead khopesh in his hand, although she knew he did not own such a thing.

Yet.

His smile, white teeth as bright as his gold skin, chilled her.

"Why?" she asked.

He snorted and turned to look down at her. The smile remained. "I do as I am commanded. It seems my Grand Archon lied to you."

She heard the words he did not speak; he had been surprised by the Grand Archon's order, not the content but by how it had been delivered. Words in the darkness. A voice he recognized, but without a face. It had frightened him, although he would never let such a thing be known.

But he was happier now. He preferred a full attack, a chance to flood the streets with his warriors and cut down an enemy that, until the Second Eldest Seer had arrived in their jungle in the south, he had not known existed.

Fires burned through the City in the Second Eldest Seer's mind. She stifled a mournful cry to see the bodies of those she knew caught in the flames. Little in the City could burn, except cloth and flesh.

"The City of the Enneads is too valuable," the archon informed her, his voice factual. "The glass itself is worth a fortune. But Grand Archon Amadi wants the portal taken and controlled, not damaged. We will not help you close it."

She felt weak, lost for a long moment in the many visions that assaulted her. A howl sounded in her ears, pained and yearning. Another shifter died. As strong as her hekau was, she could only watch, not change, the future now.

"You do not understand," she whispered. She saw him walk the tunnels around the aqueducts proudly, his warriors at his side. Their feet trampled the moss, leaving troughs in the growth. "There is no treasure worth—"

"Glass and gold are one thing, little thorn, but you have told us of another world." His grin mocked her when she regained her sight. "You will fulfill your role today, and the riches of the Enneads will be mine. You will tell me what I need to know, or more people will die."

At the archon's wave, the army resumed its march to the west. The seer did not immediately follow but, now surrounded by the ark members, turned her eyes once more toward the City in the distance. Her throat felt thick as she swallowed.

The cry she gave was not heard by any ear, but it was strong enough to reach the City. In plea, the Second Eldest Seer called out a warning, begging any who heard her to flee from the City at once, lest they fall victim to the death arriving dressed in thick lizard-skin armor.

A single vision answered; a man wearing a tattoo over his left shoulder walked out the west gates with a child as the army advanced from the east. The child wore the white jellabiya of a desert seer and, glancing back, met the seer's eyes in the vision.

Only one mind had heard the warning call, and the Second Eldest Seer of the Ennead people knew it was not enough.

CHAPTER 2

In the pastures, the Youngest Seer ran after the chez beetles, which abandoned their perches atop the scraggy shrubs to fly. The ranna herds had been taken north, where fresh pasture awaited them. The fields where Askaran led the seer had been grazed forty days earlier and were starting to regrow. The chez beetles scavenged the last of the crumbs from dried ranna dung.

When they reached the edge of the pasture, the seer ran ahead to examine the white post marker, then peered beyond.

"The grass is advancing," she remarked, checking with Askaran over her shoulder for permission to cross beyond the pillar. Askaran joined her at the marker first.

The white post, the height of Askaran's waist, had been set as part of a hundred markers to outline the borders of the land. When first they had been placed, the sand of the desert had been on the far side. Now almost a dozen strides of weak, clumped dran grains extended into the dunes. Beyond that stretch, sands took over.

Taking her hand once more, he checked, "You brought water?"

The seer nodded proudly, hefting the waterskin slung over her shoulder.

"Cover?" he asked.

"One desert wrap," she confirmed.

"Knife?"

She pulled out a tiny kitchen paring knife, and he had to smile. In her hands, it was huge, but certainly too small to be of any use except in slicing fish.

"I think we'll use mine," he replied. His two kukris sat on his hip. He had another knife, one for skinning, but thought he should wait for her to grow into the blade a little before offering it in substitute. As small as her kitchen knife was, it suited her. "How about cooking shields?"

She again nodded proudly. "Food too," she reported.

Leading her beyond the pillar, Askaran shrugged. "The desert will provide," he said. "You'd better put on that wrap. Let's go." Askaran supervised as the little seer donned her desert wrap to protect her from the beating suns and the whipping sands.

The dunes were quiet under the clear sky, Ero and Mour in slow rotation around each other in the sky. The light of Ero was red tinged in the dawn, but the paler beams of Mour beat down white and hot. Askaran wrapped his sand-cloak around his front. The wind was cut by the tight weave of the cloak, and the many light layers insulated him against the heat. The seer's wrap provided a similar service, if less well.

"Will we hunt today, Askaran?" she asked, following him along the ridge of a dune. He slowed his pace to allow her to keep up.

Askaran scanned the surrounding dunes. Most of the animals of the desert knew to cover their passage, but he could not detect even a hint of any of them.

To the east, the flatlands stretched as caked sands for blind miles. A low cloud of dust lingered over it, telling him that the native herds of tauran were moving at a slow pace. A predator would panic them into a stampede, so he assumed one of the lead females had recognized the tusked demon's presence and decided to lead the flock away. They were too far for today's hunt. If he could take a few days away, he might be able to find them at one of the oases, but his company forbid such a journey now.

"I see no game trails yet. I thought we should fish," he replied.

To the west, the dunes rolled on endlessly, but he could trace the route in his mind to the first of the chain oases. Unlike the animals of the dunes, the fish would not flee from their limited pond, and they had even been recently restocked. That was the direction they would go.

"I brought hook and line!" the seer announced, her grin huge under the cowl of the desert wrap.

"Did you know or *know?*" he asked.

The smile was pulled from her face. "You told me once it was important for the kit. You said that the desert provides, but only to those smart enough to have the tools." He suspected those were his exact words. Seers were known for having excellent memories. "But no visions, Askaran," she said sadly.

His hook and line was wrapped around his bag's strap. All of his tools for desert travel lived on him or in the little sack he kept slung over his shoulder. He never knew when a request would come for fresh meat out of the desert, and he liked to be ready. Any excuse to leave the City was welcomed.

It almost gave him a sense of freedom.

Askaran followed the arch of the suns along the dunes, reaching the first oasis as the suns turned at their plinth.

He let the conversation—the seer asking questions about everything she could think of—drizzle to a stop as he put foot to the rock nearest the water-filled valley. Without the filtering sand to drain the water away, roots found purchase and trees rose out of the wastes.

The seer went silent, like a calf heeding the mother's warning grunt. She brought herself into his shadow, and he drew his kukris.

There were five oases in the chain set, five sources of unlikely life in a wasteland. Control of the water was fiercely contended. More than once, Askaran had been forced to challenge a demon for the privilege of filling his waterskin. The seer knew that now was the time to be quiet and follow closely.

He came to the oasis from the top of the ridge, putting himself in a position to look down into the oasis valley. A flock of piper lizards, nothing more than tiny specs in the farthest shallows of the pool, drank and played in the waters. Flying reptiles called scavengers circled above them.

"Askaran?" the seer whispered, her voice tight. "Why are we—?"

"Listen to the other animals," Askaran told her. "The pipers are avoiding the better shallows at this end, and the scavengers are anticipating a kill. Something is—"

The crunch of crushed stone interrupted him, and Askaran spun to face it, shoving the seer behind him. Sure enough, a winged demon slunk out of the cover of the valley, pulling itself up the cliff to his left with the barbed fingers atop the winged forelimbs. It growled, teeth bared, and the tail flicked behind it as it took a place atop the cliff.

Askaran's instincts flared to see the demon, and the monster within him roared to life. For a moment, Askaran saw red, and the strength of the demon pulsed in him, threatening. His mind fell into the blind hate, and the scar on his shoulder, the wound that had keyed him to the demon, ached.

He fought back, drowning the monster in his meditative memories of cool water and silence. His vision cleared. He could think enough to assess the threat.

The presence of the seer made the choice for him. He shielded her now, but she could not outrun a winged demon. Fighting atop the cliffs risked pushing her back, potentially down into the valley. And he could not allow the monster close enough to harm her.

What foul luck brought him two demons in one day?

Unwilling to take any chances in defending the seer, Askaran chose to shift for the first time in more than three decades.

He slapped away his kukris and dropped the weapon belt with his bag. With one hand, he unclasped his sand-cloak and let it fall. His eyes fixed on the demon before him, Askaran shifted.

Physically, it felt like being stretched in all directions, an unsettling sensation that had become tolerable but could never be considered pleasant. His attention turned inward, to where the thoughts of the demon were released from their cage. The furious creature reared in Askaran's head, for a moment overwhelming him with fury and frustration. Mentally, Askaran created a leash for the monster and tethered the vicious presence.

When next he looked out, he was towering over the winged demon, which had shrunk back and lowered its winged limbs. With a yelping howl, it bolted into the desert, abandoning any hope of holding the oasis against Askaran and his demon.

But he could not allow it to escape.

Curling up on two enormous limbs, Askaran pounced. His bulk landed on the fleeing demon, crushing its bone into the soft terrain. Through the burst of sand, he clamped his jaw over its chest. The head was too strong to crush, but even these monsters died when they bled out. Tearing out a heart required finesse his form did not have. Instead, he ripped the ribcage apart, assuming he would tear into the heart at some point.

The sound, part growl and part squeal, steadily dwindled as Askaran held the bite. With a final moan, the flesh released. The dust of the demon settled into the sands.

Standing tall, Askaran surveyed the desert, red eyes seeking more invaders to his territory, eager to butcher another. Finding none, Askaran dragged the demon in his mind back to its cage. His body responded by returning to its natural form.

His shendyt was gone, ripped to shreds, but he retrieved any useable scraps around his waist. Even certain that he had sustained no injury, he checked himself over. From his discarded bag, Askaran retrieved a new shendyt and sandals. The wrappings from the sandals covered his lower legs to the knee. With the sand-cloak, he would be fully protected from the blown sands, but less well protected should there be another fight.

The seer's eyes were wide when he faced her, and she seemed briefly sad. He had worried he would see fear in her eyes, but she seemed apologetic as she said, "He was bigger than I expected."

She had never seen him shift before. She had not even been born when he had last shifted.

Askaran flung the bag onto his back. The strap lay across the snout of the tattoo now exposed on his left shoulder and chest, gagging the snarling face of a colossus demon. The fiery ache of his scar, buried under the tattoo, faded as the demon settled.

"I'm going to need that drink tonight," he replied.

"How come?" the seer asked, following him down into the valley's slope at the north end. Promptly, the piper lizards flittered to the shallows, recognizing the departure of the winged demon threat. By the time the two Enneads reached the waters, a game of chasing fry had ensued, and the pipers had little remaining attention for the intruders.

"Because otherwise, I won't sleep," he explained. "He gives me nightmares after any fight, and they're worse after he's been allowed out. But if I get him drunk, he forgets about it. So we need to be back in the City early."

The seer nodded, then rushed to the water's edge ahead of him. While the seer gently lowered her hook and line, without bait, into the shallow water among the pipers, Askaran set up a shelter in the shadow of three boulders. Years ago, hunters had arranged the stones to create a fishing hide, but it required a cloak to canopy it. In the shelter of the trees, which served to break the wind and keep out the sand, the seer had dropped her desert wrap. Askaran used it to complete the hide.

"It's deeper," she said, and he realized she had not been fishing; she had been measuring.

"The waterline looks higher to me," Askaran agreed. "I'm surprised you noticed." He scanned the skies again. The scavengers caught a new up current and drifted away, disappointed.

"I think the desert is getting smaller," the seer said, returning to him and sitting in the shade of the hide. She let him tie the colored threads to her hook, then cast the line into the waters expertly. Once he baited his line with thread, he cast it in.

He considered the observation. The grasses that surrounded the City had expanded beyond the marking pillars, and each of the oases seemed to be expanding. If all the areas of grass and life were spreading, the sand and dunes must be feeling squeezed. "I think you may be right. Now hush. Fish won't come if they hear you talking."

She nodded sagely and went back to wiggling her line, doing her best to mimic a larva for the fish to eat.

Of the ten gates of the City, only one was open when the army charged. Frightened herdsmen and farmers rushed through, fleeing the initial wave of Berintans, but were easily run down by the tauran riders. After a long hike, the reward was battle.

Unlike most archons, Funanya used her spear in place of her precious sword of rank. Among her warriors, she ensured she was the fiercest, and her ark was first through the open gate. With her ark, she drove back the Enneads and kept the entrance open for the rest of the Berintans to follow.

In battle, the face-paints of the warriors were vital; at a glance, she counted the members of her ark, accounting for all but one, and commanded them on. Goading her people with song, she headed deeper into the city, still over forty strong despite the initial battle. She was joined by another ark, Adeban's. Like Funanya, Adeban was from the city of Douran and served the city's highest-ranking archon, Sizwe.

"Fine day for a slaughter!" Adeban called, bowing his head in passing to acknowledge her slightly higher rank. The third clan's face paints were patterns of red and brown, but more than one was spattered or smeared. His sword—like the one she had on her belt—was edged with obsidian pieces and had been bloodied. Both were less grand than Sizwe's obsidian and wood blade.

"Keep up, Adeban," Funanya called back, hefting her spear. "Let's see who draws Farai's attention!"

They charged on, Funanya keeping herself sur-rounded by her warriors. She noted Adeban did the same. Pitched battle was a fine way of getting killed in a manner no one would suspect. Sometimes it was impossible to tell who had thrown the spear that ended an archon's life.

The Enneads provided little resistance but fled into their homes and lashed flimsy hide doors against the invaders. The warriors stormed the houses easily, and the rumors of the black skin of an Ennead being stronger than Berintan's were proven false. Only the swift avoided spear or sword in the chaos.

Adeban was still a fit warrior despite his more advanced age, and combining his warriors with Funanya's was devastating to the helpless Ennead peasants cowering in their homes. Funanya thought it would be a simple victory until she saw the monster.

The hound demon appeared from behind a home, the arm of a Berintan scout hanging like a chain of gold from its mouth. Seeing Funanya and her warriors, the demon snarled wide, spat the meat onto the glittering glass road, and lifted its bone hackles. The muscles under the crimson scale rippled as it lowered its head and stalked toward them.

The warriors gathered at once, forming a pack to face the creature as it advanced. Funanya positioned herself at the front, joining the line of spears meant to keep the monster at bay. Adeban's warriors came in at the left, forming a similar, but distinct, block. Neither trusted the other enough to stand side by side.

The demons of the desert were known to her through the briefings Archon Farai had given all his archons. Before the march, it had been forbidden to leave the jungle canopies, and for good reason. To see a demon awed her. For a moment, she wondered why the monster was loose in the city.

She corrected herself in the next thought. They had been warned about Enneads that could take the form of demons. This was one of them: a shifter.

She saw the glint of intelligence in the monster's eyes as it paused, unwilling to charge the line of bristling spears. With a final growl, it retreated, step by step, until it had again disappeared around the corner.

"Gone?" Adeban called. "That was—"

A cry went up, and Funanya spun around. Another hound demon landed among her men, having jumped in from the rooftops. Either the creature was unnaturally fast, or two had teamed up against them.

The following scramble was a blur. Funanya's warriors rotated around her, reforming the block correctly to face the enemy, knowing that to stand together was to stay standing. Adeban's ark was less organized and was quickly targeted by the demon. While the other ark scattered, Funanya's reformed the wall of spears, and, together, the line rushed in. Although the scales of the demon turned many of the lunging spears, a few found spaces between the scales and pierced deep.

A howl rose from around the corner, and sounds of battle erupted there as well. Funanya grinned to think the second monster, on its way to pin them, had been waylaid.

The wounded monster among them thrashed, pulling the spears, and two warriors stumbled forward into the teeth and claws of the furious demon.

Funanya gave the shout, and the spears surged forward again. The demon skipped back. Another howl sounded, and the demon looked toward the corner where the first had gone. In a blur, the demon was atop the roofs once more, then gone. Funanya assumed the howl had been a call, and that one demon had gone to seek the other. She steadied her spear-arm, calling for her ark to return to her.

The demon had leaped atop the building in a single bound after two spears had stabbed at least a hand's breadth into the body. If a pierce to the chest could not slow the monster, she did not know what would. She pitied the party who would meet both.

Three wounded and two dead were the final counts from her ark, and she thought herself lucky. Adeban's ark had lost a third of their numbers in a few breaths.

Hoping not to meet any more shifters Funanya left Adeban to sort themselves and treat his wounded, gathered her warriors, and headed deeper into the city.

CHAPTER 3

Sitting silently by the oasis waters proved impossible for her; the seer continued to ask Askaran questions. By the end of the afternoon, they had caught two fish, both from Askaran's line and both landed by the seer. Two others had escaped the line after he had given it to the child to work with.

The first fish was a spiked hagfish, whose meat tasted like mud no matter how it was prepared. One fish would feed one person; Askaran thought he should give it to one of the cooks for stock or soup. That would feed many more mouths and could be seasoned heavily.

The second fish Askaran could not give to anyone except another shifter. The thick-scaled silver fish was a poisonous white ruin fish. He could use it as bait safely, but it was no good to eat. It seemed a shame; they had caught a large white ruin.

He wrapped both in wax-coated leather and placed them at the bottom of his bag next to his waterskin to keep them cool. The afternoon heat was abating slowly as the sun touched the horizon, and they made their way out of the oasis.

Clouds hovered to the east as they left the valley for the dunes, dark and imposing. Askaran was surprised to see them. Rain this time of year was unusual, and with the winds moving in from the south, he should have spotted the clouds when choosing their direction that morning.

The seer was quiet until they were clear of the oasis and again among dunes, where demons were unable to sneak up on them.

"Do you like the desert, Askaran?" she asked.

"I like the quiet," he admitted, his eyes on the dark clouds ahead. Walking wet through a desert was not a bad thing, and they were not in an area at risk for flash floods, unlike the flats in the east. But he wasn't sure how the seer's desert wrap would hold up. If the storm broke early over them, he would have to make a shelter. "I like the solitude. It's hard to find space in the City sometimes."

"Enneads need Enneads," the seer informed him. "No one in the City would be alive without the others. We all have to help."

He lifted an eyebrow at her, but he wasn't sure she saw it under the cowl of the sand-cloak. "You been taking to the Eldest Seer?" he asked.

"It was Historian Belker," she replied proudly. "He was telling me about Nanterac. He asked me to watch the desert, see if it was changing. He thinks it's getting cooler and wetter. He says we've had more storms too, more rain. He says it will make living here more easy."

"Easier," Askaran corrected.

"Easier," she agreed. "Askaran, if living in the desert is so hard, why do we live here?"

The wind shifted toward him, and the cloud twisted slowly. Askaran saw no haze of rain beneath it, and it moved a little too easily on the wind.

"Because here is where we are," he replied absently.

It wasn't a cloud. The black hovering above the City was smoke, and it was rising quickly.

He stopped where he was, and the seer stumbled to a halt. They stood, the seer prudently silent, as he considered the sight.

For him to have thought it was a cloud, it had to be new, fresh, and wide. That meant multiple fires throughout the City simultaneously, else he would have seen a plume, not a cloud. The City would not burn easily; too much was stone or glass. The shades set above the streets might catch, but the rods holding them were bone or metal. He expected the people would retreat to the pastures and keep away from the fires until they abated. Nothing they had was valuable enough to waste water on fighting the flames.

He continued their walk, now wary. The seer remained at his side as they crossed through the valley of the dunes to approach the City from the west. Askaran avoided the crest of the dunes now, his hackles raised.

Once they could smell the smoke, Askaran paused again. He could hear strange noises, the sounds of metal on stone and people shouting. Somewhere in the distance, the howl of a hound demon sounded, and a chill ran down Askaran's spine. Even the demon in his mind fidgeted uncomfortably.

Something was very wrong.

"You know how to use a sand-cloak?" Askaran asked the seer as he unclasped his cloak and handed it to her.

She nodded. "Roll once to collect the sand, then lie flat or on your side beside a dune or move slowly. Shake it out when you get up."

He took her desert wrap and replaced it with the cloak. The extra cloth dragged behind her until he pinned it up in an improvised hem using the fish hooks.

"You hide here," he told her. "Right here. I'm going to investigate this. I will come back for you."

Her eyes welled with tears, but she nodded. When he pulled away from her, her hand caught his arm.

"You promise?" she asked.

"I promise," Askaran replied. "Just hide here."

As he began his cautious climb up the dune to view the pasture ahead, he glanced back and was satisfied to see her properly collect the red sand on the cloak. With a slight wind—a constant in the desert—she was invisible under the sand instantly.

He crawled over the dune, then the next one. Atop the third, he finally had a view of the pastureland around the City.

An army had trampled the pasture to the south, and some of the forces still occupied the flattened grasses there. The screams of the people floated now on the shifting winds, and the closer he drew, the more piercing they became. A shriek—a woman panicked— seemed to call to the demon within him directly, making Askaran flinch.

He held the demon in check, knowing that even the invaders on the pasture were numerous enough to kill the demon he harbored, and he did not know how many of the attackers had already made their way into the City.

He had a promise to keep.

He slunk closer, hiding in the shadows of the white markers as he traced a path to the south along the edge of the pasture. Once he reached the largest south pillar, he was close enough to see the attackers.

They were not demons. That alone made him pause. He had believed Nanterac devoid of sentient life. There was plenty of reptilian life hidden in the dunes, but nothing beyond. His mother had once spoken of parts of the world that were lush, but the Eldest Seer had never permitted exploration beyond the desert. Once, it had been to save their connection with their home-world. Askaran did not know why it mattered now, but the rules had not changed.

At first, he thought the invaders were reptiles themselves, although they had round skulls and little snouts. But those that marched to another gate walked like Enneads. The scales he had seen were armor wound with cords of leather in collars and around their joints. Their shendyts were cloth, as were the shoes they wore laced up to the knee. Their faces were painted in repetitive patterns that seemed to be associated with the group they were with. Considering the amount of clothing they wore, he could not imagine how they could march in the heat.

The Mirror Gate had been smashed in, and now dozens of the armored people guarded it, each with spear and tauran-hide shields. The demon in Askaran growled, and Askaran mirrored the sound; intruders had entered his territory.

His eyes were drawn up, and the demon nearly slipped his grasp entirely.

Enneads built low-lying houses, but one section of the City rose higher above the rest, the Heart

Hall. There, the Eldest Seer guided the City. And there, hanging from an upper window in a chain, hung ten unadorned, white jellabiyas.

Thirteen desert seers lived in the City. Ten had been killed and stripped of their robes.

Askaran took a step forward unwittingly, feeling the demon rise to the surface.

Three must yet live, he realized, and he knew where one was.

A new roar sounded over the City, and Askaran's heart skipped.

Choran, fully shifted into his winged demon form, cleared the wall in a bound and landed atop the invaders. The tusks on either side of his maw thrashed left and right, crashing into the attackers and throwing them. Hissing a challenge, he faced a new squad and charged, goring two in a single strike. Tossing his head, he threw the bodies clear over the walls once more.

One eye was squinted shut, the skin around it scalped clear from the surrounding bone. More than one spear jutted out from flesh on his back and belly, but most of the strikes from the soldiers landed on plated joints. The bone defended him, but the thinner scale overlying it was shredded. Black blood oozed from every surface, and, upon seeing it, Askaran felt his heart stop.

The enemy swarmed in, long spears stabbing. One lucky strike cut between the ribs and sank into Choran's chest.

The demon thrashed, trampling and slashing. The tail, the end like a mace, killed the man with the spear instantly, but it was too late. With the deadly blow,

Askaran had no doubt that Choran had lost control of the demon.

The kills were no longer clean; Choran smashed his way through a dozen people with a single run but took another dozen wounds. He crushed another pair of warriors under his forefeet, thrusting out his horns to gore two more. There, pinned by a dozen new spears, he sagged and stumbled. In collapsing, he crushed another invader, but he did not rise.

As Askaran watched his friend be cut down, the demon in him seethed at his inaction, but the cage remained closed. The seer expected him to come and get her. Charging into the army was fated to fail. He could not defeat so many. No one could.

Feeling a push on the cage door of the demon in his mind, Askaran withdrew.

She had to live. The little seer he had left hidden among the dunes had to be spared. He did not know where the other surviving seers were. Should no seer remain, the Enneads would perish on Nanterac, or so an ancient seer had said. The others could be facing death at any time.

Askaran turned his back on the City and made his way into the dunes.

The seer shook free the sand from the cloak as she stood before him, for once, without questions. Her black eyes peered at him as if viewing his soul, and he felt the demon in him quake. He was not sure what she saw, but he had no doubt that she was, for the first time, truly seeing. He understood suddenly why Yarr had feared her.

A single tear fell from her black eyes, glistening like the flecks of gold he could see in her irises.

"Ten robes," she said, and he, seeing no way or reason to deny it, nodded. "So one other lives."

He cocked his head. "Two would yet…" He trailed off, seeing the truth in her tears.

"Only one other," she said. "The Eldest Seer has given his life to deny them their prize. This, I *know*."

Askaran let out a long breath. He had never known a seer's visions to come so early to a child.

"But Choran shifted by the City," Askaran said, taking the seer's hand and leading her away, "and he bled there. Maybe others did too; they must have been forced into their demons. The City is not safe, not now. We'll go back to the oasis and hide there until the fires are out. I'll make sure the City is clear of demons, and we'll go back, find survivors…" He was certain there should be more to the plan. He wanted to add "rebuild," but it seemed futile. He did not know why the City had been attacked, and he did not know what would remain, assuming the enemy left at all. They had marched across a desert to reach the City. There had to be a reason.

Darkness fell quickly once the suns set. Ero's crimson light lingered the longest, casting stretched red shadows over the auburn sands as the sands settled, and a chill crept in. Driven to exhaustion by the long walking, the seer fell asleep in his arms, her gentle murmurs warning that dreams haunted her.

Askaran found the oasis in the night, reconstructed the hide between the boulders, and then laid her in the shadow of the shelter. He remembered to bury the fish, still wrapped, in the shallows to keep them cold until morning.

They were far enough away that the noises of the attack could not reach them, and the smoke plume had been lost in the darkness. The quiet chirp of the piper lizards felt wrong after the chaos of the invasion, entirely out of place, like chez beetles in the desert.

His life had just ended, Askaran was certain, but he could not bring himself to believe it. He felt like it was just another hunting trip, that he would finish tomorrow and go back and have a drink with Choran as he had promised, and be called upon again to fight a demon, and everything would be the same. He had lived that life for three centuries. It could not be different.

Somewhere in his mind, the demon was laughing.

He sat at the entrance to the hide, looking out over the water as the cold set in. The piper lizards skittered away, leaving only the glowmoths, winged insects that fed on the deadfall from the reeds of the pond. The white of the wings reflected the light of the moons like sparks across the bushes.

He felt old and, not for the first time, filled with a fatigue that went deeper than any physical strain. For three decades, he had avoided shifting, never letting the demon get close enough to him to wear him down, but the weariness could not be stopped. No shifter lived beyond four hundred, and those that got close were the weaker forms, usually hounds. No one had expected any colossus demon shifter to get to two hundred, let alone three.

The exhaustion was worse now than ever, and he wondered if Choran had been right after all; Askaran could not last much longer. Eventually, he would be too tired to hold the demon back. Before that happened, he had to go into the desert and find a way to kill himself. He could not let the demon take over, not in the end.

He hated thinking about that choice, that time. It would happen no matter how hard he disciplined his mind to contain the demon, or how often he chose to use his blades instead of his monster. He would lose the battle eventually and now wished for the death he had seen at the City under the smoke. He could have died in battle.

"I should have been there," he whispered, seeing fires in the flickering of the glowmoths over the water.

"Needed you alive," the seer's voice answered from behind him, making him jump. He turned to answer but found her still wrapped in her cloak, her eyes closed. Even the rise and fall of her chest implied deep sleep.

Askaran returned to his place by the opening of the hide and lay down. Without him, the seer would die. With him, they could survive in the desert, maybe live long enough to clear out the City and return to the aquifer there. Because he was with her, she had hope.

He did not know what she could hope for now.

Giving up, Askaran let himself fall asleep. The demon tormented him with nightmares as he had expected.

Funanya was in Sizwe's shadow as one of the five archons standing at attention. The paint on her face—zigzag patterns over her forehead and chin—itched, but she did not flinch. A few paces away, Archon Farai strode onto the steps of the central building of the Ennead city, what they presumed to be a palace, and it would not do for Farai to see her fidgeting. Farai ruled Masamba, the largest of the Berintan cities, and had been selected to command this army by the Grand Archon himself. If she impressed him, she could expect fortune to follow.

Unlike Farai, Archon Sizwe's face paint was perfect. In light of his rank as Archon of the city of Douran, the smaller cousin of Masamba, he wore full circles of keim beast hide over his chest and legs, each band a shining glow of smooth scales in the late light, but it was not blemished. Although he carried a short, thick spear, Funanya had not seen him point the tip at anything besides the sky, which explained how the weapon remained unchipped so late in the battle. His sword, an ornate wooden blade with an obsidian edge, was still sheathed.

For the assembled warriors, who were cinder-covered, dented, and bruised from their tangles with demons and frantic Enneads, the sight of their leader's perfection was irksome. It took effort for Funanya to keep her stare on Farai and his assembled warriors instead of staring daggers into Sizwe's back. He was too protected, between his armor and his surrounding ark, and the circumstances were too open. As much as she wanted him dead, now was not the time.

She forced her attention onto Archon Farai, the leader of the Berintans here. At least he looked like he had earned some of this battle; he was smeared with blood and ash.

Where Funanya expected gravel, the Enneads used glass beads along their roads, giving a rainbow hue to the path up. The surface of the building had been embossed with colored glass in individual pieces arranged to form the semblance of forests, waterfalls, and strange beasts. Some she thought looked like the ranna beasts she had seen scattering along the north desert moments earlier, their herdsmen slaughtered, and the beasts terrified by the scent of blood. Like the rest of the animals in the murals, the ranna were hairy creatures with little resemblance to the reptilian life of Funanya's jungle home.

Despite the discrepancy, the Enneads themselves were similar to the Berintan people. The most obvious difference was their skin; Ennead skin was black from their hair to the soles of their feet. Berintan skin was golden, reflecting the light in the early sunset gently. Legends claimed the Berintans had been formed from the golden sands, but Funanya did not know where the Enneads had come from. Some said from the mud of a river. Others said they were made of black sand, but the desert here was red.

Behind Archon Farai, the Ennead desert seer trailed. She showed early signs of womanhood under a simple white shift. Her black hair, dark as shaben leaves, formed a halo around her head, released from the tiny braids she had used until this day. Her skin was a shade lighter than most of the Enneads Funanya had fought on her way in. She held her arms tightly against her chest, her head bowed. At a gesture from Farai, the seer walked up the stairs, alone.

Out of the shadows of the palace, a huge Ennead male stepped up, looking imposing even in the arch of the enormous entrance. The deep coal skin was broken by a scar stretching from his ankle on his right leg to disappear under the wool shendyt he wore. He had no current wounds but was tattooed over his entire chest with raised white patterns of fissures like the cracks in the flats of the desert. When this Ennead met Funanya's stare with his black irises, Funanya felt something feral pressing toward her.

The impression faded when the smaller woman walked up the steps. The huge Ennead bowed his head.

"Yarr," the seer said, "you can stop now." The words were soft, but, surprising Funanya, in Berintan.

Whatever the man said in reply was lost in a growl.

Following the seer back down the glass steps, the Ennead male presented himself to Archon Farai. Even the imposing archon looked small for a moment, and Funanya finally realized who "Yarr" was.

This Ennead was a shifter.

The archon was all smiles as he crossed his arms in greeting to the Ennead.

"Well done, Yarr," he praised, and the shifter grinned. "I am awed by the powers of the shifters this day, your strength most of all. Sizwe! See that this man is given rest and drink of his choosing. Today, Yarr the shifter is a friend of the Berintans!"

Sizwe stepped up, crossing his arms and bowing his head in reverence as a cheer sounded from the surrounding soldiers. Funanya did not join them, seeing nothing to cheer. The shifter remained a threat. How anyone, particularly Archon Farai, could trust any creature that harbored a demon soul, she did not know.

Before the shifter moved to follow Sizwe, the Ennead looked back to the seer and said something Funanya did not understand. The words were the same as Berintan, but the accent was too thick to make out when it was spoken quickly. He clearly could understand Farai—he had responded to the commendations with pleasure—but seemed to deliberately snub them now to tell the seer something.

The shifter followed Sizwe and his retinue away, and the crowd of soldiers parted for them. No doubt, Farai had set a tent with luxuries for the shifter to enjoy somewhere outside of the city. She suspected it would work well on Yarr; the big shifter seemed easily flattered, and confirming his supremacy would appease him.

Farai watched the seer while most of the crowd's eyes followed Yarr out. Funanya heard him demand to know what the shifter had said to her.

The seer's eyes were filled with tears when she replied, "He said that two are missing. One seer, one shifter."

"Missing?" Farai snarled, mimicking the noise of the shifter earlier. "You sent him here to make sure none was missed. Every seer must be accounted for. The Grand Archon has commanded you be the last."

The seer shrugged her shoulders weakly. "The missing one is a child only," she said. "She cannot see the way I can. And the shifter is the oldest one, worn and broken by battles, only a short time away from madness."

"Find them," the archon insisted, his hand gripping the seer's forearm, and Funanya noticed the deep red of a new bruise forming under his grip.

"She travels with him and shields him."

"You said she had no power!"

"Such defenses are instinctual. A seer, from the time it is born, cannot be seen. But if we get closer…"

Farai's eyes wandered, and Funanya quickly turned her gaze away. His shouts had attracted the attention of the crowd now, and he seemed to suddenly recognize the many faces turning to him. He released the little Ennead's arm.

"Two cannot do anything against us," he declared. "The city is ours. Load the wagons!" The soldiers cheered again and began to disperse. Funanya remained at her position for a moment longer, allowing her to overhear Farai as he stared down at the seer once more. "And take me inside, little thorn."

The seer obediently marched back up the glass steps and, with Archon Farai and his entourage behind her, disappeared into the darkness of the palace.

Like her, Funanya's ark had not moved from their halted positions by the steps, awaiting her commands. "Look for chimneys!" she shouted to them. "They can't make glass or metal without a furnace. I want as much iron as you can find, whatever the form! You three, secure a well! We'll need to fill all watergourds before the wells get filled in. Take as much as you can carry but expect to be running. Sizwe's been put on scout, so you only get tonight! Tomorrow, we march to the next oasis!"

Some other arks were seeking glass, but Funanya was not confident she would be able to transport it safely when they were scouting. Metal was hardier. It would not be worth as much, but it was rare enough in Berinta that she could expect to sell any piece she managed to get home.

She beat her spear shaft against the stretched hide of her shield and her ark scattered, not a one of her warriors giving voice to their disappointment. By being sent out early, they were to be denied part of the spoils, but nothing they said could change that displeasing fact. Complaints were not acceptable to Funanya.

Funanya found Sizwe's ark colors as they made its way out the gates with its unlikely ally and promised that she would see her ark receive honors despite him.

The seer walked into the Heart Hall, her eyes fixed ahead, trying not to see the dismembered bodies around her. Yarr had done the killing; no weapon had been used. The huge tusked demon shifter, even in Ennead form, preferred to use his natural weapons. The style had no finesse, but it was no less deadly.

Farai followed her, one of his swords out and lowered at her back. When the battle had begun, he had carried one wooden sword with an obsidian edge and one ornate, fine blade of pure obsidian. Now he had swapped the wooden blade for an Ennead's ancient metal weapon, a khopesh. There were precious few of those as it was, and Farai had found a beautiful one. He had failed to find a sheath for it.

She still hoped to destroy the portal, but she did not know how. At the least, she had to know where it was. Maybe she could yet find a way to break the magic that held it open. The only magic in Nanterac was that of the mind or that of the body, of the seer and of the shifters. Once she saw the portal…

She stopped as she came to the largest of the halls. Among the pillars and mosaics, the floor had fallen away. There had once been a dais, carved in gold and silver iron. The images upon it had shown the path down through the floor to where the portal hid. Now, nothing but a huge open crater occupied the center of the room.

Pausing, the party gazed down into the pit. An expanse of water reached out a dozen paces below, the lights flickering over the rippling surface as it was broken by rubble.

This was the aquifer, hidden under the City. Here, where the aquifer touched the Heart Hall, was the pedestal where the portal orb had resided.

"Gone," the seer muttered.

"Gone?" Farai shoved her aside, replacing her at the edge of the opening in the floor. Seeing nothing, he spun to stare at her. "What do you mean, gone? Where?"

A small smile formed, first in her mind, then on her face. Although her heart felt heavy, the seer felt some part of her burden lift.

"This blast… This collapse…" she said, the visions coming to her one after another. "He used his powers against it."

In the vision, the Eldest Seer stood on an island in the aquifer. His dark eyes were fixed upon the glowing orb atop the pedestal before him. A trickle of water fell from the blue orb, dripping down the tracks over the carvings and falling to join the waters at its base, which, in turn, fell into the aquifer. She saw him reach out a hand and felt him push, like a silent shriek, in his mind. The blue orb shuddered, winked out, and dropped from its resting place. When it landed, it had become a gray igneous stone.

The air rippled like disturbed water, energy rising. The Eldest Seer looked up in the vision, and the seer felt the final message left for her.

⟨So our enemy will never have it.⟩

In her mind, the energy exploded up, the ripples of energy blasting to the ceiling of the aquifer and through the floor of the Heart Hall. The stairs leading down were torn from the walls and ripped apart, leaving a scattering of pebbles to rain down into the far waters. Stone and glass alike shattered, gutting the Heart Hall above and destroying all evidence of the reverent seats of elders and mosaics of Terac. The pedestal in the aquifer disintegrated to dust under the force. The Eldest Seer was already dead, thrown with such force that his neck broke. His body sank into the waters.

The vision paused for a long breath. The edges of the gaping hole released final rubble, creating distant, hollow splashes.

Farai had his hands on her arms when the seer brought her mind back to the present. She thought perhaps he had been shaking her but felt nothing.

"The Eldest Seer destroyed it," she told Farai. "It is gone, as is he."

For a moment, she saw a vision of Farai tossing her over the edge of the chasm into the cold waters below, but it changed as he decided against it. The command of his Grand Archon—that she be the last—saved her.

With a final curse, he released her arms.

"I hope you enjoy your new rank, Eldest Seer," he spat, storming off back down the corridor and leaving the seer alone at last.

Outside the hall, the sound of breaking glass resounded, and the seer was finally allowed time to cry. Her tears fell through the hole in the floor, echoing back to her as a gentle trickle of water.

By the time Philyre stopped to breathe, it was over. The chaos of the attack on the City dwindled to silence in her memory, leaving her numb.

She stood on the edge of the pastureland, smoke rising from the City in the distance in droves and in smaller spirals at her feet. The crops had flash burned to ashes. Her legs were etched with burns, ruby-red through her skin like hardening volcanic rock, but she could not feel it. She knew that was bad but could no longer remember why.

Some training snuck through as she stood feeling useless on the edge of the pasture. Nearby, another Ennead called out, and her mind stirred. She had a pack. Her responsibilities to others outweighed her own.

She staggered to the other Ennead and recognized him as one of the herdsmen usually tending the ranna beasts. In the panic, a ranna had kicked his shin, and the leg was twisted awkwardly, clearly broken. The man lay groaning in the ash, unable to move.

Philyre placed the splinting bandage, the rod of basic sand iron properly embedded under layer after layer of bandage. In the middle of the ministrations, the herdsman passed out, and Philyre was grateful for the silence. For a moment, all she had to think about was how to place the bandage.

"Runner!" someone called. "Have you another bandage? Or oil?"

Another Ennead approached, tall and scarred. It took Philyre's scattered mind a few moments to recognize him as Maurn, a hound shifter.

The shifter sported a hundred wounds that bled freshly in black blood against black skin, but none of them appeared too deep or deadly. Maurn stopped a dozen paces away from Philyre, but even at this distance, Philyre could see the weariness in the shifter's legs. His clothing, whatever it had been, was long since gone.

Philyre tossed over a rolled bandage and a vial of oil and returned to the splint.

Maurn went beyond the markers to where the sand struggled against the clumped grass and set about cleaning himself. The process was meticulous and extended from the soles of the shifter's feet to the top of his head.

Philyre fought with the splint, her shaking hands unable to tie the thongs. Twice she replaced it, going through the complete action of measuring, placing, and tying it. By the time she was done, the shifter had placed his own bloody bandages, used to clean his wounds, into the smoldering ashes and watched them burn. He returned to the pastureland to stand over Philyre, his wounds dry.

"Good effort, Runner," the shifter said, looking down at the herdsman. "But that bruising on his chest means he doesn't need his leg. Sorry."

Philyre looked up and finally noticed the discoloration of the herdsman's sternum. A large hoofmark was centered on his ribs. While Philyre had assumed him unconscious, it was fast becoming obvious that no heart beat in the bruised, broken chest.

She sat back, feeling stupid. After a pause, she decided she might need the bandages and removed them. One by one, she rolled them back up.

"What's your name, Runner?" Maurn asked.

"Philyre," she replied. She glanced up at the shifter. "Want me to check you?"

The shifter nodded and held open his arms. "I'm worried I missed a spot." Maurn rotated slowly around, allowing Philyre to inspect him. Besides the scratch of white tattoos along his legs and the light wounds, he was clean.

"You're safe. You sound calm, considering…"

"If I'm not calm," Maurn replied, "I'm dead, so yes, I'm staying calm. You need to bandage your legs."

Philyre looked down and saw the blisters from the fires. She shrugged. "Don't need it. Better save them for others. The blisters have stopped burning, and if they stay shut, they won't get worse."

The enemy was still coming and going from the gates, loading wagons and carts with food and prizes from the City. Philyre's rage rose. "Why? They march through a desert for what? Food? Because they can't get food anywhere else?"

"I don't care why," Maurn replied. "We need to round up the survivors and get them moving. If they take the City, we have no water. We'll head north. There's a lake there. If we're lucky, we can catch up with the hunters. Be easier to guard everyone if I'm not the only shifter."

The words made sense. Philyre's eyes remained fixed on the smoke over the City as she listened, and, at last, her legs began to throb.

"I will round them up," she heard herself say. Her responsibility was clear.

To his surprise, the shifter held her back. "Philyre, we all had family in there."

She glared up at the tall Ennead, disbelieving the serenity of the shifter in light of the attack. Shifters lived to defend the City. They had failed. The people who had relied on them lay dead.

"Shifters don't have family," Philyre snapped.

The shifter started back as if he had been struck. "I had brothers, Runner," Maurn growled. "I watched a lot of them get driven into their demons, then cut down. Yet I see more demon in your eyes than I think there is in mine. Why is that, Philyre?"

Philyre swept her eyes over the smoldering pastures. "Because they need to die. Every last one of those monsters should lie dead in a dune."

The pause lingered, but it did not bother Philyre. Once, she had looked forward to crossing paths with another runner, knowing she would meet one every fourth marker as they circled the City if her speed was right. She had preferred conversation over the silence of the wind sailing through the sands beyond the markers. She had spoken to herdsmen, farmers, traders…

But now she wanted silence. The cries of her people still echoed. Any further sound threatened to overwhelm her.

At length, Maurn spoke, but his voice was softer than before. "I agree, Philyre. But if I charge in there, I die. If you charge in there, you die. That's why my brothers are not here to help me now."

She knew it was true, as much as she did not want it to be. Although they had fought, there were too many. A thousand of the gold-skinned warriors could lie dead, and there would still be enough to conquer the City for a second time. The Enneads were not numerous. A single Ennead could not hope to make a difference, not now. She would need an army of her own.

The tiny fire of Maurn's discarded bandages gave Philyre an idea.

"Runners are good at many things, you know," Philyre told the shifter. "Our first duty is to watch for demons approaching and warn the City. We know how to recognize their tracks and trail, and we know how to hide from them when they come close." She felt a smile creep onto her face. "I'll lead one to them, and let the demon do the battle for us."

Silence lingered again. Philyre's confidence solidified.

"Help me gather the survivors, Runner," the shifter said. "Then I will release you to do whatever you want."

The burn of her legs distanced itself as Philyre dug her toes into the burned earth and sprinted away. Soon her legs were again numb, but the pain in her chest and heart gathered strength. The far-off roar of a dying shifter spurred her on.

She did as the shifter commanded. As the day closed, the straggling survivors made their way north with Maurn, a single runner sent on ahead to try to catch the earlier shifters who had gone hunting. Philyre gathered the remaining runners. Including her, only seven of the thirty who had once patrolled still lived. All six others agreed to her plan and, leaving behind the train of survivors, headed out beyond the markers to seek a demon.

After the survivors had been rounded up, Maurn watched the seven Ennead runners turn their backs on the refugees. So far, the enemy had left the escaped Enneads alone, but it would only be a few days, Maurn was certain, before someone decided the refugees made good victims and came for another kill.

He would not give them the chance. Come morning, every able Ennead would be on the path north. Already a runner had gone on ahead, trying to reach the hunters. Maurn did not much like the odds of survival if he was the only shifter, but his hope was to reach the first oasis in the north. There was an old outpost there, abandoned in the early years and used now for shifters on a hunt. It could be defended if there were enough people. The lake would have a healthy population of fish by now, thanks to the efforts of the earlier settlers.

His demon tugged at the corner of his mind as seven runners disappeared over a southern dune. He knew them capable, but they had little hope of surviving in the desert without shifter aid. He feared the demon they sought would find them all too soon.

And it would fall to him to defend the survivors when those demons hunted Ennead flesh once more.

The demon begged for release, ready to hunt down the runners before they could take on the desert and its demons, but Maurn held it at bay. The Eldest Seer was dead. There was no one to put him on trial. Who would know he had broken the law of the City?

He turned his back and walked away.

CHAPTER 4

The sound of his name woke Askaran.

He started from partial sleep, memories of demon armies and piles of Ennead corpses still vivid in his mind. Ruddy sands and a blue sky replaced the black and red sky of the burned jungle of his dreams. The edges of Ero, the red sun, had snuck over the edge of the oasis valley, casting the water in crimson. The pool looked for a moment like the oceans of his nightmares, made of blood.

The Youngest Seer sat above him, her face streaked with tears. He could not remember another time he had seen her without a smile.

"Askaran?" she called again, her voice a plea.

Rolling over, Askaran wrapped his arms around her and held her to his chest. The comfort immediately spawned more tears. She unabashedly sobbed against his chest, given leave.

Illum's soul … it had been real. The thought of white jellabiyas dangling from a cord among smoke and fire tore at his heart. He clung to the seer all the tighter, knowing she would cry enough for them both.

He let her run out of tears before leading her from the waterside shelter and into the full light of Ero. He made a smokeless fire, but she ate little of the muddy fish meat he prepared. He refilled their waterskin, scattering piper lizards as he leaned over the shallows.

The heat of the day was already well in place; he had overslept but felt like he had not slept at all. Images of black soil and burned houses haunted him, and the demon in him laughed.

Mour followed Ero over the rise, and the light became white-yellow. Knowing they would have to wait out the heat if they wanted to travel, Askaran set about cutting up the white ruin fish for bait. If they could catch something else, the mudfish would not be their only fresh choice for tonight.

The sound of scavengers squawking above made the demon in him snarl in readiness. Looking up, Askaran spotted the flying reptiles on the edge of the valley's walls. A moment was all he needed to determine that they were approaching, following something they thought would soon be edible.

"Askaran?" the seer called, her eyes following his. "Would the enemy come here?"

"No," he replied, knowing his voice sounded less confident than he had intended. "They came by the web oases. They know that route. They should follow it back."

The desert had no easy paths, but the safest ones were always the ones already tracked. Why would anyone risk an unknown way?

But the scavengers were hoping for a meal. They were following something.

"Hide under the sand-cloak," Askaran told the seer, "by the rocks over there. I'll check it out and come back."

He was struck by how similar his words were to the day before. She had no hesitation this time, but quickly lay against the rocky outcropping, the sand-cloak pulled over her. Even Askaran could not see her.

In the interest of remaining hidden, he scaled the cliffs leading into the valley instead of walking up the easier slope. He tried to avoid thinking about the winged demon that had done just that the day before. He wondered if he would surprise someone at the vantage point above, as he had been surprised.

Sure enough, as he reached the top, he heard steps on the stones above. He flattened himself against the cliff.

Bright faces peered down at his camp from the cliff face. A woman wearing a drape of tauran skin and holding a tauran hide shield narrowed her brown eyes into the distance. Every one of the faces above was painted in the same pattern: yellow and red zigzags over the forehead and chins with brown dots on either side of the lines. He could tell little of their faces besides the pattern.

"Camp there looks fresh," someone said from behind her in words that were shockingly Ennead but accented strangely. "Fire's still lit."

"Get down there," the woman said. "Search for—"

A shout interrupted from across the valley, and Askaran spotted a second party of the strangers atop the opposite cliff. From their position, his black skin against the red cliffs must have been glaring.

Spears lowered toward him, and he wondered if they could throw the width of the valley. He could be up the rest of the cliff and shifted before any spear reached him, but a falling spear might land too close to the child below.

The woman above was staring directly at him when he glanced up. She held a chipped spear in her hand, aimed at him.

"Climb down," she ordered him. "You are surrounded. Surrender, or die, Ennead."

Figuring it would be easier to tear them apart on level ground, Askaran complacently returned to the valley floor.

Seven warriors followed the woman in the tauran hide armor down into the valley, each dressed in bone-studded leather collars and heavy lizard-skin shendyts. The spears, made of long wood handles and a tip of bone, were lowered toward him as he landed at the cliff base, a step from where the seer lay hidden. *They must have been from the south jungles*, he decided, *else where had they found so much wood?*

The woman stepped forward again, her eyes searching him. Her stare lingered most on his kukris.

"Nice tattoo," she said, pointing her spear at where the face of the colossus demon lay over his scarred left shoulder.

"I thought it made me look tough," he replied, speaking each word slowly to help her understand.

She arched one eyebrow at the comment. "What is it? A keim beast?"

Askaran glanced down at the lines of white that had so faded over time. He wondered if these strangers even knew what a colossus demon was. Keim beasts were more reptilian and had longer snouts, but…

"Yes, but the artist was not good," he said. "Looks like it bred with a dredger."

The woman smiled ever-so-slightly. "You speak Berintan well," she said, her words thick to Askaran's ears but clear enough.

"I thought you spoke my language with surprising skill," he said.

She stared at him for a long moment, her eyes pinched in thought. "Speak slowly, and it will suffice," she said with a shake of her head. "Who are you?" The question became an order by her tone.

Deciding on a lie to buy him time, Askaran said, "I am a hunter. I have trade. Are you traders?"

"Traders?" The woman scoffed. "We are Berintan warriors from the south, Hunter. I am Funanya, Archon of the second ark of Douran. You," she added, poking the air with her spear to indicate him, "are now my prisoner."

At a gesture from the woman, another Berintan inched forward, and Askaran allowed them to take his kukris and belt, pleased they would facilitate his shift. The sand-cloak was already safe. If he could remove his sandals…

"You travel alone, Hunter?" Funanya asked, and he was relieved to detect no more suspicion or fear in her. She did not seem to know enough about Enneads to know no one but a shifter walked the desert alone.

"Hunts are easier alone," he answered. "Why are you here, Berintan? Why take a prisoner in the desert when it is one more mouth to feed?"

The woman's expression became a sinister smirk. "You don't know?" she said. Around her, the warriors chuckled.

"Whichever way you have come from, you have come a long way. For what?"

The woman had turned from him, and Askaran felt a knot in his chest release as she distanced herself from the hidden seer. She aimed for the small shelter and the half-butchered fish that lay in front of it.

"I might have use for you," the archon said. "Do you know the oases of the desert?"

Given permission by the slow withdrawal of the spears, Askaran followed her toward the shelter. In his mind, the demon growled softly. The predator came to the fore of his mind, ready to pounce. Askaran had been expecting it sooner. Was it sluggish this morning?

"Of course I do," Askaran replied, trying to focus on the woman in front of him and the warriors behind him at the same time. Eight of them all together, plus the four on the opposite cliff. Nothing a colossus demon could not handle.

"I would have you lead us to the next oasis."

He had to remind himself that he was not meant to know that they were but one small part of an army. He feigned ignorance once more, finally feeling like he had enough room to shift, but he hesitated, trying to figure out how to get his sandals off. He had no interest in walking the sands barefoot if he ruined his sandals. Then again, he could always take footwear from one of the dead.

"You came here that way, no? Can you not find your way back?" he asked.

When she faced him, he thought she was meeting the eyes of the demon on his shoulder. She quickly looked away.

"Sadly, the army I travel with is not careful. We needed wood for fires. Now the oases they have passed through will not take them back."

Their presence in the chain oases made sudden sense. If they had cut the oases in their wake, the web oases would not support their return. And if that were true, the passage of the army would ruin every source of water within days of the City. If the City remained contaminated by demon blood, the life of the seer was in sharp danger. Without water, there was no life.

"What stupidity brought you out so far into the desert?!" Askaran snapped before reining himself in. "Have you no…" He trailed off, recognizing his oversight.

He had never been into the lush areas of Nanterac his mother had described but knew the desert perfectly. The inverse was also true. They knew their jungle, but not the desert.

Askaran realized there was a spear at his throat. The Berintan on the other end snarled deeply like a keim beast scenting prey. "Mind your words, barbarian," the warrior said. "Do not insult our archon."

Askaran pulled the demon back under control. He could not kill them here, not if it meant risking spilling his own contaminated blood into this water. That would destroy this oasis as well. They were fast running out of water sources.

By the rocky cliff, the sand drifted upward, and Askaran spotted the seer, still hidden under the cover of the cloak, creeping up the slope. A sled waited atop the slope, pulled by two harnessed taurans. The decision was being made for him.

Askaran lowered his voice, adopting a tone he hoped sounded polite. "You were saying something about an army, esteemed Archon?"

The Beritan lowered his spear a hair.

The archon's face was impassive, a hard thing for him to understand for a woman who had helped destroy an entire city. This woman lacked emotions he expected in a sentient race.

"Yes, an army," she told him. "Your city is dead. You obey me, or you die."

The demon thought the idea was funny. Askaran caught the laugh when it was still a smile and smothered it.

"I can show you the way," Askaran said, seeing the seer continue her careful climb up the slope toward the cart out of the corner of his eye. "I know this desert. I can be useful." He tried to sound scared and eager. His words, to him, made him sound simple, but he thought that would work too.

The woman smirked. "Good," she said, finding a place beside his cooking fire. "Start by cooking. I'm hungry." She gestured, to his amusement, at the white ruin fish.

He pointed out the mudfish remains on the rocks beside the fire. Seeing her eyes narrow on him, he said, "The white one is poison. Good for bait, but not eating."

"That so?" she demanded.

Askaran felt a smile creep onto his face, and he could not stop it. "You want to try some? Your heart will speed before you have even taken your second bite, and it will stop by the third."

Her glare was thick against him, but before she could speak, a shout interrupted, "Funanya!"

The woman shot to her feet. Her retinue surrounded her at once, their spears snapping up, not aggressive but attentive.

A new Berintan had arrived at the top of the slope, dressed in keim beast hide, the scale thick and smooth. The face paint was different; this man had white around his eyes and down his nose to his chin and circles of red and white on his cheeks. The surrounding warriors, a dozen or so, matched. Askaran assumed they represented a new ark.

The new arrival marched down the slope, and none of them seemed to notice the small sandbank that was the seer. This Berintan was short but stocky and had combed his curled hair into tiny braids. They formed a mane around his head, not unlike that of a tusked demon.

"You captured a prisoner?" the man demanded. His voice was like a mother addressing a child.

"A hunter," Funanya reported. She stepped away from the fire to give the seat to the new arrival. "He has fresh meat." To Askaran's confusion, she indicated the white ruin fish.

"Ah, good," the man said. "Better than dried tauran meat." He made a face at the woman. "Should you not be setting camp?" He waved her off dismissively.

"Of course, Archon," she said, retreating.

Prodded by the woman's warriors, Askaran moved a dozen steps back. He found himself beside the archon Funanya, whose knowing smile had returned as she stood watching the new arrival sit on the stone by the water and the fish.

"I told you it was poison," Askaran said, his voice soft.

"But you did not tell him, and neither shall I. Either you told me the truth and he dies, or you lied, whereupon I kill you. Either way, today is a good day."

Every one of Funanya's warriors had been forced away from the man in the keim beast armor. Like their archon, they remained silent as the white ruin fish was cooked.

"But he is one of your people," Askaran said.

"He is the Archon of Douran," she said with a haphazard shrug, "and so my superior. I inherit the position if something happens to him."

At the top of the slope, Askaran spotted the dusty shift of the seer wiggle out from under the sand-cloak and slide under the Berintan's cart. The carts of the City used wheels over the smoothed streets, but the Enneads had never tried to take a vehicle into the sands. The Berintans had solved the problem by replacing the wheels with long planks of bent wood. Keeping the bed of the cart up avoided plowing into the sand. The seer climbed into the rigging above the skis, drawing her cloak up behind her.

Askaran's duty became clear; he had to stay with the seer. That meant staying with these Berintans. If the Berintan archon was willing to use him, he would accept servitude.

And so he said not a word to the man sitting by the hide.

Archon Funanya sent her warriors to investigate the far side of the oasis, and the piper lizards scattered before them. With no safe place to land, they took aim for the distant horizon, and the oasis was sent into silence as the scavengers circled. The smell of fish gave the scavengers a target, and the flock above grew in number. Askaran remained against the cliff, a spear against his chest, as they watched.

The man in the keim armor took the first bite of white ruin fish, and Askaran felt the eyes of Archon Funanya on him. Askaran shook his head and counted to ten.

The man was on his feet by the count of six, clutching at his chest, his skin glittering as he broke out into a sweat. He paced backward as if to retreat from the sensation but dropped to the ground by the count of ten.

"I guess you are useful after all. Come along, Hunter," Archon Funanya said softly.

The archon strode over to where the man gave a final breath and died. His warriors clustered around him, muttering disbelief as the word "dead" filtered through them.

"What is this? How has he fallen?" Funanya made a show of glaring at the surrounding people, each of which withdrew from her stare. At length, she gestured at the fish. "It must have been this food! Who could have known this fish was dangerous?"

The other clan's members stepped away, whispering amongst themselves. They did not seem distressed, surprising Askaran. But they hushed when Archon Funanya's stare fell upon them.

Not one of the warriors stood in her path as she took the keim leather from the dead man. Wiping it out with a cloth, she donned it, her grin now ominous. It did not fit well, but he understood it was a symbol more than anything. "Strip him," she ordered. "Distribute his belongings among the ranks. Mark this spot and let Archon Farai know we have secured the oasis." She glared down at the body by the rocks. "And inform the Archon that we have tragically lost an archon to poisonous fare." Her voice was flat.

The archon took the desert cloak from over the fishing hide as she left the body, and Askaran was forced by the spears to follow her. When he crested the valley and joined her beside the cart, the heat of the double suns fell upon his back.

Two paces in front of him, he knew the seer hid under the cart. Although he could now see five of the vehicles, the one the seer had selected seemed to contain basic supplies of shelters, food, and water. Several men returned to it now, their canisters—a strange gourd on a string—full of oasis waters.

"Tonight you will be bound," Askaran was informed. "Early tomorrow, you will lead us to the next oasis, and in exchange, I will spare your life. But since you are too precious of a prize to lose, you will not interact with any other Berintan. You will answer to me and no other. Disobey me, and you will be cut down. Am I clear?"

"You must already know the way," Askaran replied. "None but a madman would lead an army into the desert without knowing a way out."

The archon nodded. "Oh, she gives us directions, but finding it first is prestigious. I am now the First ark of Douran, and I intend to defend my title. You will help us be the first to reach the oasis."

"As you like," Askaran accepted. He wanted to ask who "she" was but decided against it, certain it would become clear. "And what shall I call you?"

"Archon," she said. "You now are owned by the Archon of Douran. Congratulations. Now help move the cart to the far side. I want to be positioned to leave early."

Askaran turned for the cart, his demon rearing in his mind at the thought of captivity.

But the Youngest Seer had hidden with the Berintans. Did she expect them to travel together? Was he meant to follow or rip them apart?

He held back, allowing the Berintans to go about their business, telling himself that surprise still gave him the advantage. He could retrieve the kukris from their corpses if required.

Askaran watched the archon, wondering where the people had come from on the empty planet and why they had attacked the Last City of the Ennead without warning. And how they looked so like Enneads, if he ignored their golden skin. When the planet had been searched by the first shifters on Nanterac, no sentient races had been found.

Once they were organized, he was tethered between the taurans and, with the threat of a whip to his back, he joined the beasts in pulling the cart to a place in the newly forming camp.

As soon as she left the prisoner, Funanya was joined by Dalia, one of her closest friends and warriors. Dalia offered fresh water, and Funanya traded back her old gourd, happy to have cool water again. Behind Dalia came one of the warriors wearing Sizwe's ark's paint.

Sizwe's previously loyal warrior presented himself on bent knee.

It was a formality, but one Funanya thoroughly enjoyed. She had won her place in more than one ark with similar offerings. The experience was far more pleasant when she was the one standing during the exchange.

"Our warriors are pledged to you if you wish them."

None but an archon could lead an ark. Without Sizwe's rank to hold them, the ark was immediately dropped to the bottom of Douran's hierarchy with no hope for advancement until another archon accepted them. The three other possible Archons of Douran were nearby: Sizwe's other ark leaders. None had such good prospects as Funanya.

Funanya still waited a few moments, as if giving the offer some consideration.

"I think your warriors could be great again," she said, offering her hand to the man. He placed the butt of his spear in her grip, and she brought him to his feet.

As he rose, she could not help but notice his fit form and wonder if Sizwe's warriors had sent their most attractive member to act as the emissary.

"We are in your debt," he said.

"Your name?" she asked.

"Rudo, Archon," he replied, a coy smile on his face.

"Then have your friends repaint their faces. Welcome." His expression was boyish as he bowed his head and left at a run. She enjoyed watching him leave; the shendyt he wore was designed to allow easy movement.

As they turned away, other Douran arks crested the hills by the oasis, following Sizwe's tracks. Once in the valley, they began setting up camp. The prime locations nearest the waters were already in Funanya's hands, the prize of being the first to find the oasis. The other three arks and their archons would have to set up on the sands.

"Archon?" Dalia asked, her voice steep. "I'm not sure about him. Too quick to offer allegiance. Were they expecting Sizwe to die?"

"Anyone could tell it was coming," Funanya said, spotting Tau and Adeban together for a moment atop the valley cliff. The two other archons, when they saw her watching, crossed their arms over their chests in greeting and bowed their head respectfully. She was unsure if they were saluting her victory of finding the oasis first or her success in killing Sizwe. Either way suited her, and she returned the salute, but she did not have to bow her head, not now. "Sizwe was not fit to lead," Funanya finished.

"Still don't like him," Dalia said.

Funanya thought again of the young man who had pledged the ark to her and felt warm. "I don't think I share that sentiment," she said. "Tell the warriors to set my tent. I want to be close to the water."

Without another word, Dalia bowed and left.

The camp at the oasis was silent until sunset.

They had tied the Ennead hunter to the wagon. His bag had proven to be a pitiful prize, containing basic supplies. He did not even have a spare cloak, and so was left in his shendyt and sandals by the cart in the heat. He took shelter in the shade of the cart, and Funanya ensured he was given his own water to carry.

At sunset, a group of tauran riders arrived along the marked trail to the oasis. To her surprise, the ark represented was that of Archon Farai himself.

Leaving the prisoner under the cart, Funanya received Archon Farai in her tent and offered her personal stores of chapman, although she had only local fruits to add. Dried baraka fruit, carefully hoarded for the journey back, were put on display for his use. The sparse spoils taken from the city, including half a roasted ranna beast, were begrudgingly assembled, should the archon want to eat.

Funanya swapped her armor for a fine linen kaftan decorated with tauran and dredger scales dipped in gold. The dress was held by a belt woven with tauran teeth, but she wrapped it low to let the top of her breasts be visible.

She met him as he dismounted, her highest-ranking warriors smartly at attention. Every one of them bowed the moment Farai's feet touched the rocky sand by the slope.

Archon Farai paused for a moment, assessing the scene. Apparently finding no cause for criticism, he said, "Every time I see you, Funanya, your position has changed. Rise, warrior, and get me out of this wind."

She led him to her tent, checking with every step that things were in place. Her warriors presented themselves proudly, the perfect example of discipline. Dalia alone winked at Funanya, telling Funanya she had threatened the warriors with dismemberment should they step out of line. Rudo and his fellow warriors joined in straight ranks, fresh face paint announcing their new loyalties. They fit in nicely.

The archon's entourage of bodyguards stopped at the tent, but Farai motioned for Funanya to follow him in. He performed a cursory examination of the tent, found her seat, and sat on the plush chair. She hastened to provide the chapman.

"Choked on a fish?" he asked, putting his feet up on an ottoman with a slight smirk as he took his first sip.

The general had not even knocked his boots before treading across her new Ennead carpet, or before flopping his feet onto the ottoman. She deliberately avoided thinking about what the sand from his boots was doing to the hair-stuffed furniture. Figuring it was a test, Funanya did not comment.

Knowing he would eventually hear the full story, Funanya felt it was safer to correct, "Ate a poisonous fish, Archon. A fish I have since learned is called white ruin. Very dangerous."

Farai nodded sagely. "Good of him to let us know of this danger," he said. "I will have to avoid white fish. Have a drink, Funanya. Sit with me."

Filling a second cup, Funanya sat on the carpet at his side. At least her spoils from the Ennead city kept her from having to get more sand in her dress.

"You have ever been ambitious," he said. "Are you satisfied now?"

"Perfectly," Funanya replied, keeping her expression calm despite the quiet threat she sensed. "I am now the Archon of Douran. Sizwe was a fool. The city will benefit from the change. This I swear."

The general chuckled, swirling his cup before taking another sip. "Sizwe was indeed a fool. The other arks of Douran have been vying for his position for years, and he never saw it. You, I trust, see it."

"Neither Tau nor Adeban represent a challenge," she informed the archon. "You can't be referring to Jabarl, can you? That idiot can't tell the front end of a tauran from the back." She sipped the chapman, content enough to let the fermented juices flow freely. That the general trusted her at his foot was further evidence; the campaign was a success for Funanya's ark.

The archon considered her words for a moment longer before taking another sip. "Do not think that I mention this because I like you, Funanya," he warned. "So long as the rule of Douran is under Grand Archon Amadi's control, I do not care who lives in the grand manors. But I have no tolerance for stupidity. Watch yourself, and you will live to see the end of the desert and take up residence in the Grand Manor of Douran."

He glanced about the tent once more, his eyes passing over her chest of spoils and lingering on her pillowed bed. She recognized the hint at once and, putting aside her cup, stood.

"Will you be spending the night with us tonight, Archon? My home is yours, of course."

"I will return to the city at first light," he decided, putting down his own cup. "Our little thorn needs supervision, but the way between the oases is marked this far. The army marches in two days. I want the path clear, Funanya. This is now your responsibility."

"We will find the shortest routes," she promised, bowing once more as she backed out of the tent.

"Funanya?"

She paused and brought her eyes up. The archon stood by her pillowed bed, his expression one of curiosity. "You have seen the inside of Douran's Grand Manor, haven't you?"

She knew better than to lie to the archon. "Of course I have, Archon. Sizwe was a fool in many ways."

She was pleased by the smile the admission earned her.

"Then I will sleep alone," Farai said, but he sounded impressed.

CHAPTER 5

Nightmares lingered overnight for the first time Askaran could remember, and he was no longer sure if they were from the demon or from his own memories. As he woke, images of a burning jungle—the trees and vines coated by Ennead and demon blood—hovered behind his eyes. Although he had been born on Nanterac, the vividness of the images made him feel like he had been living in the jungle while it burned, his own claws working to tear it apart.

He awoke lying on his back under the Berintan cart. Tucked up between the axles, he saw the seer. She looked older by years. Her tears were gone.

The dawn light barely crossed the far dunes as he woke, and the horizon still had stars. Askaran ensured no one was watching, then passed up the water-gourd he had been charged with. No food had been provided, but the seer showed she had brought her little bag with her and offered dried fruits. He declined, and she retreated into the shadows of the cart's undercarriage.

Beyond the cart's propped position, Askaran caught sight of movement. One of the warriors, a tall woman Askaran had seen in the archon's shadow all of yesterday, skirted into the camp. She set herself beside a fire as if waiting for the others to wake. One of his kukris, Askaran noted, was in her possession, the unique wooden handle distinctive. He made note of her appearance, memorizing her for later when he would retake what was his.

Beyond her, Askaran spotted movement. One of the other camps, belonging to people of the same city but a different ark than Archon Funanya's, was packing up. He assumed it had something to do with the prestige of finding the next oasis first.

He was happy to let them leave. Once the majority were gone, he could shift into his demon, slay those remaining, and free the seer from danger.

"We will go with the Berintans," the seer said, interrupting his thoughts.

Askaran was surprised the sentence was a statement. "If we escape now—"

"We have to hide," the seer told him. "They have poisoned the waters of the oases. and the water of the City is," the seer squinted in deep concentration, "bad." Her expression straightened. "We cannot survive the desert if the oases are gone."

She was right. Askaran was mildly grateful that she had not been able to tell why the City water was a risk now. He did not want to believe she had been so changed in a single day. A child should be a child.

Fearing the answer, Askaran asked gently, "Do you know this, Seer, or do you *know*?"

The silence was uncommonly long. For a moment, he expected new tears, but her voice was flat as she replied, "I know these things because they make sense. I just want to live. We have to go with them. Don't …

don't take me into the desert. I need these people. This is my survival."

The weight of the words settled on Askaran, and he felt his demon protest. He wanted to kill them all, take back his kukris, take revenge. He needed blood.

He forced the demon back into the corner of his mind. She was young, but she was a seer. He had to obey her and believed it was for the right reasons. She *knew* something. The Youngest Seer needed Askaran the Ennead, not Askaran the demon.

"You will live," he told her, filling his voice with confidence, "and I know that because I am going to make it happen."

She said nothing further but handed him back the water. By its lightness, she had transferred some into her own waterskin. So long as they fed him at some point, Askaran could pass food to her. The desert crossing was days, but it took longer than that to starve a shifter.

And that was where he was going: across the desert in the company of killers. The demon was not to be allowed out for now.

A short while later, the camp woke. The archon appeared, again dressed in her armor and a cloak similar to the desert wrap. One group of Berintans rode away on the back of taurans. Askaran watched them go, wondering why the Enneads had never thought of taming the beasts. The taurans' wide feet moved well on the sands and probably had served as the inspiration for the "feet" of the carts.

"Up, Hunter," the archon called, and Askaran rose. He was handed a single piece of dried meat by one Berintan while another attached a leather collar around his neck. He assumed the meat was tauran as well and tucked it into his belt instead of eating it. The rope that had bound his hands was transferred to the collar he now wore. "I have promised Archon Farai that we will find the shortest route between oases, so I want you on your best behavior. Lead us on, Hunter."

Feeling naked without his weapons, Askaran led the cart forward under the early dawn.

The cart made his typical path between oases impassable, but he still showed them the way, step by step, to the next water source. The sunrise guided him at first, but soon the tracing of a path was a careful consideration of sun position, the sight of the peaks in the far east, and haphazard landmarks that may or may not be present, depending on the shifting dunes.

The archon's warriors marked the route with posts. As each red flag faded from sight, the warriors pulled another pole from a wagon and erected it. A trail of chiming posts—for they were woven with bones and metal shards—was left behind as they made their way through the desert.

Askaran wondered what would happen to the posts if a storm passed through. Those erecting the markers were careful to set them on stone, using tools to anchor them, but if the dunes changed…

Even as swiftly as the sands moved, it would take a few days to completely cover the posts in the absence of a sandstorm.

By late morning, scavengers had appeared on the horizon, but Askaran recognized they were not following the Berintan group; they were following whatever was following the Berintan.

They had to wait out the worst of the midday heat, and the higher-ranked warriors erected pavilions for shelter. Askaran ended up under the cart again, and while it did little to encourage the cooler breeze, it worked to keep the sun off his back.

He knew he would burn. Desert wraps and sand-cloaks served to minimize exposure, but both had been taken from him. He was also going through his water more quickly than usual, and he risked severe dehydration even by midday. Still, he refused the seer's offer of water.

Once the archon had decided the air had cooled enough to allow the march to continue, she positioned herself beside Askaran. He walked on, skirting around a dune until he found the slope that allowed them to cross over it. It took three men to keep each cart moving when the taurans struggled up the slope. As he waited at the top of the dune for the sled to reach them, she asked, "Why is it you speak Berintan?"

The cadence was off, but the words were clear enough. She sounded a little childish in her inflections.

Askaran shrugged. "I do not know another language."

That earned him a sour look. He followed quickly with, "I speak Ennead. Our languages are the same: Berintan and Ennead." Having seen her the night before dressed in gowns and jewelry, he added, "We look the same as well. I thought this world empty." He avoided mention of the choice of this world specifically because it had been deemed devoid of sentient life. The histories had been clear that Nanterac had meant to be barren.

"Not empty if we are here," she told him, her head high and her eyes on the horizon. "You were mistaken."

"Perhaps," Askaran conceded. "Or perhaps we did not search recently enough." Seeing the archon cock her head toward him, he added, "We came from another world. It has been generations since we last explored outside the desert."

"Foolish to isolate yourselves in a wilderness without resources," she commented, not offering any of the history he was trying to lead her into revealing. "No wonder you had no skill with which to defend your city."

He stayed silent, feeling no need to explain their lack of warriors or dependence on the shifters to a stranger. The Berintan race had to be young; Askaran was certain the original shifters had searched Nanterac thoroughly before selecting it as a target for the Alighting Hall. But none of that explained why the two races were so similar, or how they shared a language. No Ennead was permitted to leave the Last City. Only shifters could travel beyond, and they returned or perished. That had been the way since the first of the shifters, maintained by the Elders and by the shifters since.

The wind filled the space between them, sand from the tauran's wide steps sliding down the slopes.

"What do you know about shifters, Hunter?"

Askaran flinched before he could stop himself. He could expect that she would know about them because of the siege—a demon turning into an Ennead or the other way around was too obvious to miss—but she used the term "shifters" as if it was a common conversation topic. Unless they had spoken to Enneads, how had they learned the shape-shifting peoples were called shifters at all?

"As much as any Ennead," he replied, hoping he sounded calm.

"We have a shifter among the army now, and I want to know more about him. Apparently, the rest are dead or fled north to hide, assuming they make the trek."

Knowing the path north was guarded by shifters gave Askaran hope that the refugees would survive. The duties of a shifter included escorting anyone venturing outside the walls of the City. They all knew the roads of the desert. They had never left the sands, but they could reach the edge of them in the north easily enough. Exploration there had been limited, only recently condoned by the Eldest Seer, but it was enough to give them a place to go.

The cart reached the peak of the dune, and Askaran directed them down the leading slope. The tauran obediently followed, giving the impression that they were in fact leashed to him instead of the other way around.

"Which shifter?" Askaran inquired. He felt nervous that he might already know the answer.

"Calls himself Yarr," the archon replied, eyeing him carefully for a reaction. "Keyed to a tusked demon, I hear. You know him?"

The seer's worried words about the shifter who "did not like her" came back to Askaran, and he cursed himself for not taking her more seriously.

"Everyone knows the shifters," Askaran replied mildly, "by name, if not by face. Yarr is arrogant, prideful, and powerful." Askaran wondered if the Youngest Seer was eavesdropping now. She needed to know this as well, to keep up hope.

The archon sighed into the wind, her rust-colored cloak tossed behind her. "Trust Archon Farai to win over the most powerful shifter."

"He wasn't the most powerful," Askaran pointed out. "He would probably tell you he was, but he wasn't."

"Who was?"

Although he had only overheard a small portion of the conversations overnight, Askaran felt like he was coming to understand the Archon of Douran. She was a motivated woman who thrived on taking advantage of opportunities, and her questions seemed to be aimed at better identifying or generating those opportunities. He assumed she wanted to know about Yarr because she was going to have to deal with him and knowing more about him would give her an advantage.

Yarr had betrayed his people. He did not deserve to sit around enjoying spoils. If this Berintan could wound him, Askaran was happy to help her do it.

His demon liked that line of thought, too.

"Yarr has a tusked demon shift because he went out and sought one to kill," Askaran said. "He failed to kill it, although he'll hate you for reminding him of that. He would have been slain if it hadn't been for another shifter. Askaran is his name. He harbors a colossus demon."

The archon took a short, sharp breath in. "Another arrogant bastard, if he sought a colossus demon to slay."

"It was an accident," Askaran said. "He was a boy, and the party was attacked by a colossus demon. They managed to slay it, but not before the boy had been keyed." He glanced back to check on the progress of the scavengers and was disappointed by their ongoing approach. "No one tries to bind to a colossus demon, and only the very stupid try for the tusked. The more powerful the demon, the harder they are to control. Askaran was always just a moment away from going insane. Yarr has it easier, but not by much."

He felt like his demon was mocking him now. Askaran had never confessed his struggle before to anyone, although, among the Enneads, he had assumed it was common knowledge. The way people approached him had always been cautious. He had seldom been asked to preside over justice disputes. They called on him to defend the City, not for societal pleasantries. No one trusted an Ennead who perpetually held a demonic general at bay. The women asked to share his bed because his blood could make them mothers to new shifters, but not because any of them considered him good company. He had companions among the shifters, but friends were not something a shifter expected. Friends got old and died.

He slowed his pace again, feeling his collar tighten with the stumble of the tauran. Having no desire to end up at the bottom of a dune, he changed the angle of the cart to follow a wide trough between drifts.

"So Yarr is unpredictable?" the archon asked.

"Very much so when it comes to violence, but not so much as an Ennead. He likes praise. He thinks he is better than anyone else."

"He is, isn't he?" she replied with a laugh. "A tusked demon inside, by the shour! Who could argue?"

When Askaran replied, it was for the seer, not for the archon.

"Yarr is a shifter because he was born of shifter blood, and so he was assigned a job in the City. But he is Ennead, and Enneads need Enneads. If the sandal-maker does not do his work, who will mend the sandals on Yarr's feet? And if the weaver cannot work, where will Yarr get the desert wrap to protect his back from blisters and burns?" His own back throbbed. The blisters had started. "And if the shepherd does not keep his ranna beasts out of the crops, and the farmer does not plant the seeds or weed the dran fields, or the miller grind grains, how will he make his flatbread? If—"

"I understand," the archon interrupted, her terse voice making Askaran believe he had offended her. "I had heard of this society, but I never thought one could believe in it. Do you really believe every Ennead is as valuable as every other?"

"Without each other, we die," Askaran insisted. He decided to avoid mentioning the seers. To him, they were far more valuable than any other Ennead, including the shifters.

The archon's voice became cold. "So what will do you now that you are alone? Die?"

He glanced over his shoulder again to assess the scavengers, having no reply worth voicing. The flying reptiles had gained a little.

"That is the fourth time you have looked back, Hunter," the archon informed him. "What do you keep looking for? Someone to save you?"

The irony of the question made Askaran laugh, and he thought for a moment the laughter would slip out of control. His fatigue felt like a haze in his mind, distracting him from the demon's mental cage.

"Someone to save me?" he echoed. "Someone will need to save you, not me."

She tensed at the words but seemed to realize a moment before drawing her sword that he was still a bound prisoner wearing a collar. She only had to move out of his reach to be safe.

"Not a threat, just an observation," Askaran pointed out. With his head alone, he gestured to the six scavengers circling the sky behind them. "Those scavengers follow beasts that are going to kill things. Since

I see a small dust trail beneath them, it's something moving slowly, and there's only one. Now, if the scavengers think that single something is nasty enough to kill the thirty of you, that means it's big. I'm guessing a serpent demon. It's that or a tusked demon, and tusked demons are far more likely to kick up a big trail. They like to run."

The archon paused and checked over her shoulder, leaving Askaran to walk on alone. Followed by two tethered tauran, he did not think stopping suddenly wise.

A dozen paces later, she rejoined him. "I think you're bluffing."

"I don't care. Believe me or don't. I know what I see."

She left him to walk the rest of the day without company, and he was grateful for the quiet.

When Archon Farai, highest ranked of all the archon next to Grand Archon Amadi himself, walked among the men, the warriors behaved. Upon his return to the Ennead city after a visit to the scouting camp at the first oasis, men and women alike snapped to attention, standing with their arms crossed and their heads bowed in greeting.

His first sword, gifted to him when he had been named archon, had been lost in the battle. His newer sword, shaped by his own hand the year before, was wood with obsidian shards and had to be repaired often. After the attack on the Enneads, a people he had just learned existed, he had found a fine replacement for his lost sword, an Ennead's metal khopesh, curved and made of beautifully forged metal. The previous owner had maintained it well; it showed little signs of age, even though it had to be hundreds of years old. It did not stick as well to the atra poison he preferred to use, but it worked well enough. No such metal existed on Nanterac, lending credence to the idea that their enemy's origins had not been on Nanterac at all.

Farai left the seer—now the Eldest Seer—surrounded by warriors, and her silence nagged at him. Even two days after the discovery, he could not tell if she was relieved to find the portal already destroyed or not. The loss of her people seemed to reach her superficially; she would laugh and talk as if nothing at all were wrong, but fall into deep stillness when no distractions were available. She knew they were returning now to Berinta—they had taken everything they needed from the Enneads—but that too seemed to hold no meaning for her. Grand Archon Amadi had said he wished her alive and healthy for the rest of her life. Farai was to care for her personally.

Knowing a prophet could be of use to his own position, Farai was happy to oblige. The seer's accuracy thus far had been uncanny. He was unsure she would assist him much once she started longing for her homeland, but until then, she would be interesting.

But Grand Archon Amadi had not said anything about the shifter ally they had gained. That was a prize Farai had yet to fully grasp.

At the center of the Berintan camp, far outside the Ennead city, a large tent had been erected for the shifter. As the archon approached it, the many assigned warriors rushed to and from the tent like frantic slaves in the Grand Manors, carrying fresh meat and drink, or carcasses and empty cups. Among his men, each warrior was responsible for his own upkeep and that of his or her archon. Farai had extended his authority to see the shifter provided for like an archon. Warriors from Farai's own ark were forced into demeaning positions to appease the beast Farai hoped to tame. He did not doubt the command had been resented when it had been given, and by now was wearing the warriors thin.

The warriors stood at attention when he entered the tent. Of them all, only the immense Ennead sitting at a heaped table continued to move.

Yarr stood taller than any man Farai had ever known and was built of nothing but muscle. The Ennead's black hair had been shaved to the skin, leaving a bristle over the skull. Replacing his simple shendyt, he wore a tailored Berintan linen dashiki and sokoto. The drawstring on the sokoto was left untied by necessity; even the biggest size the Berintans had barely fit around the man's waist, and the legs of it came to the Ennead's shins.

The Enneads Farai had seen so far had taller skulls and thinner features than Berintans, making their eyes look tight and small. Furthering their differences, the irises of Enneads were black, unlike Berintan brown, giving them an alert appearance at all times. Yarr's eyes were typical, except that the shifter seemed to keep his stare perpetually narrowed as if in consideration.

"Greetings, shifter," Farai called, with a gesture releasing the warriors from their tense positions. They returned to their duties. Another pile of food was swept away to be thrown to the wolfen.

Unlike the confusing Eldest Seer, Yarr seemed simple to Farai. The huge Ennead liked attention and reverence. All Yarr seemed to crave was a chance to command someone else.

Assigning him warriors who would serve him—not in combat, but Yarr did not seem to know that—had made the shifter complacent. He had disposed of all his Ennead trappings, from weapons to shendyt, in short order. The only exception was the reverence, which seemed instinctual, to the seer when the woman was present.

Farai had learned to keep the two Enneads separate. Yarr seemed happier.

Yarr smiled, his chin covered in bloody juices as he lowered a tauran leg back to the table. "What do you want?" the Ennead said. His accent was thick, the words slurred together, but they were close enough to Farai's to be understood.

How they shared a language, even distantly, Farai did not know.

"I wish to ensure you have everything you desire, shifter. Is there anything else I can get you?" Farai asked.

The shifter's nostrils flared, and he snorted. "No, what do *you* want?" the shifter insisted. "You care not, not about me. You want something."

Farai joined the Ennead in smiling. "I appreciate your candidness," Farai said, sitting across from the monster as it went back to chewing on the tauran leg. "I'll not waste your valuable time. My warriors are finishing with the city. Is there anything else we should take?"

"What has value to one has no value to another," the Ennead replied, surprising Farai. The thought was more philosophical than he had thought Yarr capable of being.

"Agreed," Farai said. "You see these hides and horns as valuable, but Grand Archon Amadi seeks riches. We know the Enneads have mirrors, glass, gold…"

"The greatest treasure," the shifter said dramatically, "is lost."

Farai's chest tightened in anticipation. "What treasure?"

The enormous shifter laughed. "Blood," he said. "But blood is…" He made a gesture like blowing out a chershire weed. Farai took it to mean the treasure had been scattered like the chershire seeds on the wind.

"Ennead blood?" Farai asked. "We've taken slaves."

"None but mine," Yarr declared, his laugh a boom. "Shifters are dead or running. Only I remain."

Farai quelled his temper. Yarr made no sense to him, but getting angry would make the brute defensive, and even Farai could not match the strength of the demon-possessed Ennead. He kept his voice even and calm as he asked, "Your blood?"

"Body power," Yarr said, taking another long drink. With the accent, Farai could not tell if the shifter was already drunk. He was unsure shifters *could* get drunk, but Yarr seemed to be trying hard to. "Body hekau. No other has it now, just me. Mind hekau, the seers have." He shrugged as if to say he thought the latter hekau irrelevant.

While their languages differed slightly in word choice and accent, the word *hekau* was entirely unknown to Farai.

Seeing Yarr smile a broad, toothy grin, Farai nodded in thanks. He did not know what to do with the information but thought it important. If nothing else, the shifter was valuable. He needed to keep Yarr.

"Come with me to Berinta, proud shifter," Farai invited. "There, you will be revered and exalted. You could have an ark all your own if the Grand Archon allows."

Yarr made a show of thinking about the offer, but Farai already knew the brute would accept; it was exactly what the shifter wanted after all.

"Fine," Yarr decided at length. "I will meet your Grand Archon. We will see who is so grand."

Farai left before he would have to address the oblique insult to the Grand Archon. He let his anger go as he left the tent. Grand Archon Amadi was the greatest warrior Berinta had ever known. No one could best him, not even an arrogant Ennead shifter. If Farai presented the Ennead to Grand Archon Amadi, the shifter might take offense and challenge the archon. One of them would end up dead.

Either one suited Farai. Such was the Berintan way.

He returned to his tent, where the seer had fallen asleep. He listened to her mumbling before heading to bed.

Led by the Ennead prisoner, Funanya's ark found the oasis first.

The second oasis was shaded but shallow. Small shrubs wove through the sands along the pool in the open plateau, with tiny alia flowers speckling deep purple in the shadows under them. Three riser trees, their thick palms casting shade over the waters, cir-cled the pool, and short reeds, the type used for making linen, covered the far end. Unlike the valley oasis they had left behind, the second oasis had little cover beyond two robust riser trees.

The exception was a huge boulder that sat, its flat surface facing the setting suns, half in the water. Unlike more typical sandstone, the boulder was volcanic and filled with pores. At the base, moss clung to these holes, while piper lizards and chitters vied for nesting places in the higher reaches. More than one of the spotted chitters, their stumpy legs almost useless over the uneven surface of the stones, came out to view the intruders before retreating back into the safety of their holes. The characteristic sound for which they had been named echoed over the oasis.

The prisoner was given another small bit of tauran jerky and dried fruits once they reached the oasis, while the scouts, still sweating, waded into the waters freely. Funanya saw the dark look Hunter gave them as he was given leave to fill his water-gourd, which was starkly empty, from the now-muddied waters.

As he bent over the pool, Funanya noticed that the skin of his back and chest had become auburn. The black was given a ruby-hue by the burn atop it. Blisters puckered the skin.

From the shadow of the boulder, Funanya watched as the Ennead removed his shendyt, his only attire besides the leather collar and rope, and touched the cloth to the waters. He flung the wet cloth over his shoulders, pressing it against the burn. With each dip—always done delicately to avoid stirring the silt from the bottom of the oasis—she saw him grit his teeth. She could imagine the pain the touch of the shendyt elicited.

Although she sweated, Funanya had wrapped herself with an Ennead desert wrap and found it more comfortable than the layer of linens they had used on the march north. Exposure in the desert had claimed enough lives already. If she could use what the Enneads had to better defend her warriors, she would.

After a dozen applications of the wet shendyt, the Ennead soaked it once more, made a pouch of it, and placed his food within, hydrating it. Then he retreated under the cart he was tied to, which had been placed on the far side of the waters across from Funanya. In the shadows, he dug a thin trench and lay, face down, in the exposed, cool sand, and waited for the dried fruits to soften.

She felt like she was watching an animal at work. His actions were simple and concise. No gesture was wasted. He ate in the shadow of the cart, one small piece of fruit at a time, chewing each a dozen times before swallowing. He sipped only. She saw in him a creature reduced to his most basic faculties.

Surprisingly, he proved how similar the Enneads were to the Berintans in the course of his brief nudity. How that was possible when the two peoples had never before met baffled her.

Her warriors were slow in settling down after their games in the waters, but soon enough the tents were pitched, Funanya's positioned in the place of best wind. Every container was refilled with water while tired tauran were released from their harnesses and led down to drink.

The other arks of Douran found their way along Funanya's red markers. A rider was sent back to tell the army to follow the red posts for the quickest route come the next day. Watching him go, Funanya was pleased to know Archon Farai would again be hearing of her victory.

Now well ahead of the army, she initially set basic sentries but, over the evening meal, her eyes were drawn back to the scavengers the Ennead had pointed out. By the end of her meal, the flying lizards hovered above the camp, and she felt unease seeping into her stomach.

She did believe he was lying to get back at his captors, but his logic had been sound.

"Adeban!" she called, and the archon of the second ark ran to attend to her. "Call your warriors back from the waters and set a watch on the north. Tonight, I do not trust the desert."

He bowed and rushed off, but not before she saw his twitch of annoyance. She knew he thought she was asserting her new authority, but, like Hunter, she did not care what he thought so long as the duty was done.

When she checked, the prisoner had fallen asleep under the cart.

The sunsets of the desert were short. The large sun lingered on the horizon as the smaller one vanished, changing the light to blue. Shortly after that, the second oasis fell into darkness, the white sun gone. The big moon was high and near full. The smaller moon slipped around the larger one and was partially hidden, limiting the light.

Uneasy, Funanya watched from her tent entrance. Her feelings of misgivings grew to see the scavengers, now numbering eight, sitting atop the boulder with their steely eyes turned toward the camp in anticipation.

Even the chitters hushed. Through the silence, Adeban's warriors began a chant to keep themselves alert.

"Torches," she commanded, and her warriors were swift to light them. The first to present the torch to Funanya was Dalia. With the torch in Dalia's hand, a wide area was illuminated. "Take them to Adeban on the north watch." Although Adeban had a pair of tiki torches already, she suspected he would need more.

Before the command could be finished, Funanya heard a hiss, followed by a surprised cry. The chant broke off. Adeban screamed a battle cry from the northeast edge of the oasis.

"Get them the light!" Funanya commanded, and the warriors with torches sprinted away, seeking the fastest route to the tip of the oasis. Funanya grabbed her weapons and called for the rest of her ark. They assembled and rushed in.

The water lay between her and Adeban's warriors, but the torch-bearers had made a rapid circuit. As she left her tent, Funanya was confronted with the sight of an enormous serpent demon rearing up. It slammed into one of the scouts, a sand burst obscuring the entire line of defenses in answer.

The warriors were in disarray; the demon had made its way between them and now bit, thrashed, and crushed with abandon. More than one Berintan lay, missing a limb or two, bleeding in the sand. The presence of a dozen wooden spears in the neck of the monster seemed to do little to slow it.

Mustering her warriors, Funanya charged around the oasis and brought her ark into a line between the demon and Adeban's people, who had managed to slink away. Dalia skittered back to the defenses, and the demon, finishing chomping on Adeban's second in command, paused to examine the new opposition. The spray of blood speckled Dalia's shins and feet extensively, but she managed to get behind the armed warriors before the serpent could aim another strike.

It reared up, instantly looming above them by three times their height. The snout, coated in thick gray scales and flanked by thin, razor horns, opened to hiss and showed the fangs, each the size of Funanya's sword. The body, legless and long, coiled back in readiness while Funanya's warriors braced their spears to take the lunge. Even if their aim was perfect, the weight of the demon crashing into them could crush the bearer.

The demon paused, glancing to the south. Funanya followed the gaze, spotting the Ennead prisoner, still tethered to the cart where he had been sleeping, outlined by the rising moon. He now stood apart from the cart as if to investigate the sudden clamor.

The serpent demon threw itself to the side, thrashing in the sand and making a direct charge at the Ennead. Funanya heard Hunter curse loudly, although it was a word she did not know. As Funanya watched, he snapped the tether binding him to the cart and took off down the dune to his right at a full sprint.

At Funanya's command, the warriors launched their spears at the retreating monster. Six bounced off the scales as the demon left the torchlight in pursuit of the Ennead.

Hunter moved faster than she had ever seen; all at once, the Ennead crested the rise of the dune closest to Funanya. He ducked under the demon as it snapped at him and skidded past it. He next came to a halt at the feet of the Berintan warriors.

For a moment, his black eyes were lit by torches, and Funanya again thought she saw an animal. This time, he was a predator, and he was on the hunt.

"I will draw it before your warriors," he told her. Eyeing the thin spears, he snorted. "You'll have to get close enough to aim between the scales. Strike up, under the chin."

With his back to the demon, Funanya had to assume the sound of a hiss told him to dodge. He rolled to the left. The demon's maw crashed into the sand where he had been.

The demon seemed to forget entirely about the Berintans in its pursuit of the Ennead. The long body slithered directly in front of them as it turned to follow the shadow rolling toward the water of the oasis.

Seeing an opportunity, Funanya drew her sword into a two-handed grip and slashed it down into the demon's back. The edge of obsidian sliced between the scales, but it could not dig deep.

The demon screeched and writhed, and suddenly Funanya had the entire mouth of teeth aimed at her. She released her sword, caught in the flesh, to fall back. Dalia, still carrying her torch, thrust the fire toward the monster's eyes. The moment the demon reared back, a small warrior by the name of Kayin plunged his spear into the jaw from underneath.

The head collapsed instantly, taking Kayin's spear with it. A shiver ran the length of the body. When Funanya rose, Kayin was tugging to free his arm from where it had been pinned under the weight of the enormous head.

His efforts were wasted. The heavy head did not move until, with the wind picking up, the flesh crumbled to ash, leaving bare, sun-bleached bones in the moon and torchlight.

With the help of two others, Kayin freed his arm from under the skull. The gray ash clung to his arm.

Halfway down the slope to the oasis, Funanya spotted the Ennead hunter. He had swung around a riser tree trunk to turn himself away from the water but now headed back up the bank. He came to Funanya's sword and lifted it out of the ash, the edge visibly chipped even from a distance.

His collar was still in place as he stepped into the light of torches, sword in hand. An arm's length of rope remained attached to the collar, its end frayed.

While the warriors tensed, Dalia going as far as to ready her torch in a sword's grip, Hunter turned the blade around and offered it, hilt first, to Funanya.

She took the sword and watched in muted awe as he turned away and walked back up the dune to the cart he had been assigned. Sand clung to his back, each blister now burst and raw.

Her attention went to the wounded, but her eyes continued to stray to the silhouette of the Ennead again asleep under the cart on the dune. Her warriors tried to collect bones as spoils, but few were small enough to carry.

She did not bother replacing his tether. It was clear she would need something thicker to hold Hunter.

After the commotion of the demon had passed, the wounded had been tended, and the camp had fallen into silence, the Youngest Seer lowered herself out from the cart. Below her, Askaran lay on his front, hands tucked under his chin, keeping his exposed back out of the sand. He did not stir as she lay down beside him briefly, hiding in his outline as she carefully positioned the sand-cloak to cover her. As she lay at his side, she heard his breathing quicken, and a short moan escaped him. She placed a hand on his shoulder briefly and felt the tension in his sweating muscles. His breathing slowed, but she knew it would not last; nightmares were haunting him again.

Knowing there was nothing she could do for him, the seer inched along like a miniature serpent demon. Leaving the safety of the cart, she crossed down the dune and up over the next.

For a moment, free of wandering eyes, the seer stood up, and the sand fell from her back. Coarse grains clung to her jellabiya, but, without beating brushes and oil baths, she did not expect to be clean again.

Her heart felt dirty now too, like her robe. The memories of her visions distanced themselves with every moment she spent under the cart in hiding. At first, they had been clear enough to shake her core, but now they faded to nonsensical pain and terror. The emotions had been strong and persistent, numbing her. Now, the seer felt nothing as she stood in the trough the serpent demon had made on its approach to the oasis.

It was a strange thought. Her memory had been near-perfect all her life. She could recite, word for word, thousands of conversations. Thoughts, feelings, and memories did not fade for her, not ever. Why was the agony of the City's loss disappearing?

Corr, the larger moon, was near full, and her smaller sister, Deva, sat at her side, hidden partially by the shadow of the big moon. With only the moons' beams to light the dark of her skin, she felt muted and forgotten. As she looked around the black dunes, all the skills Askaran had taught her seemed too far away.

Her eyes went to the moons, and there she found comfort.

The storytellers had told her Corr and Deva were named after the two daughters of Illum, the goddess of their home world, Terac. Corr was said to be a warrior woman, as fierce and determined as her brother Ero, for whom the red sun had been named. Deva had been the quiet daughter, as gentle as her mother's spring breeze. But both daughters had one thing in common; they loved to dance. In the sky, they danced, forever circling the other.

She did not know why no one spoke about gods now.

Under the light of the moons, the seer began to dance. Her first steps were simple and soft, following the light of Deva over the sand's furrow. As her muscles warmed with the motions, and her heart found joy in the movement, her steps hastened. She spun in the sands, letting her worn jellabiya flare around her, her arms in the air. Her hands followed the moonlight, and soon she leaped and twirled in honor of Corr's spirit.

Music filled her mind without touching her ears. She heard the drums of the Enneads, and her steps matched their beat. A flute joined, and her hands shadowed the sound in the moonlight, rising and falling with each thrilling note. At last came the voices, a hundred strong, singing the song into the silence of the night.

Confused, she stopped abruptly. The music vanished. The choir accompanying her disappeared, and her mind went silent.

A vision flooded in, unbidden but undeniable. A grand cavern appeared around her, carved pillars of immaculate detail holding up the arching ceiling. Blue-shaded sunlight leeched through cracks, the waters glittering like silver around her feet. No sand marred the walkways dividing the waters, never given permission to enter.

A pedestal occupied the center of the room, holding a fist-sized sphere of blue-green. As she watched, a drop of water slid from the orb, was caught in the carvings of its pedestal, and trickled down into the vastest aquifer.

The seer looked up and saw a Berintan invader staring down from the ceiling above her. He gazed at the floor, perfect, interlocking wood, and did not see through to her. He thought he was looking into a chasm. He thought the floor gone, the pedestal shattered, and the orb broken. He saw—and believed—that there was nothing of value below the City now.

As the vision snapped out of sight, the Youngest Seer heard a distant drip of water. Despite what the invader and his imprisoned seer believed, the portal orb was intact and safe.

The hollow feeling crept back in, and she was again standing between dunes under the starry sky, alone save for the dancing footprints she had left in the trench left behind from the demon's approach.

Askaran's voice returned to her in a lesson, and she rolled herself over the prints to make them vanish. Askaran might recognize them, but he would also recognize her attempts at covering them. The wind picked up, promising to hide the evidence of her midnight venture.

Her heart felt slightly lighter as she made her way back up the dune, panting from the dance but energized. She covered herself with the sand-cloak once more and crept back to her perch under the cart.

The clouds moved in over the moons for her journey back, and Askaran struggled in his nightmares as she retook her place under the cart and fell asleep.

She dreamed of the cavern and the orb she knew she would have to retrieve.

CHAPTER 6

"Get up, Hunter."

Askaran was quick to respond, clambering out from under the cart before any of his captors felt the need to come in after him. He was ashamed to realize they had come so close without waking him. He had intended to keep them at a greater distance to protect the seer from discovery, but his night had been ripped apart by nightmares again thanks to the battle with the serpent demon. The colossus demon wanted revenge for the attack, and its closeness, while he slept, brought the vicious memories of a world long since abandoned because of an ancient, brutal war.

In the gray dawn, the archon wore her stolen keim beast skin armor, her repaired sword tied to her hip. With her came two other warriors, one an unknown male and the other the tall woman Askaran had often seen at the archon's side. Although Askaran remembered the woman being spattered by blood the night before, her legs were now clean and gleaming lightly in their natural gold. Her face paint, which matched the archon's white and brown-red stripes and zigzags, looked fresh as well, although Askaran noted a smudge of black paint over the woman's left temple.

The woman held a coarse brush and bandages, while the man held a vial and a water gourd. By the condensation adhering to the outside, Askaran assumed it held cool water.

Askaran presented himself before the archon without a word, feeling worn. The battle the night before had been nothing but a short run, but combining long walking with exposure and dehydration, then topping his day off with demonic nightmares, left him struggling to stand.

"Turn around and kneel," the archon ordered.

Seeing none of the Berintans had a weapon in hand, Askaran obeyed. His demon growled lightly in his mind, warning that a weapon coming at him now would result in a shift. The demon played with the idea of tearing the archon's head off, amusing itself with the idea. It took force to remind the demon of its place, and the assertion was met with bemusement. If his life was endangered, they both knew Askaran's exhausted hold would slip. The leather collar would probably not hold against a shift.

But Asakran knew the demon questioned that certainty. It hesitated.

In place of a weapon, the brush was set against his shoulders to remove the sand from where it clung to his crusted wounds. It stung fiercely over the blisters that had burst in his roll down the dune the night before but served to scrape away dirt and dried fluid.

"Why did the monster go after you last night?" the archon demanded as the warrior cleaned him.

"If this is meant to be torture," Askaran replied, "you're doing it wrong. You're not supposed to help me."

The archon laughed—she had understood his quick reply—but it was short and stifled. "You do me no good lying dead in a dune," she said once she had regained her composure. "Why did the monster leave my warriors to attack you?"

The brush raked across his shoulder, and Askaran flinched. While the brush continued to work down his back, water poured over his shoulder and new hands rubbed ointment over the injuries. The sting vanished. To his amazement, the wounds felt instantly cool.

He saw no harm in the truth here.

"I'm Ennead," Askaran said, remembering to slow his words so she would understand. "Any demon will seek to kill an Ennead unless directly threatened. Lucky for you, Berintan, that does not appear to be the case for Berintans."

The archon came around to stand in front of him, and he peered up at her. For a moment, he thought about crushing her between two claws.

He was slow to realize she was holding the desert wrap in her arms, the one that had been taken from Askaran. The Ennead in him thought it important, but the demon continued fantasizing about tearing the Berintans apart.

"I came out to see what the commotion was," Askaran told her, which was the truth. "If I'd known it was a demon, I wouldn't have. Demons like to kill us too much."

"You broke your tether," she pointed out.

"I bet you could break it too if you had a serpent demon charging you."

"You outran it."

"I was well motivated, Archon," Askaran said. "I was trying to avoid being killed. Are you not just as fast? I thought our races similar."

A long moment passed, and Askaran let his head lower. His exhaustion had sapped his patience; he no longer cared what she thought, so long as she did not check under the wagon beside her. The scar hidden under his tattoo seemed to mock him.

She dropped the desert wrap onto his lap.

"We will be staying here a day," she informed him as she turned away, "until the army catches up. Expect to leave early tomorrow and lead the way." She paused, her voice containing a raised eyebrow. "You know the way fully across the wastes, do you not, Hunter?"

He nodded. "Never went that far, but I've seen it. I know the way. You need to fill twice here; the next one will not be reached in a single day of walking."

"Good," she said. With a sharp pivot, she left him to the two healers.

Once in the light of the dawn, Philyre viewed the Berintan camp from afar. Behind her, the six other runners crouched low, their cloaks spread in the sand. Although they were not as good as sand-cloak, the desert wraps camouflaged them well from a distance.

The bones of a serpent demon were left behind as the Berintans headed off to the south-west once more. Philyre was pleased by the blood-stained sands near the body, knowing it had taken some of the enemy with it, but it was not enough.

Five dead, she mused as she crouched down once more, plus at least that many wounded by the demon. She had hoped for twice that many when she had found the serpent demon to lead to the enemy, but the Berintans disappointed her with their prowess.

"We need something bigger," Philyre said as she flopped onto the dune, facing north once more. "Really big."

The six faces of the runners who had followed her into the desert stared back at her. Mout, Dessen, and Charn each sat in silence, their eyes averted. Their confidence in the plot had dwindled steadily since they had found the trail of the serpent demon. Philyre had expected them to pick up now that they had succeeded in luring the demon into the company of their enemy, but the minimal success of the venture dampened their spirits once more. The other three had been brimming with energy throughout, but now even Neiltan and Kalut seemed to draw away. She knew little about Neiltan or Kalut—they had always been on the same circle as Philyre, so their paths had never crossed—but she had appreciated their enthusiasm for her plan. She was sorry to see the confidence fade.

Closest to him, Erosan crouched, his bright teeth huge in grin. "Tusked or colossus?" he asked.

"Whichever we find," Philyre replied, standing and heading directly east now. They could not follow on the enemy's trail lest they be seen, but keeping back allowed them to follow, nonetheless. The Berintans seemed to have little skill for hiding their passage.

Erosan leaped up with a laugh. "Let us continue our madness! Out into the suns you lot! Onward!"

The other five rose slowly. With a demon dead so close to the water, no one was willing to fill their water-skins there. They carried enough water for now, but it was clear getting back to the City was no longer certain.

But they followed her into the desert, Philyre knew, because they had no choice. There was nothing to return to. Forward was the only direction.

As she climbed down the dune, Philyre paused. In the valley, a spattering of strange tracks decorated the sands. She could not decide if the overlying tracks belonged to multiple Berintans or a single one running in circles. One footprint looked small, like that of her little sister, who had been cut down in the City two days earlier.

She kicked at the prints, then led the way onward.

After another full day of walking in the sands, they were forced to camp without water. For one night, they were spared the company of the other arks. The wind picked up in the dusk, and even the thick layers of the tent could not keep out the dust. Funanya left much of her belongings packed in the hopes of keeping them clean.

As the dark settled, she went to her chair and sat back. Her armor had already been oiled by Dalia and her sword checked for cracks or chips by Kylin. Her food was prepared, water and chapman out, her pillows and bed set. It had been many years since she had been forced to do her own chores.

She sent for Rudo.

The fit man arrived in a brightly patterned dashiki and sokoto set, one that matched his new ark colors mysteriously. He left his weapons at the door, as was expected. Seeing him, she thought the pattern of her ark on his face suited his features better than Sizwe's had; his wide eyes now looked worldly instead of bugged.

He was too far beneath her for Funanya to offer drink or food, but she let him take a place at her foot. He leaned one arm onto the ottoman, keeping his sand-covered feet off her precious carpet respectfully. His eyes never left hers.

"How long did you serve Sizwe?" she asked idly.

His broad eyes sparked when he laughed. "My archon seeks information?" he said. "I am glad. I had feared a seduction."

Funanya felt herself warm slightly. The thought was not unpleasant. Mindful of the strategies she had used when the positions had been reversed, she smothered the idea. She had seen the inside of the Grand Manor of Douran through Sizwe's bed because Sizwe had been blind. If Rudo or any of her bed partners ever had goals of becoming archons, the positions, both in the bed and out of it, could too easily be reversed.

"Feared?" she asked, goading him. "I am so repulsive?"

He took a long, thick sigh. "Far from it, Archon, hence my fear. But I will be pleased to serve however I can. I followed him four years."

"And before that?" she asked.

He cocked his head. "You seek information about me, not Sizwe?"

"Sizwe is dead," Funanya pointed out, "proving I knew enough about him. I accepted you and yours into my ark. I want to know the extent of what I have earned."

His gaze penetrated into hers further, and it made Funanya's chest tighten. She could not decide if she was a tauran under the predator eyes of a keim beast or a tauran cow being faced by the bull. It felt too suggestive to be deadly, unlike the beastly stare of the Ennead hunter during the demon attack. Rudo seemed to be focused on her as if nothing outside the tent existed, and she was, for a moment, pleased by his attention.

"I came from the Night Road," he said, his voice soft, but firm. "Most saw that as a curse, but I enjoyed the freedom. I traded my weapons to whichever city needed me. Sizwe picked me up in Douran during a festival match four years ago. I was glad to have an ark but am happier to have a strong leader."

"Sizwe was Archon of Douran," Funanya mused. She dared not break the stare, fearing it would somehow show weakness. She had not missed the mention of the Night Road, the very place Funanya had awoken for the first time, but she ignored it. In taking the title of archon, she had abandoned the life of the unlabeled and houseless. Few enough even knew of her unlucky start to life, and she had no intention of sharing it.

Rudo laughed, and his teeth showed brightly. He had a surprisingly perfect smile.

"He gained that post by luck!" Rudo said. "Did you know the previous Archon of Douran?"

She nodded.

"So, you know how he kept all competing arks at bay by assassinating their archons? He only left the ones he did not feel threatened by. He let Sizwe survive because he didn't care! Then he slipped on scented oil outside the bath and cracked his head on the bedpost! Sizwe inherited!" At last, Rudo let the stare break. He rolled his eyes at the memory. "And our illustrious leader tried to get out of it!"

"Who talked him into it?"

Rudo went sharply silent. When his stare returned to meet hers, he glanced away swiftly.

Funanya had known Sizwe before and after his rise. Before, he had thought keeping his head down was his only hope for survival in Douran and had gone to great efforts to keep from attracting attention. He had no love of authority, his or anyone else's. Rumors hinted he had even tried to kill himself to avoid taking the seat of Archon of Douran.

But he had taken Archon Sefu's ark and power with confidence. In one night, he had become arrogant. At first, Funanya had believed Sizwe's earlier cowardice had been nothing but an act, but as his foolishness persisted, she decided the voice of authority belonged to someone else. Unfortunately for the voice, the combination of confidence to command and a lack of finesse had limited Sizwe's support and, in the end, his life.

Rudo, being on hand for four years, had to know the voice that had driven Sizwe to see himself above his fellow arks. Having arrived after Sizwe's rise to power meant the voice could not be Rudo's.

"You'll kill her," Rudo finally said.

"If I believe your answer, I will either have her work for me, or I will kill her," Funanya replied. "I did not reach this place by letting a golden tongue sit unrecognized and ungagged among my warriors."

He struggled to find words. Whoever the woman was, Rudo had served with her for four years. In battle, although there had been few, camaraderie was powerful, one of the reasons Funanya made sure she always fought alongside her own warriors. Rudo had fought with the woman. He might have even been saved by her.

At length, he met her stare once more. The smile was gone, but he did not frown. "Abeni," he said. "Her name is Abeni."

Funanya leaned back into her chair and sipped her cup. "What would you do if I asked for her head?"

"I would take my dagger to her tonight," he flawlessly replied. His stare made her heart return to fluttering. "My weapons belong to my ark, and you are the archon. I am yours to command."

She held the stare, a thin smile on her face until he again looked away.

"I will speak to her," Funanya decided. "You may go."

He left slowly, as if not wanting to go on his way into the night. She blamed the blustering wind and dust for his hesitation, suspecting all the while the cause had been disappointment.

CHAPTER 7

As they moved on, the Berintans replaced the hair rope that had bound Askaran with braided leathers. Tethered, Askaran was forced twice overnight to roll the cart out from the drifting sand to avoid being buried. By morning, the wind was still strong, and a new bank of sand had piled up beside him. The seer wore the sand-cloak over her face and said little, despite the privacy the wind brought them.

They resumed the march in the morning, trekking off into the wind. All the scouts now wore long robes against the sand, making them look like walking dunes. Moving the taurans on became difficult; when confronted, the beasts clumped together and put their backs to the wind. Askaran was limited to directions that were not into the wind, and, by dusk, the party stopped; any step except one into the wind would be the wrong direction.

"How can you tell in this?" the woman called Dalia asked Askaran in the red light of the sand. "I can hardly even see the suns!"

"Light," Askaran replied, glaring back at the woman who still carried his kukri. "Mix of light tells the time. Just follow, Berintan, or be buried."

They marched on, fighting against wind and sand with every step.

"Cover the taurans' eyes and noses," the archon commanded. "Lead them by hand." Soon, each of the tall reptiles wore linen cloth over their eyes and nostrils.

Askaran was impressed; with their eyes covered and their noses protected, the beasts walked better into the wind. Blindly, they followed their Berintan masters over the dune.

"Distance, Hunter?" the archon called through the wind.

"Another hundred paces to the rocks," he called back. "Keep up!"

He saw Dalia go to the archon's side. He knew her eyes were on him under her shaded brows and felt certain Dalia's words were not kind.

He did not care. She would be the second to die, according to the demon in his mind, after the archon. Askaran wondered if the demon was sentimental about the kukri, or just happy to be making a list.

A howl in the wind made Askaran pause, and he turned his back to the wind to listen again. Every Berintan following him froze. The archon even held a hand up to Dalia, and the warrior was forced into silence.

The sound came again. This time, it had formed into a roar.

His gut lurched as the demon in his mind slammed against the cage. It knew that sound.

Askaran closed his eyes, forcing coherent thoughts. He turned his head slightly into the wind. The sound was traveling a long distance in the wrapping gales, but it was ahead of them.

"Faster," he called, pivoting into the wind and driving himself onward. He was surprised at how quickly they followed.

A hundred labored steps later, the shadow of the three columns he had been seeking came out of the dust. He brought the party into the lee of the immense pillar and, for the first time since morning, they were free to pull the wraps from their mouths and faces to breathe. The tauran were unblinded and allowed to rest.

The sand here came in because of the wind carrying it. The footing beneath their feet had become gravel as they moved into the reg desert.

Dalia went back to the archon, her eyes of dark poison on Askaran once more, but before she could say much, Askaran called for silence.

"Why should we listen to him?" Dalia demanded. Her face had been caked by dust and sand, giving her a glittering hue beyond the light of her natural gold skin. Her black hair was speckled blond by the sand.

"Because something big is out there," Askaran replied. "I don't think you want it to find you."

"Don't lie to—"

The thump of a step stopped Dalia's next tirade cold. Collectively, the Berintans held their breath.

A shadow moved along the edges of their wind-swept view, crossing along the last dwindling edge of the dunes beyond. It lumbered on thick legs, walking steadily despite the bluster of the wind. Long forelimbs hung at its side, each the width of the legs and tipped with claws the size of a Berintan's leg. The squat head did not seem to notice the sand whipping across its ears through the curled horns arching above them. The tail dragged behind, the club of the tip digging deeply into the sand.

Askaran watched it go. Red light drifted over a vine-swept waterfall in his mind, the buzz of insects and lizards humming in the roar of the sand. The demon marched through the undergrowth, its nose to the ground as it scented prey. Ennead voices echoed through the trees ahead, and the demon growled low in pleasure.

"Hunter?"

Askaran jumped, cutting off the growl that had been rumbling in his throat. The shadow had faded into the more distant cloud of sand and wind, leaving him with an audience of Berintan warriors.

"Hunter, what was that?"

The archon stood beside him, her dark eyes peering into the sand and wind. By the curious, but unconcerned, look in her eyes, he knew she had not seen it.

"Big," he replied. "I suggest you take a break here. Give it time to leave. Then we can go on. It's not too far now."

"I make the decisions," she reminded him.

He turned his eyes back to the receding shadow. He felt the rumble of the earth under his feet with each step the colossus demon made.

"I know," he said. "That's why I said 'I suggest.'"

"Watch it, Hunter," the archon replied, her voice heavy. "Not everyone likes you."

He snorted laughter. "She fears you," Askaran replied, knowing at once who the archon was talking about. "But she fears most having me help you."

He settled into the gravel, leaving his back to the archon and her warriors. Somewhere back the way they had come, a red-topped post tossed its tethered bones in the whipping sand, but only the shifter's eyes could see it through the dust.

He closed his eyes, breathing deeply despite the sand and dust, and refused to open his eyes until he could be certain he would not see red.

From the first pillars, worn by the invariable winds of the area, the terrain became rocky. Funanya changed from sandals to thick hide boots. The travel became slow as the carts quickly jammed and stuck on the uneven gravel.

The oasis lay hidden among stones, half buried by rockslides off the nearby mountain. Dry stones crumbled down the inclines in the spiking wind, clattering from a height steep enough to endanger the lives below. They all kept their distance until they were safely at the water.

Funanya's warriors claimed the best locations, out of the path of falling stones. As night fell, Tau's ark finally followed the last of the red posts in, but Funanya was quick to notice that they were not marking with their own brown posts. Where once two dozen warriors had traveled, seven walked. None bore wounds, but their expressions spoke volumes about the disaster they had witnessed.

Tau was not among them.

A single warrior reported to Funanya at the oasis. His words were shortened by a throat parched by the wind and sand.

"Hound demons," he said. "At night, a pack of two. Only we live."

She gauged their exhausted faces and directed them to the water and rest. They washed their faces clean in the waters, in a single night erasing Tau's brand.

"Dalia!" Funanya called. "Set a dozen warriors on the trail these men left. Be ready for demons." Dalia appeared, then disappeared, at the directions. Little preparations were needed. They were still on a war march, their face paints freshly done that morning and their weapons sharp.

A chant started, with each voice the energy building for battle.

Alone, Funanya made her way to the wagon where the Ennead prisoner lay.

He had braced himself between stones at the far end of the oases, using his shendyt as a prop for his chest and leaving his legs dangling. His sore-covered back aired in the brisk wind. So far into the stony valley, little sand reached, and the breeze felt cooled by its passage over the water and plants.

Hunter did not rise at her approach but looked up mildly.

"Hound demons," she said.

"What of them?" he asked. Although he often remembered to speak slowly enough to be understood, Funanya was getting better at deciphering his words when he slipped up. The more tired he became, the more it happened.

"Two just attacked Tau's party. Seven survivors."

He pushed himself up slowly, giving a yawn. "Then they are tracking your survivors," he told her. The fact did not seem to upset him.

"Would they be intelligent enough to leave survivors, to follow them? Or were they just not hungry enough for all—"

When he laughed, the sound was bitter. She glared down at him as he rose. Hunter brought his shendyt with him and tied it in place, but was careful not to stand over her despite his advantage of height.

"You dare laugh at—"

"Demons don't eat, Berintan," he interrupted. "Why would you come out here, not expecting this? How did you get this far with such ignorance?" He scanned the skies. "Or such bad luck?" he finished, his voice dropping.

She followed his gaze, spotting half a dozen scavengers in the distant sunset. "I'm beginning to dislike those reptiles," Funanya muttered.

"To meet one demon on a trek is bad luck," he said, his eyes still on the specs in the sky. "To meet two is exceptional bad luck. To meet three…"

"They will follow the survivors to us?"

Hunter brought his eyes to her, and she stood square before him. Even though she had left the armor behind for the moment, her draping dress was decorated with the talons and claws of powerful beasts. She was no less a warrior without her keim beast armor; she had not needed it when she had first earned her way into an archon's rank.

She thought she saw him defer slightly.

"They will follow the survivors to you," he agreed.

"You knew how to kill a serpent demon," she said, stepping up to stand directly in front of him. Although he was taller, she felt him shrink back. "You hunt these things! How do you kill a hound demon?"

His face was pensive for a moment, as if she was a familiar face he could not quite place. "You show how little you know," he replied, a tiny smile sneaking in. "Very well, Archon, I will answer your question, but I want you to answer one question of mine."

She looked again at the silhouettes above and thought the scavengers were closer. Archon Farai was relying on her to mark the path. Her party of scouts was relying on her to defend them from the desert. She had to know.

Funanya ensured her glare was full of venom when she again met his eyes but did not think it unnerved him as much as she wanted. The Ennead watched her with patient eyes for the reply.

"Fine," Funanya decided. "Give me your question."

"You asked about the shifters; how do you know about them?" he asked. "No Ennead would discuss them with outsiders," he continued, "even if we had met Berintans before."

"Your hidden weapon?" she remarked.

"Our greatest shame," he shot back. "Answer my question, Berintan, or face the demons alone."

Since gaining the rank of archon, Funanya had seldom been forced to do anything. Even Sizwe's orders, if she had not arranged them, were manipulated to her advantage. The Ennead's need for water had brought him under her control, but now her need for information moved the power to him, and she despised him for it.

"We were told about the shifters. We had to know about them, to be ready at the siege," she confessed.

"Who told you?"

"The desert seer," Funanya replied. "Now tell me how to…"

She trailed off when Hunter's face fell. The mild smirk he had been holding vanished. Nothing replaced it—his face was blank.

Funanya waited, feeling the scavengers soaring in at her back, following an approaching demon or two. She held a grip on her sword.

A hundred heartbeats later, the Ennead finally roused enough to recognize she was still present. When his eyes focussed, she pressed, "How do you kill a hound demon?"

His voice was flat, the words without energy, when he replied, "Easier to attack from behind, since their teeth can cut through an arm without effort. The vein on the inside of their back leg is not plated. Get a blade under, and you'll bleed them in six steps. It will use five of those steps to kill you if it can."

He sank to a seat on the stone he had used to prop his head and was quickly lost in thought again.

She hurried back to her warriors to spread the information.

After dusk, with the scavengers taking roost above them, the other scout parties filed in, leaving their trail of blue and green posts. The seven survivors of Tau's ark were divided; Askaran saw individuals pledge alliance to all three remaining arks. Only one went to join the scouting party carrying the green posts.

The three arks joined forces to guard the path into the oases overnight. The chant slowed into one or two voices for lengths of time but did not stop. They knew battle approached. It reminded Askaran of the runners atop the walls, goading the shifters on, although the words were different. Here, the warriors passed the song around, listing deeds of greatness and names of warriors they were serving with.

As the moons set in the early dawn, their vigil was rewarded by the arrival of two hound demons. The battle was bloody in their tiki torchlight.

Askaran watched from beneath the cart, feeling forgotten and grateful for that. The demon seethed in him, a monster clawing at the door. Askaran could not tell if it was more in frustration at being kept from the demons or from the Berintans. He dared not move, unable to do anything beyond clench his hands and focus his strength against the cage of the demon that so desperately wanted out.

At length, the screams of battle dissipated, and the wind dispersed the ashes of the demons. At least one had bled out from a wound to its back leg. Askaran felt distantly sad to know he had helped kill the monster.

The thought terrified him the moment he recognized it. He rolled over, digging the stones of the valley into his back, and the pain stabbed his mind into dehiscence. The sympathy he had felt was knocked from his mind.

Feeling blood seep from his back, Askaran scampered clear of the cart. He felt his fogged mind snap to attention; fresh black blood was being shed near a desert seer. He had wounded himself.

His fatigue had worn him too thin. Fear of rising demon emotions drove him to instinctual denial; pain had seemed the simplest choice. But shedding blood near the seer threatened all he was defending. Pain gave the demon more motivation to stay near the surface of his mind. Askaran's exhaustion smoothed the path to a loss of control.

Tearing a strip from his shendyt, he waited for the blood to dry before doing his best to clean the wound with the cloth. He dared not return to the cart but carried the strip with him, thinking of finding a place at the end of his tether to bury it.

A desert seer, the archon had claimed. A desert seer had told the Berintans about the shifters. But she had not told them everything. The Berintans did not know that Enneads traveled the desert only in the company of shifters. She did not know that none save a shifter dared tangle with a demon, any demon.

Black blood could not be poisoned, after all.

Askaran slept the rest of the night in the lee of the stones facing the water, the bloody cloth clutched in his hand.

The Berintans scavenged the bones of the hound demons they had slain. By morning, the bones of the demons decorated robes and armor alike. The archon wore a pair of teeth on her necklace as a trophy.

When the army came into view for the sentries, the orders came to pack up once more. The supplies on the carts looked sparse now. Askaran wondered if they had intended to collect meat from the desert to feed their men. Their behavior made fishing impossible. The ruckus they created scared game, and the demons left no meat when slain. Even the tiny scraps of jerky and dried fruits the Berintans shared with him were getting smaller.

In the morning, he led them onward, pausing to bury the cloth far from the oasis.

Behind him, the scavengers fed on the slain Berintans.

Philyre and her team ranged far from the Berintans after the death of the hound demons. The main forces closed in on them from behind, putting them at risk. They waited out the wind in the lee of standing stones, the world a blur in the sand and dust.

The others were sullen as the dark became the cool dawn, tired from running and stinking of the keim beast blood they used to hide their scent. They could run all day, but baiting demons incessantly was too much of a wear on their sore muscles and on their patience. Philyre knew it.

Mout and Dessen, sharing a look, turned away from the camp as the wind lessened and made the desert passable. Together, they walked back into the sands from the reg desert, no doubt seeking a way home. Philyre saw the indecision in the eyes of the others. Traveling back to the City would be straightforward enough, but finding the others less so. When no others rose to leave, she was certain it was only because survival would be easier together.

Philyre ignored the departures, keeping her eyes on the scattered stones around the enemy's camp. She checked twice more, needing confidence in her discovery before announcing it.

Erosan brought her food, then joined her crouched beside a pillar of stone, looking out over a wide flat expanse of reg desert.

"Footprints?" Philyre finally ventured.

Erosan scanned the same gravel Philyre had but then shrugged. "I don't see it."

"There," Philyre said, pointing back a dozen paces to her left. "Then there," she added, pointing in front of him. "And one more." The last one was again a dozen paces to the right.

Erosan squinted, then adjusted the hood of his desert wrap. "Just three prints?" he said.

"Only one thing has a stride that long," Philyre replied.

She watched the realization dawn on Erosan. It started as a pensive expression, moved onto surprise, then quickly to excitement.

"Colossus?" he nigh-on shouted, jumping up. "We've found a colossus?"

The others came forward hesitantly, hunched close to the ground to protect them from the wind. Even died down, it was strong.

"What say you all?" Philyre asked them. "One last run. If we can lure the colossus in, our job is done. We return home."

They took turns checking the tracks Philyre had found, but slowly accepted the plan. One final run, a trail of Enneads set to lure the demon to the enemy. Keim blood kept their scent hidden, their sand-cloaks prevented their silhouette from being distinctive when they needed it, and their sandals were made for running. They would bring doom to the Berintans.

CHAPTER 8

The wind settled in the darkness as the final night of their march across the desert drew to a close. The last oasis lay at the base of the Keim Mountains, a day from Berinta. Keim beasts, fierce predators that traveled in mated pairs, were known to roam the area but, unlike the demons, tended to avoid people. The oasis had been abandoned by the time Funanya and her scouts found it.

The area, closing in on the edge of the desert, stretched three times the distance of the other oases. Two small ponds were connected by a deep creek flowing with red sandy waters that tasted like metal. The north pond seeped from deeper waters, and the underground river dipped under the solidly packed rock at the south end.

In the wide spaces of the final flats oasis, the three leaders set their tents close together. For the first time since her promotion, Funanya had time to sort through her chest of Ennead metal goods, discovering a strange mix of eating utensils, pots, platters, daggers, chains, and shackles. She had failed to find a sword of metal to claim but was content with the spoils.

Pulling out the utensils, Funanya hosted Adeban and Jabarl in her own tent. The two other seats, meant for Sizwe and Tau, were set but left conspicuously empty.

Having sent a runner ahead into Berinta, Funanya had the meal prepared with fresh foods from the nearby city instead of the dried and preserved goods they had lived on for the days of marching. After the meal was done, stewed baraka fruit made a pleasant dessert for the archons.

Their city was still three days away, and they discussed traveling there as soon as they were released from Archon Farai's festivities in the city of Masamba. The spoils of the Enneads would be paraded for days through the streets, but they were not sure if they would be expected to remain for the demonstration. Funanya had seen enough of Ennead things and was eager to return to her new home, the Grand Manor of Douran.

Jabarl remained largely silent through the meal, a typical thing for him. Of the three, Jabarl had been promoted last and his ark remained the smallest. The fact that two archons had died in the desert had elevated him to third, but he seemed ill-prepared for the change. In him, Funanya saw another Sizwe. One day, he might inherit the entire city by accident, if the two higher-ranked archons managed to kill each other.

Unlike Jabarl, Adeban was well-spoken. He was a second-generation archon, although he had been forced, like them all, to gain the rank on his own. His exposure to his mentor's position of authority growing up had created a more formal man than either Funanya's Night Road beginnings or Jabarl's warrior lineage. Timing alone had favored Funanya; had she been but a few months later in being assigned to Douran, her rank would have been below Adeban, and he would have been sitting in the largest seat at the table.

Adeban lifted his cup in salute. "To walking in straight lines!" he called. "And to the red markers that blazed that road."

Jabarl fumbled to raise his cup as Funanya lifted hers in acceptance of the tribute.

"To returning home in victory," Funanya added.

"And to no more sand," Jabarl murmured bitterly.

Having lived in the jungles of the Berinta, forbidden from entering the desert before they went to war, Funanya appreciated the final toast most. She did not know why the territory had been opened to them, but she was hoping it would close again. No doubt, she would be finding sand in her belongings for years to come.

They all drank small sips only, then sat in contemplation, the desert winds howling around the tent.

"I cannot fault you the results," Adeban said, breaking the silence as he put down the cup and pushed away his empty bowl, the metal spoon clattering, "but I have to wonder, Archon, where did you find that Ennead?"

She was unsurprised that Adeban had spotted the Ennead, and she was equally unsurprised by Jabarl's aghast expression.

"Ennead?" Jabarl exclaimed. "You had an Ennead working for you?"

Adeban laughed aloud, shaking his head. "Did you think she had covered one of her warriors in mud, Jabarl?" he asked. "No, that was an Ennead leading her. I had thought we had been sent out too quickly to pick up slaves."

Thinking lies would lead to more trouble, Funanya decided on the truth.

"I found him," she admitted. "He had nowhere to go, and so became a slave."

Jabarl's jaw sagged open. "But I thought we had to have slaves inspected."

"Speak clearly, Jabarl, else no one will ever believe you are an archon," Funanya chastised.

Adeban's eyes narrowed. "How interesting. Does it speak? I heard they were meek, useless people. Certainly seemed to be in the streets we stormed! I saw his tattoo. The details are faded. Rather poor quality."

"They can mark their bodies however they like, but that does not make them strong," Funanya replied. She scanned their stares and saw an opportunity. "Shall we bring him out as tonight's entertainment? Dalia!"

The woman warrior swiftly passed into the tent at the summons. Funanya was sure to watch the other two men for reactions. Adeban looked suitably interested in the attractive woman. Jabarl appeared embarrassed by his own thoughts. Funanya was satisfied.

"Fetch me Hunter," she commanded.

Dalia rushed from the tent, not even showing her usual displeasure. Funanya was well aware that Dalia had come to hate Hunter, and it was rare that the woman made an effort to hide that fact.

A short while later, Hunter arrived at Dalia's spear tip. His hands remained at his side in fists while Dalia held the rope tied to his leather collar.

Adeban circled him, and the slave stood at easy attention, his eyes looking vacant. Jabarl shrugged when Funanya invited him to inspect the prisoner as if not knowing what to do with him.

"He's scarred over his back," Adeban pointed out. "Blisters, scratches…"

"The road has been rough," Funanya told him. Seeing a new wound, she asked, "You scrape your back on something, Hunter?"

"I rolled over onto a stone," the Ennead replied, his voice impassive, but his words deliberately polite and slow.

"And it speaks!" Adeban exclaimed, his smile now broad. "What a trick!" He spun to Funanya, his grin widening. "How is their tolerance for pain? I couldn't get a sense of it during the battles."

Hunter's face remained blank, but Funanya thought she felt his presence tighten.

The Ennead had stepped out of line when he had refused her command for information on the hound demons. Such insubordination had been tolerated at the time for the sake of the information she needed, but now that time had passed. Now, she would punish him.

"Shall we find out?" she said.

"Ten lashes?" Jabarl suggested.

She waited to see Hunter's fear, but nothing rose. As they took him outside and had him kneel in the sharp red stones of the flats, he bowed his head and closed his eyes.

Dalia secured his rope to the nearby cart again while Adeban took the whip. Funanya clearly saw joy in him as he brought it across the slave's back and made a note of it; motivations to cause pain could be dangerous to her but also could be manipulated.

Hunter tried, but failed, to stop from crying out to the touch of the reed whip, but he did not move away. One by one, the lashes landed against the blistered skin, tearing open the black and exposing flesh beneath it. Sweat covered him, glittering in the newly lit torches, and his cries became harsh enough to form growls in his throat. The whip lashed into the tattoo twice, etching thin lines over the snarling monster on his shoulder. His blood, dark in the dusk, covered his back by the time they finished.

He held himself on his hands and knees and did not move.

"Looks like they bleed as much as any of us would. Are you satisfied now?" she asked her guests.

Although he was winded by the exertion, Adeban's snarling grin remained. "I am. I thank you for the meal and the entertainment, Archon. I look forward to our return to Douran." He glanced at the immobile shape of the Ennead. "I guess he'll die once we reach the border. No use for him then." He shrugged. "Good night, Archon. I will see you in the morning."

Crossing his arms and giving a final bow of his head, Adeban departed. Jabarl's farewell was short and less eloquent. Both archons returned to their tents, led by torches. Soon, the camp was dark except for the lit edges guarding the trail.

Funanya went to the Ennead and crouched briefly at his side as Dalia hovered nearby. Hunter's breath came in broken gasps and his arms trembled, but he did not move. She was unsure if he heard her when she said, "This is what awaits slaves who do not know their places. Remember it, Hunter."

Funanya left him there, kneeling in the rocks by the riser trees. She headed back to her tent and dismissed Dalia. At the entrance, she paused.

Hunter slowly moved. He first examined his hand in the moonlight, then loosened his shendyt and threw it away to one side. With great effort, he lowered himself, naked, into a seating position with his lashed back straight. There, lit by moonlight, he froze again.

Funanya grew bored and decided sleep was a better use of her time. Closing in on the homeland, she thought Hunter's assistance of limited value. She had not decided what to do with him yet but thought he would be useful as a prize.

Askaran heard the shuffle of sand and stone but did not turn. He dared not even let himself think of danger for fear of the demon.

The demon rattled its cage in his mind, roaring in outrage, demanding retribution for the pain. It wanted that Berintan, wanted to tear her apart, then rip through her camp and slaughter every Berintan around the water. The terror would be absolute, the reward vast. He could taste their blood against his tongue, hear their cries…

But with the next calming breath, Askaran eased away that fury. The seer snuck up in the dark. His mind had fixed upon her the moment the lashes had begun, and now she filled his head. He denied his demon, lash after lash, for her.

"Stay away," he whispered.

"Stay away?" her gentle voice echoed. "Why?"

He did not want questions now, not when the demon hovered on hand, pushing at the limits of his mind. He could not find the words.

"You're hurt," she added, her voices coming from closer. "And no one is around. No one can—"

"I will be fine, little flower. But I need silence. Please. I'll explain when you're older, I promise." His heart ached to deny her even a conversation, knowing the last five days had seen only a dozen words between them, but he dared not tax his mind now. He had no strength left to hold the demon.

He felt it snarl, and the pressure in his bones rose. Askaran forced another breath through his aching muscles, soothing the monster away from the cage door.

"Black blood flows," the seer whispered.

Askaran had the terrible feeling that she understood. She was too young. Seers came into power as they became adults. He could not expect her to understand the visions if they came so early.

Her voice withdrew into the darkness as she added, "Hold to me when the blood is dried and brushed into the wind."

She slipped away.

Askaran remained sitting, his back straight, as he waited for the blood to dry. Sleep overcame him because it could not be denied. The dreams came again, a bloody war raging through dense jungle. Demons prowled with weapons, organized into squads. They set ambushes and prepared battle plans. Their hunt for the Enneads was calculated and fierce, and, for once, Askaran woke more rested.

He felt sick when he realized that was because the terror of the demons he had seen in his dreams did not upset him as much.

CHAPTER 9

Come morning, for the third time, the two Berintans were ordered to help Askaran; they cleaned his back, stitched two of the deeper lashes, and applied the cooling ointment again. He felt no guilt in letting them clean the black blood from his skin. The woman Dalia was vicious in her ministrations, but in her thoroughness, he could be confident that the seer could again touch him. Askaran suspected the archon continued to assign the woman to the duty solely because the woman hated him.

The energy of the scouts was festive. The archon had revealed that cities were the next stop. A handful of men and women went on ahead, but the majority of the party was assigned to hold the oasis and prepare it for the arrival of the full army that was two days behind them. The talk turned to the prospect of good food and comfortable beds. Askaran saw almost normal sentient beings emerge. He found it hard to understand how these Beritans, who now spoke and acted Ennead-like, had butchered a city days earlier.

They forgot their weapons as they moved about. Although sentries guarded, the warriors around the oasis relaxed.

"Then what?" he asked the wind when he sat alone beside his cart.

The shy voice answered from behind him as he sat by the cart; "Hide," the seer replied. "We need to stay with them, get inside their lands. The desert will kill me."

Askaran watched the archon pass, her long kaftan tattered by stones as it dragged behind her. The warriors hushed when she was near, crossing their arms and bowing their heads respectfully. The archon met the gaze of the Archon Jabarl, and the lower-ranked man quickly averted his stare.

"Best to stay with her," Askaran said. Archon Funanya had proven she could take what she wanted. If he was challenged, he thought her the best ally to have.

But once they passed out of the desert, his usefulness would fade.

The demon laughed, happy to show him how he could make himself useful by making a drum out of the woman's skin. It was tempting. Retaliation for the pain of his back, the empty gnawing of his stomach, the burns on his shoulders…

Askaran snapped to attention. The archon had called forward a warrior. The handsome man was one Askaran recognized.

"Rudo," the seer whispered from behind him. "He is called Rudo."

Certain no one was watching him for the moment — their eyes were on the archon and her summoned warrior—Askaran checked behind him. He could not see the seer. She had again donned the sand-cloak and was invisible in her position, lying prone below the cart, watching.

To hide her further, he leaned back against the cart. His back ached initially but soon became numb. He fiddled with his collar, feeling the leather crack. The archon had again tied him to the cart, this time with a thick leather rope.

Rudo was given orders, and the crowd adjusted to expose another warrior, this one a woman. Like Rudo's, her face paint was fresh. The pattern was that of Archon Funanya's ark, but the bright colors made it clear the association was new.

Rudo and the woman were soon isolated from the jeering crowd. Both lowered their spears in open threat. The woman spat words at the warrior, who was now squared against her, but Rudo did not seem to notice. He lunged. The woman blocked the spear with her shield and jabbed her own attack down at him. Rudo dodged wide.

"They were allies," the seer said. "Now the archon wants her dead, so he will oblige. All lies. Allies…"

The duelers continued to circle each other, making smaller attacks to goad, but the stone tips did not come close. Around them, the crowd pounded their shields and gave hoots of encouragement, like battle cries released too soon and cut short.

"How do you know this?" Askaran asked quietly. He feared the answer would be visions.

"I have been listening and watching," she said instead, allowing Askaran a small smile. "She is Abeni, and she is clever. I do not think the archon likes her."

"Since she has arranged to have her killed, I agree, little flower."

Rudo threw his spear. To protect herself, Abeni had to duck behind the shield, and for a moment her vision was blocked. Rudo followed his spear, brandishing a thick, but short, club of wood. His weight landed on the shield as one hand batted aside Abeni's spear. When Abeni looked out from the shield cover, Rudo smashed the club into her skull.

She was dead instantly. Proving their barbarity, Rudo decapitated the body and offered the head, like a present, to the archon. With his rough dagger, it took a lot of sawing to free the head from the body.

Askaran shrugged and crawled under the cover of the cart next to the seer. It did not matter to him who killed whom. All the duel showed him was that the archon was in control. She remained the ally he needed.

Dalia, long braids dancing as she emphatically gestured, was less impressed. When Rudo presented the head, Dalia's face was twisted in disapproval. Although he could not hear them, Askaran was certain angry words were exchanged. Like a scorned lover, Dalia tossed her hair and stormed away. Even from a distance, the archon looked amused.

Seeing nothing else of interest, the group dispersed. The archon returned to her tent, leaving the head behind.

Askaran tried to settle down to sleep on the second night, but the nightmares were too vivid; he started awake. He felt the pressure in his bones and was forced back into the plateau beside the cart, where he could sit and try to trance.

The suns had dipped under the horizon, Mour lingering behind his red brother by a few moments. The camp fell to silence, and the stars, speckling the sky, quickly emerged. The large moon Deva hovered behind the hills, casting bright moonlight, but tonight, Cor hid behind her sister.

Askaran watched the many Berintans go to their beds, the torches of the sentries hazy on the distant ridges. He counted stars, listening to the swell of the rocky plains that edged the desert as the sounds of life faded. The soft running of water became a seductive lullaby.

In the silence of the deep night, a night Askaran dared not sleep through, the water became a steady sound. Then it changed, gathering strength until it was a strong rush of a waterfall, and Askaran was sniffing the ground under a dense canopy, the blood of the Ennead driving him on, his hunger burning…

The demon laughed.

Askaran felt the cage door crack open.

He slammed his strength against the monster in his mind, but the demon did not retreat. Instead, it pushed back gently, as if in tease. Even the slight effort was sufficient to knock Askaran aside. Askaran's vision went red.

His muscles thickened, his heartbeat now steady. He felt the pull of the shift come over him and, for a moment, was relieved.

Panic struck back. Remembering the child under the cart, he kicked out. The demon stumbled, temporarily forced into the cage in his mind once more.

He could not stay. The shift would take him. He had to release the demon. Even if he hunted keim beasts in the wastes, he had to let the demon out.

He could not be near the Berintans, or the seer would die.

"Here."

Askaran turned his head to see the tiny paring knife extended toward him, and he weakly smiled. The question was answered; he would go.

He stripped down, leaving his sandals and shendyt beneath the cart. With the little paring knife, he cut the collar.

"I have to go," he told the seer behind him, hardly recognizing his own voice through the strain. "I will be back."

"You promise?" her tiny voice answered, sounding again like the child he kept forgetting she was.

"I promise."

Ducking out from the cart, Askaran made his way beyond the stony ridge and behind. Skirting along the cliff where he knew the sentries' positions, he made his way north. He waited for the shadows to move in the moonlight, then followed them north. Well beyond the sentries and the camp, Askaran set himself among the stones.

As his fear for the seer faded, the demands of the demon thickened. He had heard of a shifter bringing out the demon to relieve the pressure before—Yarr had been renowned for utilizing the strategy—but Askaran did not trust the demon enough to bargain with it. If he let it slip, it would run away with him.

A croaking sound interrupted him, and Askaran found three dozen scavengers sailing above him. In the dusk, they would be all but invisible, except to a shifter's eyes.

Perceptive reptiles, he thought, *to detect the presence of a colossus demon, when it was in Ennead form.*

The rumble under his feet corrected him. It was not him they had come to watch, he realized. The wind changed, bringing the distinctive smell of a demon to his nose. He recognized it at once.

Colossus demon.

Luck no longer mattered. Askaran could accept having a pack of hound demons not far from a serpent demon, but the presence of this beast finding them during the trek out of the desert could not just be misfortune. Something was drawing them in.

He could not allow the demon to reach the seer. A colossus demon would be attracted to fire and noise, even if it did not know an Ennead was among the Berintans. It would seek to kill them all, the Ennead first but certainly not the last. He might be able to drive it off, but if he waited, the Berintans would think he was defending them, a sure cause of suspicion. He could not risk it.

"Protect the seer," he told himself in a whisper, pushing himself up from the stones where he had been sitting. The demon surged within him, pushing at the cage with steady, intractable pressure.

Perhaps it had known. Perhaps this was the best chance he had of appeasing his demon and saving the seer.

He took a slow, deep breath and sought focus, but it was a slippery thing. As the cage cracked, Askaran tied the leash around the monster in his mind. Knowing it was better to have control, he consciously released the demon.

At first, he thought little had happened. The shift pulled at him, stretching his body and sitting heavily on his mind. He felt nothing for a moment more and in that moment, realized something was wrong.

He felt nothing because the demon was not struggling; it was rushing ahead, no longer tethered. Instead of battling with the mind of the demon, Askaran had been overrun.

Askaran knew his chest swelled and rumbled with the roar of challenge. The keen nose of the demon followed the scent of its enemy over the cliffs of a valley, and down into a chasm. The faintest hint of keim beast blood was mixed in the valley's air, making Askaran suspect a hidden Ennead was nearby. His people used keim beast blood to fool a demon's nose, and only when it was being applied did the scent come without smell of flesh or decay. The demon lacked the deductive power of an Ennead's mind and did not recognize the pattern, thinking the keim blood irrelevant.

An Ennead? But where? And how had one come so far from the City?

At the end of a long canyon, the demon spotted the huge shadow lumbering on in the dark, requiring no sleep and no light. Its movements were slow and steady. With each step, the stones crackled underfoot. It was heading toward the oasis, instantly becoming the focus of both the demon and Askaran himself.

Askaran felt his chest heave in another roar, answered by the other demon as it turned its red-bright eyes onto him. Instincts overwhelmed him; he positioned himself atop a stone to look down on the creature, puffing his chest wide and snarling. The other demon matched the display, hackles up, and stomped both forelimbs onto the stony ground. The many layers of cliffs around them shook.

Small stones tumbled down the nearby slopes.

The demon that was Askaran answered with a frenzied charge at the colossus demon, and Askaran was pulled along, helpless.

Crashing stones, like the collapse of a mountain, woke Funanya from a dream of darkness and cave-ins. At first, she sat up bewildered, unsure what had been dream and what had been truth, her heart pounding in fear of the answer. The roars rolled over the camp, followed by more rumble of stones falling.

Rising quickly, she left the tent. She could not see the source of the ruckus in the shadows, but she felt it under her feet in the very stones of the oasis field.

Trying to plan without knowing what was going on was impossible.

"Warriors to me," she called. "Armed and ready now! Await me here!"

With the warriors who answered swiftly enough, she left the torches and walked by moonlight for the sake of going unnoticed.

Well beyond the view of the camp, they crested a rise, and the enormous shadows of two demons appeared ahead of them in a chasm between cliff walls. Each was the size of a hill and swung arms the size of trees. The clubbed tails smashed stones when they landed, sending chipped shale flying. In the moonlight, the glow of the red eyes lit the scene.

They were matched. Identical in size and strength, only time would tell which colossus demon would kill the other.

Hunter had said demons would attack Enneads unless their lives were directly at risk; would the two colossus demons choose an Ennead, not a Berintan, over each other if her party was detected now? Before, the Berintan seemed too unimportant to warrant attention, but there was no Ennead this time to distract them.

The thought of the Ennead made Funanya pause. Even if the Berintans remained unseen, the victorious colossus may yet come after the camp once its opponent was dead. An alternative target would be of profound benefit.

"Rudo," she called quietly, "send someone to bring the Ennead. Keep him behind this ridge, but ready to move. We need a decoy."

The warrior selected a messenger and sent him back to the camp. He did it without moving his stare from the battle before them.

One demon lifted a boulder to crush the other, but a swing of the club tail shattered the shale, dropping the shards onto the first. The demon lunged, throwing its weight against the other. The second demon ducked and rolled, throwing the first off. The weight of the creature cracked the stones and shook the ground beneath them, but it was soon up once more. Horns, each the size of riser trees, lashed across the scaled flanks, but the darkness did not show if there was an injury.

Like two tauran bulls, the demons charged each other. They collided at full speed, skulls cracking and falling together in a tangle. One club tail flailed wide, crashing into the cliff face. With their eyes on the monsters, few of the watching warriors seemed to recognize that the vibrations had shaken loose stones from the hilltop behind the Berintans and that the limited space was bringing the stones down upon them in a rockslide.

"Scatter!" Funanya warned. The warriors dispersed.

Funanya cleared a ledge and took refuge behind it, joined soon by Rudo and another warrior from Sizwe's ark. Stones crashed down around her, one bouncing over the back of her head and narrowly missing. She crouched low, her hands over her head. Beside her, Tamrat was less fortunate, and a stone flicked off the nearby cliff to strike him on the side of his head. He went down heavily.

Rudo pivoted sharply to dodge a similar ricochet and positioned himself over Funanya, his arms extended around her and his chest shielding her head. Gravel fell around them like stone rain as the landslide ended, only small pebbles making it through Rudo's protection to bounce off Funanya's keim beast armor.

Another roar sounded. The demons beyond the rise continued their war, and the earth trembled at the thought.

"Get back to camp," Funanya commanded as she rose, having to untangle herself from the protective "embrace" of the warrior. "Collect everyone before the damn mountain comes down!"

She came to her feet in time to see one demon pick up the second and throw it, limbs flailing, into the cliff face.

The entire side of the mountain came down.

The seer lay beneath the cart as the camp emptied, and she watched them go. She heard the commotion in the distance. Askaran was there. He would come back, and that was all that mattered. Until then, she would wait.

Only one moon was high in the shadows, illuminating the return of one of the warriors after the sound of roars had been replaced with crashing stones. The stranger passed the sentries, aiming for the cart where the seer lay, and where Askaran was meant to be.

Askaran had given her no instructions, and the Berintan was fast approaching. The seer had Askaran's shendyt and his sandals, but if they did not find him here, what would they think? Would it be so hard to decide he was the demon when they already knew of the shifters?

Surprising herself, the seer discovered she had her fishing line in hand. Her absent-minded fingers tied a loop in the end.

She threaded the longer end through and created a lasso. Hidden by the cloak and the skids of the cart, the seer hung the loop over the abandoned clothing and went back to waiting.

The Berintan was named Otieno, and he was an old warrior. From listening, the seer knew he had been part of Sizwe's ark from the beginning, but he had no love for his dead archon. He had followed the others into the new ark, and some of the others suspected he would soon try to woo the archon. He had always thrived as a close companion of the powerful.

"Up, Hunter!" the Berintan called as he arrived at the cart. He crouched to peer under the cart, and the seer felt his eyes pass over her hiding place under the sand-cloak. His eyes narrowed on the shendyt. Leaning forward, Otieno reached for the clothing, as if planning on shaking the Ennead awake.

His head slipped through the loop as he reached.

The seer yanked hard, drawing the string tight, then hooked it around the tread of the cart. Otieno lurched back, and the line tightened further. His hands clawed at the fine rope that had dug into his skin, but he could not loosen it. When he tried to stand, it dug deeper in.

The seer did not move from her place as the Berintan panicked and then collapsed onto the stone. When she was satisfied that the scuffling had not been heard over the clatter of stones in the distance, the seer slipped out and retrieved her fishing line. Not knowing what else to do, she climbed back into the undercarriage and waited for Askaran's return.

Erosan was the fastest of them, leading the demon the farthest through the remaining desert. In a chasm of shale, Philyre was the last decoy, standing high on a cliff to lure the colossus the final distance. The demon spotted her, lowering its head and blasting a roar of frustration.

Was it clever enough to recognize it had chased four different Enneads, or did it believe it was facing one incredibly fast one? Philyre did not even know what drove the beast to pursue Enneads, but the desperate need to hunt Enneads was predictable.

Once she had the monster following, Philyre dropped down and ran the length of the chasm. The mountain path bent to the south at the far end. From there, unless it chose to cross the cliffs and mountains, it would follow the chasm to the oasis and the Beritans there.

To her dismay, the demon slowed as Philyre turned the corner. She knew she could not be scented with keim beast blood, but the vision of demons was superb, even in the dark. It must have known she was an Ennead. Why did it delay?

She checked behind her and stumbled back in shock. Another colossus demon had appeared between her and the first. It had its back to him but was a scarce thirty strides from her.

Philyre dropped down, throwing the sand-cloak over herself. It had been primed with the red sands of the desert and not shaken out. Although it matched the cliffs poorly, she had never known a demon to notice such a thing.

She hid as the heavy footsteps nearby made the earth tremble. The new colossus demon was too close to risk attracting its attention, but if she could convince *both* demons to follow…

The demons turned on each other. It was not until one was thrown that Philyre fully recognized her oversight. The chasm walls were high around her, and the force of the confrontation was bringing them down.

Daring not to wait, she broke from hiding and ran, quickly scaling the chasm walls. She did not stop even to look back until she was out.

One colossus demon slammed the other into the cliffs. The second pounded its enormous fists against the cliff, and a large section of stone balanced above came crashing down.

Dust and shadows fell with the shale until Philyre could see nothing more. Both demons were gone, buried under the rockslide, and so useless to her.

Cursing, Philyre turned away. She dreaded going back to the others in failure, but she had promised one final run, and it was finished. The Berintans were nearly clear of the desert and all its demons.

From atop the cliff, the glimmer of their fires beyond the ridge of the chasm was visible, and she cursed that as well.

She had run out of time. They had escaped her.

Askaran felt nothing and saw nothing. He was aware of the sounds at first, of the roars coming from his lungs. He heard the landslides. Someone screamed, and the sound woke his tired mind.

He pushed back enough to see through the demon's eyes. Where the demon ignored the scattering Berintans who fled from one cliff's ledge, the mind of the Ennead in the demon sharply noticed them. The scream was one of pain. Falling stones had landed on someone.

Given something to focus on, Askaran evaluated the scene. The other colossus demon was too strong to overpower, its scales too thick. This battle could go on forever unless Askaran found a way to tip the balance.

The falling rocks gave him an idea, and he gifted that idea to the mind of the monster controlling his body.

The demon liked the suggestion and quickly put it to action.

It slammed its opponent against a cliff face. Instead of beating at the other demon directly where scales and iron-bone would blunt it, the demon pounded its tail and fists into the wall of the cliff. The vibrations climbed above to a large outcropping.

The entire wall gave out. Black and red stones came shattering down.

The demon had misjudged its own size and, caught in the landslide, it briefly panicked. The stones would crush even the victor's thick hide.

Askaran was ready. While the demon reacted to the dangerous crash of boulders around it, Askaran formed the cage around the mind again and slammed the door shut. In a final act, he kicked the demon's legs against his enemy, pushing off to drive himself away from the slide. He fell, tumbling down the chasm's slant. By the time the movement stopped, he was again an Ennead, lying on his sore back, staring up at a twinkling sky. One moon shone brightly down.

For another long moment, Askaran felt nothing, but soon the pain of his back brought back focus, and he was able to push himself up. The wounds from the demon were mere bruises. Nothing had been broken. The only blood was from the abrasions to his back, a result of throwing himself out from the landslide.

Inside his mind, the demon howled, clutching at the side of its cage and rattling it. But the energy of the monster had been spent, and it could no longer force it open.

The chasm's end was filled with rubble. A bone stuck out from the debris, already sun-bleached despite the moonlight illumination. The ash of demon flesh floated away with the dust of the slide.

Seeing its opponent dead, Askaran's demon settled. More satisfied now than it had been in days, the demon calmed, and Askaran, at long last, could breathe. Exhaustion settled back in, and Askaran sank wearily against the stones.

The thought of a child wearing a worn white jellabiya made him start.

"Get moving," Askaran told himself as he checked the sky for directions and forced his feet to lift. "You promised."

Hearing the echo of the seer's voice in the word drove Askaran onward. Knowing he could be missed at any time, he broke into a long sprint to retrace his steps to the camp and back to the cart.

He knew he should have been aghast to find that the seer had strangled a Berintan in his absence, but Askaran saw the necessity of it and did not want to further worry the seer. Without questioning her, he lifted the body and found a place to hide it.

As he left the cart, the limping archon returned to her tent, fleeing the rockslide and ready for the next battle.

How little she knew.

They returned to the camp, the entire chasm collapsing behind them. Funanya did not care who had buried whom. Even if one survived, she expected it would follow their scent, as the hound demons had, to kill the camp. She hoped the confrontation with the other colossus demon had weakened the survivor, else her warriors had no hope of saving themselves.

A bruised ankle, sustained when her foot slipped over a stone on their retreat, was the extent of Funanya's injuries. Rudo had been scraped along his shoulders, but Dalia remained unwounded as they rushed back. Upon their arrival at the camp, Funanya ordered every warrior out of their beds to take up posts of readiness and await the colossus demon that might follow them back. She was uncertain if the monsters had spotted them, or if it would be in the mood to follow a trail, but could not take a chance.

Even with all forty-three warriors ready, Funanya thought her chances low. The other arks would have to react as well, their numbers flowing out from the tents, but it still seemed too little.

Once in her own tent, Funanya dismissed Rudo, propped her spear against the central post, and let Dalia bind her foot. She absently accepted a gourd from Dalia and, with a swallow of water, tried to chase the dry apprehension from her throat. Satisfied she would be able to stand on the wounded foot, Funanya went to retrieve the spear, with every intention of returning to her warriors.

Weakness crept into her from her chest, a sinking feeling rising even as her legs trembled. She fell with her hand outstretched to grip the spear shaft, falling short. She gasped for breath and knew the hot air filled her lungs, but it was not enough. She gasped again.

Through the haze of her mind, Funanya was certain of only one thing; she had been poisoned. The spear, still in its cradle, seemed to drift farther away as she collapsed onto the carpeted floor of the tent.

Dalia came into view, and Funanya watched her take the spear from its cradle and face her. Unable to move or speak, Funanya stared up at the woman who had been her friend and servant for four years. Her mouth tingled, telling her where the poison had been from.

Holding the spear in one hand, Dalia drew a knife casually, like a hunter going to skin the already-dead prey. Through choked lungs, Funanya stuttered, "The hunter?"

The laugh that came from Funanya's warrior was bitter and unlike any Funanya had ever heard from Dalia. Even the voice sounded darker than usual as she answered, "I would kill you because I don't like your Ennead pet? Oh no, Archon. This has been coming for years."

The mark of an archon was their sword, but as Dalia's knife advanced toward her, Funanya knew it would fail her. The sword was too cumbersome for her dead arms and legs.

The Night Road had never been a kind place. Even after a decade away from the life of an unlabeled, Funanya had not given up all the habits born there. Her tired arms, almost too heavy to lift, hung beside the sheath where a tauran trainer's strap knife still lay on her calf. It was meant, in honorable lives, to cut leather straps for trapped animals or people if they fell from their mount. In the unscrupulous, it was hooked for the cutting of purses.

Her numb fingers found the grip of the knife as Dalia reached around to slice through Funanya's windpipe.

Yanking the blade free, Funanya slashed at the arm, and the hooked blade caught the flesh, cutting a deep gouge in Dalia's arm. Dalia's knife fell from her hand.

Desperation kicked Funanya to her feet. She lunged. The hooked blade caught on Dalia's chest, tearing her breast open to the ribs. As Dalia stumbled back, Funanya slashed again, and the blow landed on the woman's throat. Blood spurted one last time. Dalia crumbled.

The burst of energy ended. Funanya collapsed.

She struggled to bring her thoughts together. Instincts released her now that the immediate threat was gone, but she still could not draw breath, and she felt unconsciousness creeping in. She knew blood coated her and that it was not hers but also knew she would soon surrender, wound or not, to the poison. Her head swam like she was drowning in the air.

She needed help.

Funanya dragged herself by her arms alone, her legs limp behind her. Under the flap of the tent, she pulled herself into the moonlight, seeking someone but unable to call out.

To her relief, Rudo stood by the tent entrance as if expecting her. Seeing the archon prone, he quickly searched the area and kneeled beside her, a gentle hand on her head. She thought he spoke, but she did not understand what was said.

With no breath remaining, Funanya could not cry out when his grip tightened on her hair, and he dragged her away. Gone was his pleasant smile and eager demeanor. She was nothing but a body as, following the curve of the tent into the shadows behind it, she was pulled to a hidden corner of the camp.

Nothing remained; she could not lift her arms or force her voice to obey. She expected fear but found instead herself turning to disappointment. After decades of effort, her life would end just as any life from the Night Road expected: cut down in the dark. The training, the plotting, the games she had played had all amounted to nothing in the end. Now, she was just another death caused by misplaced trust.

Rudo said nothing, but positioned himself over her, holding her hair to keep her neck extended. Another fine obsidian knife cast a shadow in the moonlight, aimed at her exposed throat.

But before the blade could touch her skin, Rudo gave a cry. Funanya's head reefed to the side as he stumbled away. In her fall, Funanya cracked her skull against a stone. The world spun around her.

A shadow stepped over her, advancing on Rudo. The silhouette was so dark that even the moonlight could not brighten it.

Gasping, she lost consciousness.

CHAPTER 10

The suns were glaring in her face when Funanya opened her eyes.

Her head ached in the bright light, and she winced her eyes shut. She tried to bring a hand to her temples, only to discover her hands were bound.

She pressed her head back against the stones behind her, trying to remember.

Dalia's poison and Rudo's attack inched back into her mind. She had expected to be dead. The pain was evidence enough that she was not, not yet.

Forcing herself to ignore the pain in her head, she opened her eyes again. She was bound with torn carpet, her hands fixed to each other and bound to her feet. The carpet had been left entire enough to create pouches over her clenched fists, preventing her from even trying to release the knots. Although she was still dressed in armor, her sword was conspicuously missing from its sheath on her belt.

She had been propped in a corner of a stony valley, with the eastern sunrise shining as if to illuminate her alone. The red and brown stones of the crumbling mountain stretched in all directions. She was alone except for the lounging figure in the shade of a stone a dozen paces from her.

Hunter lay with his feet propped up on a ledge and his shendyt forming a pillow under his head. Four empty bottles, their corks lost, lay scattered around him. He had balanced a piece of carpet over his head to shield it. He was again nude, even his collar gone.

"Good morning, Archon," he said, tilting his head toward her. His eyes were bloodshot and sunken in the light of the morning. "Feeling better?"

Funanya breathed deeply, feeling the residual tightness of the poison there but was glad to feel the air rushing to and from her lungs.

"Atra poison," she said, hearing her own voice rough. She coughed and spat to clear her throat. "Diluted in water, it's never enough to kill, just cause collapse." Squinting into the light, she searched the area. She did not recognize the valley and saw no other signs of life. The camp could not be far. The mountain was the same one. "Makes it easy to kidnap," she finished.

"Or kill," he said, rising and tossing the carpet aside. He held a skinning knife—it looked like Dalia's—in his hand as he advanced toward her.

Funanya shook her head in dejection. "You wait for me to wake, just so you can do what they—"

He cut the carpet threads from her wrists and ankles. Spinning the blade over, he extended the hilt to her.

"Just didn't want you to wake early, find me asleep, and come to all the wrong conclusions."

She gingerly accepted the blade from him and watched in muted shock as he returned to his stone "bed" and collected his shendyt.

"You drank my spirits?" she muttered as she stood and recognized the bottles. "Four bottles of it? On your own?"

"It's called qileeo," he corrected, his voice groggy. "Fine Ennead quality. And yes, four bottles. I didn't feel like sharing with any Berintans." Now wearing the basic wrap, Hunter scooped up a watergourd and offered it to her. Seeing her hesitate, he chuckled.

"Collected last night from the oasis. As you pointed out, I could have killed you last night. You think I waited this long to do it in a tricky way?" She took the gourd and drank, finding her mouth dry as soon as the water touched it. "And your sword is over there," he added, pointing to a stone another few paces to her right. "Not sure what I'd do with the damn thing, anyway."

She drained half the water before coming up for air. After retrieving her sword, she felt enough like herself to face Hunter once more.

Instead of looking at her, he had returned to his bed, propped his feet up once more, and placed the carpet over his head to provide shade. She put herself too far to one side to cast a shadow over him, forcing him to squint up at her.

"You tore up my carpet," she said.

"I needed something to tie you up with. It was an Ennead carpet anyway," he pointed out. "Nice weave."

"You snuck into my tent, stole my … my drinks, tore up my carpet… The least you could do is stand up and address me properly."

He was slow in rising.

"You're hungover," she said.

"I did drink a fair bit."

Funanya had no answer, feeling lost. Nothing made sense. Her closest allies had sought to kill her, and her enemy had saved her. Would the suns swap places too?

"Why?"

"I wanted to get drunk," Hunter replied, straight-faced. "First good sleep I've had in days."

In her frustration, she lashed out. Her slap was light against his shoulder, but he flinched like a much stronger blow had been delivered. "Not that! Why help me?"

He winced. "Could you let me take you back without making me answer that? It would be less complicated."

"No," Funanya replied. "Answer me, Hunter. What happened last night?"

He sighed in surrender. "I went to your tent to get drunk. I thought you were going to kill me as soon as you were back in your own lands and figured being drunk might make that not so upsetting. And I knew you had all that qileeo from the City in your tent, and that you were out looking at something. So I was sneaking in, but you showed up. And then you were crawling back out, and Rudo was there, ready to stick you. That's when I realized I had to change my plan." Hunter gave a helpless shrug. "I can't go back. The water's gone. And I can't go forward, seeing as I don't think the Berintans will like me much. But then I thought maybe they would put up with me so long as I belonged to someone, and that someone had enough clout to force them. The problem is that Rudo isn't powerful enough, that haughty Adeban doesn't like me and Jabarl is … well, an ass."

"An ass?" Funanya asked, bemused.

"He's an ass," Hunter repeated. "So I was left with you, only I wouldn't be left with you if you was dead … were dead I mean. So I figured I should save you and maybe then you'd want me around a little bit longer."

He paused and at last met her stare.

Funanya chewed at her lip in thought and regarded the Ennead once more. "You killed Rudo? He was a good warrior."

Hunter made a face of disgust. "He didn't see me coming. Pretty heads crack against stone just as nicely as ugly ones do."

"Where's your collar?"

"I cut it loose when I decided to rob you," he replied, showing no hesitation or remorse. "Sharp stones. Anything else you want to know before I lead you back to camp and let you get back to your comfortable, carpet-poor tent?"

Funanya stared at him for long moments more, seeking a flaw in his calm demeanor. She generally did what she could to ensure others owed her favors and hated having the roles reversed. She did owe him something. Had it not been for his timely aid, she would not have made it through the night.

"I have a pack of wolfen at home," she said. "I use them for hunting on the grounds outside the manors. My handler is also, as you so eloquently put it, an ass. Maybe I could have you handle them instead."

To her surprise, lowered his head in a perfect Berintan bow. "I would be happy to serve."

"Lead me back," she ordered, and he quickly gathered the remaining supplies, leaving the empty bottles scattered in the little valley.

He led her out of the hiding place, and she found herself staring down at the camp. They had been a hundred paces from them the entire time, but invisible in the little corner of the mountains.

She paused at the crest of the hilland, staring down into camp. Her eyes narrowed on her tent. There was only one other archon's tent present now

"Hunter, why did you say Jabarl is an ass?"

He chuckled behind her. His voice was still placid as he perched atop a boulder at her side.

"Because when night fell, only one ark was still alive, and it was his. My understanding might be limited, but I thought that meant he had cleared out those above him. That makes him a murderer, and I think all murderers are asses."

"So the other ark … Adeban…"

"Dead," Hunter said. "What happens when you go in there, Archon?"

She placed her hand on her sword, the fine chitter scales of the hilt warm under her fingers. Upon the reminder of her authority as an archon, she lifted her chin and squared her shoulders.

"Depends on if I accuse him of the murders," she said. Although her voice was gaining strength, it was not quite as powerful as an archon's was meant to be.

"Does it help if I point out that Dalia had black paint on her? Or that a young warrior who once wore the striped brown and red paint of Adeban now has black on his face, too?"

Only Jabarl, of all the arks of Douran, used black.

Funanya let out a slow sigh. She had to assume Jabarl had been feigning incompetence, but after that, it all made sense. Dalia had come to her shortly after

Jabarl had arrived in the city four years ago, the same time she now knew Rudo had joined Sizwe. A spy had been in each of their arks.

She had thought Jabarl shy in his dealings but now recognized that he had been avoiding interacting with Dalia. He had placed his spy and exploited the opportunity the trek across the desert had given him.

"Go back to your cart," Funanya ordered the slave. "Your support will hurt my position. But if I live through this, I will make you the handler of my wolfen pack."

She made her way down the rocky slope alone but felt the eyes of the Ennead on her each step of the way. She made sure her sword was in hand as she reached the edges of the camp and sought out her warriors.

When she looked back, he had vanished from his perch.

Askaran watched the archon go, not sure if he was wishing she would be cut down or welcomed. He had given her a long tale of lies, but the truth remained that she was his only hope of entering Berinta.

"You made it work," the seer said, and Askaran cracked a smile. The little girl seemed to have taken a liking to hiding and spoke to him from the camouflage of the sand-cloak. Seers were known for being mysterious. This one seemed to be enjoying it.

"I lied a lot," he said, feeling strangely giddy and blaming the alcohol. He wasn't sure he wasn't still drunk.

"I didn't think it would work," the seer said.

"It sounds like we can go back to the cart," he answered, dropping from the boulder to land beside her, working to focus. "Can you stay under there a few more nights? Once we get into Berinta—"

"I will go play in the forest!" she declared. Wide eyes peered out at him from the pile of stones where she was hidden. He saw the glint of the kukri as she tucked it under her. Even without the second, retrieving the blade Dalia had stolen filled some of the void he still felt from their absence.

Having no idea what awaited, he saw no reason to correct the seer's assertion. His idea of winning over the archon had been desperate, but he was glad he had succeeded.

Biding time, he promised himself. He would figure out the details later, once he had drank some water and had another nap. He needed the seer to grow up.

Until then, he accepted servitude.

In his drunken bliss, he thought it was not so bad, so long as he stayed with Archon Funanya. Her, he understood.

Four of her warriors, called in from the defensive line that was still awaiting a colossus demon from the north, guarded Funanya's tent against all intruders. She gave them instructions to tell no one of her return but refuse requests for access. Jabarl himself tried to visit and had to give up.

Taking it upon herself to clean the tent—although she noted Dalia's body was nowhere to be found—she tore up the remaining stained carpet and washed away the blood. The tainted gourd she marked with charcoal and placed on a hanger in the tent as a reminder. She cleaned and sharpened her spear, something she had not had to do herself since before becoming an archon. The distantly familiar ritual settled her nerves.

Finding the hooked bone knife on her torn carpet, Funanya cleaned, sharpened it, and replaced it in the sheath against her calf.

She sent no messages. The four warriors she had selected stood like statues at the entrance for the day and a half it took for the main forces to join the scouts at the final oasis. Without confirmation one way or another, Jabarl did not know if she lived still, or if the warriors were obeying another. She wanted him confused.

At nightfall of the next day, Funanya donned her finest clothing and jewelry. Without assistance, she drew her ark's war paint on her face, feeling every line like a scratch over her skin. The sword of her office looked out of place where it lay against the royal blue of her dyed kaftan but it felt right.

When she felt ready, she called the four warriors and sought Archon Farai's tent.

He admitted her but rejected her warriors. She entered alone.

Farai's tent had been ornately added to with Ennead spoils. Woolen carpets, not unlike the one Hunter had ruined in her tent, covered the floor space completely. Mirrors, each as tall as a man and wide as two, had been erected against the tent walls, casting perplexing reflections like she was in a hall with a hundred rooms, a hundred chairs, and a hundred Archons.

Farai sat on his demon bone chair, his feet propped up comfortably. The drink he had in his hand was in a glass bottle, making her believe it, too, had come from the city. Even the chiseled glass goblet he held spoke of the conquest he had achieved.

She bowed low to Archon Farai, but he sneered as she rose from the diminishing position.

"You claimed to be content, Funanya, yet Adeban lies dead. I am not pleased," Farai said.

"It was not by my hand," Funanya answered. "I came here to ask your permission to kill Jabarl."

The swirling glass of the archon stilled. Farai sat up slowly. "The fourth ark of Douran?" he asked.

"Now second," Funanya said. "On the night Adeban was slain, I was attacked twice by spies from his ark. It is one thing to let our warriors duel, but I consider overt assassination poor behavior for an archon. I mean to set it right."

The Archon considered Funanya for a long moment as if analyzing every tooth and talon she had donned, most of them from her kills over the many years before becoming archon. She had chosen a dark blue deliberately; it was the richest color. She would not be taken lightly.

He pointed to the place beside him, giving her leave to kneel at his side.

"You are certain?"

"My warriors would not simply murder me, Archon. I noted flaws. Even now, you will find a new warrior among Jabarl's soldiers, one everyone will tell you was loyal to Adeban yesterday."

"He could have changed oaths."

"Without knowing if I live, no warrior has offered Jabarl their oaths, Archon. Jabarl's tactics are subtle. The warriors do not think him strong. Adeban's ark is waiting to see if they can join me, but I have not been available. No oaths have been made. You can ask them if you want." Funanya smiled. "Now may I kill him?"

Farai shook his head. "We cannot have archons killing each other openly. Grand Archon Amadi will be very displeased if he has to assign four new arks to Douran."

"Then let us acknowledge the fine warriors of the conquest and name three new archons," Funanya suggested. "All I am certain of is that Jabarl cannot be allowed to keep his rank." She cocked her head at Farai. "Is this why he was moved to Douran, Archon? Why he has never stayed in any city long enough to be the First Ark?" Farai's smile confirmed her theory.

"Still," Farai said, "Grand Archon Amadi will not allow one of his chosen leaders to be slain." It was a given that they would plot against each other. But only a poor assassin was caught.

"Which makes what Jabarl did to Adeban unaccept-able," Funanya insisted.

Farai nodded. He pushed himself up, leaving the glass goblet on the armrest. "Walk with me," he told her.

Funanya hurried to follow.

They left the tent behind and passed through Farai's ranks, filled with more spoils and excited war-riors. Hidden among these, they came across a small, unmarked tent, and he ducked inside.

The space was entirely occupied by a single cot and the Ennead, barely a woman, who sat curled on it. She had removed the white shift she had worn in the city and now was dressed in a Berintan kaftan and beaded necklace. The combination looked strange against the pitch-dark skin.

The black eyes that fixed on Funanya when she lifted the tent flap made her flinch. Despite the decoration of bones and talons and teeth she wore, Funanya felt weak and naked. No armor, not even keim beast skin, could have protected her from the penetrating stare of the young woman.

"What do you see?" Farai demanded to the Ennead.

The desert seer continued to stare at Funanya for a long moment, her eyes wide and fixed. When she finally blinked, it was slow, almost sleepy, and it broke the gaze. Funanya felt the tension release.

"Twice her trust has been betrayed," the Ennead said. "The colors drawn on their faces were wrong."

"So she spoke truth to me?" Farai asked, and Funanya's heart skipped. She ran over their conversation, wondering if she had lied and would be caught at it. Lying to Farai would be a death sentence. She had wanted to keep Hunter out of the story, but if the Ennead seer could see his involvement, would the omission count as a lie?

The ebony eyes drifted away from Funanya and fixed themselves on Farai once more.

"Every word. The ark of Jabarl has murdered its way to the top. Now you will see him killed."

Done, the Ennead pulled her arms around her legs and placed her chin atop her bent knees. Her wrists were pink in the sunset, showing where shackles had torn her skin.

Farai grinned at Funanya. "So we shall. This way." He left, passing under Funanya's arm as she held the tent flap open for him.

The Ennead glanced up at Funanya before she followed Farai out. "You should be grateful to your warrior," the seer said. "Had he not been there to push the killer aside, you would be dead."

"My warrior?" she wondered.

"He is strong," the seer said, her eyes narrowed in thought. She seemed, for a moment, confused. "He alone will not betray you," she whispered. She replaced her chin on her legs. Her deep eyes closed.

My warrior, Funanya thought as she chased after Farai. Hunter was no warrior of hers. Had the seer been unable to see the skin of who had saved her?

Funanya found Farai at a huge tent that was a dozen paces farther into camp and followed him through the flap. The well-lit space was filled with trophies, from keim beast claws to winged demon tusks. Another Ennead, lying long across a couch, greeted them with a grunt. For all his size, his legs, from the knees down, hung off the seat.

The black-eyed stare of the Ennead shifter had a similar, but unique, tension as the seer's. Where the eyes of the seer had been piercing, this stare was blunt and brutish. Funanya felt more pushed than criticized, and she found the sensation much easier to resist. She squared herself formally, making herself strong under the pressure.

"What is this?" the huge Ennead growled.

"An offer," Farai said. "She has found a traitor, and I need him dead. I cannot kill him directly, but if a monster were to attack the camp and slay him, that would be perfectly acceptable."

The Ennead pushed himself up, and Funanya spotted the long scar along his leg once more. The wounds he had suffered in the city had faded to nothing, leaving his dark skin a shadow in the lamplight. His smile was bright and feral.

Farai nodded his head. "This way, mighty Yarr."

Funanya stepped aside to let the shifter out into the night and did not follow Farai as he showed Yarr his target. The alarms sounded, and the cries rang across the waters. Funanya called her warriors back to form a defense along the edge of her camp, where they watched and waited.

They did not engage the tusked demon that rampaged through Jarbarl's forces, but it took Funanya's authority to keep her warriors in line. More than once they flinched away, fearing the next blow would be directed at them, but she forced them to stand their ground.

Farai joined her in time to see the shifter finish. The screams were dying down as he stood at her side and looked into the rubble of Jabarl's ark.

As tall as the serpent demon ready to strike, the tusked demon towered over the tents as it rummaged for survivors. Lifting its maned head pointed the enormous tusks to the sky, and it roared at the moons, sending deep vibrations over the onlookers and making more than one quake. Refusing to look away, Funanya saw the form change. The layers of spikes along the creature's back shrank into smooth skin, and the bristled tail was pulled in. Soon, even the towering, muscled body vanished behind the tents.

Yarr, naked and blood-covered, walked out from between the tents and to his own like a man heading to the market.

She understood killing. Funanya had been born among murderers and criminals, and killing others was a part of her life she had never questioned. Her warriors trembled, but she refused to. This, however, made her quake within.

Once she was certain the danger had passed, she faced her warriors.

"Let it be known that the allies of Archon Farai were offended by Jabarl's transgressions. And may none of us ever offend again," Funanya shouted.

She dismissed them all.

Once they stood alone in the moonlight, Farai cleared his throat and said, "Eight archons have died in this campaign. Thankfully, the battle has given many warriors a chance to prove themselves. We will name new archons soon. I will assign three new ones to Douran."

"I am pleased it does not have to be four," she replied.

He gave her a small smile and left for his own warriors.

Funanya returned, shaken and exhausted, to her tent. Without orders to put her warriors on watch, she allowed them to relax. Now, that calm would create rumors. She wondered if those rumors would surround Farai and his shifter or her.

Once she had settled, she called for Hunter.

Askaran watched the tusked demon among the Berintans from the safety of the cart that had been his home for the crossing of the wastes. No rope tied him now, but he stayed within reach, tethered by his promise to the child underneath. He remained ducked low as he watched, keeping his silhouette and his scent concealed from the monster. He wanted no additional attention now that he had nowhere to run.

His demon was placid from its night of drunkenness. It took little interest in the tusked demon's presence, which surprised Askaran. Even recently sated, the demon usually hated to have its territory infringed upon.

Watching the demon methodically work its way through one corner of the camp helped Askaran understand what the demon had already known. It was too perfect, too calm, too planned. Demons raged and were chaotic. This manifestation was calculated.

As soon as the single ark was destroyed, the monster vanished, and Askaran had his suspicion confirmed. The demon he had just watched was a shifter.

His demon was not offended by shifters.

"Never did like him," Askaran muttered, feeling a stronger need to remain hidden. Yarr could scent him from a distance if the wind changed. He could not let that happen.

At length, the camp settled. Askaran assumed Yarr had gone to sleep. The night fell in earnest.

"Hunter," a warrior called. "The archon wants you."

He glanced back, but the Youngest Seer was not visible below the cart. Satisfied, he followed the warriors to the archon's abode.

He did not know the man who escorted him to the archon's tent, but none of the warriors lowered their weapons at him. Instead, the men and women now wearing the archon's colors on their faces seemed to accept the Ennead, who marched among them untethered. Once he stood before the archon, they unquestioningly left him alone in her presence.

He thought the deep blue kaftan she wore, decorated with tassels of talons and beads made of bones, was meant to make her look powerful, but in it, Askaran saw only death. Some of the horns were from dredgers, huge but harmless beasts. He could be impressed by the keim beast teeth but saw no prestige in killing dredgers.

The demon bones she wore sent a shiver down his spine, not because she had slain them, but because they reminded him of the monsters that still roamed the desert.

In her hand, she held a hinged ring of metal, which she lifted when he halted before her. He allowed her to place the circle around his neck.

"A new collar?" he asked. "No tether?"

He placed a hand to the cold metal, tight like the poised hands of a strangler.

"I found it in my goods," she said, lifting a key in one hand as she pulled away, leaving the collar in place. "It will stay with you now, marking you as mine."

It was clearly Ennead in construction, but he had to wonder why the Enneads had made such a thing. The metal was old, likely from the days before Nanterac, when demons had been trapped on occasion. His mother had told him about those who had studied the monsters, discovering what they were and the effects of their blood before the shifters. This had to be a restraint for a hound demon or similar.

Now around his throat, the pressure of the collar made it difficult to swallow.

"Will it be removed?" he asked, pressing his finger to the metal.

"Only if I wish it," she replied, shaking a key at him. "I do not wish it, not for now, Hunter. Kneel," she commanded. Askaran lowered himself onto his knees, placing his hands firmly on the torn carpet of the floor. Strangely, she had left the carpet scraps and hung the poisoned gourd from the central post. This was someone who did not want to forget the lessons she had learned.

He watched her place the key onto a lanyard and hang it around her throat like a necklace. He could not stop himself from chuckling.

She rotated gently to regard him, her expression curious. "I have locked you up and now you laugh?" she asked. He thought he saw an amused shine to her gaze.

"It is the symmetry," Askaran said. "You hang it around your neck, you see, on a chain. Mine has no chain. Ironic."

Her smile darkened slightly. "I have been seeing much irony. Ironic that I have come to trust my enemy when I cannot trust my allies, for instance."

Askaran started. "Trust me?"

"Trust that I can control you," the archon replied, her smile strangely sincere. "You are a slave of my ark. Any warrior may demand whatever they wish from you, and you will obey. You belong to me."

He found the words meaningless, but he showed the obedience she expected by crossing his arms over his chest and bowing. For now, it was good enough.

Interlude

CHAPTER 11

The seer watched Farai pour another cup of chapman, the floating fruit visible, bobbing through the steam. She had lost track of the number of goblets she had consumed, which could only mean one thing, Farai was trying to get her drunk.

She slumped back against the stretched hide seat, her hand pressed to her hot forehead. Visions flickered in her mind, and her eyes followed them. Somewhere in the jungle outside the Grand Manor windows, a pair of lovers had found a secret place. She watched them sneak below the bridge; her face beamed, but his watched for spying eyes. His movement was practiced, hers unsure.

With force, the seer focused on her host and the goblet he was extending. She took it, happy that the visions were of nearby Berintans who seemed ready to enjoy themselves.

"Have I been talking in my sleep?" she asked, hearing her voice bobbing like the fruit in the chapman. She could hardly see the sitting room or feel the cushions under her through the haze and was glad.

If she did not feel, she did not think. It was a strategy well used over the last six years since the razing of the Ennead City.

"A little," Farai confessed, giving her a wide grin and catching her hand when it tipped the cup. He squeezed beside her in the seat. They had once been able to sit side by side without difficulty on the same chair, but now the space was cramped by the seer herself. The rich foods of the Berintan, such a contrast to the scarcity of the desert, pleased her, and living in a haze of foods seemed to keep her visions quieter. Seers were born of pain—a father long dead before their birth, a mother who perished moments before the child was brought into the world—and the seer had hoped plenty would dampen the magic she had been cursed with.

"Did I say something nice?" she asked.

"You talked about my death," he replied, helping her lift the cup. He did not seem upset by the topic she had chosen in her sleep, and she wondered if that was true or just a ruse. Talking to the archon about his death was bad, she was certain.

She never saw the face of his murderer, not in any of her visions, so had to assume the person or the event was too far for her powers to reach. Details had been sneaking in when she was unable to keep them out, be it by food or drink, but she had deliberately kept those details to herself. She didn't want him knowing.

She didn't want him avoiding it. His failure in the desert had made him lose face, although he still commanded other archons and had the blessings of his Grand Archon. Seeing him fall further from grace would bring her great satisfaction. Already, his hold on Masamba was tenuous and often challenged.

The seer pushed aside the cup. "I am done for tonight," she said. "I can hardly keep my eyes open." The statement was true; the soft blue cushions of the sitting room made the lamps seem dark under their colored glass. It felt like the room was filled by the same moonlight the lovers explored.

Her mind flashed back to them. The woman whimpered and shook her head, but the man held her shoulders firmly and kissed her. The woman tried to pull back but could not release the grip of the man before her.

The seer pulled her mind away from the pair. She had no desire to share in the woman's fear.

When she felt hands on her, she started, unsure if her mind had slipped again to the lovers by the river outside the Grand Manor. To her surprise, Farai held her fast.

"You said my death would come from someone near to me," he hissed, his face a hand's breadth from hers. His hands, as firm as they were, could hardly reach around her plump arms.

She laughed. "It will come from one of your own Grand Manors," she answered, giddy. "Foolish man, your own archons…"

Suddenly realizing that she was saying aloud that which she had told herself to keep silent, the seer stopped.

He did not seem to notice but stared at her, his expression incredulous. Her laughter renewed at seeing Farai's wide-eyed stare.

His face held fear, and she thought it wonderful. In six years, she had been unable to harm him. He catered to her, used her, bedded her when it pleased him to, and she could do nothing. Hiding in artificial pleasures, she had padded herself with armor in the form of fat, but it failed to discourage him. Her only weapon had been her silence, but now saw that her greatest blow had been delivered by words.

The Berintan who had betrayed her, destroyed her City, and nearly driven her people to extinction was afraid.

Outside, the woman rolled free of her lover. Her kick took him across the face, and his head slammed back into the bridge. He went down heavily. Collecting her kaftan, she ran into the jungle and left him with blood pooling on the stones under his head. Like the seer, the woman outside was no longer afraid.

Farai gripped the seer harder, and the vision fled from her. "Who?"

The Eldest Seer knew her smile was darkened by the shadows cast by the lamps, but it felt right. No lie could pass her lips, but she had no intention of giving him any more details.

"Do you think knowing will prevent it?" she asked him instead. "Or will knowing cause it?"

His grip released, and she staggered away into the dark, her smile for once victorious. The visions stumbled alongside her, following the escaped lover for a bit, then watching the cru lizards among the trees where they were hunting for chitters.

"Just tell me!" Farai called after her. "You hate this life. Tell me, and I will release you!"

Her vision was tossed by walking when the drink was so deep tonight, she struggled to look back and saw him standing in the doorway. His swords of status hung on the wall behind him, ornate and useless. She knew what he meant when he said "release," and it was not letting her leave the Grand Manor of Masamba. He would kill her.

Although she hated the life she had been sentenced to, the seer had never considered ending her life. Her mistake had cost her people greatly, but to die—to leave the Enneads without any seers alive at all—was to certainly damn them.

Somewhere across the desert, maybe new seers had been born. Certainly, enough men had died in the raid. Childbirth was dangerous. If even one pregnant woman perished soon enough…

But how many pregnant women would make it across the desert with their child yet alive within them? Or carry a child to term in their struggle in the desert, denied the life-giving waters of the City? Until the seer knew for certain that another desert seer lived, she could not let go.

She left him behind, letting her mind wander on and about, unable to focus on any vision for longer than a moment. In the distracted attention, she found an uneasy silence. Every sensation, good or bad, was short. Nothing lingered as her mind drifted. Her feet wandered toward her room absently, enjoying the buzz of the chapman.

In a single blink, the visions went silent, and she saw a small blue ball—a glass orb—atop a pedestal, lit by a single beam of natural light. Water trickled from the object, dripping down the pillar into a vast chamber. Arching ceilings, supported by intricately carved columns, stretched over the endless pool of water. The light played over the ceilings briefly, casting the artisans' vines and wildlife in shimmering shadows.

The vision was gone in the next instant.

The seer tried to chase it, but it withdrew in the mist of her drunken mind. Had it been the past? She recognized the orb below the floor of the Heart Hall, the portal that had been destroyed, but it had felt real. For a moment only, it had felt current and real and awful.

She dismissed it. The City and the portal once residing below it were too far away for her visions in the haze of the drink. It had been a memory, she decided, from before her trek across the desert, and her ill-fated bargain with the Berintans. It had to be. The portal was gone.

When she found her bed and finally slept, her dreams were strangely empty.

Philyre jumped back and the hound demon's glass-sharp teeth missed her leg narrowly. She scrambled across the red-hot sand, scalding her exposed hands and wishing she could wear gloves and still manipulate her spear. Two other Enneads rushed in, cutting off the next hound demon's lunge. One warrior stabbed at the eyes—a worthless strike—but the other slashed at the back leg. The spear bounced off the plates on the haunches, the scraping noise like a growl. But the demon turned to retaliate, aware that it was vulnerable.

Feeling the sands fall behind her, Philyre glanced over her shoulder and found the second hound demon. It lay dead in the sands, the blood and flesh already becoming dust. A spear stuck out from the ribcage, although that was clearly not what had killed it. Philyre's hand was only a finger away from the pool of blood that had been spilled from the hound demon's back leg.

Erosan stood over the demon, the trickle of red blood on his arm. He held a kukri in his hand, the black blood on it dissolving. His opposite hand, where the blood trickled, was empty.

Tense and ready, he faced the other demon.

Emboldened by the presence of the experienced Ennead, Philyre rolled to her feet and pulled the spear from the hound demon's bones. This was not the first hound demon pack they had felled, and it would not be the last.

The boy who had attacked the front—his name was Themba—slid back on the sand. The hound demon ignored him, turning to bite at Chean. It knew its weakness as well as they did.

Chean was ready for it, turning the spear and thrusting at its face. The demon pushed through the attack, knowing its tiny red eyes were impossible targets for their larger spears, and attacked. As he leaned back, Chean fell into the sands, the snarling demon above him.

Seeing no alternative, Philyre leaped atop it.

She came down on its neck, pushing the head down into the dune. Red sand burst around them, briefly hiding Chean and allowing him to retreat under the monster. Philyre rolled forward, over the hound's head, and landed on her back. Looking up, squinting through the prick of sand in her eyes, she bounced the butt of the spear against her knee to change its direction and jabbed it at the underside of the demon's jaw.

While the spear tip could not pierce, the effect slammed the jaws shut and stunned the monster.

It was long enough. In the settling sand, Philyre made out the shape of Erosan, now behind the demon, crouched in readiness.

As soon as he could see clearly, Erosan cut up, slicing under the leg.

The black blood burst out, chasing Erosan as he pulled away. With the opportunity, Philyre properly braced her spear and stabbed hard through the skull between the eyes, where the bone was the thinnest. The sound was like a baraka seed being cracked.

The beast collapsed before them.

They all paused.

Chean slowly joined them, shaking free his cloak. Themba stood and brushed himself off as well, but cradled his shoulder from the fall. Bruising would soon form, but no skin had been broken.

Erosan kept an aggressive stance as he watched the body, only relaxing when the dust began to form, the skin and scales released.

"My kill," Erosan said, his grin wide enough for two.

"I get the assist," Philyre grunted, rolling up. Her sand-cloak needed a lot of shaking to free it from the red sands it had collected.

Erosan lifted an eyebrow at him. "From down there?"

"I'm the only reason it didn't tear you apart," Philyre replied, becoming aware of their audience. Chean and Themba were two of the six who had attended the hunt. Three others were about to reach them, although it would be too late to help. Luring the demons into the trap had worked, although the monsters had discerned the ploy early when they heard Themba fidget. To save him, Philyre and Erosan had attacked before the others had joined.

The final member of the party lay dead over the dune, having failed to move fast enough to escape the demons. They would have to go back to retrieve some of the supplies, but that was a chore Philyre would do herself, else assign to Erosan. The newest residents of Hope did not have to experience that disappointment.

Philyre eyed Erosan's wound. "You all right?"

In experimentation, Erosan flexed his fingers. Philyre could see the muscles move in the wound that had pierced his forearm, but all five fingers moved.

"Needs treating," Erosan said. "We have any jannu sap left?"

Philyre shook her head. "No, but I can gather some. You take the runners home when they get here. Chean, Themba, and I will find some." She eyed Themba, the bigger boy antsy on his feet even now. It had been that impatience that had brought the hound demons upon them too early. "Gives me and Themba a chance to talk about how a sand-cloak works and when it won't."

Erosan nodded and headed back to the north. Philyre struck out east, looking for one of the rocky spots where the jannu plant would grow. Kept clean, she expected the wound to do well. Philyre had been cut just as deeply on a previous skirmish the year before, and it had healed with the jannu plant sap. So long as any infection was kept out…

She brought her attention to the newest members. "Sand-cloaks offer no sound protection, Themba. The next time I tell you to stay still, don't squirm!"

Yarr sat cross-legged on the smooth floor of the Berhanu Grand Manor basement with his eyes shut and his teeth clenched. His jaw ached now, but he used that distracting pain to keep his hold firm. Although he had turned his attention inwardly to converse with the tusked demon in him, he and the demon both heard the approach of feet on the stairs into the cellar. They were of medium weight but well-balanced and steady as they approached, showing no fear. Alone, that would have allowed him to recognize the Grand Archon Amadi, but the conclusion was confirmed by the scent of shaben leaves flowing on the fresh air from the hall above.

"I asked for silence," Yarr growled without opening his eyes.

"And I gave it to you," Grand Archon Amadi replied. The footsteps paused at the bottom of the stairs, and the smell of the shaben tree, musty and tart, permeated the cellar. It made Yarr's nostrils flare, but the demon in him seemed pleased by the scent. The tusked demon thought it familiar.

Yarr opened his eyes and fixed a glare on the small Berintan who stood before him. Although they called him "Grand," Amadi was shorter than Yarr by almost half, and his physical prowess had been diminishing over his many years. Yarr had asked but had not been able to find the age of the old Berintan. He knew it had to be over a hundred years, which seemed to be unusual for Berintans, but nothing further.

Grand Archon Amadi's clothing was made of shroud, a cloth of woven shaben leaves finer than even the best linens of the Enneads. Without being prepared properly, the shaben leaves leeched out toxins that could be absorbed through the skin and make even a strong man perish. To wear it was risky and a sign of immense wealth, something Amadi seemed to flaunt at every turn.

In addition to the shroud cloth itself, Amadi wore leaves from the shadow tree to form almost scale armor over the man's chest and legs. Unlike natural plants, the leaves did not rustle. The shaben tree was known for standing silently no matter the wind or weather, a fact that had lent itself well to the mystic powers thought to be associated with it.

A small piece of shroud—a square of cloth no bigger than his hand—hung over Yarr's shoulder. Over six years, he had earned the mark of rank and wealth through battle. Had he been Berintan, he expected he would have been given the rank of archon, but it seemed obvious no Berintans wished to join an ark led by an Ennead shifter, and that the shifter had no desire to lead one.

The Berintan's eyebrows and wrinkles had been covered permanently by paint, leaving Yarr often wondering if he even was the same man from day to day. It was possible that a dozen different Berintans took turns pretending to be the Grand Archon. Yarr could not see enough of the man's features, not even his eyes, to be sure.

"Not enough," Yarr replied.

"Is your demon not happy?" Grand Archon Amadi asked, his expression lost under the layer of white and blue paint that covered every surface of his skin.

Yarr had taken his tusked demon recently out hunting keim beasts near the desert borders, and Yarr considered the monster well satisfied. He had long since learned that giving the demon an outlet on occasion made it more complacent. He traded times of freedom with the demon for obedience. Although he was certain there would come a day when the demon simply refused to return control, since coming to the Berinta he thought that day was distancing itself. The demon seemed more content with shaben leaves and hunting trips than it ever had with battling demons and patrolling the desert.

"It is satisfied," Yarr said with a sigh, leaving behind the "conversation" he had been holding with the demon. Their minds, despite their proximity over a hundred years, did not share a language, making actual conversation between them impossible. Yarr had learned how to interpret the demon's emotions and thought that much was mutual.

"Has it a name yet?" Amadi asked, a smile barely visible under the white paint that encompassed the entire face. The Berintan's teeth were worn by age.

"Not yet," Yarr replied. The archon had suggested he name the demon when they had first met after the fall of the City, six years earlier. While Yarr could not remember any rules forbidding it, the thought of giving a permanent name to the monster in him sat uncomfortably with him. He could not bring himself to do it.

It was easier to delay the archon than put words to his worries.

The small Berintan paced as if considering addressing the deflection at last, but when he paused once more at the bottom of the stairs, he said, "I have an assignment for you."

Yarr and his demon both became attentive. Since his first meeting with Grand Archon Amadi, Yarr had been impressed by the Berintan's ability to select appropriate jobs for him.

"You will be joining Archon Farai's forces for a tour of the lands."

Disappointed, Yarr snarled. "Send a spy," Yarr replied. "I have no interest in prancing between arks like a pet."

He turned and slumped back.

"Yarr," the Grand Archon said, his voice smooth as the shroud cloth, "this needs your skills."

Yarr checked over his shoulder, trying in vain to read the face of the Berintan leader. The voice was as plain as the painted face.

"Farai has control of the last desert seer, and his patience with her is slipping," the Grand Archon said. "He must not be allowed to kill her. I also know he will be going north across the desert, and I want you with him. He has unfinished business there, something he must remedy. If Farai is guilty of treason, deal with him."

Yarr grinned widely. He remembered the Berintan he had first met in the City. "I will go," he said. "I would like to see Farai again."

"I have no doubt," Grand Archon Amadi answered. "You must take him back to the Ennead City, Yarr. He must retrieve that which he failed to bring back last time."

Cocking his head, Yarr growled. "The portal? I thought it was…"

"It was deception," the Grand Archon replied. "I do not care how he does it, but he must bring me the portal."

"I will see to it," Yarr agreed. He thought of the desert and nodded. "A good run, a chance to hunt."

"More than you know," the Grand Archon said. "You will have to hurry. He is touring his holdings now. You will catch up with him in Douran." The smell of shaben trees distanced itself as the Berintan leader retreated up the steps, leaving Yarr to his meditations.

"So be it," Yarr muttered. The demon seemed oddly content.

Part 2

CHAPTER 12

The smell of baking hung in the air in the sunrise. Funanya had set her chamber above the kitchen for that reason, forsaking the more traditional, and larger, archon's chambers in the stone rooms of the Grand Manor of Douran. The single room had been designed for an honored warrior and suited her better. Her trophies covered the riser wood walls, from Ennead kukris to keim beast skulls. The sheets and drapes had been dyed in shour black but held no trace of the actual plant. The only true shour cloth she had was in a head-dress she seldom bothered to wear.

Beside her, Funanya heard movement, and she turned her head to watch the Ennead hunter rise from the bed. His dark skin had lightened over the years under the canopy of a forest, but still had a hue darker than the younger stock. Even after six years, he seemed as spry as the first day she had claimed him as a slave.

"You're not as good as Lesedi claimed," she called after him, rolling onto her side and pulling the sheer sheet over herself.

His face was devoid of emotion as he faced her. Among her warriors, she preferred deference and formality, but she missed the honesty she and Hunter had shared in the desert. In six years, she had never seen him as raw and exposed as he had been in the valley outside the oasis after saving her life. Their conversation then had convinced her to offer the position in her ark, but nothing similar had been exchanged between them since. His manners suited the warriors well, but Funanya kept looking for a glimpse of his more flippant side.

"You've only requested me three times in six years," he replied as he tied a breechcloth around his waist, followed by his legs. "I am still learning your preferences."

Lesedi claimed the Ennead was a lover to rival the best in Berinta, but Lesedi had also been making use of the slave as frequently as she could. At Funanya's command, Hunter was to obey any member of the ark, from the haughtiest warrior to the newest recruit. His willingness to submit made him seem docile, like a proud keim beast taught to perform for festivals. While Funanya enjoyed the fruits, she found his quietness disappointing.

Hunter slipped a finger over his collar with a brush of his hand testing the metal.

"Six years and you're not used to it?" she asked.

Although she was certain he did not mean to, he glanced at the cabinet where she had stashed the key.

"It is what it is," he said. "I am expected at the wolfen pens. Am I allowed to go, Archon?"

With the dawn's light trickling through the window, bringing the smell of fresh flatbreads, she could not blame him for wanting to leave. Hunger pulled at her stomach as well.

She did not immediately answer, enjoying the advantage of her rank by forcing him to wait. The sex of the morning had been a pretense, anyway, if an enjoyable one. They had unfinished business.

"Hunter, why have you not tried to kill me?" she asked.

She wanted a reaction from him, be it shock or denial. Instead, his façade did not so much as twitch.

"Should I have?" he asked.

Standing, Funanya grabbed a nearby kaftan and donned it. She added a belt so that she could wear the sword of her rank. She took to tying her cropped hair into a tight bun as she answered, "Every other adult Ennead we took as a slave has rebelled against their masters, and they were artisans and laborers. You are a fighter of a sort, and yet your behavior is perfect. It is uncanny. I would know why," she said.

"Is it so hard to believe I am happy here?" he answered.

"Happy?" Funanya echoed, an ironic smile coming to her. "If you've laughed or smiled once since coming here, I have not heard of it. You cannot be happy, yet you trudge along with exemplary behavior not shared by any but the young of your race. It does not follow."

His hesitation was so slight, she would not have noticed it in any other. Hunter never seemed to so much as question an order, his reactions always instant. For a rare moment, he paused. When the moment was over, his expression had not changed.

"I never liked living in a city," he said, and she noted that he had not said "the City." For the Enneads, there was one city—the City—but he seemed loathed to call it by name. "Here I am given leave to run the woods. My duties are not difficult." Finally, for a blink only, his eyes lit. "Some duties are even pleasant."

The glimpse of emotion from him appeased her, and Funanya finally felt relaxed enough to wave him toward the door.

"Go on. We are expecting a shipment today," she told him as he turned from her. "I want you in the Grand Manor at midday."

"New wolfen?" he asked, his head tilted like the beasts he tended.

Going to her cabinet, Funanya unlocked it and selected a jeweled dagger to thread through her bun. The key lay on the shelf in front of her, the chain now embossed with gold thread and glass beads.

"Females arrive today," she told him, glancing back to watch for a reaction. "The wolfen you've bred are the best hunters we have ever had. Fortunate that our ark has such a proven stock, don't you think? So I have bought another three females from—"

"Archon!" a warrior called through the door. Hunter quickly stepped back, giving the entrance to Idir as he rushed in, breathless. "Archon Farai and his retinue have been spotted in the Emeka hills, on his way to Douran!"

Funanya's heart leaped into her throat, but she could no more show Hunter her surprise than he showed her his. Using a calm voice, she closed the cabinet and faced her warrior, saying, "Well, if he thought to catch us by surprise, he will be disappointed. Assemble the warriors in full dress. I will join when I have bathed. Hunter—"

"I will be present at midday," Hunter said, admitting that he was now a prized specimen meant to be flaunted. Farai would have no way to know Hunter was not a slave who had changed hands after the fall of the Ennead city. But Ennead slaves were very rare still.

"Get him a shirt, Idir," Funanya commanded as she strolled past her warrior and slave into the hall.

Armed with an embroidered dashiki, Askaran left the manor. He placed the shirt carefully in a tree's nook, thinking it easier to shake off chips of bark than dirt and wolfen stench. The archon would be displeased if he presented himself before Archon Farai dressed in filth.

After turning the wolfen pack loose, he headed into the forest. The pack split to run both ahead and behind him, half watching for Berintans following and half eagerly clearing the way. More than one gave a chirp to tell him they had found a trail of game but he refused them pursuit, and they instead joined him as he headed deeper into the woods. Today, the panic about Farai's imminent arrival kept the Berintans from watching him as he went about his routine.

Routine was the most important thing. Simple actions required no thought and, most importantly, no emotion.

Following trails brought Askaran a clearing in the thick jungle, where a large stump dominated. Sitting down on the stump released the wolfen from their work, and they created games of their own, running in circles to chase each other or sprint after the chitters they disturbed. A few of the older wolfen watched over the younger's antics, still keeping a wary eye on the edges of the forest for intruders.

The demon, for so long an overbearing presence, was quiet. When he had first felt the monster settle, Askaran had been certain that it was gathering its strength for a sudden assault. But then the demon had tried to shift. The metal collar had choked the Ennead throat before the completion of the change, threatening to kill them both. Surprising Askaran with its sudden restraint, it had abandoned the attempt part way through, giving control back to Askaran.

He had never known any demon to give up control.

Since then, the demon had remained a dormant presence, only rearing its head during emotional times when it seemed unable to help itself. Askaran had learned swiftly to keep his emotions steady. No matter the goading of the archon or the teasing of the other Berintans, Askaran would not react. He had drilled the techniques for keeping his head clear of panic since a young age, but had applied them so often in his initial year among the Berintans, he could now enter his meditative calm within a heartbeat.

He knew it made him appear cold, but he did not care.

As he took a brief assessment of the demon's state—another instinctual process he had perfected over the last six years—Askaran heard the shift of grass behind him, too soft for even the wolfen to hear over the games.

"Good morning, little flower," he said.

Askaran heard a rough snort from the girl who had been sneaking up behind him.

"What gave me away?" she asked as she stood up from the grass. Her skin matched the yellow grass of the meadow, the mud drawn in lines to shadows. In the hot jungle, she wore scraps of cloth over her chest and hips, leaving her long legs free. The same cloth had been tied over her head to hide her sheared black hair.

"Rustling," he said, facing her and standing. His heart felt lighter at seeing her, and he allowed that joy through cautiously. For her, he would show happiness. "You on the prowl today?"

The desert seer skipped back a few steps and retrieved a stick of impaled chitters. The striped skin of the girl and the lizards matched as she presented it to him. "Already been hunting. They don't hear me rustling like you do."

The six chitters on the stick were enough to feed her for the day, but Askaran still offered her the bag he had brought with him from the Grand Manor.

"Sweet fruits and a handful of cracker nuts," he said. "Tastier than chitters."

"But not nearly as much fun," she replied, smiling broadly as she dug at the roots of the stump to reveal one of her stashes. The seer placed the bag where she had coated the surrounding dirt and wood with riser tree sap to seal it. The scent of fruit would be hidden well. "Are you here for long?" she asked, her hand hovering over another stashed item, the wooden kukri blades he had carved for her years before. His old kukri lay wrapped beside them, protected with a waxed cloth.

"Long enough for a spar," he replied, and her face lit up. She snatched up both sets of wooden blades and nearly threw two at him in her haste. Turning her back, she hopped several steps like a ranna calf, then pivoted again to face him. She held each wooden blade in a reversed grip, the "blade" part lying against her wrists while the "hilt" was held in her hand. He kept one blade bared but copied her defensive hold with the other.

As Askaran stood slowly, the seer crouched into a fighting stance. He envied her balance; she had taken to the poised stance of a warrior from their first lesson. Seers were known for their ability to learn anything, but even he was amazed at her aptitude for battle.

He swung slowly with his fake weapon to come at her head. What her arms lacked in strength, they made up for with speed; she slapped aside the strike and brought her other hand toward his face, tilting the blade enough to stick the edge out from its guard position.

Matching her speed, he tapped her strike wide with his defensive left blade. Rolling his wrist let him slide his right blade out from her block and stab it back toward her left side.

She adjusted her weight, and his slash missed entirely.

The combat continued along a similar vein: block, block, swing and miss. The seer had long since learned his best tricks and how to avoid them. Now, her time alone in the jungle had given her the opportunity to practice, and she tested new tactics against him. He matched her, keeping the blunt wooden blade from so much as tapping his skin.

In the meditation of the spar, the demon did not raise its hackles. It seemed too bored with the simplicity of the combat and the knowledge that it would never amount to more.

"Archon Farai's coming in," Askaran said as one wild swing sailed over his head. When he stabbed the kukris forward, the seer was already out of his reach.

"I remain in the forest then?" she said. "As opposed to wandering into the Grand Manor?"

In six years, she had never left the forest.

He cracked a smile. From the corner of his mind, he felt like Askaran, the Ennead he really was, woke a little.

"I'll have no gallivanting around from you, young lady," he replied, skipping onto the stump. He towered over the small woman when on level ground and found the higher position a hindrance. In her crouched stance, she was now even farther from his reach, and he had given her a new target, his ankles.

He jumped over and around two slashing kukris before skipping off the stump.

"Little flower, you are too small!" he told her as he came down. His foot hit a hidden root, and he stumbled over. A wooden kukri slammed into his left shoulder, bruising the nose of the demon tattooed there.

The seer paused, peering down at him as he lay in the grass. Obi, the white wolfen, flicked his tongue over Askaran's ear, making the shifter flinch. The demon jumped, for a moment snarling at the little wolfen and wanting to snap at it.

In the space behind a blink, Askaran brought his mind into a sharp calm. The monster quickly went silent once more, but Askaran felt its thoughts; it could not shift now, anyway.

"I am not as small as I once was," the seer replied, not seeming to notice his brief lapse. She whistled lightly, and Obi abandoned Askaran to join her. As she ran her nails over the scales of the creature, Askaran rose to his feet.

"No," he said once he stood over her once more. "No, you're not."

She had turned fourteen this year and was fast becoming a woman. Between her hunting and the limited food he stole for her, she was kept lean, but living among the trees and woods made her fit. Her thin frame seemed to have trouble supporting the curves of a woman, but the changes were still there. It would not be long before Askaran would have to stop calling her little. Even now, she could become a mother and...

Sitting back down on the stump, Askaran put down the kukris. The seer's expression fell in disappointment.

He was afraid to ask the next question, knowing that the visions of seers could not be controlled when they first came. If she did not know the answer, he would be reminding her again of her unfulfilled responsibility, and that would remove the smile from her face for days. But if there was any chance she did know, he thought it worth the risk.

"Do you *know* the way home?"

With the main oases destroyed by the army passing through them, there were no known paths back to the City. The simple fact had trapped them among the Berintans for six years and threatened to keep them there for years more.

She did not balk, but let her stare unfocus. Askaran held his breath. There had been glimpses of her power before, although it had gone dormant for a few years after their arrival here. The visions were becoming more frequent as she aged, unpredictable though they were. She could not control the mind hekau she held.

After a few moments, she squinted her eyes as if trying to focus on something distant and frowned.

"I see the first steps," she whispered, "but not the entire path. But the steps lead on, not to an end. The desert weeps, and the tears form new paths through the sands. I know there is a way, but I do not know how to find it yet."

The seer startled from her trance, blinking like clearing flashes from her eyes. The chill in his chest released, replaced by the jungle's sweltering heat. Nearby, the wolfen chirped, bowling each other over in their games. Askaran weakly smiled.

"That is the most you have ever divined," he told her, and she straightened proudly.

She returned her kukris to the stashed location and cocked her head at him. "I have been trying to trance," she confided, "but the shifter's way to meditate does not fit well. It is getting better. I am seeing more. I hope to see—" She paused, her eyes going vacant again, then flashing with golden light in sparkles. Her expression confused, she said, "Stay near windows, Askaran. And go now."

Heeding her words as a seer's prophecy, Askaran whistled for the wolfen and immediately trotted from the jungle.

He was pleased to learn that Archon Funanya had sent warriors to fetch him. He met them on his way out, safely distant from the hidden desert seer in the woods.

The Youngest Seer, for even as she grew, she knew no other name, saw the warriors on their way. In a single blink, she saw them find Askaran in the forest clearing. They would see her tracks, find her stash under the stump, and know all the secrets Askaran had hidden from them. She would be hunted, Askaran slain, and the Enneads, without seer, would vanish from the world.

But with two words, "go now," the entire thread was cut. Askaran met the archon's warriors on his way out of the jungle. The secret remained hidden. The Enneads of Nanterac were saved.

It amazed her what two words could do.

The wolfen followed their master from the meadows, as obedient to him as he was to her. Once more, the desert seer was left alone.

She took back up Askaran's kukris, which he had left on the stump in his haste to obey her, and played with them over her palms. She brought the brief spar to her mind and repeated it twice, once from her own perspective and once from Askaran's. She repeated it a third time, every swing, feint, block, and strike, and modified some of the steps. Finding a more suitable response, she memorized it.

As the noonday suns pushed through the canopy, the seer stopped her practice and, filled with sudden certainty, collected her belongings from the stump, bid farewell to the meadow, and headed into the Grand Manor grounds.

CHAPTER 13

As Asakran left the forest, he nearly ran into Idir, who chastised him for cutting his arrival so close and forced him to don the shirt they had prepared. While Berintans rushed about with perfect face paints and shining weapons, Askaran washed his face and pulled his hair into a trio of braids. That was as dressed up as he intended to get.

The long Grand Hall was lined with mirrors, each one an Ennead trophy. It was set on the south side of the manor, in the best position for long sunsets and glorious natural light. Lamps, fixed along the wall facing the mirrors, could be lit to further illuminate the hall for viewing, showing off the grandeur of the mirrors and the various trophies set between them. The windows took up the entire length of the hall on one side, while the mirrors up the other.

Outside the huge windows but down a story, the garden stretched out to the edge of the forest itself. The mirrors gave the illusion of a wider hall, but also more of a crowd now that the entire ark had been gathered.

The warriors wore their face paint and armor, and each carried their spears. They formed ranks at the far end of the hall, overseen by the archon's most honored warriors. The archon herself stood by the main door at the end of the room, adorned in a kaftan of royal blue that had been layered in Ennead wool and decorated with demon bones. In coming through a side door, Askaran avoided crossing her path.

Moving down the hall, the ark had been organized by rank. Slaves were positioned at the far end, and Askaran went to join them next to one of the huge windows. A breeze drifted through the opened window, which overlooked a drop into hedges.

After an agonizing hour, the Grand Hall became silent. The prestigious visitor entered the hall.

The commotion at the far end was slow in approaching. Archon Farai arrived, recognizable because he wore the shour leaves over his shoulders. Askaran remembered the Berintan from the desert. Then, the Archon had been an ally of Funanya's. Now, the way he eyed Funanya implied a change. Askaran thought him suspicious.

Archon Farai moved down the line of the ark members, inspecting each group individually with Archon Funanya watching formally at his side.

They were still among the servants when Archon Farai paused, his narrowed eyes on Askaran at a distance. Askaran averted his gaze, imagining himself as innocuous. Being Ennead was obvious, but he could still look humble and meek, like a proper slave.

His plan faltered when an Ennead woman stepped up from among the archon's accompanying warriors. Her black eyes locked on Askaran's and, despite the wear of years on her face and the change in her girth, he recognized her.

"Seer," he stuttered in surprise.

The now-Eldest Seer's eyes went wide, her jaw for a moment slack.

"Shifter." The word choked in her throat.

The visiting archon reached for his sword, the body-guards rushing in to surround him. Faster than them, Archon Funanya spun to face Askaran, charging with her spear already lowered.

He did not wait to see any of their actions through. Knowing the window was open behind him, Askaran threw himself out and down into the gardens.

The hedge he landed in scraped at his shirt and breechclout, like sticky fingers clawing him back. In a leap, he cleared the plants and ducked around the corner of the Grand Manor. The drop would save him from the swords perhaps, but a well-thrown spear remained a real threat.

Clearing the corner nearly collided him with the Youngest Seer, who was climbing out of a window. Her swift sidestep saved them from impact.

For a moment, Askaran could not think of any-thing to say but stared at her. She had never left the forest, to his knowledge. Her sliding out of a kitchen window with soot on her face and smoke rising behind her seemed impossible.

Her smile was content, like a girl with a new bauble, when she faced him beside the Grand Manor.

"Fire," she said brightly.

Looking past her, he saw the flashing of fire. With the ark in the long hall, no one was in the kitchen to know that the flames had left their place to crawl through the walls, toward where Askaran knew powdered dran grains were stored.

And dusted grains such as dran had a tendency of exploding in fires.

Grabbing the seer's arm, he dragged her away from the open window.

"You can't shift in the collar," the seer said.

Askaran paused. His hand went to the collar around his neck, the metal cold against his fingertips. There was not even enough room to slide a finger under it.

"Shour," he cursed. He felt the demon grumble, and the sound echoed into his own voice.

"You'd best go get the key," she told him.

He had been running away from the archon, not toward her. Knowing what he was, it seemed logical she would surround herself with her bodyguards, worsening his chances.

"She's not wearing it, Askaran," the seer said, following his every thought. She handed him his old kukri and the wooden handle fit into his grip perfectly.

The archon had left the key, he realized, in her chambers that morning in the cabinet. And he was standing below her balcony even now.

"You come into your own, little flower?" he wondered, scanning the surface of the building for handholds as he tucked away the kukri. The lower windows were paned and paneled, so he could plant his feet there for a leap. The balcony was set back over the lower story.

She tilted her head as if she did not understand the question and said nothing.

"Stay out of sight," he warned her, and she nodded absently. Grasping lightly, Askaran climbed up the muntin bars of the window, hooked his feet over the header, and stood up to reach the railings. With little effort, he pulled himself onto the balcony.

The archon had ever been cautious; she had locked her balcony. That made Askaran smile. Pleased to finally be allowed to break something, he slammed open the doors and strode into the darkened room. The demon paced in his mind, held not by a cage but by its own restraint. It wanted the key, and the desire was so potent, Askaran could not differentiate the demon's emotion from his own.

It had gained strength over the years.

As soon as his foot touched the smooth wood of the room, a blast from below shook the building, sending him reeling off his feet. When he brought himself to his knees, flames were visible under the door to the hall, and a Berintan—Archon Funanya herself—had entered the room, running for the cabinet.

Askaran did not think about it; he charged the archon.

○

Shifter.

It didn't matter if the accusation was true or not. The moment the charge was made, Hunter had to die. Funanya lowered her spear and charged.

He was too fast. Before she could strike, the Ennead, who had flawlessly served her for six years, dropped out a window. She rushed after him, aiming a throw, but he had vanished around the corner of the manor before she could loose.

She spun from the window and sprinted through the hall. She knew where he would go. The key was not around her neck. He had to get it.

Hiking up the kaftan, Funanya ran through the Grand Manor of Douran. She had cleared one stairwell when an explosion rocked the ark and the stairs she had left behind seemed to evaporate under flames.

Smoke billowed from the opening, followed quickly by fires. The loss of the stairs took out the warriors who had been keeping up with her, leaving her alone on the landing, for a moment stunned and staggering.

Even without knowing how he had done it, Funanya blamed Hunter for the fire. Gripping her spear all the tighter, she ran down the corridor and burst through her bedroom door.

He kneeled by the balcony, knocked off his feet by the same explosion that had destroyed the stairs. She had the advantage as she rushed to the cabinet and grabbed the key.

A flick of her wrist detached the key from the chain. In a flash, she tossed the chain over her head as if to wear it once more, but her free right hand instead slipped the key into an inner pocket, a feature she had sewn into all her clothing as a memory of the Night Road. She had her hand on her spear as she turned, ready for Hunter's charge.

He had a kukri in hand, although where he had found it, she had no idea. He was a hunter, but his skill in combat surprised her when he parried her spear with the kukri and lurched in as if seeking to catch her unprotected hands. She sharply pulled away. Taking a step back, she coiled and then thrust the spear forward.

It seemed to take little effort for him, fiercely grinning, to tap the spear wide. The glint of reflected fire from the hall made his eyes look red as they stared at the chain around her neck.

On the next parry, Funanya spun the spear and swung the shaft at his head. His casual dodge became pressed; he leaned back, and the shaft whistled past his face.

She thought his weight was too far back, but he shocked her by kicking out. His foot struck her hands. Refusing to drop her weapon, Funanya turned with the impact, bringing the spear's tip around in a perfect circle.

Fast as a striking serpent demon, he came up between her and the spear, their bodies inches apart. His open hand caught her arm, and the stab halted. He held her for a moment, then twisted his grip. Her wrist reefed, Funanya released the spear.

His knee snapped up into her ribs. Winded, she saw stars as she fell back, gasping for air and inhaling smoke. When her head struck something, the stars vanished to black.

The strength of Berintans was nothing compared to the power of demons. Armed with the familiar kukri, Askaran had little trouble disarming and disabling the archon. The demon seemed to lend him strength, their purposes in agreement for the moment.

He needed that key.

The crash of collapsing wood shook the room as Askaran pulled the chain from her neck. Throwing the chain over his head, he aimed for the balcony, then paused.

There was no key on this chain.

The fires were eating their way through the doorway when he looked back, with fresh flames sneaking around the floorboards and igniting the bed.

He rushed to the cabinet and searched it.

No key.

At the foot of the bed, the archon still lay prone, her chest rising and falling in uneasy breaths. He was losing sight of her in the smoke.

The demon laughed. Death by fire. She had damned the City to such a fate.

Covering his face, Askaran crawled to her side, roughly trying to search her as the smoke took vision from him. His lungs were burning now, coughs racking him. He felt around her neck and in the folds of the kaftan, finding nothing.

Frustrated, he grabbed her arm and pulled her between new blazes to the balcony. Once in the open air, the fires now hot at his back, he lowered her over the balcony and climbed down.

"Into the trees," the seer said, seeming unsurprised by the presence of the archon. "Her too."

With no time to search further, Askaran hefted the archon over his shoulder once more and followed the seer as she fled back to her jungle, hoping all the while that the key would not fall loose, wherever it was.

The cries of the Berintans as they fought the fire faded once they reached the protection of the trees. Soon even the smoke plume over the ark was hidden behind the jungle canopy. They did not break stride until they had reached the seer's hide deep in the woods.

Lying the archon on the forest floor, Askaran searched the still body again, pulling off beads and bones as he sought the little metal key meant to release him. He found, to his immense frustration, nothing.

Sitting back, he looked up at the seer. "So, you knew they were here, that another desert seer was present," he said.

"Bits," the seer replied, her voice shy. "Not clear. I can't chase it."

Askaran nodded in understanding. Eventually, seers saw possible futures. With training and practice, they learned how to aim the visions, ask questions, and have them answered. They called it "chasing" a vision. That she had seen that much when a desert seer was involved was impressive enough.

"Any chance you know how to remove this damn thing? Or where the key is?"

She shook her head.

The collar prevented his shifting. He would have to find cutting wires or a smith. He could not imagine a Berintan smith would help him.

Maybe not Berintan.

The demon agreed, and Askaran felt uneasy. He hated when he and the monster matched purposes.

"How about a way home since I asked you this morning?" he asked.

Her smile was sweet. "No, but I know where to find it. We will walk the Night Road to the next city. From there, there is a path. The desert continues to weep. I will follow the tears home."

He let out a long sigh and, for the first time, noticed the three bags against a tree next to the seer, bags meant for traveling.

"Water?" he asked.

The seer nodded proudly, going to the sacks.

"Cover?" he asked.

"Two desert wraps, and I still have your sand-cloak," she said, pulling the cloaks out of the first bag and throwing him one. He fitted it over the collar. She next tossed him a woven scabbard and chest strap. Once he had donned it, he sheathed the kukri.

"I have my knife too," the seer pointed out, holding out her paring knife. "But maybe we should use yours." She chuckled at the remembered jest, but his mind felt too cluttered to join her.

"Food?"

"And cooking shields," she confirmed. "The desert will provide."

"Once we reach it," he replied. He glanced over at the collapsed archon. "What shall we do with this one?"

The seer stared at him for a moment, looking confused. "As she has heard everything we said, she must come with us. Once beyond—"

"Heard? She is—"

"Awake," the seer said. "Has been since we arrived here."

The archon gave a snort as she pushed herself up, giving up on her ruse of sleep. "Shour…" she grumbled.

"Indeed," Askaran answered.

He drew his kukri and felt the demon rise, ready to enjoy the pleasure it might provide. "Well, Archon, you don't have to come. Tell me where the key is, and I will let you go."

He measured her stare as she turned it against him. Although she sat below him, it was as if she was armored and armed, so confidently did she meet his gaze. She knew he was lying. He had no intention of letting her live, key or not.

"Save me from fire to kill me anyway?" the archon said. She sat back, leaning against a tree and tenderly checking her head. No blood came away with her hand; the injury was concussive only.

"You weren't a threat when you were unconscious," Askaran replied, "but now you are. I will not allow anyone to threaten—"

"She comes with us," the seer flatly said, as if their words had not been spoken at all.

He thought to argue with her as the shifter of the City would have any citizen, but as he opened his mouth, Askaran stopped.

She was no citizen of the City. She was a desert seer.

"As you wish," he said instead. "You got rope in there too?"

The look the seer gave him made Askaran feel like an idiot, and he saw why; the archon's dress was too long to run easily without being lifted. If he bound her hands, she would only walk, slowing down their escape.

Both problems had a single solution.

The archon sat in fuming anger as Askaran cut her kaftan dress at her thigh. The strips of cloth were easily braided into rope. He pulled off the demon bones and tossed them into the jungle. The wools, he stashed in her sack.

"Better than carpet threads," the archon muttered as Askaran bound her hands.

He felt satisfaction at the memory of the last time he had bound her. Despite the great changes that were happening, he smiled. Those were fond memories, and the demon agreed.

It felt like waking up.

"This way," the seer called, carrying one sack already and gesturing deeper into the forest. "I know the path."

Keeping his blade on hand, Askaran prodded the archon to her feet, then scooped up the other two bags. "Quickly now, Archon," he told the prisoner.

She marched ahead of him, her jaw clenched in fury, as they made their way to the Night Road.

The building's wing collapsed, burying anyone left behind. Farai himself stood back in the shelter of the jungle, an easy run to the river should it be required. The servants and ark members came and went like waves, some beating blankets and others tossing dirt and water. The fire had spread quickly. It seemed unlikely they would save the Grand Manor of Douran.

Farai fumed as he waited for the fire to burn out. The Eldest Seer sat behind him, surrounded by Farai's personal guards. She had gone silent. While he was certain he wanted to hear what she knew, she seemed determined to keep the information from him. Occasional words snuck out in her distraction, but they were too fragmented to make sense of.

He had found a shifter hiding in one of his own Grand Manors. Even if she would not confirm it, this had to be the source of danger the seer had mentioned in her dreams. It certainly had come from his own archon; Funanya had made this mistake.

He would kill the shifter, and he would kill Funanya for her part in this. Blind fool, she had disobeyed their orders. Had this slave been properly examined, they would have known he was a shifter. It would never have gotten his far.

Funanya had to be punished for disobeying him, else the other archons might decide to challenge his authority as well. He had to show the woman her place, but the presence of a shifter posed a problem. Still, Farai had killed demons before. A shifter, particularly one so far from home or support, was little more than that, and he had his poisoned sword.

He would have to hunt her down.

One of his warriors approached, hunching his shoulders in regret as he interrupted. "Yarr has come seeking you," the warrior said.

Sure enough, the large Ennead waited beyond Farai's men, impatiently pacing the line of warriors. For him, these men did not exist. If he wanted to move through them, he would. It was as simple as that.

Tailors had finally made a dashiki large enough for the imposing Ennead, but no tailor was good enough to make the loose-fitting shirt flatter the man. His dark skin had become lighter over time, now barely a dark brown. He still wore sandals and had his scrap of shaben leaves tied to his leather chest strap.

He didn't look ready to shift, Farai thought, not so finely dressed. And last Farai had seen Yarr, the Ennead had been living with Grand Archon Amadi. It stood to reason the shifter was here now at Amadi's behest.

But in case he was not, Farai readied his khopesh. It had been laced with atra poison as always. He had been assured by the seer that it would fell any demon or shifter as surely as it felled a Berintan.

"Let him come," Farai ordered.

Once the order had been delivered, the shifter walked up to Farai, his lips held in a sneer. "I came to deliver a message, but it seems you have a problem," Yarr said coyly.

The winds shifted, and now Farai could smell the smoke. His eyes stung, but the wind moved the black smoke along soon enough that he could stifle his cough.

"An archon has misbehaved," Farai admitted.

"Grand Archon Amadi asked me to join you for a while," Yarr said. He spat, clearing his mouth of the taste of the smoke. "You must return to the City of the Enneads." He grinned a wide, feral smile.

Farai frowned. "Why the city?" he asked. "What lies there now?"

"You have unfinished business," Yarr replied, sniffing the air. "Perhaps that is where your renegades are heading,"

The mutterings of the seer, so recently mentioning a drip in the expanse of water in her sleep, made sudden sense.

"How?" Farai grumbled. He turned to face the seer, who sat under a tree a distance away, lying so far back she was probably sleeping. "How did she hide the portal?"

Yarr shrugged and stood by, waiting for more of a response.

Farai found his bearings. He needed this dealt with swiftly, and if he could kill Funanya and her renegade shifter along the way, he would. Yarr would be an asset in that.

"I welcome your aid," Farai answered. He eyed the enormous Ennead. "We were waiting for the smoke to clear before setting the wolfen pack on them. Can you find the scent sooner? We can track them as they flee and dispose of them along the way."

Yarr snorted. "She travels with a shifter," Yarr replied. "That scent, I can find anywhere. But we should not allow distractions. Shall I run them down now?"

Farai considered it. It would be easier by far to have Yarr do the hunting and bring down the shifter and his wayward archon. But what show of authority was that? It would never strengthen Farai's position, rather it would confirm the superiority of the Grand Archon and his shifter ally. If he wanted to regain any of his wounded pride, Farai would have to go on the hunt himself.

And now he had to go north, anyway. It was clear he was meant to embark immediately on the quest for the Grand Archon. He had no time to prepare.

"No," Farai decided, putting a hand on his favorite sword. The metal in it was stronger than any of the wooden blades his people carried, regardless of the stone they embedded in the edge. He had earned his position by battle. It fit that he would hold it by that means.

Ironic that the same poison that had elevated her into a place of authority would be the cause of Funanya's death.

"I shall go as well. We will hunt together. You will take down the shifter. I will handle Funanya," Farai decided. "Then we will continue on to the city."

Yarr's smile was doubtful, but he shrugged his wide shoulders. He had a small bag slung over his shoulder, Farai noted. If the man had come all the way from the Grand Archon's Manor, wherever that was, with only that, he must have shifted for some of the journey and hunted. Yarr could not expect hospitality from a Berintan in his travels.

"As you like," the Ennead said, his eyes flashing to where the seer sat looking off through the smoke. In turn, Yarr faced the fire as well and again spat. "But hurry. They will expect us to give chase."

CHAPTER 14

Hunter dressed her in the desert cloak, which wrapped over her fine, but torn, kaftan dress. Then, in an act that left Funanya fuming, he washed her face of the painted ark markings, leaving her as bare as an arkless.

Both Enneads wore cloaks as well, covering themselves in the dun-colored cloth and concealing their skin. Hooded and hidden, the small Ennead girl showed the party the way to the opening to the Night Road.

It was strange to follow the smaller Ennead. Funanya had seen the children of the Enneads and considered them similar to a juvenile tauran, the ones that learned to walk with staggering steps and required the assistance of their parent for months before being accepted into a flock. But those children had fled from the Berintan attack, and Funanya had given them little thought since that day. Now, it seemed odd that a people similar to Berintans would have juveniles at all when Berintans did not.

And wouldn't these juveniles be weaker than the adults? Why did Hunter defer to the younger Ennead?

The entrance to the Night Road was unlit, although the glow of blue-green moss along moist areas provided soft illumination within the tunnel. Clever travelers painted words in the plant, sometimes marks of territory or tithes, sometimes directions, so the patterns were ever-changing. Fire and smoke in the tight spaces of the tunnels, especially those that were dug near the sulfur fumes, were deadly. Thus, as night fell and the girl brought Hunter and Funanya to the opening, entrepreneurs sold jars of the glowing moss for the new arrivals to carry in place of torches.

With the shifter watching and Funanya forced to follow, the Ennead girl bought a jar of glimm moss and delved into the Night Road. Not three steps from the entrance, a young Berintan in a full-body cloak approached her. Funanya figured he was one of the local "guides" who made their money by making even simple journeys through the Night Road last days and sometimes leaving their charges robbed. He looked clean and small, probably very new.

Hunter was instantly between the girl and the approaching stranger, catching the Berintan's reaching hand.

The guide leaped back, craning his neck but failing to see Hunter's face under the cowl of the cloak. "Just offering services," he said. "Was asking if you need a guide."

"No," the shifter said, his voice a growl. "No, you were not 'just' asking, and no, we do not need one. Back off."

The guide nodded and pulled away. The shifter let him go but was still watching when the guide glanced back over his shoulder. He seemed to walk away all the faster.

Fast as a hound demon, she thought. *Or is he one of the winged ones?*

The disappearance of the sky brought tightness to Funanya's chest. The air of the Night Road stifled around her, making each breath heavy. She saw Hunter pause as if to smell the stagnant air. When he spotted his charge marching on obliviously, he pulled Funanya up between them and pushed her forward. With her hands still bound behind her back, Funanya joined the Ennead girl. Together, the three walked the dozen steps to the first crossroads.

Two other "guides" sat there, but Hunter's attention seemed to make them reluctant to make their offers. They slumped against the wall instead, each displaying their knives to discourage Hunter from trying anything of his own.

The code of the Night Road was simple, and Hunter seemed to have little trouble adapting to it. What could not be defended could not be kept. As newcomers, being forced to fight was almost inevitable, although there would be a degree of sizing up of the opponent first. Funanya had always thought of it like tauran bulls bellowing to scare off other males before resorting to their horns.

At the first junction, the Ennead girl paused. "You can see?" she asked Hunter.

"I see well in the dark," he replied.

"Do you two even have any idea what you are up against down here?" Funanya interrupted. "Every cut-throat of Berinta walks these roads. You'll be robbed, raped, and left for dead by morning, being Ennead. You cannot possibly expect—"

She did not see him move, but Hunter was suddenly directly in front of her, looming with a predator's presence she had not seen in him since the oasis battle against the serpent demon.

"Archon, you are alive only because she asked you be. Endanger us again with your words, and I will cut out your heart." His voice was a snarl.

In the glow of the glimm moss, she saw only blackness under his hood.

"This way!" the Ennead girl called, pointing to the left at the junction. She flashed Funanya a wide, cheerful smile, her face visible. "Just like going home."

Before Funanya could find any reply through her surprise, the girl had headed off. At a prod from Hunter, Funanya followed.

She knew? Impossible. Even Funanya's closest allies did not know about her beginnings in the dark of the Night Road. No one could have told her. No one knew.

As they walked on, Funanya watched the Ennead girl closest. Who was this child, who a shifter deferred to?

Without the suns above, the walk down the dank corridors of the Night Road lost the passage of time. Askaran followed the seer onward, trusting in her and trying to smother his doubts.

She was still a child and one without training. She might think she knew something and be wrong. The paths, to him, looked identical.

But she led them on, at first with enthusiasm and then with determination. When her steps began slowing, Askaran suggested they rest.

He propped the archon against one of the alcove walls, where a huge hand had been drawn in white on the wall. The seer settled across from the Berintan and handed Askaran water from her bag. After he had drunk and given it back, she offered it to the Berintan.

The archon pulled down the cowl of her cloak and eyed the seer for a long moment.

"I just drank it myself," Askaran pointed out. "You think it's poisoned?"

Reluctantly, the archon took the gourd. "I still don't understand why you're keeping me alive." She drank long from the water.

Picking a piece of dried meat to chew, Askaran slid into a seat blocking the alcove, placing himself between the seer and the rest of the tunnels. He assumed such alcoves were for resting, being defensible.

"You must come with us," the seer said simply, following the statement with a yawn.

As much as he wished to know why, Askaran could see the seer was exhausting herself already. "Rest, little flower," Askaran invited. "I'll watch."

As she lowered herself onto the stones, pillowing her sand-cloak under her, the seer mumbled, "For now…"

They waited in the shadows, the glow of the seer's glimm moss jar casting weak shadows. Despite her obvious fatigue, the archon did not close her eyes but stared across at Askaran relentlessly.

He dared not sleep, not with her watching. A trance would help, but even sinking into himself would dull his awareness. He could not trust the Berintan.

They sat across from each other as the seer fell into fitful sleep, her head next to Askaran's hip. Without the suns above, he had no way of measuring dusk or dawn and counting the hours, but he knew hours passed as they sat there, staring.

Movement in the main corridor interrupted their standoff. Five Berintans approached down the corridor, carrying a single glimm moss bottle between them for illumination. They wore the cloaked style he had come to associate with Night Road travel—a cloak of black not designed to keep the weather off but to provide camouflage. Weapons, from slings and knives to a chamba axe of twisted wood and obsidian stone, were openly displayed like the warning colors of chitters. Their hands were painted white.

He watched them out of the corner his eye but made no move, hoping they would move past. He was disappointed when they paused.

The archon, despite a desert cloak to match his, had left the hood down and fixed the approaching strangers with a suggestive smile.

Askaran gathered his feet under him in readiness, the kukri drawn under his cloak.

The archon moved first, darting from the wall and into the corridor to take refuge behind the strangers. Knowing grabbing her would make him vulnerable to the new arrivals, Askaran let her go. He had time.

"A thousand orzo for my freedom," the archon said, hiding behind the bulkiest of the five Berintans. "I am archon of a powerful ark. Great riches are yours for the death of these two!"

Askaran rose in a stalking crouch, feeling the demon in him eagerly smile. He was already envisioning the archon's head dangling by her hair off his talon. After six years of mocking servitude, he was looking forward to the prospect. Even five Berintans would not stand in his way.

"Need her," the seer whispered, her voice a murmur in her sleep but loud enough for Askaran's straining ears to hear.

He glanced at her, but she did not seem to have wakened.

The largest of the five stood at the center, acting as a shield for the archon, his beady eyes narrowed on Askaran. His smile was broad in the shadows of the lone jar of light the group was carrying.

Beside him, the seer shifted slightly, and her jar of light rolled beneath the sand-cloak. The shade of light differed; the new light was a washed-out blue.

The demon snarled in frustration to be denied his prize, but Askaran saw no alternative. He would not disobey the seer.

"This prize is not worth your lives," Askaran told the intruders.

"Lives?" the central man said with a sneer. "You? Against us?" He laughed and lifted his axe. "How about you step aside and let us take that little plaything behind you and…"

The man's voice trailed off as Askaran slowly brought forth his kukri. He thought they had paused because of the weapon, but Askaran quickly recognized that something else had caused their hesitation.

As he brought his hand out, his skin was visible.

"Enneads," one of the other Berintans said. "Worth a fortune by himself!"

To Askaran, the tensing of their muscles was a glaring warning. All five adjusted their weight forward, ready to strike.

The demon started laughing in Askaran's mind.

Askaran threw the kukri, not caring if it hit tip or hilt, and the impact smashed the light jar. The moss, spread too thin, went out and plunged the tunnel into complete darkness.

But red eyes could see through the darkness.

Askaran darted forward, catching the central man's throat with one hand before the man could so much as twitch his axe. Askaran squeezed and twisted, crushing the man's windpipe. With a choked breath, the man died.

Askaran was already moving. He slammed the next woman's head into the wall, feeling the bones give way under his grip as the skull collided with the stone behind it. The third man swung to face the sound of bone cracking, making it easy for Askaran to slip, unseen and unheard, around him. Askaran hooked his arm around the man's throat from behind, trapping it in his elbow, and squeezed. He released almost instantly; in the crush, he broke the man's neck and did not need to wait for suffocation.

The two remaining Berintans vaguely pointed their weapons toward the sounds of their compatriots dying. Snatching up his thrown kukri, Askaran finished the two with a slice across the throat each.

As the last Berintan collapsed to the ground, light leached from the alcove. The seer sat up calmly, her jar of light lifted out from the cloak. The archon's face was cast in bright white-blue hues. It made her face glitter as if silver instead of gold.

"Rest now," the seer said, nestling back against the rock. "Long way to go. Need you." Her eyes were soon closed once more.

Askaran collected the weapons as the archon remained apparently too stunned to move. When Askaran pointed to the alcove and told her to sit, he was surprised how quickly she did so. He wondered how much of his demon was showing. He thought he saw fear in her eyes.

But as they sat across from each other, neither of them willing or able to sleep, Askaran doubted his assessment. In the light of the jar, her wide eyes were intent, interested.

Three years after he had come to live among the Berintans, the archon had used Askaran and the wolfen pack to hunt a particularly aggressive keim beast that had been killing tauran stocks. After six days of tracking the beast through the mountains, they had thought it trapped by a lake, only to find it circled the water. When the tracks had led back onto themselves, even Askaran had been forced to admit defeat. The hunting party had made two laps of the lake before deciding that the beast itself had left the lake, having used its own trail to confound the hunters.

That night, Askaran had seen the archon looking back toward the lake from camp, her expression one of similar interest. Then he had thought it disappointment, but seeing it now, he thought he had misread her all along.

Maybe it was respect.

Within the first day, the Enneads made the mistake of resting in a claimed area, and they met one of the gangs. The five who challenged them died.

They died as efficiently as Funanya had ever seen. Funanya followed her captors in silence from there. She had seen the flicker of red in the eyes of the shifter in the light of the glimm moss and felt that lurking threat. Five Berintans had died to show her how proficient this shifter could be, even without taking his bestial form.

In the darkness, neither of the Enneads spoke but trudged on blind and hopeful. Rest was taken when required. The girl slept deeply, although she often muttered words in her sleep that the shifter keenly heeded. Hunter himself did not seem to sleep at all but sat cross-legged with his hands placed on his knees and his eyes mostly shut. Funanya always felt watched, as if his rest was shallow enough to be ripped apart should she move even to blink.

He always woke first and decided when it was time to move on. Funanya lost all concepts of time but assumed that he was letting them sleep as long as he dared.

And so the pattern went on for days.

The last day was spent in infrequently traveled tunnels, following the little Ennead girl with no regard for the labeled paths of the Night Road. Funanya expected them to meet a dead end as they wandered the unmarked tunnels. To her surprise, they emerged into the light of the evening.

The tunnel mouth was small, forcing Funanya to pass through on her knees into the sunset. The cool air of dusk made her shiver for a moment as she gazed out over the stony expanse. They had emerged onto a cliff edge, and the little Ennead girl was already standing on the ledge, looking down. The shifter had positioned himself between Funanya and the girl once more.

With her hands still bound, Funanya was not sure what he was expecting her to do. He had refused to release her even as she wiggled through the hole, but climbing would be truly impossible.

"No…" the Ennead girl muttered, prompting the shifter to look over the ledge.

Hunter grabbed the girl and pulled her away roughly. Whatever he had seen below must have been a larger threat than Funanya, for he hid the girl behind him, toward Funanya.

"Demons," he snarled. His stance stiffened, like a wolfen raising hackle scales in threat. He then took a forceful, long breath and seemed to deliberately settle himself.

Keeping a distance between herself and the shifter, Funanya made her way to the edge and peered down. She swiftly retreated.

The canyon was two hundred paces across but marked by sheer cliffs in all directions. The thin river that had cut the path through the stone was a distant thread, surrounded by rusty red monsters—demons of all descriptions—and black-shaded pillars.

"Pillars?" Funanya wondered aloud. She reviewed the glance in her mind. The river extended in both directions through the canyon but widened into a small lake directly below them. At perfect pacing, a dozen pillars of unknown black stone surrounded the lake. Between the pillars, demons of every type milled. Their snarling growls were raised on the air, distant but distinctive when she trained her ears for it in the canyon's wind.

"Of all the places…" The shifter was cursing, staring down as if unable to look away. His lips were curling back in a snarl. "Alighting Hall."

Funanya turned away from the ledge, thinking heading down a foolish thing. But as she checked around, she could find no handholds above them, and the cliff top was still two dozen paces above them. On either side, the cliff face was a sharp drop. Even if her hands had been free, there was no way up.

"Great choice of exits," Funanya grumbled at the Ennead girl. "Do you have any thoughts on how…" She let the sentence fall.

The girl was huddled back against the cliff by the tunnel, crouched among the stones, her head in her hands. She was muttering something and clearly not listening.

For a moment, Funanya did not know what to do. The shifter had not moved from examining the demons below and seemed to be oblivious that the Ennead girl was cowering behind him.

Having both escorts so frozen would be a problem. With her hands bound behind her back, Funanya needed the Enneads to be useful.

"Hunter?" Funanya prompted lightly. When he did not respond, she snapped, "Hunter!"

He started and faced her sharply. Funanya indicated the scared girl, and Hunter's stern expression instantly softened. He rushed to the girl's side.

The mumbling became coherent when Hunter gently placed an arm over the child's shoulders.

"I didn't see them…I didn't know…"

Cradling the girl's head to his chest, the shifter ran his hand over her shorn head, pushing down the cloak hood.

"You couldn't have, little flower. No one expects you to."

See? Funanya wondered. They had never been to this place before. She could not have expected to see…

It made sense in an instant. The little Ennead girl had seen the path to take through the Night Road. She was the reason Hunter had been perfectly behaved for so long. She knew of Funanya's life on the Night Road.

She was a seer, a young one and one that seemed to have blind spots, but a desert seer nonetheless. Like the woman Funanya had met twice at Farai's side, the girl was infinitely more valuable than even Hunter.

When she looked at the weeping child, Funanya didn't see the great power of the seers. She had none of the deep, portentous strength that Funanya had seen in the seer with Farai. How could this child even know what she was seeing? She could be a woman soon, but was so young still!

If she could get the seer back to Grand Archon Amadi, there might be a way to salvage this terrible situation. How could he deny her a position of respect if she delivered to him this great prize? With or without the shifter, the girl was the means for Funanya to buy back her position.

For now, that meant getting past demons.

Giving the pair their space, Funanya decided that, since up and side were not promising, she would check down again. This time, she ignored the demons around the lake below and tried to assess the cliff itself.

It was doable but would be difficult. She knew their supplies included rope. Other ledges like the one where they were perched extended down the cliff, giving them a path down.

Down to where a hundred demons argued loudly about the water. Among themselves, the demons did not seem to be coming to blows, but she was unsure why. Thankfully, the three travelers were far enough up to be unseen by even the enormous monsters; there was a colossus demon in the mix.

"Not to upset this touching moment," Funanya said, "but it's getting dark, and I don't want to be out here when the demons go hunting. Particularly the winged ones."

The shifter glared up at her, and she felt herself shiver once more. The hackles seemed raised again. She had to remind herself that the collar around his throat would stop him from shifting, but then remembered that he didn't need to be a monster to kill her; he was armed, and she was not.

The girl began stirring and, supported by her shifter, came to her feet. With him holding her firmly, she approached the edge and again looked down. Funanya watched her carefully, wondering what she was seeing when her black eyes became vacant briefly. The Ennead girl winced, then looked again. Her focus was obvious, if fruitless. At length, the girl shook her head.

"You need to rest," the shifter said, leading her away. "Traveling at dusk is folly; their vision is better than yours. We will wait for tomorrow, when the light is high, and they are quieter."

The child seemed to wilt when she was allowed to sit back down. Fatigue? Funanya wasn't sure. The girl had been away from the light for days now, and the Night Road had a way of sapping energy, but until now, Funanya had seen no sign of that weakness. Now the girl seemed deflated.

Wanting to put some distance between them and the demons, they made their way back into the corridor of the Night Road. Funanya selected a place by the exit to prop herself, her bound hands against her back but allowing her to lean against the stone to sleep. Through one half-opened eye, she watched the shifter deliberate over whether to place himself nearest the exit to the demons, or the Night Road. He chose the demons.

He fiddled with the collar that hung around his neck once more before setting himself in his cross-legged position. Funanya thought his posture was more slumped than the first few days. Bags under his eyes had become heavy. Even the tension with which he moved was worse.

She saw in him the wear of the Night Road, and it pleased her.

CHAPTER 15

Askaran had never used the trance to replace sleep entirely, but he saw no alternative. With the archon among them, he could not trust himself to sleep. The trance provided renewed focus and calm, but as he settled into the position by the tunnel's exit, he recognized that it was not satisfying his fatigue. He felt thinner than usual, and the thought worried him.

For six years, the demon had been silent. Without stimulus—without demons to hunt and Enneads to constantly defend—the demon had been easier to control, but seeing the demons milling around Alighting Hall had woken it fully. He felt like the demon had been readying itself for all those six years. When it rose now, it did so with greater strength than ever before.

And Askaran was tired already.

The trance settled his mind, and he forced the calm into his body. By command, he made himself find his own peace, one without a demon. It took more effort than before, but he found the deep calm waters he visited in his mind, where the wind showered over the ripples and he was alone. The double suns shone down over the bright lake, goading him into the serene waters.

The waves crashed, and the jumping fish leaped after flickering insects gliding across the shallows. He felt the peace of the water soothe his weary soul, and the thoughts of demons faded.

In his mind, he floated in the waters for long moments, not wanting to return. Eventually, the suns went dark, but the silent darkness did not trouble him. No stars flickered above. The wind died down.

Suddenly aware that he had fallen asleep, Askaran flew to his feet. His senses flooded back to him; noises in the corridor were approaching. There was light where none had been previously. Even the smell of plants and sweat warned him that the three travelers were no longer alone in the corridor.

He recognized that a group of Berintans took up the corridor leading into the Night Road. He noticed that one of them held the seer already and had placed a knife at her throat. He knew the Berintan was speaking. He suspected the man was threatening to kill the seer. Askaran did not bother to hear him out.

In the light of the glimm moss, Askaran darted forward and slammed his right hand into the Berintan's forehead. His left hand snatched at the blade, effortlessly removing it from the position near the seer. As the man fell back, Askaran yanked the seer from the enemy's hold and tucked her behind him.

Only then did he realize there were another dozen intruders, and they had their spears poised.

The demon lurched in Askaran's mind at the danger, and it took all of Askaran's concentration to rein it in. He could not allow the shift. The tight corridor had no space, and the metal collar would choke him if he tried.

"About time!" the archon interrupted, stepping into the glow of the glimm moss from behind Askaran, her hands still bound behind her. In a stride, she stood ahead of Askaran, facing the Berintans. "Cut my hands free! Who's in charge here?"

The Berintan Askaran had struck stepped back up, blood from his nose joining with the painted pattern of his face. The colors were muted in the green light of the fluorescent plant, but the archon seemed to still read them as the man gathered himself from the surprise attack.

"Archon Farai himself has taken an interest, has he?" she said. "Well, cut me loose and take me to him!" She turned to show her bound wrists to them.

Askaran felt the seer leave his back, heading for the opening out. A faint touch of dawn light trickled through, casting a gray shadow. He held his place, giving her time to escape.

The narrow opening might slow the group down, but where to run? Into demons?

"Not today, Funanya," the warrior answered the archon, surprising Askaran. The Berintan smeared the blood aside and grabbed a spear from one of his warriors.

The archon's head tilted at her name. Like her, Askaran acutely noticed the lack of title.

"What nonsense is this?" she demanded in a voice Askaran had seen few resist.

"Archon Farai has commanded you die alongside your conspiring Enneads," the Berintan declared, his blood-streaked grin wide but his voice nasal. His new spear inched forward, forcing the archon back a step and into Askaran's reach.

"My Enneads?" Funanya snapped, her posture straight. "I am a captive of theirs, Ekene. The archon must know as much!"

Askaran thought he heard her voice crack slightly.

Ekene, the warrior, shook his head. "He doesn't care, Funanya. And I am ever his—"

"Let me see him," she replied. "Bring me before him! I will prove to him—"

Ekene inched the spear forward once more, and Funanya, prodded, eased back another step. "No such permissions were granted," the warrior said.

Without moving anything other than his arm, Askaran placed the hilt of the knife he had stolen into Funanya's bound hands. In the darkness behind the glimm moss, her fingers tighten over the grip.

For the first time, it seemed their needs aligned.

"The archon must be close by," Funanya insisted. "To send in his arks without—"

Ekene chuckled, enjoying whatever expression he was seeing on his captive's face. "He will arrive in time to examine your corpse. Those were his orders, Funanya. It's your fault for hiding in this dead end, expecting that our search would not flush you out like the tauran cow you are."

Funanya twisted the knife, slicing through the bindings on her hands. Although she did not move, she had her hands free. Ready, she changed her grip to bring the hilt of the knife firmly in her palm, still behind her back.

Frustration slipped into Funanya's voice.

"Ekene," she said, "don't do anything you will regret."

The warriors and their spears tilted in. Ekene himself showed a bright smile in the light of the glimm moss. "I will not regret this. You have nowhere to—"

She lunged and, ready to take advantage of any assistance, Askaran did the same. With his single kukri, he batted aside a spear and sprang at a warrior. The spear failed to turn fast enough, opening the way for Askaran to slash at the warrior's neck. The warrior leaned far back, and it was enough of a change in balance for Askaran to exploit. He hooked his heel behind the man's ankle and let the warrior trip himself backward.

Showing surprising speed, Funanya darted under Ekene's spear, pivoted backward, and slammed her dagger into Ekene's chest. The noise was like a waterskin being popped. The man screeched and tumbled. The path was opened for Funanya to continue her spin and knock the light jar from the hands of the nearest warrior.

Following her example, Askaran threw himself at the man holding the other light jar. In a tackle, he knocked the jar into the stone and broke it.

Darkness landed. With red eyes, Askaran watched Funanya sharply turn and bolt for the exit. She fumbled as she approached it. Askaran's sensitized eyes could easily see where the seer had draped the sand-cloak over the exit to hide it. The Berintan approaching had no way of knowing there was a way out at all.

But Funanya already knew, and she found the cloth. Pulling it aside, she crawled into the light.

When the Berintans shuffled after her, homing in on the light, Askaran caught them. In the darkness, he slipped the kukri through the spine of each in turn as he made his way. Positioning himself to the side of the light, he waited like a hunting hound.

The demon chuckled, pleased by the smell of blood and the ease of spilling it. But the Ennead knew he could not continue. They had seen the light. They knew.

The speaker of the group was still raggedly breathing as he lay across the tunnel's path, but more people were coming and Askaran did not have time. Overruling the determination of his demon, he quickly squeezed through the opening. Pivoting, he slammed his shoulder into the tunnel, shifting one of the stones to narrow the opening further, but he could not seal it entirely.

Turning, Askaran found the seer and the archon standing on the ledge, looking down into the valley in the early dawn. Below, the roar of demons echoed distantly. He joined them, trying to find a path down the cliffs that would not allow the Berintans to follow. Rope was dangerous; they would cut it. Up was impossible. He could kill some, but how many were coming? Perhaps if he killed one as they came out…

"Come here," the archon commanded, surprising Askaran. As he faced her, Funanya reached down the side of her kaftan.

Askaran opened his mouth to refuse, but the seer's light voice interrupted. "Trust us," she said.

Muttering a curse to the women he had tied himself to, Askaran hesitantly approached the Berintan.

When Funanya withdrew her hand from her hip, she held the tiny collar key.

"You had it all along?" he snapped.

"Shut up," she said, "and bend down."

It took effort, but he did not move when she placed the key into the collar. She held the collar with her other hand, barely brushing his skin, and it seemed a lifetime as she fitted the key. Could it tighten further? She could kill him if that was the case. But the seer had said to trust her. He fought to remain still.

With a loud *click,* the collar opened. It took Askaran both hands to pry it wide after its six years of inactivity.

Gone. Finally, the collar was gone.

Meeting his stare, the archon squared herself up. "Now get us down this cliff, shifter."

He did not require additional prompting. Handing his kukri to the seer, Askaran opened the cage of the demon and let the monster's form take him.

Funanya was numb. Farai had commanded her death. Hatred swelled into the void of emotions. Killing those who tried to carry out the order did not upset her. Survival was the only goal.

But even her hatred could not stay when she saw Hunter shift for the first time.

She had expected a hound but had been hoping that maybe he was one of the winged demons and that he would be able to carry her and the little Ennead girl. She had never thought for a moment that in shifting, he would tower over the ledge and make the stone bend.

He was a colossus demon.

The ledge, unable to hold their weight, cracked sharply and gave way.

Before she could even scream, Funanya felt a rough arm snatch her up, and she was pressed against the scale and hair hide of a great crimson monster. Next to her, she found the Ennead girl nestled, clinging to her bag desperately and burying her face against the chest of the shifter.

They skidded and clamored down the cliff, bouncing from stone to stone but ever cushioned by the monster. When he landed on the valley floor, his claws dug gouges into the granite and had him standing firm.

Funanya glanced out. A dozen demons, each snarling wide with bone-white teeth and glowing stares, looked up at her.

But the shifter was bigger. Hunter's great, maned head reared back, and he roared at the lesser demons, making them all duck their heads in hesitation. Before they could decide if they wanted to challenge him, the shifter dug his claws in and sprinted away three-legged, carrying the Ennead and Funanya against him.

In a few long strides, the shifter left the other demons behind. Moaning cries chased them.

Over rocky banks and through the chasm, the shifter sprinted. Funanya clung harder to the chest, fearing she would be tossed from his crushing hold and fall onto deadly stones. Her grip brought her closer to the Ennead girl as the girl muttered, "Stop, Askaran. You've got to stop."

Even directly beside the girl, Funanya had hardly heard the words. It would be impossible for Hunter to hear them over the clatter of his running.

He pounded down the riverbank, his long pace making them seemingly fly over the boulders of the valley. Thick claws dug hard into the struggling moss and reeds, slicing them to ribbons.

"Stop, Askaran," the Ennead's soft voice said again. "If you don't stop now, you never will."

Funanya raised her voice to her most powerful shout. "HUNTER!" she called. "STOP!"

The monster stopped so abruptly, he skidded over a boulder and landed on one large knee, cracking through the shale of the river's stone beach. With haste, he released the girl and Funanya and, for a moment, stared at them as if surprised they were there at all.

A colossus demon. A full-sized, huge colossus demon stared down at her. The nostrils of the monster flared wide, and Funanya felt a shiver run through her. The lips were curling back in a snarl, showing fangs the size of her leg.

"Askaran?" the Ennead girl asked.

The stare of the demon turned to the girl, and Funanya saw the red-eyed stare soften. The great eyes closed slowly, and the demon gave a single, long sigh.

The shape twisted before her eyes. The red skin faded to black, and the scales folded down into skin as the body returned to that of an Ennead. Unarmed and naked, Hunter soon stood where the demon had, his dark skin coated in sweat and his chest heaving from exertion.

"How...?" Funanya regretted speaking when his eyes snapped to her, his stare still potently crimson. With a snarl, he lunged and caught her by the throat. She hit the ground hard, his weight atop her and his grip on her neck tight enough to make her see sparks. A growl rumbled in his throat, an echo of the roar of the monster he had not quite left behind.

"Askaran! Please!"

Again, the shifter's expression eased at the sound of the Ennead girl's voice. The hand holding Funanya's throat released. His breath still coming in pants, his eyes changed once more, losing their red color and darkening to an Ennead's usual black. Funanya felt his muscles slowly release their tension as his senses returned. A dozen heartbeats later, his breath calmed, and recognition finally came to his face.

She waited another dozen heartbeats with him pressed atop of her, the hand that had been on her throat released and forgotten over the nape of her neck. In his lunge, he had hooked his other hand onto her hip to hold her down, and she became sharply aware of that contact. The press of his heated, pitch skin against her bare legs made her stomach knot, and it was not just fear.

"Move your hand, Hunter," Funanya said as calmly as she could.

To her relief, he pulled himself quickly away. She thought he even looked embarrassed.

The shifter stepped toward Funanya and extended his arms side-to-side. "Check me for wounds," he said. When she did not immediately leap to her feet, he added, "I crashed into the cliff face in that fall. I must know if I am bleeding."

Shaken, Funanya pushed herself up slowly and approached him. She was surprised when he did not pull away.

"A deep gash … on your back," she reported. "You don't feel it?"

His dark eyes were cautious when he replied, "Everything is numb after a shift."

"Here," the seer called. When Funanya checked on her, the girl was extending a basic stitching pack. Funanya and her warriors carried the supplies in battle, but where the Ennead had stolen it from, Funanya did not know.

As Hunter did not fetch the package himself, Funanya marched over and took it from the girl. Laying it open on a stone, she selected a sponge, dipped it in water, and began cleaning the wound.

"She can't do this?" Funanya asked, eyeing the Ennead girl as she located a mossy rock and sat down. While most people would avoid sitting on the plant, the girl chose the very center of the moss and sat with her knees up. With wary black eyes, she watched Funanya and Hunter.

"Black blood is poison to her," Hunter replied.

Funanya turned the sponge over in her hand, surprised to see the fresh blood was indeed black, not red.

"Black?" she muttered. "How did I never…"

"When you beat me, it was dusk," Hunter answered her unfinished question. "Every time you dealt or saw my wounds, it was in the dark, or days later. What you thought was old blood was, in fact, fresh. My great secret."

Returning to cleaning the fresh wound, Funanya tried to smile. "Demon blood is black," she said.

"And black blood is poison to an Ennead," he agreed.

Putting down the sponge, Funanya located the stitching needle and the thin line meant to close wounds.

Hunter gave her a weak smile as she showed him the tools.

"Thank you," he said and, without a word of complaint, let her stitch his wound.

It had stopped bleeding after her stitches were in place. She placed a bandage over it, but they had no spare shirt for him. Thankfully, the Ennead girl produced a breechcloth from her bag, and Hunter wrapped it around his hips. She also produced a pair of sandals for him.

"Got more in there?" Funanya asked. "Because if he shifts again—"

"If I shift again, I might not come back," Hunter interrupted, giving Funanya a glare. "Archon, I barely got out of that one. The demon is more powerful than ever, and I am too old and tired to argue with him."

"Old?" Funanya said, snorting. "You've not aged since we met, and it's been—"

"I am three hundred and forty-eight this year," he informed her, rotating his shoulders as if to test her stitching. He winced and placed a hand gingerly to the side where the gash had opened him to the muscle. "Old."

"Ah," was all Funanya could think of to say. He still looked like a hale adult. "So you won't be shifting to climb out of the valley? Or to run on across the desert?"

Softly, Hunter shook his head. His smile was bitter. "No. Maybe once I'm more rested. Maybe."

"And we need not climb," the Ennead girl called from her place in the moss.

Hunter paused and checked with Funanya before moving toward the girl. "It is safe?"

"You are clean," Funanya reported. He seemed to hesitate once more, but with a final wince, joined the Ennead in the shade. Funanya followed but chose to sit on the stone instead of the wet moss.

"So, how do we get out of here?" Funanya asked. She wasn't sure if the seer would know, but the girl had found a way through the Night Road blindly. A valley didn't seem nearly as much of an obstacle.

"We?" Hunter asked.

"Archon, you are free to go if you wish," the Ennead girl said. "We can no longer keep watch over you. Askaran must sleep. So, if you wish to come with us, you may, but we will not force you. Go where you will."

"Well, I can't very well go back up that hillside and into the Night Road. I will come with you until we get clear of the valley. Then I will head home."

The Ennead girl nodded as if already having known what her decision would be. "Then welcome," she said.

Seeing Hunter's narrowed glare, Funanya did not feel welcome, but she chose to ignore the shifter's animosity for the moment.

"We will follow the river out," the girl said, pointing upstream. "This is the Valley of Vaseil." She looked meaningfully at Hunter.

"Where the Alighting Hall was anchored," he said with more understanding than Funanya felt he was justified in using. He seemed to search the stones and boulders around them as he glanced around. "The shifters set up hides along here, so we should be able to find shelter."

"Hides? Why?" Funanya asked, seeing the Ennead girl stand and follow her. Kicking water free from her feet, the little girl skipped off the moss and onto the stony bank, leaving wet footprints for a dozen steps.

"Because the demons had to leave the valley to reach the desert," Hunter replied. "And the only way out was along the river."

The Ennead girl slung her bag over a shoulder and began walking, followed quickly by Hunter, who had lost his bag in the escape, including all their pillaged weapons.

The logic took a moment more to make sense in Funanya's mind.

"Are you saying the demons all come from Alighting Hall, Hunter?" she demanded, chasing them until she could fall into step beside the Ennead male.

"Once, yes," Hunter replied. "And I am Askaran, Archon. If you cannot call me that, call me Shifter."

Funanya paused, wondering what name she felt suited him better. "Shifter" seemed to match "Hunter": simply identifying what, not who, he was. His actual name seemed … familiar?

"By the shour!" she cursed, catching up to him and tapping a slap into his right, untattooed shoulder. "You told me about yourself! Askaran! You said 'Askaran' was the most powerful of the shifters, even more powerful than Yarr! You told me your name!"

The Ennead girl ahead of them stopped for a moment, laughing. Funanya could not tell if it was at Askaran's disgruntled expression or Funanya's outrage.

"And you? Have YOU a name?" Funanya snapped.

The laughter quieted quickly, and the girl's black eyes became distant. Gold flecks flashed in her gaze briefly. Beside her, Askaran seemed to be waiting for the reply with as much interest as Funanya.

"I am a desert seer," the girl replied. "I am the Youngest Seer."

Askaran nodded approvingly and made to move on.

"I cannot be calling you 'Youngest Seer'," Funanya said, deciding to keep ahead of him and trekking on. "He calls you 'little flower.' For now, you will be Dana."

Behind her, she heard Askaran echo, "Dana?"

Funanya glanced back at the pair. "My favorite flower. Pretty little blooms. Grows in the dark best."

The Ennead girl was smiling broadly, but Funanya pretended not to notice the bright stare on her as she picked a path along the river.

"I like it," the Ennead said. "Dana. I think I will be called Dana. What do you think, Askaran?"

Hearing no reply, Funanya again looked back. She found the little girl peering up at the Ennead who could become a demon, somehow looking curious, not afraid.

Askaran shrugged and joined Funanya along the water. She wasn't sure but suspected Askaran had decided not to answer because his reply would upset the girl.

Farai was the last to lower himself down the ropes the warriors had laid along the cliff face. As he stepped onto the rocky chasm floor, he first checked on the seer, who he found sitting in the shade of a stone, her breaths heavy. In the six years since coming to Berinta, she had hardly walked more than a dozen steps in a row, and the trip through the Night Road had worn her profoundly. Mentally, she seemed brighter. For the first time in years, he thought he could see the flicker of visions in her stare. Although she did not openly discuss them, he had heard her talking in her sleep and what she said had helped them track the fleeing shifter when the trail had been tricky through the Night Road.

She panted as she rested, her face shining in sweat and her large body slumping. He thought he might have to create a pagoda for her if they were to keep pace at all.

As he watched over her, waiting for the scouts to determine which way the colossus demon shifter had gone, a cry went up. A scout returned at a sprint.

"Tusked!" the warrior called, quickly joining the party as they assembled.

"Behind…" The warrior gasped for air. "…following…"

Sure enough, step by huge step, Farai felt the ground shake.

As Farai reached his warriors, leaving the Ennead desert seer hiding behind the boulder, Yarr stepped out of the gathering of warriors. As he moved, the shifter's naked form expanded and blurred. He had taken his demonic form by the time a tusked demon rushed over the rise from the river's shore.

Both monsters were as tall as an ark and covered with thick-plated scales. The mane around the head of the demon wrapped around its shoulders and extended down the spine, tracing a twisted path between enormous spikes. The shifter's mane was black while the demon's had a ruddy red sheen to it and, if Farai squinted, he could see Yarr's scar traced over his back leg even in the shifted form.

The warriors assembled behind the shifter, lifting their hide shields and bringing their spears into throwing positions. Farai was slow to draw his swords, thinking it probably unnecessary. He had seen Yarr fight more than once and had always been impressed.

The shifter, in his own demonic form, stood firm before the demon as the tusked demon bellowed its challenge and tossed its head in warning. All Yarr did was lower his head in readiness for the charge. Incensed, the demon tucked its horned skull low and stormed toward the shifter.

From a safe vantage point on the cliff walls, Farai had seen the tusked demons in the chasm perform similar exchanges all afternoon. One would initiate the attack. The other would answer with horn waving and bellows. Eventually, one would back off or it would come to blows. Like tauran bulls, they would charge in and clatter their horns against each other, trying to hook one of their tusks against the other to throw them off their feet. Whoever succeeded was deemed the victor, and the loser gave up the ground.

Yarr was different. He did not wave or posture. He did not charge the demon, but instead let it come. He did not meet the horns with his own, even though he seemed more than capable of withstanding the blow. Instead, Yarr ducked as the tusked demon barreled into him and caught the weight of the demon's chest against his shoulder, avoiding the horns and tusks entirely. Heaving, Yarr threw the demon off its feet and into the stone cliff beside them.

Before the beast could rise, Yarr charged and sunk both horns into the demon's underbelly deeply, pinning it against the cliff. The roar of agony ripped through the valley, echoing a dozen times before drifting far enough to allow Farai to lower his hands from his ears.

The demon gave a single shaking tremor, then flopped. The flesh instantly disintegrated into dust and was scattered by Yarr's snort of victory.

Once he had untangled his horns from the skeleton of the tusked demon, the shifter returned to his Ennead form and re-joined the warriors by the ladders. One of the warriors presented the shifter with his clothing and weapons, never once meeting the red eyes of the

Ennead who had, with a single blow, slain one of the most powerful demons known to them.

"Nicely done," Farai commended, making Yarr shrug.

"Predictable," Yarr replied, donning his dashiki and shour, followed by the sokoto.

In the distance, new demonic howls called.

"Can you get through them?" Farai asked.

The enormous Ennead grinned widely. "They are demons. Keep them apart, and I can kill any one of them."

"Any of them?" Farai mused. "Are you capable of killing a colossus demon?"

The shifter adjusted the patch of shour he wore on his shoulder as he licked his lips. "Demons think like demons. I am Ennead, and I think like an Ennead. I can kill any demon, even a colossus," Yarr said.

"Good," Farai said. "Because the beast we hunt was seen to be a colossus demon." A scout arrived quietly, indicating with his head that he had found a trail to follow. The warriors sorted themselves into groups and headed out, instantly assigning positions among them as they went. Years of battle had trained them well; Farai expected no less.

Yarr did not carry any supplies but headed out into the chasm with long, confident strides. Two other warriors stirred the seer and prodded her onto her feet. Yarr paused to watch her take the first of her tired steps down the path placed in front of her. Farai joined him for a moment, happy that the warriors had distanced themselves and would not hear the question or the answer.

"If the shifter we chase thinks like an Ennead but is a colossus demon, do you think you can handle him?" Farai asked.

Yarr's teeth-baring grin did not waver. "He is Askaran," Yarr replied. "No other colossus demon shifter exists. And since he is Askaran, he is tired. Had you waited a few more months before your invasion, you would not have met him at all; he would have already walked into the desert and found his way into death. His hold on his demon weakens with every day. When we fight, he will be thinking like a demon. And I will kill him."

"If he was months away from death six years ago, why does he still live?" Farai wondered. He looked back at the seer, thinking she might be a better recipient of the question. Even if she did not answer immediately, he could hope to hear some divinations in her dreams.

To his surprise, Yarr chuckled. "You cannot figure it out?" he said. "It is obvious, Berintan. Your desert seer cannot see them well, can she? Her glimpses are weak. That tells you why Askaran lives still."

Farai watched the seer stumble on, her face worn. He had assumed the deficit was because of the distance between her and the target, or her own lying stubbornness, but even in her dreams, her instructions had been unreliable. The shifter had been unaware of their approach and had still evaded them. Stumbling across the fugitives near the exit from the Night Road had seemed an accident; the seer had been as surprised as the runaways.

"I do not understand," Farai admitted.

Yarr showed his teeth in his joy at being able to lecture the archon.

"There are only two things seers cannot see. Demons are one, but Askaran is too old to be in his demon so much. No, she cannot see him because she cannot see desert seers, Archon. Askaran lives still because he defends a seer. He will not let himself die until he has seen her returned to her people." The grin grew sinister, as if blood was already dripping from his teeth and he enjoyed the taste. "That, or when he loses control and kills them all."

Yarr checked on the slow progress of the seer. "Come," he said.

As Farai followed the warriors in their pursuit, he wondered if Grand Archon Amadi had known how useful the shifter would be to him. He had thought it had indicated a failing faith in him, but now wondered if Amadi had somehow known about the shifter they would be chasing on their way to the city.

Had the Grand Archon known the fugitives would run for the city as well? How much of this journey had been predicted by Amadi?

After the day of walking, Askaran found a cave off the main river bank, and the seer, now insisting her name was "Dana," made camp. He fished in the river until his eyes grew heavy, then returned, unsuccessful, to the cave.

The two women sat in the dim light of the jar of glimm moss, but their talk simmered to a halt upon his arrival. The archon handed him some geru nuts, scavenged from the rocky cliffs, and Dana threw him a water gourd.

Curious, he removed the cork and investigated it. He had come from the river and had drunk before leaving. He needed no…

"Dredge," the seer cheerfully informed him. The stench of alcohol from the bladder was potent.

"Dredge?" the archon echoed, her face bright with a slight smile. "I forbade that stuff! How did you get some?"

Seeing the camaraderie between the women, Askaran surrendered. If the seer trusted Funanya now, he had to follow her example. She would know of treachery.

He folded his legs, sat down, and drank deeply from the gourd. The potent drink had no flavor except that of the alcohol's burn.

"I watched the cook. He made it. Took chapman and reworked it many, many times. It loses its color and instead—"

Askaran coughed, blinking several times as his eyes watered. When the tears cleared, he found Funanya smirking at him.

"Instead, it becomes potent enough to strip bark from trees," Funanya finished for the seer. She watched Askaran as he took another drink. He closed his eyes and leaned back, waiting for the drink to settle and calm his mind. The demon already seemed happier.

After a pause, her voice quieted and Funanya said, "You were drunk that morning outside the final oasis."

Feeling the strain of six years release itself, Askaran laughed aloud. "I *had* been flaming drunk the night before. The best sleep I'd had all crossing was that night. Drink shuts the demon up."

So long without alcohol had an advantage, Askaran thought. Two swallows and his head was already drifting in bliss. The stiff muscles from the crazed run through the valley faded as he leaned away from the light and let the silence comfort him.

Whatever dredge was, it was acting quickly. He would not need another mouthful. Without knowing how much the seer had brought with her, that was good.

He sat in delightful tranquility for long moments before the archon's voice came again, soft and questing.

"Does the demon have a name?"

"You have an obsession with names," Askaran replied without opening his eyes.

He heard her shrug.

"We have nothing but our name," she replied, but her voice had none of her usual lecturing tones. "Our name is our fame."

He opened one eye to regard her, and his vision took a long time to focus. Thinking back to the Berintans, he recognized the truth of her statement. The merit and skill of the individual were all that led to advancement. Wealth and connections seemed to hold little value. He thought the concept almost Ennead, if the Berintans could also give up the idea of advancement and prestige. Enneads had to be happy where they were. No Ennead was more important than any other, but Berintans spent their time trying to become just that, important. He thought it a sad life.

Askaran closed his eye once more and let his mind drift. He no longer cared what she knew. "Of course it has a name," he said. "Askaran."

They fell into silence, which satisfied him. In the haze of the drunkenness, Askaran slipped into sleep, and the demon was pleasantly silent.

CHAPTER 16

"Shifter?" The voice called him from by the cavern entrance, and he ignored it. "Shifter?" the archon called a second time, her voice still soft and not urgent. He ignored it again.

"By the shour, Askaran!" she finally shouted, and Askaran rolled over.

Funanya stood in the cave mouth, her hands on her hips over her torn, partially shredded kaftan. The gray light of dawn seeped in behind her, casting a tiny shadow but bringing with it the smell of water and moss. In the cave, the air was stagnant and almost metallic. He enjoyed the reminder of the river.

"Good morning, Askaran," the archon said. "Sleep well?"

Feeling like a well-fed keim beast, Askaran stretched out before rising. He located his sandals, and, by habit, went looking for his kukri. It took him a moment to realize he had given the seer the weapon for the shift on the cliff. He was unarmed.

When Askaran put out his hand, the archon rolled her eyes and produced the stolen Berintan blade he had given her and handed it over.

"Careful with it," she warned. "It's the only blade we appear to have unless that girl has something else buried in the bag. It's not in mine."

Finding a line in the bag, Askaran tied a small loop to the knife in case it slipped from his grip. The archon had a good point about losing the blade now.

"Anyway, I thought I could see movement on the horizon. I'm not sure if it's a demon but regardless we should—"

Askaran stopped listening to Funanya when he scanned the cave. He did not see the seer or her bag.

"Where is the seer?" he interrupted. He turned his glare to the archon, the demon rising. If the seer was in danger because of this Berintan, he would tear her limb from limb.

She seemed to see the red in his eyes and backed away, her hands raised in surrender. "I slept outside, shifter. She didn't come out past me. Relax. She's sleeping probably. The cavern goes back a ways. She must be back there."

Peeling himself back, Askaran called, "Seer!" and headed for the back of the cave.

She did not answer.

Turning his attention to being a hunter, Askaran found the scuffs indicating the passage of feet along the stones and followed it back. Between the two large boulders that made the back wall of their cave, he found a gap.

The archon joined him there, holding up the glimm moss container. As Askaran took it from her, he noted for the first time that it was an Ennead glass jar, likely pillage from the City. She'd watered it, making it brighter than it had been overnight.

With the light, Askaran searched the wall and found the trace of fingers in the dust. She had run her hand down the side of the boulders, toward the gap.

It would be a tight squeeze for him, and he was not certain he would be able to turn around at the far end. The prospect of trying to wiggle through a crack backward sent his demon howling in terror. Like him, the monster feared the small space.

Because it could not shift there. A shift within the gap would crush him. Once in the space, he was trapped as an Ennead. He would be helpless. The demon balked at the thought.

He glanced at the Berintan with him, and the archon shrugged.

"She didn't get around me, and I slept by the entrance. She must have gone down there. Shour only knows why."

Askaran growled, feeling trapped even before setting foot into the crack. It was possible the archon was lying. He could kill her for that. The idea had merit.

Need her.

The seer had said they needed her. She had asked that the archon come with them. The night before, they had been laughing together. Askaran was not yet sure he could trust the Berintan, but it had pleased him to see the seer—Dana—making a friend. And he could not disobey the commands of a seer.

But had it merely been a request? Hope? Did the seer even know what she was seeing?

He had to trust.

"Need you," Askaran muttered. "You first, Berintan. You can tell me if it gets too narrow for me."

The archon scowled at him and shook the glimm moss jar in scold.

"If I have to call you 'Askaran,' I get to be called 'Funanya,' I am not merely 'Berintan.'"

Askaran cocked an eyebrow at her. "Not 'Archon'?"

She darted back a little as if he had stabbed the paring knife toward her. When he saw her face, he recognized the comparison was apt; he had wounded her.

After a moment or two to gather her confidence, she replied, "I have been stripped of title and ark. I am Funanya, and that is all, Askaran."

"You go first, Funanya," Askaran said. "And let me know if it opens up deeper down."

Funanya handed him her bag and approached the cleft. Squeezing her belly and chest in, she slid into the opening.

He gave her a chance to get ahead, trying to breathe deep and calm. The seer was missing, and he had to chase her down a tiny crack in the rock. His demon wanted to tear the stones out of the wall and make the opening larger, but Askaran knew that could destabilize the opening entirely, maybe even crush the seer. Was there another way?

"It's a bit wider here," Funanya called. "Opening further… Oh! A bigger cave. But you kept the glimm moss, you ass, so get down here! I can't see a thing!"

Tucking the jar into the bag, and positioning it behind in his wake, Askaran took a final breath and forced himself into the crack.

It was slow going, in some places the gap was no wider than he, and he scraped his arms and chest along the rough stone. More than once, he felt the ground below pull away, and he was crawling along between two walls by footholds. A look down revealed that the crack extended down for seemingly forever.

The demon whimpered like a scolded wolfen and then kept quiet. He felt the fear and shared it. Falling could kill them both. Being crushed could kill them just as easily.

Creaking step by step, he shuffled along the stone.

The gap opened bit by bit. After a point, he no longer had to suck his belly in to advance. He felt the rock that scratched at him pull away, and his foot found firm setting. The crack closed below him, and he pulled himself onward, emerging from the wall into a tunnel.

Funanya was facing him, although her eyes looked through him when she tried to see him in the dark. Her expression had set itself, but he thought the tightness of her muscles implied fear. She was smothering it, as he was. Neither of them would show any more than absolutely required.

He brought out the jar, and she reached for it with primal need. Understanding her fear of the dark, for he likened it to the fear of tight spaces, he let her have the container.

"Check me for wounds," he directed, and she stiffly nodded.

Leaving the woman to examine his roughened elbows and shoulder, Askaran turned his attention to the ground, hoping Funanya had not been moving around enough to upset the tracks. To his dismay, the ground was perfect stone. There was not even a hint of a scuff to tell him which way the seer had gone.

"You're clean," Funanya declared. "No broken skin." She eyed him. "You're paranoid."

Ignoring her, Askaran investigated the tunnel. Supported by set, smooth cementum stone, pillars lined the path. Both directions looked identical.

Askaran circled the gap once more, searching, but in the end stood in the middle of the tunnel, unsure. He tried to smell her, but the air was heavy in sulfur and musk, and he found no trace of Ennead.

"She went this way," the archon said, pointing to the right. When Askaran narrowed his eyes on her, the Berintan brought the jar of glimm moss down to the ground and pointed. Askaran saw no print, just the skittering of black tiny maggots.

"Glowmoth larvae," Funanya explained. "They are attracted to light and heat. It's why glimm moss glows in clumps; it's meant to attract the larva. There was heat here. Her footstep."

Askaran placed a finger near one of the black maggots and watched the tiny worm slowly inch toward him. It bumped into his nail three times before giving up and trying to circle his finger.

"They eat the dead moss and spread the seed for the live one. But they make it easy to track someone. Probably how Farai's men found us once we left the main trail in the Night Road," Funanya said.

Askaran eyed her suspiciously. "You are being strangely helpful," he said.

For the first time in many years, Askaran thought he saw Funanya genuinely smile. Her other smiles had been political strategy, or vicious grins announcing a sore victory. Here, she was purely pleased with herself.

"I need you to get me out of the valley. After that, Dana said I could go."

Askaran rose from his crouch, muttering, "Dana..."

"Oh, it's prettier than 'the seer' all the time. It's like calling me 'archon' or 'Berintan' or calling you 'shifter.' That's a title, not a name. Now come on," Funanya called, skipping ahead of him by a step. "We've got a desert seer to catch. I'm sure you're looking forward to scolding her fiercely for her disobedience. What would possibly possess her to come down here? It reeks!"

Hiking up the bag, Askaran followed Funanya onward, smiling weakly.

There had to be a reason, and Askaran thought it was the silhouettes Funanya had spotted on the horizon beyond their cave. If the seer had known they would be overrun by the Berintans chasing them, she might seek a different path. What he could not understand was why she had done so without notifying him.

He followed the glimm moss light as Funanya trotted down the empty, ancient tunnel.

Yarr stopped cold by the river. The Berintan trackers were circling, looking for the trail they had lost, but he did not join them. Leaving the seer on a stone by the river, where she flopped down like a broken toy and said nothing, Yarr put his nose to the ground and searched.

All demons used a sense of smell to hunt, and the tusked demon was one of the strongest. In the shifted form, each scent was easily identified: wet earth, newly dried from where they had moved a stone in search of bait for fishing; cold ash from their small fire; the sting of alcohol someone had packed; the sweat of a Berintan woman; and the musk of a raging colossus demon.

Had he lost control right here? Yarr could smell Askaran's demon powerfully. The monster had been furious. There was blood, demon blood, mingled in the ash. He had burned the cloth he had cleaned himself with. That meant Askaran had survived to return to Ennead.

He found the scraps of line; someone had stitched a wound. Demon blood lingered on the line; someone had stitched *Askaran's* wound. Yarr didn't think it had been the seer. The scent was Berintan.

Following the scent, Yarr walked on. By morning, he located the cave where the escaping Ennead and their accomplice had spent the night. The scent of drink was heavier here, and he found where Askaran had lain overnight. The scouts found the gap in the stones that led down.

With their weapons and armor, the Berintans could not follow. Yarr himself was too large, as was the seer.

He shifted back to Ennead and returned to Farai.

"They will have to head toward the exit from the valley," Yarr told him. "We cannot follow the same path, but we know their destination." He pointed west.

The archon followed the gesture, staring down the long, winding river valley.

"You know this valley, shifter?" Farai asked.

"It is the Valley of Vaseil, home to the Alightening Hall," Yarr replied. He looked at the seer, but she had slumped down and did not seem willing to join the conversation. "Shifters used to patrol here. There is only one way out, following the river. The Enneads once built tunnels running along it to allow them access in several places without having to enter the valley. It has many openings along the valley, but one exit, one that points toward the City."

Farai seemed to consider the information for a long, solid moment, then nodded. "I will send most of the warriors to the valley's opening and have them wait there. We will seek another path into the tunnels, one where you can fit." He made a disgusted face but nodded toward the seer. "Her too."

Yarr shrugged in acceptance, not caring. The shifters who had long ago abandoned the valley had deliberately made their openings difficult to keep the demons from following them in, but plenty of time had passed. A rockslide or a cave-in might have opened a new way in.

The seer's eyes were distant once more, flickering in gold. He was certain she saw visions, but she said nothing. He thought he saw a tiny smile on her face for a moment as she was shoved to her feet.

After another hour of walking, the seer's scream cascaded down the tunnel. Askaran broke into a run, the tiny paring knife in his hand.

A dozen paces ahead, a tattered hide door had already been hooked aside. Askaran rushed into the room beyond.

The wall had been cracked open on one side, allowing thin sunlight to filter in. Inside the gap stood a winged demon, its horns lowered in readiness for a charge. The wings were flared wide behind it as it sought balance on the crumbled remains of the decorated but collapsed wall.

Across from the demon, the seer had flattened her back against a wall and was staring wide-eyed. Chests, barrels, and debris littered the floor, but nothing of enough substance to slow the demon if it chose to charge.

Askaran launched himself into the path of the monster, skidding to a halt with his knife raised as the demon took its first step. It paused, surprised into brief hesitation. Askaran was unsure if that was because it had not seen him coming or was just shocked that an essentially unarmed Ennead would confront it.

With a loud snort, the demon aimed its plated head and charged.

The only place that Askaran's knife would be able to penetrate was the eye.

He held his ground, waiting for as long as he dared before leaping up, catching the horns of the monster, and swinging himself over the head. He landed facing forward on the plated neck of the demon, brought the knife down, and pierced through the socket.

The demon roared and bucked but was thrown from its charging trajectory and careened into a wall instead of where the seer was cowering. Askaran pulled his leg over the dead of the demon and let himself fall to the ground to avoid becoming pinched against the wall. The cavern stone shook heavily, and a spattering of pebbles fell, but the wall held against the assault.

When Askaran got to his feet, he realized his hands were empty. The knife had remained in the socket but was too short to reach the brain of the demon. Besides blinding the monster on one side, making black blood pour down its face, the blade had done little.

"Dana!" he heard Funanya call. "Get behind something! Askaran! Here!"

As he backtracked away from the demon, which was shaking off the pebbles and turning to face him,

Askaran glanced toward the voice. He found Funanya inside the hide door, holding an ancient bent spear. She threw it to him in vertical lob, then grabbed a second from a nearby rack.

By the entrance, the walls were lined with weapons. All around him, clothing, sacks, and tools hung from pegs in the stone or were laid atop stone chests. Dust and dirt had fallen over everything, but otherwise, the room appeared to be in good repair.

He lunged to grab the spear and held it in two hands as he faced the demon. The bent tip seemed to sag.

The demon charged, and Askaran dodged being trampled by moving to the blind side. The horns passed by, Askaran's counterattack bouncing the tip of his spear harmlessly off the scale plating. Almost as soon as it was beyond him, the monster pivoted. Askaran skirted around it, ducking under the tail to come up behind its back legs as it turned the front winged ones awkwardly. The spear was too long to turn against the slightly thinner underneath from behind. He emerged on the other side and used the demon's own movement to mask his retreat.

Funanya stood a dozen steps back, her spear lowered in a firm stance. "Weaknesses, Askaran?" she shouted.

After six years, he had to run the information through his mind to bring it forward. A winged demon's weight was about three times that of an Ennead, and it could walk on either all fours or the two hind limbs, to free the upper winged limbs for striking with their claws. The neck was plated like that of a tusked demon, and they shared similar horns both from their jaw and from their forehead. The front end was too protected. The answer had to be in the back, but that part of the demon was heavily plated. His kukris could have sliced between them, but he lacked the finesse with the spear and feared the old horn shaft would not sustain the force required.

The colossus demon within him had an easy solution, but Askaran fought back mentally, shoving the cage door in his mind shut with all his force. He could indeed slay the winged demon if he took colossus demon form, but then where would he be? His last shift had almost been the death of everyone, including himself. He dared not, not until he had recovered more.

It was just a winged demon. Even when traveling alone, he had slain them before with his kukris.

As the archon waited for him to answer, Funanya shifted her grip on the spear comfortably, testing the weight.

She knew spears in a way he did not, Askaran realized. She could land the blow.

"It will chase me," he called back. "Get behind it and drive the spear between the scales on the underside!"

Not waiting for a reply, Askaran leaped aside. The monster swept its head to the side, aiming to catch Askaran on one of the largest crown horns. As black blood sprayed from the bleeding eye, Askaran ducked low and rolled clear. He deliberately stayed on its visual side this time, baiting it to follow.

The demon circled to pursue.

He would have liked to lead the winged demon into a good position, but Askaran found himself instead completely on the defensive. His spear saved his life when he was caught near the jaws of the demon. To save its good eye, the monster decided not to lunge in for the killing blow.

While he maneuvered desperately, Askaran was aware of Funanya in the room, but he could not track what she was doing. More often than not, she seemed to get behind the demon, but time and again the spear was deflected by the thick scales. Askaran heard Funanya spit out something that sounded like a curse.

Taking advantage of the boost from a supply chest against the wall, Askaran threw himself over the demon's back and to the other side. The demon followed to its right, toward the wall, and had to spin to catch up. The tail, heavy as a mace, grazed against Askaran's shoulder as the demon came around. By the time Askaran had landed, rolled over his sore shoulder, and regained his feet, the demon was facing him and charging.

Funanya came in from the side, moving as fast as he had ever seen, and slid onto her back in the path of the demon. Askaran froze for a moment longer, delaying just long enough to see her cram the end of the spear into a crack in the stone underfoot. The demon—its goal Askaran—barreled onward.

The moment the demon was upon her, Funanya kicked the tip of the spear up. Braced against the stone, the spear sank into the chest of the demon. At some point, she rolled clear of the impact and came away wearing a tiny spattering of black blood that was dust by the time she stood up.

Askaran threw himself out of the way when the demon went careening past him and collided with the wall, sending clothing flying when it burst open a stone chest.

As the dust settled, Askaran waited for the demon to rise. Nothing moved. The dust was, partially at least, that of the dead demon. Bones were visible amongst strewn clothes.

Funanya had retrieved another spear and came up beside him, holding the new weapon. She nodded her head back toward the entrance.

"There are some knives over there, too. You want your knife back?"

He stood, stunned, as the demon in him settled back from the cage walls and gave up. The threat was gone.

Getting no reply from him, Funanya shrugged and made her way toward the bone pile in the rubble. "Well, I'll grab it. You check on Dana. " She waded into the skeleton, her spear in hand.

The mention of the seer brought Askaran to his senses, and he searched the room. It did not take long; she stuck her head out from behind one of the stone chests. Considering the black blood that had been spraying, Askaran was grateful she had hidden herself.

The seer came out but sat atop the chest instead of approaching. Askaran checked himself over and found a gash, probably from the grazing blow of the tail, on his shoulder.

Funanya returned and handed him the knife. She was covered, from her tiny black braids to her bare feet, in dust. Most, he assumed, would be from the body of the demon. Without the winds of the desert, the dust settled where it could and tinted Funanya's golden skin silver.

"Water there," the seer called, pointing to troughs that had somehow survived the crashing demon. She then pointed to a pile of waterskins.

"Would you mind grabbing it?" Askaran asked Funanya. "I am bleeding. I must not contaminate the water."

Snorting, the Berintan trudged over to the water-skins and selected a few. "Because the spraying blood of the demon wouldn't have done that?" she asked. She peered at the troughs, her nose wrinkled. At the end of the rank, she found a covered one and selected it. She filled all three water-gourds. She threw one to the seer before heading back to Askaran.

So long as she kept clear of the water, where the blood might linger, the seer could move safely through the room now that the demon blood had gone to dust. Her goal was as of yet incomplete, and she lowered herself from the chest and resumed pillaging the room. Askaran watched for a moment before Funanya cleared her throat noisily and lifted the sponge and sewing kit again.

He smiled weakly and took a seat, so she could easily reach his shoulder.

She had scrapes of her own, presumably from sliding along stone to get under the demon, but her red blood had already dried. Her dress was torn to nearly unusable shreds; they would have to find her a change here in the storage room. The sight of a spear in her hand nearby should have upset him, but Askaran instead found himself impressed. She had perfectly timed the blow from under the monster and still managed to get herself clear of being trampled. She possessed similar battle skills as the shifters, but she had none of the shifter assets. How had she moved so fast?

"Stop staring at me," Funanya said after a few moments, and Askaran consciously turned his gaze. He had not meant to simply stare but now realized that was what he had been doing.

"You are dirty," he replied.

The look she gave him made his smile strengthen. "Right, that was what you were looking at," she said. "I get the impression you have never seen a woman fight before."

"Only shifters fight," Askaran explained, feeling guilty that his attention had been so obvious. "It has been many years since a woman shifter walked among us. So no, I have not seen a woman fight in centuries. No other Ennead ever does battle. "

She lifted an eyebrow to him as she cut the thread of the stitching and pulled out yet another bandage to apply over it. "Why not? Did you have so many shifters?"

Askaran shrugged, but that reminded him about the slash on his back. "We never had enough shifters, but the only battles were with demons, so it had to be shifters. No one else could safely fight."

Once she had placed the new bandage, she gestured for him to turn around and, for the first time since they had met, Askaran did not hesitate in turning his back. She removed the bandage from his shoulder to examine the slightly older wound.

"Different," she muttered as she worked. "Among my people, everyone has to fight. There is no other way to advance." He had to assume his back was still holding well, for Funanya replaced the bandage without adjusting the stitching.

When he faced her again, Askaran felt the colossus demon rising but without anger. Her kaftan had slipped and was torn, exposing one breast and most of her legs. Under the powder of demon and stone, her smile was wide. Every muscle she had was outlined by the white, amplifying her form and strength. Askaran was shocked to find the demon wanting to reach for her.

"Well, shifter?" she said, one hand resting atop a hip. "You are clean. Shall we gather some much-needed supplies?" Her eyes ran up and down him briefly. "Or should I let you cool off first?"

He wanted to be ashamed, but the fact that she recognized his sudden excitement only made the demon smirk. Strength, Askaran was slow in realizing, was desirable to the demon. Funanya was the first woman he had ever met who demonstrated such prowess, and it made him lust for her potently.

"I'll get you cleaned up first," Askaran forced himself to say, trying to take a step away in his mind. He was still the master of the relationship between him and the demon. He would not allow it to overrule him, even if it was with desire instead of anger.

Rummaging through the debris, Askaran located a ranna hairbrush. "We've water enough. And we can get you fresh clothing."

Her smile brought a grin to Askaran's face. To his delight, she took her turn, presenting her back to him for assessment, dropping the kaftan off her shoulders.

Using the brush, he cleaned her skin of the dust and debris. When he was finished with her back, Funanya pulled up her kaftan and gave Askaran a leading look.

"I can handle the front, thank you," she told him, snatching the brush before he could find words. "Just find me something else to wear, would you?"

As much as his demon wanted to argue, with words or with claws, Askaran smothered the emotions and backed away. He found the seer, her bag newly packed, waiting. Atop her bag, she had folded a simple blue-dyed linen dress. When he arrived at her side, she extended her hand for Funanya's bag and began filling it anew.

"Food?" he asked.

"Nothing that survived this long," she replied. Askaran consciously kept his back to Funanya as they spoke. "But a change of clothing for you, and sandals for everyone." Cocking her head with a smile, the seer added, "And there are weapons by the door, better than the ones you stole from the Berintans. Why don't you pick up a few? I'll give Funanya her dress."

Askaran watched the seer snatch up the linen dress and dart away. Below it, he found the original wood-handled kukri and took it. Thinking better of glancing at the women, he aimed for the weapon racks and selected a second kukri to complement his mother's old one. It made him miss the second kukri she had given him, but that grief was six years old and not fresh enough to bother him. There was even oil, and he collected it with plans to hydrate the stiff leather bindings as best he could. By the time he was done, Funanya was dressed and was inspecting the weapons. She had left her last spear in the demon. Askaran assumed it was too damaged to be of use again.

It was odd to see her without bones, beads, and claws decorating her. Where the Berintans wore patterned cloth, Ennead linen gently wove between colors, drifting in hues but not forming patterns. The simple dress hung from the shoulders to the ankles, the only break in the pale sky color the lashes over the shoulders to hold it in place.

The Berintan was in the process of tying a man's belt over the fine gown. The contrast made Askaran wince.

"Definitely not designed for battle," Funanya informed him, cinching up the belt. She placed her retrieved knife into the holster she had threaded onto the belt, then hiked up the dress. After testing the stretch of the fabric, the archon cut a slit in the dress to free her legs. To properly gain full mobility, she had to cut one in each side, leaving her golden skin visible from ankle to hip.

She caught his stare on her leg and added, "This is why we don't fight in kaftans. Miss my armor, but at least this fits. The rest of the outfits here don't allow for breasts!"

"Designed for shifters," Askaran admitted, fitting his own new belt in place and placing the kukris in their new home. He selected another dagger to add to the collection, a short blade practical for skinning or eating.

"If only shifters came out this far, why is there a dress at all? Shifters liked dresses too, did they?" Funanya asked, pursing her lips at him and lifting her hem as an example.

"One of the women's," Askaran replied. "We can trim it if you want it shorter. The seer has found you sandals, too. We'll bring wraps to cover our legs once out in the sands." He paused. "Of course, you probably don't need them. You won't be crossing into the desert with us."

"We'll bring them anyway," Funanya said, testing the balance of a new spear expertly. Askaran had left the spears behind, finding their use too foreign for him. He had never thrown a spear accurately in his life but preferred the close nature of the arched, wide blade of the kukris that better matched the demon's claws.

"We don't know where these tunnels will bring us out. Could be I will have to cross some sands." Funanya glanced at Askaran down the shaft of the spear as she checked for bends. "What women? You said women didn't fight."

"Women wishing to be chamoot," Askaran replied.

Funanya decided the spear shaft was too twisted and replaced it. She selected another as Dana helpfully added, "The women wishing to be mothers to shifters."

Funanya examined the new spear with a raised eyebrow to Askaran. "They mothered you?"

"Women who wished to bear shifters. To bear a child with shifter blood," he clarified.

Based on finding a dress among the supplies in the cavern lining the Valley of Vaseil, he had to assume the practice of the chamoots had been among the Enneads since the first shifters.

Despite living among the Berintans, Askaran had never seen a Berintan child. The jungle people matched up for fun, yet none were ever pregnant or nursing children. The youngest he had seen had been a young man looking about sixteen who had arrived with a caravan, although he'd not been able to ask about it in his role as a slave. He'd decided that children must be born elsewhere in their society, although now he doubted even that.

Funanya cracked a huge grin. "They had a breeding program for shifters? Like picking the best bull for a herd of taurens!" she exclaimed. Selecting her spear, she found knives to add to her collection as she added, "You enjoy that, shifter?"

Askaran shrugged.

CHAPTER 16

The demon was strangely content as they left the room, but Funanya seemed to be looking at him differently. Askaran was not yet sure what to make of it.

CHAPTER 17

The halls that led out of the room were no longer cut from the stone but built up in bricks. Here, intricate murals made panels on either side, the open grooves showing where precious metals would have been laid. The scenes were waterfalls and lush jungles, with ranna beasts roaming in open fields and strange furry flying creatures skittering along the trees. Although Askaran and Dana seemed determined to press on without pause, Funanya fought to examine the decorations as she walked under glimm moss light.

There was immense skill in the shape and detail of the cementum stone carvings, and each was unique. She saw Enneads in the scenes as they moved along, usually children playing with odd toys in ring shapes, or families harvesting fruits from strange plants. Clouds drifted on clear skies over the woven canopies, which reminded her sharply of the forest of her home.

But as she examined the details, there were profound differences. No wolfen or tauran were depicted; all the beasts had hairy coats like ranna beasts instead of scales. The leaves on the trees were thin and long, unlike the broad leaves of her jungle. Where she expected cattail plants along a stream, she saw tiny spiny trees.

The corridor branched and opened into rooms at random. The seer led the way, picking a path that walked them into more corridors and more rooms. Although they found the occasional intact chest or bag at first, as they progressed, the rooms and halls became entirely empty, stripped of all useful things centuries before. Under the dust, carvings remained.

After hours of walking empty, deserted halls, Funanya finally asked, "Who made these?"

The shifter glanced back, with his unnatural eyes easily seeing through the shadows between them. "Enneads," he replied simply, before continuing down the hallway. They passed another room, but it was starkly empty. A few trap lizards had made a home within; their sticky nests were arranged around the cracks in the walls, awaiting grubs but coating the walls in fibrous white webs. The dust proved that nothing besides the lizards had moved in the room for a long time.

"I thought you didn't leave your city," Funanya replied, skipping after the Ennead when she realized he was not waiting for her to finish checking out the room they had passed. Another tattered hide door across the hall showed a similar scene of abandoned, empty rooms. In the hallway, a new mural stretched on in the pale light. The trim showed chisel marks, Funanya assumed, from taking the gold trim out of its inset.

Askaran glanced over his shoulder, then shrugged and carried on, leaving Funanya and Dana walking side by side.

"Enneads are fine crafters," Dana replied, holding back long enough to let Funanya catch up. "We weave, smelt gold, create glass—" Her eyes went to the next carven panel, where a huge creature, looking like a hairy keim beast with fangs like a wolfen, was depicted. "—and we carved natural stone. In the desert, we lost that art. Cloth could be made from ranna beast hair, and gold dug from the sand, or the sand melted into glass, but we had little stone once we dug down as far as we could. So we have not made carvings for years."

Funanya lifted the light over the snarling visage of the creature in the panel. The eyes still had gold in them and glittered like a Berintan's skin under the glimm moss.

"What is it?"

Dana paused beside her, peering up at the short-nosed creature with tall, vertical ears tipped with tufts of hair. Its wide stare had the look of a predator.

"I think it's a hound," she said.

"Like the demon?" Funanya replied. This beast seemed larger than any hound demon she had seen, and it had fur, not bone plates, but the resemblance was there.

"The demon was named after it. Some say a binding of souls created the demon from the animal, but the eyes—"

"Seer," the shifter's voice gently interrupted from down the corridor, "those are stories." Funanya thought she heard disapproval in his voice.

The look Dana gave the shifter made Askaran stand a little straighter, for a moment uncertain. "Hiding, are we?" she said, her tone heavy and not entirely her own.

"Hiding things. Things I cannot see. So all I have are stories."

The shifter seemed to contemplate saying something more but after a long pause, simply turned down the dark corridor and walked on.

Dana scowled deeply and muttered, "I can't see seers and demons. This is one of those. You don't want to talk about it. But you know, Askaran. You know. You just won't tell me."

She followed Askaran down the hallway in silence, leaving Funanya for a moment alone with the hound.

The glittering eyes of the beast stared through her.

The day passed in silent corridors, but as the march ended, the seer led them to where the desolate path opened into a huge hall.

While Funanya's tiny jar of glimm moss carried light only a few paces, Askaran's sight easily extended well beyond. The hall was a cavern, vast enough to make the ceiling out of stalactites as long as he was tall. Pillars reached up, each a unique construction. Here the patterns were vines and tree trunks, as if the ceiling would reveal leaves and follon apes among the pretend canopy. Various tiny animals were concealed in the patterns, peeking out from behind cover to watch the intruders. Their golden eyes gave them away.

Askaran waited as they entered, allowing the seer to go first. She paused, her eyes passing through the huge space. He assumed the manner with which she examined the room required no light.

She chose a direction and walked on. Under their feet, cracked shale and pebbles made spattering echoes that carried forever uninterrupted.

For once, Funanya was silent, and Askaran was grateful. He dreaded answering either woman's questions.

"We have to stop, take food and water," the Berintan objected after another hour had passed without any indication that the seer was looking for a place to set camp or sleep. The day had passed; they were approaching dusk. The seer seemed ready to walk on and on.

Their camp would be sparse and required nothing but somewhere to sit and lie flat. The food they carried would have to be eaten as they had it; they had no fuel except small fire starters with which to cook, and no sun overhead to use a cooking shield. Water would fast become their most prized resource. Already they were through a quarter of what they could carry and had seen none since leaving the river-side room at the start of the day.

The seer seemed surprised at the interruption, but once she had focused herself, agreed with the Berintan. Beside a pillar, one carved as a twisting shaben trunk, the bark in peeling strips, they sat down.

Askaran eyed the glimm moss jar as Funanya set it to one side, freeing her hands to undo her sandals.

"How long do they last?" he asked, indicating the jar.

"Several weeks usually," she replied with a shrug. "We'll water them in the morning; no point in having brighter light while we sleep." She slipped down the pillar and sat propped up with her spear across her knees. Strangely, he did not feel threatened.

The demon within him snarled, but the emotions were mixed, like a tauran male scenting a female in his territory. On the one hand, he wanted to drive away the competition. On the other, he could never have off-spring if he chased away all others of his species.

Askaran shook his head to clear it. She was no demon, and so no threat. The threat had been dealt with earlier today, and although the presence of the colossus demon lingered in Askaran's mind, there remained little anger.

As he made to sit and remove his own shoes, the seer presented him with a water-gourd and a knowing smile. Uncorking the gourd, Askaran took a long drink of dredge before even bothering to eat.

Funanya raised one eyebrow.

"Getting drunk again? Did I fail to notice you shift?"

Between chews of tauran meat, Askaran replied, "Had to fight a demon. My demon hates that."

"Askaran hates that?" she asked, goading him with a smile.

"More than anything," he admitted. "Askaran is territorial."

He liked the glimmer in her eyes as she leaned for-ward from the pillar.

"Any excuse to get drunk," she said, lifting the gourd from his hand and taking her own swig. Unlike him, she handled the alcohol smoothly, smacking her lips once before corking it and leaning back. Askaran sat dumbfounded for a moment. "I guess you were right," Funanya said. "This stuff does make the demon quiet."

Heeding the warning, Askaran ate sparingly and found a place to rest near the seer. He was not sur-prised that she, while he and Funanya bantered, had propped herself against a fallen pillar, wrapped the cloak around herself, and immediately fallen asleep.

He watched the seer as an excuse not to look at the exposed legs of the Berintan with them. The seer's energy was clearly wearing thin, yet she did not seem to have noticed. Had Funanya not prompted them to stop, the seer would have kept going with no regard for the failing of her own body. She had become strong in the jungle of Douran, but that strength was fading quickly. He had thought it a product of the darkness of the Night Road, but now it seemed more than that. She had fallen asleep without eating or drinking. Askaran could not remember if the seer had eaten the morning meal either.

As he stared at her, the seer drew a sudden deep breath and released it as a slow whimper that made Askaran's heart ache. In a muttered voice he had learned to heed, she said, "Don't let her fall."

Askaran glanced at Funanya, but the Berintan had not moved and did not seem to have heard the seer's instructions. The words had been meant for Askaran alone.

Fall? Fall from their influence? Fall in death? Askaran did not understand.

Promising to monitor the seer's health a bit more closely, Askaran positioned himself facing back the way they had come.

The sight of Funanya sitting propped up, her legs bent and exposed, her cut dress falling between her knees, was the last thing in Askaran's mind as he drifted off.

The demon remained oddly silent.

Funanya instinctually swung at the person who prodded her awake, but the person caught her wrist and pulled her up short. Before she had managed to open her eyes, a hand was covering her mouth, and she felt the press of a body against her, keeping her prone.

Memories of the Night Road and the tunnels of the Valley of Vaseil cascaded into her blurry mind. She opened her eyes and found Askaran, his hand pressed carefully over her mouth to keep her from making a sound. Behind him, the seer crawled up, keeping to the cover of a fallen pillar.

Funanya nodded to show she was awake, and the shifter pulled away, leaving her skin warm where he had touched it.

"We must go, now," Askaran whispered. "Someone is in the cavern. They are heading on a tangent to us, but we cannot risk staying here."

It was a simple thing to collect the bags and, staying low, slink away. They kept the glimm moss jar covered and moved in the darkness by touch. Funanya did not see their pursuers but followed Askaran's lead, counting on him to see far enough into the darkness.

She felt the air freshen as they left the shadows of the pillared area and could make out the dark silhouette of a structure ahead of them. That there was sufficient light implied some moonlight or sunlight was sneaking through the cracks of the stone, making Funanya believe that the surface was not far.

Funanya felt her spirits lift at that prospect.

As her hope rose, the tiles beneath her feet gave way.

Lunging instinctually, Funanya threw herself as far forward as she could, but she found nothing beneath her and dropped. Her flailing right hand, for a moment, felt the edge of the hole but the smooth tiles gave no handholds, and she felt the cold stone slip across her palm.

She fell long enough to recognize the fall and know with defeated frustration that she was going to die in the dark after all. But before she could decide which curse to use, she struck a ledge, and her thoughts were jarred loose. She slipped off that outcropping, but it slowed her enough that, when she next bounced into the uneven surface of the walls, she managed to catch a handhold and stabilize herself. Her bag thumped into her hip and made a tinkling noise, the glass within shattered.

The stones of the floor she had so recently been walking upon continued their fall. It was another long while before she heard them strike bottom.

The slight moonlight from the room above was gone at this depth. By touch, Funanya found the edges of her ledge and discovered she had been uncommonly lucky; the ledge was a hand's width wide, and barely long enough for her to sit upon while being solid enough to hold her weight. While she felt her shoulder and left arm had been badly bruised, it did not feel dislocated when she tested its movement.

She rummaged in the bag, hoping she had been wrong, but found only glass shards and moist moss. Spread thin, the glimm moss did not have any glow left.

Looking up into the darkness, Funanya could see the irregular hole where she had tumbled. A darker shadow—someone's head—briefly appeared at the opening, giving her finally a reference for the size of the opening and, by assessment, how far she had fallen.

The head withdrew without a word.

Of course, he would say nothing, Funanya thought. Even if the shifter could see her, their pursuers were too close to risk speaking aloud. They would have to work silently. They had rope, although how she would see it to grab it, Funanya did not know. The irregularity of the pit would make it difficult, without a doubt, for anyone to climb, and she didn't think any approach would allow them to pull her up, even if they…

For a moment, Funanya relived the feeling of falling. There was no reason for the shifter and Dana to aid her. They had recently found a balance in their relationship where neither attempted to kill the other, but taking on the risk of rescuing her when the Berintans chasing them were so close on their heels was foolish. Askaran would defend the seer. He had always done so. Now, that meant leaving as quickly as he could.

The dark felt heavy around Funanya. She had lived in the Night Road without fear, but this darkness was thicker. She felt, for a moment, that the walls leaned in, each side just far enough to be out of reach but close enough to press against her, stifling her air. And below her was a crevice, an impossible drop that would give her time enough to contemplate the terrible end before smashing her bones into the depths.

She was trapped. Her only comfort was the fact that she could leap to her death before dying of thirst.

Turning her back to the drop, Funanya felt again at the wall behind her. The stone was vertical, made of splintering stacks of weak rock. As she groped for footholds, the stone gave way in her hands, too fragile to hold her weight. Her hands came away wet.

With the water, she would not die of thirst either. So it would be hunger or the fall.

Torchlight appeared above, and Funanya shrank against the wall further. This time voices were present, and the words carried a Berintan accent. More silhouettes appeared overhead, the details of their golden faces lost in the glare of the light. Their voices were distorted by the echoes of the uneven surface of the crevice, but she heard their conversation clearly enough.

"Fresh," one hunter said. "Someone was here."

"You think they went down?" the second replied.

Funanya shuffled back as far as she could, feeling the cold damp of the cliff against her exposed back. The first hunter lifted his torch, shining the light as far down as he could.

"Maybe…"

To her horror, they released the torch, their eyes following it down into the dark.

Funanya dropped into a precarious crouch, grabbed the hem of her skirt, and pulled it over her head from behind, hoping that the dusted gown had lost sufficient luster to blend into the stone. At the least, she would not look like a human shape.

The torchlight gave her, briefly, a glance at her surroundings, and she felt her heart drop. Across from her, the cliff had an enormous overhang a pace above her level, which jutted out to a distance almost two strides away. The rest of the crevice was wide until the top, where it had been tiled over. She assumed the water seeping through the stone had eroded the weaker stone, leaving a thin layer—the tiles—above. The others had been lucky to avoid stepping on the weakened part, but Funanya's weight had brought the floor down.

She dared not peer down after the torch, afraid of making a silhouette for the hunters above to see, but she was disappointed by how long it took for the clatter of the torch to reach the bottom of the long well.

"If they went down, they're dead," the first hunter said. "Come on."

The heads withdrew, and a second light went with them. Soon, only the dim glow of the filtered moonlight was seen above, and Funanya was plunged back into suffocating blackness.

With the overhang, she was not even certain Askaran could have seen where she had fallen. Even if he had wanted to help her, he probably believed her dead.

Funanya drew back her skirt and sat on the ledge. The cold of the stone seeped into her bones, but she ignored it, looking up at the moonlight in frustration.

For the first time in decades, Funanya felt tears burn in her eyes.

When the clattering of the ground giving out reached Askaran, he immediately grabbed the seer and dragged her away from the weak floor. He covered her mouth, stifling the cry she gave at seeing Funanya plummet through the floor, but it was not enough; the distant torchlight of the Berintans they had been fleeing adjusted to investigate the noise.

"Stay hidden and silent," Askaran commanded the seer, shoving her behind a pillar made in the likeness of clouds. Sprinting, Askaran made it to the hole and discovered that one side was solid for his weight, while other sides continued to crumble if he so much as leaned toward it. He quickly peered down the hole that had been created.

While the hole itself was narrow enough to be jumped, the gap below expanded quickly to several strides wide. Directly below him, the cliff was straight and sheer, but after a dozen paces, it slanted into an outcropping. Below the peak of the overhang, on the opposite wall, he was unexpectedly pleased to see Funanya.

She was bleeding from a series of cuts but stared up at him, her eyes narrowed in annoyance at her predicament.

Below her, the pit continued infinitely, even to his eyes.

The voices of the Berintans came to him, and Askaran withdrew before their light reached the pit, scuffing the trail both to and from the pit as he went. Joining the seer behind the pillar, Askaran hid.

When the seer stared up at him, Askaran felt her fear. He had expected her to give him directions but soon recognized his mistake. The seer had come to quickly like Funanya. Perhaps it was nothing more than the desperation of a lonely child who had at last met someone who showed interest in her, but Funanya was now the girl's friend.

Commands were not required. It was obvious to the girl, to Dana, what had to be done.

Don't let her fall.

Working in silence as the Berintans approached the pit and inspected it, Askaran retrieved the rope from the seer's bag and roughly measured it out. It would be close, and he did not think there was enough length to both reach Funanya and tie it around her. With her injuries, could she hold on long enough? He could risk not tying the end at the top and brace it himself, but if his hands slipped, she would fall. And he still wasn't certain he could get the rope to her on the far side of the well. The area above her was too fragile. How could he toss it accurately and expect a woman sitting in the pitch dark to catch it?

The only way, Askaran realized, was to climb down himself. He could tie the top but make up the lost length himself. He could carry the rope to her.

He waited for the Berintans to leave after they had tossed a light down the hole. Askaran wondered what he would do should they discover Funanya. Would he fight the Berintans? He could shift, but his duty to the seer was unfinished. Still, Askaran kept thinking of Dana's voice in half-sleep, repeating, "Don't let her fall." Did that mean he would have to fight these Berintans if they made an attempt at killing Funanya?

The problem never manifested. Seeing nothing, the Berintans returned to the track they had been following.

Askaran skirted around the pillar in silence. The Berintans moved on, apparently following no given trail except a general sense of the direction their quarry was traveling.

After a hundred paces, they decided loudly to rest and allow more of their party to catch up.

Askaran secured the rope to a part of the pillar's cloud formations, then tied the end around himself so that he could easily grasp it later in case he was wrong about the distance. Leaving the seer hidden, Askaran slithered along the ground to the solid side of the hole and began the arduous climb down.

In some ways, climbing down was harder than climbing up. His muscles, he was certain, were designed to go forward, not backward, and he found it awkward to lower himself down the cliff, struggling to control his slide along the outcropping. He had made it to the tip of the outcropping when his rope went taut.

Finding a solid foothold, Askaran stood tall and released the rope from around his waist. He held the end in one hand and extended himself over the out-cropping, reaching his hand to Funanya.

The Berintan stood on her ledge for a moment staring toward him, but not at him, unable to see well enough in the darkness. He clearly saw her expression of dis-belief. Tears had left tracks down her usually composed face, but her eyes were wide and determined now.

"Give me your hand," Askaran said. When she reached out blindly, he had to direct, "Higher. You have a bit more space on the ledge; come forward." She shuffled her feet forward cautiously, her hand lifted above her head.

For a moment, Askaran was struck by her faith in him. He could have lied to her, told her that she should lean forward and let her fall. He could kill her without ever having to lift a weapon against her.

Don't let her fall.

Askaran crouched and, reaching one final inch, grasped Funanya's wrist. She instantly grabbed at his and, with absolute confidence in him, allowed him to pull her across the drop and onto the outcropping.

She threw her arms around his shoulders, using his steady footing to balance herself. Releasing her, Askaran tied the rope once more around his waist.

"You'll have to hold onto—"

Berintan voices came from overhead.

Askaran glanced up. The light of approaching torches reached over the hole, lighting the distant ceiling in amber. The senses of the demon allowed Askaran to hear them talking.

"Heard something over here," someone above them said.

Askaran turned sharply. "Hold on," he told Funanya. He checked that she had a good grip around his neck but, once satisfied, grabbed the rope and used it to give him handholds on his way up.

She lay against his back, her legs hooked over his hips, and said nothing. With the strength of demons helping him, Askaran hardly noticed her weight, but he did think it odd that the demon within him had not yet reacted to the presence of enemies. He had fought with the demon throughout their flight that morning, but now that the enemy was about to be standing above him, the demon had gone silent. Instead of being rankled by the Berintans, the demon felt … content?

Askaran had to convince himself to be ready for combat. He had spent so much time placating such emotions, it felt unnatural to be cultivating the ideas.

He could not be in the hole when they arrived, he decided, climbing swiftly. He would be seen, and the Berintans would have the advantage. He needed to be within reach of them by the time they saw him, but as he pulled himself up out of the pit, he knew he would not be fast enough. Instead, they would reach the hole at the same time that he reached the top.

"I'm on it," Funanya whispered. Her breath on his ear made him notice not her weight, but her closeness. Hooking her hips tightly around him briefly, she released one hand and reached for his waist. She freed one of his kukris from his belt and brought it up to her mouth.

He understood perfectly. For a moment, he felt like he was fighting alongside another shifter, someone he had known for decades. He knew what Funanya was planning and knew how to complement it.

They reached the crest of the cliff. Forgoing the rope, Askaran planted his grip on the edge and held firm, allowing Funanya to climb up him, onto the solid tiles above, and immediately attack the Berintans.

Everything happened in a blink. She was up and among the party of four Berintans instantly. Askaran pulled himself up, but already two Berintans were dead on the tiles, their throats cut. The third faced Funanya, while the fourth tried to come up behind her. In doing so the Berintan put his back to Askaran. Askaran's strike with his second kukri neatly disconnected the man's spine. The Berintan collapsed sideways, slipping into the hole and vanishing.

No longer taken by surprise, the last Berintan was matching Funanya's skills with his spear and shield. He could not, however, match Askaran's strength when the shifter crashed against the shield, knocked the man over, and cut through his shoulder. He silenced the cries of agony with a final stroke.

He checked the surroundings but saw no other signs of Berintans yet. Finally, he let his guard down and turned back to Funanya.

The Berintan woman briefly opened her mouth as if to say something important, but hesitated. Instead, with a toss of her head, she declared, "I'm not used to your silly knife. Give me a spear, and I would've had all four by the time you got up here."

She tossed the kukri to him, then dropped down to pillage the remaining bodies. "And try not to throw loot away like that," she said, gesturing to the hole where Askaran's first victim had fallen. "So wasteful."

Askaran smiled, and the demon in him growled as if taking offense at his amusement. Funanya was so busy searching the bodies that she entirely missed the approach of the seer, who threw herself at the Berintan from behind in an enthusiastic hug. Both women were soon on the tiles, tangled. Funanya squawked in outrage but was laughing too hard for the ire to be believed.

"I'm on it," Askaran replied, wading in to pull the seer off. He set both women on their feet.

For a moment, he met Funanya's eyes, and he again felt that connection of camaraderie.

It was not a feeling he trusted, not after so many years alone.

He pointed the way they had been heading and said, "We need to get going. There will be more of them."

The party moved on, but Askaran noticed they all had more energy in their steps now.

CHAPTER 18

The exit from the caverns approached as an intensifying light. With every step, like an artificial dawn, the light brightened. The thought of being out of darkness lent strength and speed to Funanya's steps. She felt ready to skip in her excitement.

"Will you come with us?" Dana asked. The shorter girl was verily jogging to keep pace with Funanya's long strides.

"With you?" Funanya echoed, a little surprised. As she considered the question, it lost its unexpectedness and gained value. "Where?"

Dana glanced back at the shifter, who nodded approval. Although Funanya herself still did not understand the question, it was evident Askaran did.

"Well, you are free to go," Dana said cautiously. "You said you would go until the desert. This leads to the southern edge of the desert. You can go south, you see. You could. But we're going to go north, back home. I want you to come. I know you'd like it."

"Do you know?" Askaran asked from behind them. "Or do you *know*, Seer?"

The girl bobbed her head lightly. "I *know* Askaran." She held Funanya's hand gently. "I also *know* why I am needed in the City." She glared at Askaran pointedly. "And I would appreciate a friend there to help defend the City from the enemy." She smiled at Funanya widely, her eyes childlike once more. "I also *know* that you don't understand us, Funanya. I *know* you don't believe in the seers. But please believe me when I say that you belong with us, not with them. I … I don't exactly know how or why yet, but it's true."

Funanya's throat went dry, despite having recently refilled their water from their pursuers. The young woman was so damn sincere it pained her. How could someone so tied to war and fear be innocent like that?

The big dark eyes looked up at her, pleading.

She could go back, she thought. Without her face painted, Funanya could invent a name and start again. She would probably have to fall back on her Night Road beginnings. Archons did not favor people from the Night Road for that reason; without references, they could be anyone. They could be failed warriors or thieves. In her case, they could be a deposed archon.

But with her skills, she could still become powerful and influential. She had done it once already.

The seer's sweet entreaties twisted the thought in Funanya's mind. The Night Road, although familiar, contained no such friendly faces. She would be alone again.

When she glanced behind her, that thought hurt more. Askaran tilted his head toward her in query, meeting her gaze and still wearing a slight smile.

No one in the Night Road would have risked so much to help her out of a pit. No one would have waited for her.

"I will come with you," she said.

Dana squawked in joy and grabbed Funanya in a hug without breaking stride. Feeling like she had been tackled, Funanya struggled to keep her feet moving.

"I am so happy! You are important, and you are my friend. Thank you for staying with us!"

Funanya could not decide which state—important or friend—was more unexpected.

They walked awkwardly for a few steps before the seer finally released the embrace. Funanya thought she had simply decided to carry on without tangling her feet, but the girl came to a complete halt. Before Funanya could ask what was wrong, Askaran had moved up beside the girl. Funanya spotted a blade in his hand.

"The light…" she whispered.

The shadows must have been huge to impede the light at this distance, but it was unquestionably there and then gone.

Something large had come through the entrance.

Askaran's eyes were bright red as he gazed ahead, his monster obviously rising.

"A demon," he said, his voice tightly controlled. She had heard the tone before. When a fight loomed, Askaran became rigid. He could still move with the speed of a keim beast, but the action was precise and short as if no room remained for anything else.

When the sounds of voices reached them, it became obvious that the demon ahead was not alone. Berintan voices cast echoes into the large hall, bouncing between the pillars but unfailingly coming from the exit.

"Can we go around?" Funanya asked Dana. "Is there another exit?"

The seer's expression was crestfallen, her eyes wide and brimming with tears.

"She can't see it," Askaran explained. "It involves a demon and, if my suspicions are correct, a seer. She would have seen it sooner, when the shifter was in Ennead form, unless a seer was with them."

With Askaran joining them, the three fugitives stood side by side, staring toward the flickering light. Soon enough, the flickering stopped. The light, calling them on, remained.

"He's done it on purpose," Dana whimpered, her lips pressed together in concentration. "He shifted, so I couldn't see."

"Yarr can move quickly," Askaran warned, placing a hand on each woman's shoulder and guiding them to the left. "Get going. Funanya, lead her on. She's blind to their movements, so don't count on her to know the way until you are through the exit." As he spoke, Askaran stripped off his shendyt and removed his kukris, handing them to Funanya for safekeeping. Stark naked, he turned to face the light.

"You're going to do what? Fight him?"

"Delay him and distract them all," Askaran replied, his voice like a taut hanging line, tense but at the same time mundane. "Kill him if I can." The shifter glanced over his shoulder, his eyes deep, blood red. "Run. Please, get her home."

A roar shook the air, then the stones. Parts of the ceiling crumbled, and sections of the unstable tiled floor collapsed in the distance. Water had worn away the stone beneath, leaving jagged edges of stone and debris like the pit Funanya had found earlier.

In the distance, a huge shape loped toward them, delayed by the crumbling floor but not for more than a moment. Leaping and clawing its way through the debris, knocking pillars as it went, a tusked demon barreled down on their location.

Knowing such a monster could follow their scent even if they concealed themselves, Funanya pulled on Dana's arm and led the girl away at a sprint.

Dread crept over Funanya. Askaran was bigger and stronger. Why had he said, "Kill him if I can?" There should have been no doubt.

But he was still avoiding his demon, Funanya knew. His choice to accept it sounded like a decision to never return.

Assuming he kept the enemies busy for long enough, Funanya and Dana could skirt around and reach the light. Once in the desert, she thought the girl would be likely to gather her senses and lead the way, even if she could not see where the pursuers were.

She ignored the logical part of her mind that reminded her that a demon would be hunting them across the desert and that any tusked demon could easily outrun a pair of women.

Without an alternative, Funanya pulled the seer along behind her. Counting on the battle of demons to distract the other Berintans, she swung around the pillars and made a run for the light.

Dana followed, tears streaming down her face. "Goodbye, Askaran," she whispered.

At first, it seemed the demon would not come out to Askaran's command. As if teasing him, the colossus demon leaned back in the shifter's mind, watching the approaching tusked demon with interest and little emotion. But once the women had made their escape, the colossus demon seemed to wake. It looked around as if looking for something and, annoyed at not finding it, snarled.

Using that frustration, Askaran brought the demon to the front of his mind and, tying his mental tether to the monster, let it loose.

The shift was faster than before, his body stretching and changing painfully this time. The demon's mind lurched into action, straining Askaran's tether. He had to dig in his heels and set himself against the pull lest he be pulled off his feet and out of control.

The strain on the tether was more than he had ever felt before. He had expected the demon to be strong—it always was—but the creature had been run recently and had been quieter than usual until now. He had thought the journey had pleased it, but he was quickly recognizing the truth.

The demon within him had been biding its time. It knew exactly when Askaran's strength had waned suf-ficiently. It had been awaiting the moment.

The tether snapped in Askaran's mind.

Driven by fury and no longer contained at all, the colossus demon charged Yarr, and Askaran watched on from within their shared mind, helpless. The demon didn't consider the floors, stumbling more than once as parts of the tiles gave out under its titanic weight. Its size, too large to fit down any of the rifts it created, saved it from falling into the distant abyss. It plowed down the pillars, crushing centuries of craftsmanship into dust and destabilizing the distant ceiling further. The tusked demon came to a halt, knowing that to charge back was not in its favor and, like the clever Ennead it was, positioned itself to deflect the impact.

Sure enough, when the colossus demon crashed its immense shoulder into its target, Yarr turned the blow off his plated shoulder. Askaran crashed into a pillar instead.

Without the momentum of the charge, now it was claw, horns, and teeth. Clumsy in fury, the colossus demon relied on its thick hide to take the cut of raking claws. Yarr was skilled; he angled the attack up, finding a gap in the plating and hitting skin. Black blood seeped from the wound. Askaran wailed in frustration and surprise.

It was not accustomed to pain. In all the battles with the demons, few had ever managed to score a hit against them.

Askaran's beast retaliated, slamming both forelimbs down upon Yarr's neck. The long spikes over the spine there pierced into the colossus demon's hands, and Yarr managed to duck aside before the strike landed beyond that. So fast was he, the weight of the colossus demon fell past him.

The tusked demon rotated, slamming its tail into the colossus demon's face, slashing his cheek open. Askaran caught the tail, pulling Yarr back from his quick escape, but just as he thought the demon would be able to slow Yarr down, he realized that Yarr had deliberately allowed the grapple. It kept the colossus demon from being able to adjust his weight.

Moving in a manner Askaran had never seen, the tusked demon folded down and twisted. Following his tail back, he was suddenly under the colossus demon.

And with its front legs extended, Yarr could stab his mammoth tusks into the sternum, aiming for the heart.

Instincts saved the colossus demon. It launched itself backward, delayed by the hold on the tail but abandoning any chance at attacking back. The blow to the heart missed, but the tusk rammed into his chin instead. Askaran felt jarred, his mind fuzzy.

When he regained his senses, his mind felt strangely quiet.

The demon's mind had not recovered as swiftly. For a moment, Askaran had control.

He knew fighting Yarr was death. An Ennead's mind was faster and cleverer than that of a demon. If the colossus demon stayed, it would be killed, Askaran with it. He had only a moment before the demon regained control.

But the roof was already unstable. A cave-in favored neither of them.

Askaran charged the nearest pillar and tore it down. He managed to destroy one more before the ground gave out from under him, the entire world tilted, and he was falling, surrounded by a crumbling ceiling, tiles, and pillars.

He had wondered how deep Funanya's pit had been. Trapped in a crashing rain of stone that, with finality, destroyed the floor of the cavern, he found out.

Dana started crying before they reached the light, certainly knowing more about what was happening behind them than Funanya did. Still, she feared the worst and fought to press on. The entire cavern was coming down around her. All she could hear was Askaran's voice repeating, "Run. Please, get her home."

When Dana's feet slipped, Funanya scooped the girl up and pulled her along. Eventually, she threw her over a shoulder. She had carried warriors in this manner, those sworn to her. The small girl was nothing by comparison.

She stopped trying to watch for the other Berintans she knew had to be somewhere near the entrance but just ran. Instead of people, she was dodging falling stones and uneven tiles. She caught glimpses of the others on occasion, but they were on the run as well, too busy escaping the collateral damage from the demons' battle to chase her. The final crash, followed by a howl of rage, deafened her as she burst out of the underground hall and into the full light of the sun.

The ceiling crashed down behind her, burying anyone who had not been as quick. She spotted two other survivors, each too occupied to pay her heed as she bolted from the area.

Funanya aimed for the desert and resumed her run, Dana sobbing on her shoulder. She spotted an Ennead woman, rotund and dressed in a colorful kaftan, sitting atop a short pillar where the broken road ended. Her black eyes seemed to bore into Funanya with every step the Berintan took, but the woman made no move to rise from her seat. Funanya rushed by her, pleased she did not have to fight her way out. The Berintans were too occupied unburying each other.

It was not until after, when Funanya and Dana had reached the rock-ridden, windswept edge of the desert and taken refuge behind the buttes and columns, that Funanya realized the Ennead on the pillar had spoken. She had seen the woman's mouth move, but Funanya's ears had still been ringing from the roars. She had no idea what had been said.

Once her legs would carry them no farther, Funanya threw the sand-cloak over their hiding place and waited until her heart stopped thundering. With the blurry memories of their run—of dodging collapsing stone and skirting along floors—she tried to make some sense of the last hour, but it all kept going back to the Ennead in the kaftan by the entrance.

At length, as her mind calmed and sanity returned, Funanya recognized the woman as the desert seer who had been with Farai.

If she were an ally of Farai's, why had she not tried to stop them? She had spoken to them, not sounding an alarm or calling for others.

When there was no sign of pursuit, Funanya pulled off the sand-cloak and slowly eased from hiding.

If the seer were not an ally of Farai's, would she mention she had seen the two women escape the cave? Or would she lie? Would they believe Dana and Funanya were dead?

The wind circled the column where they had taken cover, picking up stones and prickling Funanya with them.

"Come on," Funanya said, rising and pulling out the desert cloak. She wrapped herself in it, then adjusted the seer's sand-cloak so that she was well protected from the wind and sand. "We can make good use of the chill of tonight to get some distance under our feet."

Mute, the girl nodded. Her dark eyes swept over the hamada like a hunter scanning for game. Her chin lifted proudly. Dana began walking. Funanya followed, keeping one eye behind them for pursuit and one eye on the sky for scavengers. She had not forgotten the trick Askaran had taught her about watching the animals of the desert.

They walked in silence until the suns had vanished. Once it was quiet, they walked on in the desert, and Dana started humming a tune. When the wind lost all heat, they were forced to rest.

Finding a crag to duck behind, Funanya prompted the seer to eat some dried fruits and take some water. Then she bundled the girl up in her cloak against the sharp cold of the desert. She dared not risk a fire and had no wood or dung to burn, even if she had wanted to.

They lay side by side for warmth, the sand-cloak facing out to hide them. The desert's rustling became audible under the gusting winds. The sound of chitters across the sands and glowmoths taking to the skies tickled the silence. It was a sound Funanya found strangely comforting after the cold, dead dark of the underground.

As her mind drifted to sleep, Funanya had to ask, "Can you see him?"

"I see no future for Askaran," Dana replied, her voice hollow. "None ever again."

Funanya squeezed Dana in a hug, knowing the girl needed far more than that but not knowing what else to do. "I'm sorry," she said.

"I loved him," Dana whimpered, nuzzling her face into Funanya's shoulder. "He taught me. He protected me. He guided me. I can't do this without him."

Funanya sighed. "I've heard it said that the Enneads will all die if they don't have a seer to lead them. Isn't that right?"

The seer nodded, her face still buried against Funanya. "Silly old saying."

"Silly old saying or not, you have to help your people. They need you. I'll get you there."

"Why?" the seer asked, pulling her head up to peer at Funanya. "I don't understand you, Funanya. I wanted you to come with us, but I never thought you would. This is not your fault. This is not your fight. You choose to remain, but I cannot understand why."

Casting her eyes into the darkness around them as the first of the moons rose over the crags nearby, Funanya did not have an answer, not immediately. She had thought her willingness to leave behind her people had simply been self-interest. Farai had marked her as a traitor. Her own people would seek to kill her. When Askaran had been with them, she had a better chance of survival out in the desert than among the Berintans.

But without him, the opposite was true, and yet she had no intention of leaving Dana.

"I like you, Dana," Funanya replied, "and I liked Askaran. You two Enneads seem more ... more real than anyone I have ever met. I want to be real like you." Shaking her head, Funanya snorted in annoyance. "That makes no sense."

"It makes perfect sense," Dana corrected, her voice gentle. "Thank you." She let out a soft sigh. "We will go together to the City. Those who follow us will go there. We all now seek the same thing."

Funanya leaned back, trying to look down at the Ennead girl. "What is that?"

"The portal to Terac," the seer replied solemnly. "And whoever gets it will dictate the fate of both worlds."

They fell into an uneasy silence, the whispers of the winds and the skittering of life in the rocks around them their lullaby.

When the two shifters collided, Farai withdrew. Once the stones crashed down, he left at a run. His warriors followed, but he had positioned a dozen deep in the caves to flank the enemy. These could not get out before the cave-in closed the entrance.

Once he had caught his breath, Farai gathered the survivors outside. The seer had taken a seat beyond the cave-in, her dress not even dusted by the rubble, though pebbles and boulders were strewn on either side of her. He was surprised she had predicted the outcome that accurately and was angry she had not deigned to inform him of the consequences of Yarr and the shifter Askaran going head to head. The supplies, left with the seer, were untouched at least.

Of the two dozen warriors he had started with, Farai was down to six. Two others lived but had injuries that limited their usefulness and would require them to return home.

"Well?" Farai demanded to the seer once they stood outside the entrance, their backs to the desert. "Where are the shifters? What about Funanya?"

The seer's stare became introspective, like a well without a visible end. Her voice was bitter. "I see only Yarr emerging from the waters," she said. He thought she smiled slightly, but it passed too rapidly to be sure.

"Waters?" Farai demanded, looking around the desert's edge. Here, the bare ground still had scraggy shrubs, but the rocky expanses covered the horizon. There was no water to be seen. "What of the other? Their shifter, the one Yarr called Askaran?"

The seer shrugged. "I see no shifter beyond Yarr," she said. The seer looked up, her dark skin glistening in sweat, and she smiled at him in earnest. "This way," she said cheerfully.

Put off by her smile, Farai followed her around the broken, collapsed gates into the caverns. They left the desert, followed by the surviving warriors, and moved down among rocks and rubble. Waddling, the seer led them between outcroppings and down a trail only she could see.

"What about Funanya?" he called after her. "What of the other seer?"

The seer paused, grinning over her shoulder. "What would you have me say? If they are dead, my visions cannot see them. If they live, I cannot see them, for she travels with a desert seer. I cannot see them, Archon. I only see Yarr."

Begrudgingly, Farai followed her onward, the warriors carrying the supplies down the trail behind them.

It took an hour, but after they had descended into a valley beside the cave-in, Farai heard the sound of rushing water.

At the bottom of the crevice, a river ran like a torrent from a small opening in the cliffs. Rapids were interspersed with falls for a few dozen paces before the water vanished underground once more.

The seer settled onto a stone beside the river, her face drenched in sweat but her smile still in place. "Wait," she said.

Farai sent the warriors to investigate the crevice, but they had nothing to report. The river lasted above ground for this short distance. The opening in the rock at the head of the river was large enough to crawl up, but the pressure of the water was intense, and the speed of the flow was liable to crack a person onto the rocks should their footing slip. The only way in or out appeared to be the thin path the seer had led them down.

As the seer sat, Farai became restless. He had not seen her smile like that in years, not even when drunk. In fact, the last time he had seen her smile, she had been predicting Farai's death. What had changed? Perhaps this distraction was a ploy. Would the waters swell, flooding the crevice and killing them all?

Since he had used the seer against her own people, Farai had found the seer uncannily accurate, but cagey. She tried to hide things from him when she could, but she was never wrong. Looking back, he could not find a time she had lied to him, even when she knew the truth would aid him. When she spoke, it was with regret and hatred, but it was never a lie.

Had she been leading him on? But if she was speaking truth to lead him astray in the future, why not try to hide her hatred? Why now pretend to cooperate? The seer was never shy about resenting Farai or the way he pressed her for information. She hated him and herself and made sure he knew it.

If she was right, Yarr would come from these waters.

The suns set, and Farai set camp beside the river. At the least, he did not have to go far for water, but he doubted his ability to sleep next to the roar of the rapids. It did have the advantage of preventing conversation. None of the warriors tried to do anything except their duties, then went to sleep.

And the seer sat by the river, grinning.

For two days, they remained by the river. In between watches on the seer, Farai gathered the remains of spoils from his dead warriors from the rubble where he could and divided them up among the survivors. There was more than they could carry alone. Farai ordered a stash put aside by the cavern for later retrieval.

Around midnight on the third night, Farai woke to the sound of a wet cry. Alarmed, he rushed to the water's edge with a lamp. In the shadows of the moon and the light, he found the source of the cry; an Ennead lay across rocks beyond the beginning of the river.

The seer stood, her smile finally gone. She pointed at the surviving shifter.

Yarr glared into the light, his eyes drifting between black and red like dark sands over a clay landscape. He was stark naked and clung to a stone with a waterfall pounding onto his back, his body bruised badly enough to be visible through the dark skin.

Slowly, the black took hold of the eyes, and he could assess the river in Farai's lamplight. He released his stone, allowing himself to drift down to another set of rapids where he heaved himself out. Blood dripped from open wounds still, his body bruised extensively.

The archon passed him a blanket. After drying himself with it, Yarr wrapped it around his waist.

"What became of your opponent?"

Yarr pushed past him, heading up the slopes to where the warriors had set their beds. "Only an Ennead could get out of there," he shouted over the roar of the river, "and Askaran's no Ennead anymore."

Done, the Ennead took another blanket, wrapped the upper half of himself in it, and promptly went to sleep. The seer stayed watching from a far distance, her eyes seeming to track each drop of black blood that fell.

Trapped spending another night by the river, Farai went back to his own small tent. Seeming satisfied, the seer finally left her vigil by the river and joined the beds. She gorged herself on food, no longer having to be rationed in the plenty caused by missing mouths to feed. Bloated and content, she too drifted off, but he noted she drank only from water gourds, never Farai's chapman.

Farai did not sleep, too disturbed by the river's thunder. And where sleep should have been, he instead found contemplation.

He was down to six men, plus Yarr. Askaran, the shifter that had posed the largest threat, was now dead. Funanya could yet live. He needed to know. He could not have her survive.

The seer's joy continued to nag at him. Why had she been so pleased to show them to Yarr? Why bring the shifter back to those who would use him? There was little threat to the woman herself.

She had to be up to something, but Farai could hardly fathom the idea. She had been complacent, showing little desires beyond those of flesh and sustenance. He did not trust her calm; he was used to frustration and anger. Those emotions ... he could control. This was different. Why would she develop the motivation to act on her own now?

Deciding he was missing something, Farai left the shelter of his tent and crept to the seer's side to listen.

She muttered in her sleep, her demeanor strangely bright for having skipped so much sleep.

Would it be safer to kill her now? She had been useful, but the older she became, the more she hid her visions from him. Would the Grand Archon be angry? Would he even know?

One mumbled sentence came out clearly from her soft ramblings, "Under the City, the water runs pure; under the City, the portal stands open."

In the next breath, she was again lost in mutterings.

He sat back.

It confirmed Grand Archon Amandi's belief, but left Farai annoyed. He had one last thing to do. He had to go to the Ennead city. If Funanya went there as well, he would finish his revenge. Or perhaps, if Yarr had been right, Farai could capture a younger, more impressionable desert seer. And even if he could not, the portal was a thing of great power. With it, Farai himself could be the next Grand Archon.

Crossing the desert was no concern, not with Yarr and the seer. The City of the Enneads had been left in ruins six years before. Would they have returned? And even if they had, the seer was one of the last of her kind. They revered desert seers. He could force her to get him the portal as the Grand Archon had commanded. Considering the state they had left the city in, Farai doubted the Enneads would have stayed. They would have perished with the first sandstorm, assuming starvation did not strike first.

Not waiting for dawn, Farai allowed the shifter and the seer to rest a short while but woke the party before light. He directed them to pack for a long journey across the sands, planning to stop for the midday heat for more of a rest. As they began their trek, Yarr snorted, but smiled, wrinkling his nose as he scented something.

"I am not usually impressed by you," he said. "Two days at least," he said, "but your little Berintan is hardy, is she not?"

Farai nodded and tried to make it look sage. "Of course, she escaped," he said. "I taught her much of her skill. I need her head on my spear yet. But we now head to the city itself, Yarr." He lowered his voice, not wanting the seer to hear him. "My renegade archon will be only one part of this."

Yarr shrugged and peered off into the distance, tracking a trail in the sands and stones that Farai could not fathom. "You don't want me to just run her down?" he asked.

Farai again considered the idea, thinking it had merit. "Can you find the city?" he asked.

For the first time in his remembrance, Yarr looked embarrassed briefly. The expression was quickly replaced by anger.

"I know not this path. Too much has changed." He glared at Farai. "Your people poisoned the oases. They may not even be there."

"Follow her; Funanya is our guide," Farai directed. He paused, then asked, "Do you still believe she travels with another seer?"

"The only way she'd find her way across would be a seer or a shifter who knows the road. Asakran's dead, so she's got a seer," Yarr replied, his voice solid with reason and giving no room for disagreement.

Farai glanced behind him where the seer was walking unassisted over the cool sands. Her expression was once more unreadable, but it was enough for Farai that she was not pointing the way; Yarr was leading. She was displeased they had set their road into the desert, disappointed no doubt that her distraction had failed.

"Following Funanya will give us a direct route," Farai said. "Assuming you can follow her, mighty Shifter?" he added, prompting Yarr.

Yarr growled. "Of course I can," he grumbled. "Keep up."

The dry heat of the desert enveloped them as they crossed into the dunes.

CHAPTER 19

$\mathbb{P}$erched atop an exposed outcropping, Philyre watched the horizon. She knew the lay of the dunes in the distance would allow a demon to snake between them without cresting the dunes, but once they reached the closer reg desert, even the hound demons would be visible to her before she was to them. Being downwind in the swirling gusts of the desert was not possible here; Philyre accepted smearing keim blood over her hair to mask her scent instead.

She would see them first. She would bring the others against them. No demon would enter her territory.

Erosan, similarly dressed in a dust-covered sand-cloak and wearing keim beast blood in his hair, slunk up to Philyre from the windward slope. His footprints left little disturbed; here the sand had been swept away by the wind decades before. Although it would encroach along the edges, the main part of the reg desert was bare stone and gravel too heavy to be moved by the light tap of an Ennead's footstep.

They faced each other, perched in a crouch. Bringing up their hoods, they created a tunnel between them. Erosan dropped the collar away from his mouth first.

"Two travelers approach," he reported. "An Ennead woman and a Berintan female. They're on their way to Hope." The bigger Ennead sat back on his haunches like a poised colossus demon, chewing on the jannu root that would help keep him hydrated in the desert wind.

Philyre pulled her collar down.

"A slave and master? Why would the master come?" The sounds of her voice, even only a whisper in the wind, helped give her thoughts substance. Philyre had seen Ennead prisoners six years ago when she had observed the Berintan army. Maurn, when the shifter visited from the north, had warned them about the threat of Berintan slavers. He had also reported a few others who had escaped their captors in the years since the destruction of Hope, but for every dozen, only one survived to make it back to the Enneads. "Why would they bring the slave?" she added.

"What difference does that make?" Erosan snapped, chewing on the root aggressively. "You want to go deal with it? I'll keep watch here. They're getting close to the markers, coming in from the south, third marker to the east. The others are waiting for you."

Of the Enneads who had initially come with Philyre into the desert, only Erosan survived. The team had been replenished by others who followed Maurn down from the Ennead's hiding places in the north, but none of them knew the desert as well. Most survived only a few seasons before a battle with a demon was too much for them and they fell. Erosan and Philyre were the most experienced, but Erosan had no patience for talking. The only thing that satisfied Erosan was killing demons, and that focus had become fervent of late. Perhaps he wanted revenge for the wound he had been dealt the last time a hound demon had crossed their paths. Perhaps the death of a demon was the only way Erosan could feel they were making progress.

The reconstruction of Hope certainly did not instill Philyre with feelings of accomplishment. But then, the rebuilding of the great Ennead city seemed an exercise in futility. Despite the many streets they cleared, the Enneads would not return. Their society was built around the shifters and seers. They had only three shifters left, although two more had come out of the descendants and were waiting to be keyed. They stayed with the main group of refugees in the north, with Berro and Maurn taking turns searching the desert. Only Maurn ever visited the group in Hope, and his visits were short.

But without a seer, no one had the confidence to settle anywhere, let alone in the ruins of their abandoned City.

Why Berro or Maurn had not seen these two travelers approaching, Philyre did not know. Without Maurn here, it fell to her to deal with it. She had no intention of letting a Berintan into their home again.

"You watch. I'll go," she said. By way of warning, she added, "There's been a colossus demon seen in the regs."

Philyre pulled her hood away from Erosan and adjusted her collar, hiding her face from the wind. If Erosan spoke again, it was lost in the wind.

Thankfully, it seemed unlikely that even Erosan would try to take on a colossus demon himself. He might be arrogant enough to test himself against a hound now. He had survived six years of fighting the monsters. Not all of his arrogance was bluster.

Philyre still felt a thrill of unease pass through her as she looked over her shoulder. It was a brief sensation, and it left nothing behind. She thought for a moment she would not see Erosan again. She did not consider Erosan a friend, more of a colleague or fellow warrior now, but she did not want to lose the man. They had grown strong together and had a reputation among the new arrivals. They were veterans of the sands, part of the originals. Dying would sully their reputation.

Assuming the feeling was because she was going to face a Berintan once more, Philyre turned her back.

A little vengeance was due against those who had destroyed their people.

Collecting her shield and pack, Philyre followed the crest of the next ridge, down through the valley and to where the river broke the surface of the gray-brown rock. The pool was stagnant and hot, baked by the suns and flowing too slowly to remain fresh. Still, there had been nothing but a mud slat there the year before. Now the water could be drawn out and drunk if allowed to settle. It tasted like stone and chalk, but it was water where there had been none.

She reached the markers and moved east until she found the south pillar. She ran her hand over the brow of the stone, which came to her chest now, by habit. It was lucky, the runners had always claimed, to touch one of the eight direction markers, but none of them would have ever dared lay a hand on the writing identifying it. Hands could wear down stone after enough time.

The passage of hands over the stone had worn the top instead, paired waves denting the stone, one on either side. Philyre recognized the action had been nothing but a means of keeping the otherwise menial job of the runners more interesting, but the habit was ingrained. She ran her left hand over the stone, for she was traveling east, and trotted with the stones on her left along the double, overgrown path.

As she passed the first of the markers beyond the direction stone, she wished that her life was more menial now. Six years ago, she had hoped for excitement. She had wanted to be the one to see the demon first or spot a returning shifter. She had wanted to be useful. Now, she wished she could be running circles around her City, knowing that if she missed something, a dozen more runners would report it. Now, she would have given anything to be boring.

At the second marker, Philyre pushed the past from her mind and checked her weapons. In addition to her kukris, two throwing spears were strapped to her back, tied too well to wiggle in her trot. She had rigged a set of trick knots and had proven she could loose a spear before one of the others could reach her from only ten paces. Being quick had saved her life more than once. She could never be as strong as Erosan, but she could be faster.

At the third marker, Philyre met up with the rest of her team. Unlike Erosan, who had been seasoned by countless long, cold nights and close brushes with demons, these ten were young and naïve. Maurn had taught them basic skills with a blade and spear, but only one or two showed any promise of lasting more than a season. Unsurprisingly, they all looked to Philyre for directions when she arrived.

Maurn always sent only boys, and these ten were no exception. The females were too valuable to be released into the desert, yet Maurn had never suggested Philyre return. She had started this effort. She alone would see it through.

"Erosan said a Berintan and slave were approaching," she prompted.

"Coming this way, moving in from the trench. Will be here in an hour," one of the boys, Chean, reported. He was an average would-be pilgrim for Hope but had his hair cut too short for walking in the sun. While the others could work outside for some time, Chean had to wear a hat the moment he stepped out from cover, else his head got burned. He seemed to be trying to grow out his hair now, but it was a slow process.

"Come with me to the ridge," Philyre commanded, frowning at them. "I will confront them while you all hide nearby. I need you ready for a fight."

"Fight?" Chean said, following her closely as she led the way deeper into the desert, into the rocky plains. "But one is Ennead."

"Ennead or not, be ready," Philyre warned.

She led the way, picking a familiar path between stones. The boys scrambled behind him, disappearing one by one into the surrounding sand, stones, and dirt. Each of them had a sand-cloak, an easy way to conceal themselves, but some were better at choosing their positions than others. With ten separate "piles" of stones, none of them stood out too obviously in the terrain.

Philyre chose a boulder to sit behind and went still. She listened, but for a time, the only sound was wind and the bounce of pebbles over the rock. Rarely, one of the others would shift their weight, and a stone would fall loose from the sand-cloak.

This silence was one Philyre had learned to love. Raised among people, Philyre had once feared silence.

Now, the only silence was in the dead of night, when even the demons never approached, and in the calm before battle. These snippets of silence were the only relief she had.

All too soon, the silence was interrupted by the scuff of feet on stone. Neither of the strangers seemed to be moving cautiously, but the steps were measured and steady, like travelers along a long road. They almost moved in pace, out of sync enough to have the beat shift continuously.

Philyre did not move but kept her sand-cloak covering her and her spear in hand, laid flat to hide its shape. She was expecting to have them pass her and move into the canyon where the others were concealed, but the steps stopped unexpectedly.

"What?" a voice, heavily weighted with a strange accent, asked. She assumed it was the Berintan, but was surprised the word was recognizable. Would they not have their own language?

The Ennead answered gently, as if she was soothing a wild ranna beast. "Patience."

Although she did not know how they had figured out she was ahead, Philyre realized the two would not move on now. Figuring she would have to talk to them before long regardless, she left the boulder and stepped onto the path between the uneven rises of stone.

She was taken aback by the Ennead. Erosan had said she was a woman, but she had expected a meek slave. This woman stood tall, her black hair tied back in a dozen braids. Her skin was deep ebony, darker than any Ennead she had ever seen, and she had an impossibly potent stare for a young woman. Her clothing was simple, although she wore a sand-cloak over it and had wrapped her legs for travel in a distinctly Ennead fashion. Most women Philyre knew were more dumpling-like, soft and warm. Children were raised by the entire City, and her defnition of a woman was limited to that: a slightly plump, laughter-filled, doting mother.

This woman was lean and muscled like a male. Her legs were long, her shoulders broad, and her expression strict. She appeared to be unarmed, but the very thought that she was checking her for weapons struck Philyre as odd. An Ennead slave should not be armed. Why did she think to check?

Philyre had to force herself to check the Berintan, knowing she was the greater threat. She had seen the Berintan women fight like their men, and so was less surprised by this woman's muscled form and her spears. She had dressed like the Ennead: a simple tied dress, short like a runner's, wrappings for her legs, sandals, and a less-impressive traveling cloak.

Odd that the master would give the slave the better cloak, Philyre thought. So many things about this pair made no sense.

The Berintan glared at Philyre without fear. Her grip shifted on her spear as she asked her companion, "This what we were waiting for?" Although the words were sloppy and slow, Philyre understood them well.

"Stand fast," Philyre said. "You have entered Ennead territory. Berintans are not welcome here."

The Berintan cocked her head, her dark eyes narrowed as if translating the words.

"We lost this territory, Philyre," the Ennead woman said, making her jump. "A band of ten cannot claim this land for the Enneads. You are bluffing. Do not challenge Funanya, please. She is not a threat to you or your group."

Philyre paused, acutely aware of the use of her name. The others had not met this pair yet, and she did not recognize the woman in front of her. Perhaps they knew each other from the days before the fall of the City, but she was unable to place her. An old friend? She was only a bit younger, not quite twenty. The daughter of the baker? Perhaps Serina's younger sister?

But she could not know about the others unless someone had told her.

In complete disregard of her weapons—perhaps dismissing an armed Ennead woman as Philyre had done—the Ennead walked on along the path. Her words had a light accent as she spoke. "Hope cannot be rebuilt without me. You were just thinking that." She let the thought trail off, but Philyre was not sure if it was to let her finish, or because she could not bring herself to say more.

Philyre stared at her as she walked fearlessly past her. She had called it Hope. If she had known Philyre from the City before its destruction, she would not have said "Hope." How could she know what they called the ruins?

The answer struck her like a spear's thrust.

"Desert seer," she choked out.

She followed the woman with her gaze, unable to think of a suitable action.

The Berintan laughed, and Philyre realized she had lowered her spear, opening herself to attack. By the time she raised it and adopted a defensive stance, the Berintan stood close behind her. She could have easily put the spear through her chest.

"She got it!" the Berintan said, her spear in a relaxed hold. "Smarter than she looks, this one."

Flashing her a bright smile, the Berintan—Funanya the seer had called her—rejoined her companion, taking a position protectively at her back.

Like a guard, Philyre realized. The Berintan was protecting the seer.

"Get up!" the seer called, looking at each of the concealed Enneads and their sand-cloaks. She knew where every last one was. "All of you. Get up."

Of course she knew, Philyre thought. *A desert seer…*

"You heard her!" Philyre called, coming up on the other side of the seer and addressing her group. Cautiously, the others peeked out. "Obey the Eldest Seer. Come to your feet!"

They muttered with uncertainty as they stood. Like Philyre, they kept a weathered eye on the Berintan, but their eyes were wide in awe when they glanced at the Ennead seer.

The seer tilted her head toward Philyre. "I am not the eldest, Philyre."

"I do not understand. If another…"

"I will explain once we are out of the wind," the seer stated, leading the way to Hope. Philyre thought to offer her a guide, then chastised the thought. She needed no help as she unfailingly took them to the markers and into the City, the Berintan at her side every moment.

With every step, Philyre's elation faded. At first, she had thought her the end of the long dry days in Hope, toiling uselessly in empty streets and empty houses. She had, for a moment, glimpsed freedom from responsibilities. She could be a runner again and circle the City, looking for danger…

But the seer *knew*. She *knew* everything. She *knew* every doubt Philyre had ever had. She *knew* every death she had witnessed, and all the ones she thought she could have prevented. She *knew* how much Philyre hated Maurn for bringing new Enneads down into Hope, even though they were the only reason Philyre still lived. Some part of her hated Maurn solely for keeping her alive.

None of them spoke as they followed the seer through the overgrown fields outside of Hope.

The Berintan alone seemed to have the courage to break the silence, "Must have had some nasty storms. Looks like flood damage here. Washed out fields too. Markers are still good. Those must run deep." Since no one commented, she carried on in her odd accent. "It's colder here. The dirt is cool. Strange."

The seer's voice was flat. "The desert is dying."

"Cheery," the Berintan said. "Dana, is that why the water is farther out? The grasses extend well beyond the markers."

"Water is poison to the desert," the seer replied.

"Dana?" Philyre asked. "You call her…"

"My name is Dana," the seer said in her flat voice.

"That is not a name," Philyre answered without thinking. She felt like she spoke to a child playing make-believe. Perhaps she also thought the City was run by taurans in costumes. "You are a desert seer. You are—"

"Would you call me the Second Eldest Seer?" the seer said, stopping and staring at Philyre. Her perfect confidence broke like the mud over a dried river bed. "You know one is elder to me. Were she to come before you now, would you obey her before me?"

Taken aback, Philyre stammered, "Yes, that is what—"

"Wrong answer," the Berintan interrupted.

The seer's calm expression shattered, and the swell of emotions was visible. "Then wait for her," she snapped. "She comes behind us, in the company of Archon Farai and the shifter Yarr. They come to kill me and take the source of life from our City, from our Hope. They come to finish what they started six years ago with their siege of the City."

Without giving Philyre a chance to reply, the seer pivoted and strode away, passing through the gates into the City.

A seer was once more present. It was the City again.

Bewildered, Philyre looked at the Berintan. The thought of losing this young seer made her heart sink, but she could not understand how the pursuers could include a seer, let alone the Eldest Seer.

The Berintan shrugged her golden shoulders and grinned. "Seems to me some of your traditions are going to change," she said. "She'd rather be called Dana for one. I'm Funanya." The Berintan crossed her arms in greeting but did not stow her spear, making it clear she still felt she needed the weapon.

Philyre, still too confused to act except by instinct, mimicked her greeting and said, "I am Philyre." She blinked at her in confusion. "Did the seer teach you to speak as we do?"

The woman laughed and hitched up her spear. "No, but I'm getting better at sorting out your accent. Strangely, we share a language, Philyre." The Beritan glanced at the gate where the seer had passed. "Dana spoke more like an Ennead the closer we got to the City, maybe to give me practice. Can hardly hear the

Berintan years in her voice now." She cleared her throat and faced Philyre squarely. "You in charge here?"

"As much as anyone is," she replied.

The Berintan laughed again, and, together, they followed the seer in. "Good answer! I'm going to tell you what we have been through, Philyre. Then maybe you can understand why you upset her."

As they walked the empty streets of the City, she listened to the Berintan's story. In watching "Dana," she recognized her as the Youngest Seer all those years ago.

Six years. Only six years, but she was not the young woman running around the City on alert for danger, delivering messages, or providing first aid care, and the seer was not the innocent child asking a million questions, seeking knowledge from everyone in the City.

When the Berintan confessed she had been part of the raids against the City, Philyre began to believe her tale. Would she not have denied it if she sought their sympathy? Instead, Funanya detailed the Eldest Seer's journey to Berinta, then back across the desert. Yarr's betrayal at first filled her with anger, but it quickly faded. She had seen hints that a shifter had been among the enemy forces. For all she knew of the shifters, Yarr seemed the most likely.

Knowing the seer trusted this Berintan, Philyre accepted the woman's words. She saw the truth of the enemies approaching and knew she would have to intervene to protect the seer.

The fact that she had upset her gnawed at Philyre. Her fear was gone. Dana *knew*, she remembered. That meant she knew everything about everyone she met. Philyre felt great sympathy for her and understood why the Berintan was there, following the Ennead and carrying her spear at the ready.

This desert seer had to be protected, for she was fragile.

Her duty was decided. This seer—Dana—had to be kept safe from these killers. The Eldest Seer had betrayed her people and no longer held Philyre's heart. Dana gave her purpose, and she would not fail her.

The group of Enneads who had taken up residence in the ruins of the city mostly stayed in a block of houses near one of the gates. They had closed all the other gates and blocked them, leaving only the nearest gate functional. The others could be … if only someone would clean the sand from their hinges.

Funanya was impressed by what the dozen boys— for they were all younger than her by a decade or more—and their hardy leader had accomplished. They maintained their water source and took turns cooking, hunting, and cleaning in a coordinated schedule. The only two above the schedule were the eldest, Philyre, the girl who had met them, and an older boy called Erosan.

The seer led the way to the encampment, knowing the way without guidance. She was showing off, Funanya was certain. Dana had to prove herself now, no longer able to lean on Askaran. She had the impression Dana was overdoing it, but it wasn't until after dinner, which the residents provided proudly, that she had a chance to talk to the seer in private.

Whether Dana had known Funanya would seek her out, or had simply wanted some time alone, Funanya did not know. But once she was certain the locals had settled into their evening routines, Funanya left them to follow Dana. She found the seer atop a roof, looking over the moonlit city. Annoyingly, she had found a place in the wind, as if the sheltered air were somehow stifling her.

"You should take it easier on them," Funanya said, joining Dana at the edge of the roof and looking out. The Ennead city itself looked dull compared to the last time she had visited. Many of the wool awnings were gone or had become weighted by sand, their canopies tattered or missing entirely, scavenged by need. The glittering roads of glass were faded, scuffed, or hidden by sand. In some ways, the city was partially buried already, like a corpse half in the grave.

"I want them to realize what I am," the seer said softly, "and at the same time, I wish I wasn't what I am. I didn't want to do this alone."

Funanya placed an arm over the girl's shoulder. She had not brought her cloak up, and now her bare shoulders were open to the wind. Goosebumps speckled over her arms and shoulders.

"I think that Philyre is paying more attention than you give her credit for. She's green but has lots of potential. Watch out for Erosan, though. He's not balanced."

"Darkness follows him," Dana agreed. She gave Funanya a weak smile. "I like Philyre."

"I don't," Funanya said pridefully. "She's clever but too young! Still has some idealism in her; I don't have the patience for those who keep dreaming when the dream is dead."

Dana cocked her head toward Funanya. "Do you think the dream is dead?"

"It's not my dream," she said.

She pulled away and turned around. From this rooftop, she could see out into the desert. The markers around the city, a set distance away, reflected the moonlight as if lit with glowmoths. Only the lack of stars showed where the dunes covered the horizon.

She had done as she had been asked. Dana was home. She had new defenders. They were a good group.

"They can't protect me," Dana interrupted.

"You knew what I was thinking," Funanya grumbled. "That's a little disconcerting."

"I'm sorry. I sometimes *know* things. And you wouldn't say it aloud."

"No, I wouldn't," Funanya said. "But since you already *know*, you *know* I'm not sure what to do now. They are your best chance to get away from Farai. They can take you north. That makes sense to me. The rest of the Enneads will come back now that you are here, will they not? With the entire city back, Farai will need an army. It will buy you time. You can rebuild." Funanya glanced up, but the light was, like the city, dim and muted. "You don't need me," she finished.

She waited in the chill wind for Dana to say something. She expected the girl to argue. Under her facade, Dana was still a child in many ways. She would cling to the familiar things. She had grown up in the City, but the forests of Berinta were more home now, and Funanya knew it.

But the silence dragged on. When Funanya finally turned around, she found Dana staring up at the sky.

The two moons were side by side. The big moon loomed over the city, the second moon partially tucked behind it. They were both half-moons.

"The big one is called Corr," Dana said. "She's the warrior. She's fierce. The smaller one is Deva, the sweet one." Dana met Funanya's stare with a small smile. "If Corr was not there, Deva would fall from the sky. Corr loves her sister and wants her to stay in the sky. So they dance together, Corr pulling her little sister back up every time she falls toward the planet. But Corr's arms will get weary over time, and one day Deva will fall. When she falls, she will die."

Unable to find words, Funanya looked at the moons. Both glowed in orange tonight, the lights of the distant suns mixed.

"Funanya, I cannot see beyond a day right now. Tomorrow, something is going to happen. Please ... stay until then. Help me find my footing on this steep path. I need you to keep me from falling."

A chill ran over her. Funanya wrapped her arms around her shoulders, but it did not help.

Funanya nodded.

If Dana could not see, it was a demon or a desert seer that approached. Either way, Funanya feared the youngsters below would be unable to handle it. They had boasted about the demons they had killed, but she did not know if they could be trusted.

"I will stay for a few days," Funanya agreed, heading back to the stairs, hoping to get out of the cold wind.

She stopped when she found the Ennead Philyre atop the stairs, her spear in hand.

"We would appreciate your blades," Philyre said tentatively. "We have spotted a campfire in the desert. You told me a desert seer and shifter were with a Berintan general, seeking you out." The young woman's expression was grim. Her face was broad; it seemed better suited to wide smiles than these deep scowls.

"Yes," Dana replied, her voice timid, as if afraid she would be scolded.

Funanya watched the Ennead for a reaction, reading every gesture she did or did not make. She had sensed Philyre's excitement upon recognizing the seer. Now she saw cautious devotion in her. She had known warriors such as her before. She had found this cause after a time living in basic survival. Funanya also saw desire, both for what Dana was and what she appeared to be.

Interesting that she could see the difference between those two. The others had not.

Dana tilted her head, peering at Philyre as if seeing her for the first time. "They seek to claim the gate beneath us."

The woman nodded solemnly as if knowing that something meaningful was hidden in the sentence she did not understand.

Funanya was less willing to simply play along. "Explain, Dana. Are we going to have to fight them? And what gate?"

Dana smiled, her voice soft as she spoke. "I know of a gate that was supposedly destroyed, only it was hidden instead. Farai came here for it those years ago. Now he returns in pursuit of his pride."

"He's chasing us to regain his pride," Funanya corrected.

"He has learned the great secret. He knows the city here has the gate. He knows that to give it to his master, he must kill Funanya and me. So he comes."

Funanya lifted an eyebrow at the seer. "That's new. You *know* any more?"

Dana nodded, shivering. "If we stand aside, he will take the portal. If we fail to stop him…"

When Dana trailed off, Funanay took that to mean the future was not worth discussing; it was bad.

"So we confront him," she said. She smiled broadly at the Ennead. "Farai is a warrior and a fine one. I am best suited to fighting him. You and yours will be needed against Yarr, I assume. Can you kill a tusked demon?"

"In all my time here, we have never felled one. I assume this one will not be turned from your trail," Philyre admitted. "We have seen a colossus demon lurking not far from Ho… from the City. We could draw it in."

Philyre looked at the seer, seeking approval.

Funanya saw the pain in her eyes. Like her, she assumed, Dana felt a throb of pain at the mention of such a monster. The reminder of Askaran was too sharp.

"It might work," Funanya said, her voice sounding thin to her ears as she fought to push memories out of her mind. "But Yarr has slain a colossus demon before."

"Even if he is victorious but weakened," Philyre explained eagerly, "we will be able to best him. If we can lure him into the City, we can restrict their move-ment. We could attack from the tunnels."

Funanya gripped her spear tighter, eyeing the spears still held over Philyre's shoulders. She went over her memories of the Ennead city from when they had attacked. Tunnels had never been mentioned.

"What tunnels?" Funanya asked.

Philyre and Dana shared a knowing smile at her expense.

"The aqueducts," Philyre said. "The parts of the city even the raiders never knew existed. Where exactly do you think we fished?"

Funanya remembered the many pieces of jewelry of the Ennead, finely woven fish bones. She remembered finding rations of dried fish hung in the desert air in the city. Then, it had not occurred to her how strange that was.

"I assumed the oases," she admitted.

"We are built upon the lake. It is sustained by the portal," Dana said.

Funanya checked with Philyre again, but the young woman looked lost this time. She even shrugged. "I know nothing about a 'portal,' but if the seer says it is there, I believe her."

Dana blinked repeatedly, her attention present again.

"Visions?" Funanya asked.

Dana nodded slowly, a pensive expression settling on her face. "They never told the others," she said. "Only the desert seers *knew*. And the shifters. But they never told a desert seer. We just *know*."

"So why are you worried?" Funanya asked.

"Because I can see Archon Farai approaching in the morning," she said.

This time Philyre checked with Funanya. "Why is that worrisome? We knew he was coming."

A knot formed in Funanya's stomach. "Because he's with a desert seer," she said. She looked back at Dana, understanding the girl's bewilderment. "And Dana can see him."

"Desert seers cannot see other seers," Philyre said.

"Hence the confusion."

"It could be an illusion. The portal was hidden by illusion," Dana warned.

"Or she's helping us," Funanya said. "She did not stop me as we left the Valley of Vaseil. Could she drop her protection? Deny Farai her powers?"

Dana thought for a moment more, her lips pressed in thought. "I do not know."

Philyre hefted her shield onto her shoulder once more. "Well, I think we had best be moving, just in case. I will send a scout out to follow them. They can send us mirror signals to keep us informed. Erosan and I will lure the colossus demon in once we have a target. It's been a while since we coaxed one into attacking something other than another demon, but…."

Funanya cocked her head. "A while?" she asked, suspicious.

The Ennead shrugged. "Not since the Berintan army left."

Askaran had said that the crossing had been uncommonly unlucky. Seeing one demon was bad. Seeing three…

"The army! You lured the colossus into my camp! I was there!" she exclaimed, but the Ennead stared at her blankly. Funanya pointed at Dana. "So was she!"

Philyre's face fell. "I did not—"

Dana sighed. "Of course, you did not know, but Funanya no doubt appreciates the explanation. Admittedly, driving a demon into Yarr is probably our best hope."

Funanya nodded. "Best send a scout out now, so we can find out if what she's seeing is real."

With a stiff nod, Philyre left them, heading down the sandstone stairs into the darkness.

Funanya waited a moment more to see if Dana had anything further to add.

The seer gave it some thought. "Defend her, please." Shyly, like a virgin asking advice, she added, "I think I like her company."

Deciding she was not the one to lecture Dana about her choice of companions, Funanya moved for the stairs herself. She left Dana staring up at the sky.

The seer's voice was a whisper as Funanya reached the door, but Funanya still heard her. "It must be an illusion. It cannot be you. Not you, not Askaran."

Funanya fought to ignore the way her heart skipped at his name.

He was dead. Reminders only hurt.

CHAPTER 20

The scouts confirmed what the seer had told them; a party camped half a day from the City. Philyre sent another scout out north, in the hopes of having them come across Maurn or the other shifters. Maurn was due for a visit, yet none of them saw any evidence that he was in the area.

Perhaps he was tracking the colossus demon, Philyre thought. Was that not what shifters did—monitor demons to kill them or drive them away from the City? It was their most sacred duty, continued despite the fall of the City and the loss of lives in the desert.

Before the suns rose, the Berintan Funanya came to Philyre and asked her to show her skill with the spear. At dawn, the seer joined them in the streets, where Philyre had accepted practicing with the Berintan.

"She is a good teacher," Philyre told the seer when she spotted her watching from the shelter of their house.

Funanya gave a dramatic scoff. "You're self-taught. Anything is an improvement!" But Philyre sensed the jest in her voice, a camaraderie she had forgotten existed. Only Erosan had known her long enough, but that side of the other Ennead had fallen away. They had been performing their duty with no time to laugh with each other.

Funanya cracked her spear shaft against hers, jarring Philyre's hands and bringing her attention to the spar. "Keep your hand position consistent. You want the balance of the spear to be predictable. Eventually, when you know all the angles of the shaft and the weight of the blades, you can adjust it. For now, consistent!"

Philyre took her advice and moved her hand back into the hold she had suggested. She threw the spear, rocking onto her front leg and launching it with her full strength. It cut into the wall of the house opposite, sticking in the sandstone. She had been able to throw that far before, but never with enough strength to do damage.

"Bring down your elbow," Funanya corrected, showing her how to drop the arm after the throw. "You'll throw better for longer."

Philyre thought to be proud of the throw, for the power of it had clearly increased, but sensed she would get no such approval from Funanya. Instead, she glanced at the seer for her thoughts.

She cocked her head. "It is strange to see weapons in the hands of an Ennead."

Philyre moved to retrieve the spear, seeing she would have no praise from either woman. "We had to survive without shifters," she pointed out, checking the edge of the spear as she pulled it loose and quelling the sudden embarrassment that rose in her.

"Something ... something about that worries me," she replied.

"We are defenders of the City for when the Enneads return," she proudly said.

She mutely nodded as she moved off, leaving Philyre wondering if she had said something wrong.

Thinking it would spare lives, Philyre left the rest of the team setting up the tunnel where they planned to lure in Yarr should the colossus demon fail to kill him. She chose a stretch of corridor narrow enough to prevent the demon from entering but short enough to allow a spear's throw. Even if she was not yet ready to use the spears that way, she suspected Funanya could. If she could kill Yarr with a single blow when he was in Ennead form, the invaders would be kept out.

As the suns rose over the horizon, Erosan reported that the colossus demon had been seen again, and Philyre went to join him. The seer seemed saddened by the news but not overly worried.

"So how does this luring thing work?" Funanya asked, following Philyre as she made to leave the house. Philyre noted the woman had her leg wrappings on once more and was carrying a spear.

"There must be two of us," she explained cautiously, seeing the seer watching their conversation and wondering if Funanya was asking questions because the seer dared not. This affair concerned demons. Dana would not be able to see it. "Demons are drawn to Enneads. If it sees or scents one of us, it will follow. We trade off, hiding our scent and letting them follow us when we desire. So long as they can't smell us, the sand-cloaks work."

Taking out a pot, Philyre painted her hair with keim beast blood once more.

The Berintan wrinkled her nose at her. "Smell indeed!" Giving a sigh, she peered into the pot. "I don't suppose I need it. Demons do not chase Berintans."

Philyre raised an eyebrow at her. "You are coming with us?"

The woman hefted her spear. "You can lure in the demon, but only I can lure in Yarr and his party. You are going to need me, or so I am told."

Philyre checked over her shoulder again, and the seer still sat against the wall. She held a kukri in her hand, turning it over like an artist with an unfinished piece. She felt sad when she saw her familiarity with the weapon. Was she familiar with weapons as Philyre was?

"So be it. Keep up, Berintan, or be—"

"Philyre, you are a good person, but if you call me that again, I will box your ears," Funanya replied.

Philyre's heart sank. "It was not an insult. A statement of—"

"It's not what was said," she interrupted, passing her on the way to the doorway. "It is who else used to say it."

She was outside in the next moment, leaving Philyre with the seer for a moment.

Dana—she was still not used to using her name—narrowed her eyes on her and handed her the kukri.

Although she still had her own two, Philyre accepted the weapon. "I do not expect to need another," she said.

With vacant eyes, the seer replied, "I hope you will need it. Hope is all I have." She shook her head and smiled apologetically. "Perhaps this will make sense soon. All I know now is that there are too many possibilities. Funanya will set the outcome. Watch for her."

"We can trust her?"

Dana's face shone as she smiled in earnest. "She is the only one we can trust. Others come and go. Only you and Erosan remain, and Erosan we cannot—we must not—trust."

A chill ran over Philyre's core. This woman was a seer. She would only speak the truth. Philyre had known Erosan for six years of battle. She had trusted the Ennead with her life more than once, but if Dana did not trust him, Philyre felt she could not either.

It was strange. She had known Dana before, although their paths had crossed only a handful of times. Then, she had been the Youngest Seer. Philyre had been a runner of no note. But now, when she looked at Dana, Philyre felt a profound sense of duty. Like an original colonist, today she had awoken in a new world, where nothing was as it had been. Now, her life was tied to the woman in the sand-cloak. For her, she would die.

Today, she was in love with the Youngest Seer of the Enneads, and she thought that a wonderful thing.

Love had always been uncommon among Enneads, although not frowned upon. A marriage could be for love, although most were for practical reasons. Children came from love or from necessity. If it was right for the City and for the Enneads, it would be done. So long as love and duty did not conflict, no one begrudged lovers their attachment.

But Philyre had never been in love before and now wondered why others had not been honest about the emotion. She felt happier than she ever had before, and at the same time was terrified. She wanted to impress Dana and earn her affection but dreaded the thought of disappointing her. Nothing was simple. Nothing was balanced. She was either elated or devastated. While it made her ill, she wished it would never end.

Love had always been there, an option, a possibility, neither good nor bad. It was, at the same time, both. While it confused her, she smiled as she followed Dana out.

She was purpose and light to her. Philyre was complete now.

As she crouched on the distant dune, Funanya wished for her jungle. Without Dana to distract her, all she could think about was sand and the hot suns. Her skin chafed from the constant sand and stones, and her mouth was dry. The Enneads with her constantly argued, although they tried to do it in whispers, so she would not hear it. As a result, she knew it was about her.

Erosan judged everything she did. She felt his constant gaze. Among Berintans, competition was fierce, and hatred was common. She was used to recognizing it and using it where she could, but this wasn't the same, not in an Ennead. Even Philyre seemed to recognize it, and something about it troubled her.

Together, at first, they hunted in the dunes. It was a short while before they caught sight of the tracks of the enormous creature. They split, Erosan and Philyre working in overlapping patterns to draw the monster away from the city and toward the southern enemies before the suns rose in earnest and limited their movement. Philyre had promised that, once they were close enough, the demons would scent each other, and the decoys would not be needed. Colossus demons were territorial, and the smell of Yarr would draw the colossus demon in. They had taken even the wind into consideration.

For the better half of the day, despite the midday suns, they worked. Funanya kept herself hidden, knowing all the while that it was probably wasted effort. The demon had no interest in her.

But this demon did not behave as they expected. As they tried to lure it, the monster kept turning away, moving back toward the city instead of following the Enneads toward the enemy.

"We'll have to get closer to it," Philyre told the two of them when they, for the third time, lost the demon's interest. Funanya could still see the enormous shoulders as the monster headed out over the dunes, north, toward the city.

"Dangerous," Erosan replied, but his tone did not imply he was against the idea.

Like Funanya, Philyre stared out across the desert, watching the demon. "We have to be a better target than whatever it's going after. I've never seen one so determined."

Erosan snorted, stretching as he prepared to run once more. "It's a colossus demon," he said. He cast a suspicious eye at Funanya, his stare showing how much he wished she was not present. Still, he said the words. "We've not lured one in years, Philyre. They're smarter. Probably just got lucky on the last one."

Funanya remembered the mountain slope around the last oasis of her long crossing of the desert where she had seen two of the enormous creatures do battle. It was obvious now that one had been Askaran defending the seer. The other … now that she understood that these Ennead children had been luring demons into her party, it seemed likely the last colossus demon they had lured had been during that crossing.

Now, she thought, *they were beginning to under-stand how close they had come to killing the seer in their overzealousness.*

"How close do you need to get?" she asked.

Philyre shrugged, her face tight. "Too close. Erosan's right. We'd be dead."

He looked south. Funanya knew the enemy was probably no more than an hour south, likely to reach the walls before sundown. The scouts had been using mirrors to track them, and Funanya knew Yarr and his group had been moving north as expected. By now, they would not be far.

"Or maybe…" Philyre muttered. She let out a breath, and Funanya realized the Ennead was holding her water gourd. "Maybe we need to be more tempting."

Before she realized what Philyre was doing, the Ennead had dumped the contents over her head, washing the keim beast blood out of her thick weave of hair.

Erosan took a large step away. "Idiot!" he snapped, spinning in search of the demon. It had vanished over a dune. "He'll smell you!"

Shaking herself, Philyre stood tall. "Get a head start," she told Erosan. "I'll move as fast as I can. You need to be ahead to keep him moving once he catches me."

A long growl carried over the dunes, coming from the north where the demon had recently disappeared. The wind, meant to carry Yarr's scent north, was now helping Philyre be detected by the demon.

Erosan did not wait a moment more; he bolted south through the early sunset.

Funanya paused, peering at Philyre. It made little sense. They were still too far away from Yarr and the others. She had seen a colossus demon run. No Ennead could escape it.

Seeming to sense her question, Philyre shrugged. She slipped free her sack and handed it, and its spears, to Funanya. It left Philyre with the sand-cloak and shendyt.

"For her," she said.

She saw it, love. Philyre was in love with Dana. Foolish and rash, that was young love. Love was not a thing that could be negotiated. Funanya took the sack and swung it over her back.

Philyre began to trot in the direction she wanted the demon to follow, and Funanya pulled away from her, running in parallel. With her long strides, she kept pace with despite carrying double packs.

A roar erupted behind them, and the dust cloud of the approaching demon rose, the earth shaking with each step the demon took. No longer was it a shambling trudge, the demon was running.

Angling herself to lead it away from Erosan, Philyre broke into a full sprint, and Funanya mirrored her.

Sure enough, the colossus demon crested the dune it had recently left. It quickly disappeared again, sunk into the valley between dunes, only to emerge on the other side, already a dune closer. It growled once more, its head lowered as Askaran's had been the day he had carried them down the cliffs into the Alightening Hall.

Philyre was fast, but the demon was too big to outrun. It was not long before the monster was atop her.

But Philyre was more agile. She dodged sharply left, and the demon missed her. It turned to follow, only to be confounded again when Philyre stopped too suddenly. The sand became the demon's downfall. It slid down to the base of the dune before being able to stop, and Philyre was already taking off along the crest of the dune at a full run.

Funanya fought a shout of victory. She was drawing the demon in the right direction.

When the demon again reached the top of the dune, barreling down after the Ennead, Philyre skipped off the crest. Angling her feet, she slid down the slope, quickly outdistancing the demon. She had chosen a long dune, giving him a head start.

The colossus demon roared in outrage and ungracefully tumbled after the Ennead.

Funanya kept following but was wondering how she was going to keep up now.

Philyre's victory lasted only to the bottom of the slope. Hitting a hidden stone, her feet went out from under her. The controlled slide became a fall. Bouncing wildly, sand clouds flipping up behind her, Philyre plowed down the dune and landed, limp, on the wind-swept slope near the bottom.

Although the sand-cloak hid her as she landed at the base of the dune, the demon crashed toward the prone Ennead, following the scent.

Taking a leap off her own vantage point, Funanya raced to beat the demon to Philyre. She unslung the pack as she ran, thinking the Ennead should have her spear. Even if she could do nothing, any warrior should die fighting. She felt a sudden fear, not for herself, but for Dana. She had already known the loss of Askaran. How would losing her new allies affect her?

The affection Philyre felt for Dana had been partially reciprocated.

The demon caught on the same stone that had been Philyre's failure, pausing on the jutting rock to peer down at its prey. Its pause gave Funanya time to reach Philyre, flip her over, and check her breathing.

She was alive but dazed. She would not be able to fight.

Picking her spear from its holster, Funanya sought firmer footing. She found it above Philyre, where the sand had been worn away from the stone beneath. Philyre must have knocked her head, Funanya decided. That which had harmed her ally now would help her stand and fight.

"For her," Funanya muttered as she set herself before the monster. The winged demon in the tunnels by the Alightening Hall had ignored her. Looking back, the serpent's demon she had fought had also ignored her until she had become a direct threat. Would this one do the same? Even if she was given a chance, how could she find the weakest point? The colossus demon was coated in scales. She knew of no soft place for her spear, and reaching anything above the scaly feet would be nearly impossible.

This colossus demon, she noted, did have a wound she could target. Under the chin, the scales had been opened and raw muscle was visible. Another wound, older and mostly healed, stretched across its shoulder on the left. Others, bruises and cuts not able to get through the scales, decorated it. If she could get it to lower its head…

She paused, faint recognition stirring. She had once stitched a wound that would cause that scar on the shoulder.

The demon's eyes finally focussed on her. It leaned back, growling as if in uncertainty. She could not believe it thought her little spear a true threat but did not know what else would hold it back. It needed only to leap.

The nostrils flared, taking in the scents, and Funanya saw the monster look beyond her at the Ennead. But when she adjusted her grip, making the spear in her hand twitch, she immediately had the demon's attention once more.

Dana had said it was possible. It was an illusion, surely … but if it wasn't…

"Askaran?" Funanya asked. She could believe the blackened and bruised scales were from the cave-in. The wound under his chin … had Yarr done that?

The demon before her flinched. Then it snarled, leaning forward and showing her a maw of teeth like a wolfen defending its cubs.

It didn't matter, she realized, tightening her hold on the spear. Even if it was Askaran—or had been Askaran—he was gone. He had told her there would be a time when he could not come back. They had nearly reached that in the Valley of Vaseil. That he had been brought back then had been a miracle.

The demon moved slowly, dropping down on all fours and stalking forward, its teeth bared. Funanya held her ground. If it lunged and she was fast enough, she might be able to strike under the chin, into the wound, like the serpent demon those many years ago. She could be that fast.

Like the serpent demon Askaran had coached her into killing. What if it was him? What if he could—?

Remembering what had dragged Askaran back from the brink once before, Funanya decided there was nothing to be lost in trying.

Standing tall, she met the blood-red eyes of the demon in front of her and raised her voice to a command meant to carry across a battlefield.

"ASKARAN!" she shouted. "GET YOUR SORRY ASS OUT HERE."

The demon stopped, its snarl gone. The red eyes bored into her, no longer distracted by the Ennead she was protecting. It stared, the whole of its attention on her and her alone.

Heartbeats skipped by as it considered her. Funanya stood firm despite how it briefly twitched as if thinking of advancing but reconsidering. After two such false starts, it roared, sounding frustrated, and, to Funanya's shock, changed.

The first thoughts Askaran had were groggy. He felt as if he had been sleeping after a long battle and still did not want to wake. He could not see and could not hear, but he could feel.

He felt frustration. He was filled with it. Deep desire coursed through him, driving him on, yet the thing he wanted, whatever it was, he could not have. Frustration moved to anger but then retreated. Anger would not help. He might hurt her. And so the frustration remained.

Slowly, his vision returned. He was seeing through red-tinged eyes. He was in the form of his demon, and he ached. His head still swam, but he recognized the Berintan before him. Funanya. She was standing on a stone on the edge of a dune, her spear held ready. Her muscles stretched the wraps of the cloth binding them. She was coated in sweat and wore an angry expression. He hated that he had made her angry.

In his mind, he felt something prod at him, like a child poking an elder for attention. Trying to clear his thoughts, Askaran sought the sensation.

He felt a question, a plea. He wanted something. No, the demon wanted something. *They*, the demon corrected, *both wanted something*. The demon could not get it. Only in Ennead form could they get it.

Funanya.

The realization came slowly. The desire was lust. Askaran wanted Funanya. More than that, the demon wanted Funanya. But a demon could not expect to touch someone so small.

I do not bargain with demons, Askaran thought, knowing the monster within him would never understand the words. But the meaning … it would know what he was trying to say.

Sadness came through. Not a bargain. Not a trade. Genuine. Desire. Compromise.

You would take Ennead form? Askaran asked. *You would obey me?*

Eagerness. Excitement.

For how long? Askaran asked himself. Making deals with demons was fated to end poorly. His mother had taught him that … insisted on it. Others had made bargains with their demons. Any Ennead who had thought they could trust their demon had been betrayed. The demons were creatures of instinct and forgot or ignored promises.

But looking through the demon's eyes, Askaran saw Funanya, and that was becoming hard to ignore.

It wasn't just the demon, he realized. He wanted her, too, if she would have him. Never had he met a stronger female. She intrigued him, challenged him, and brought out so much more in him.

And although he knew it probably would not last, he wanted it.

Agreed.

The vision changed, and he felt himself shifting. As he returned to Ennead form, the excitement of the demon within him rose. Without containment in his mind, the emotions of the monster were just under his skin, overwhelming his own, or perhaps mirrored in his own in a manner he had never recognized. He could no longer tell which emotion came from who.

But more than anything, he knew he wanted her.

His vision was clouded and disoriented as he shifted. He knew they had come down the slope. With a swat, he had disarmed Funanya, more powerful in the partially shifted form than she was. He drove her back but was surprised that she did not fight. He pressed himself down upon her and finally was fully Ennead in physical form.

But the lust still raged within him, no less his own than the demon's. One hand held her hip as the other held her fist down.

He froze there, forcing his mind to pause. He brought Ennead thinking forward. The instinct was strong, but if he hurt her, she would be angry again. And if she did not want him…

The demon objected. He could smell her lust. She wanted him. It prodded Askaran—pushed him harder.

Lusting and wanting are not the same things, he corrected. He had to know…

Funanya adjusted under him, bringing her face toward his. She nuzzled his chin, gently biting him.

"Funanya," he forced his voice to say, "I am not sure I can stop. If you don't want—"

Her free hand hooked around his neck and brought his lips to hers. The demon and Askaran groaned in pleasure, his body melting down onto her.

She released long enough to say, "If I hadn't wanted this, you idiot, I would have put the spear through your skull." She arched her back, pressing her hips firmly into his. "But we'd better make sure Dana's friend is alive before taking up too much time."

It took great effort to ease away from her, and he could do nothing else. The demon objected. Askaran reasoned with him; if Funanya was angry, she would never let them touch her. It had to please her.

It waited, shaking in anticipation and desperation, and obeyed.

Once the other Ennead had been wrapped protectively and placed in the shadows of a rocky outcropping, Funanya returned to him. She spread the desert cloak onto a flat ledge and lowered herself on it, spreading herself before him.

He wanted to warn her. The demon was not contained, not now. Now it roamed within him, a part of his consciousness and a part of his emotions. He did not know where it stopped and he began. He did not know if he would be able to temper it.

But she dragged him down beside her, rolling suddenly to pin him under her, her legs on either side of his hips and her body arched to keep their mouths joined. She tasted like iron sand and salt but felt perfect.

He had misjudged both her and the demon. The three of them were a fine match.

CHAPTER 21

Philyre awoke to familiar smells. The fire was cooking a string of chitters, a special treat, and the tray in the embers baked a huge snapshir fish seasoned with hot spices and sugar of cannus twigs. A chain of dried white ruin fish meat hung beside the fire to be used as bait later.

The sounds of home surrounded her from the scuff of feet as the watch changed to the dull thuds of a needle and sinew working through a hide cover. Someone nearby was sharpening a blade.

She blinked her eyes, forcing them to open, and found herself looking up into the light of the two moons, Corr and Deva. The stars were dim surrounding the moons, the light of the fire at her back.

"Welcome back," the Berintan's voice said, and the bustle of the others stopped.

Rolling over, Philyre faced them, finding all eyes on her, the Enneads all frozen mid-action around the fire. Funanya had been sitting across from her. How she had known Philyre was awake, she did not know. Now that she was, everyone seemed determined to stare at her.

Pulling off the gentle sheet protecting her from the wind, Philyre slowly got to her feet. Her muscles ached, and she remembered the mad run over the dunes. She remembered the earth-shaking steps of the colossus demon following her and the racing beat of her own heart. She remembered falling, then she remembered nothing.

The seer—Dana—her eyes sparkling, handed Philyre a cup, and she drank. The water had a sour tang to it, spiked with jannu plant sap. It would correct her dehydration and help her headache.

Once her tongue was softened by the water, she said, "Why am I alive?"

Dana smiled at her, and Philyre's heart leaped. She usually hated the way the Enneads looked to her for an answer, but this time, Dana's smile filled Philyre with relief and confidence. Happiness, she realized. Because Dana was happy.

"Because it wasn't time to die," the Berintan said. The others, appearing sheepish to Philyre, went back to their tasks.

Funanya prompted the seer with another look.

"Archon Farai has made it to the west gate. He plans to make his way in come morning," the seer said.

"The Heart Hall," Philyre muttered, yawning and regretting it. She wanted to focus, but her eyes still were filled with sleep, and her head was slowly sorting itself out through a throbbing ache.

"Precisely," the seer said. "The portal lies within, and that is what Farai wants more than anything."

"Do we know why?"

"Yes," Dana replied.

Philyre waited, but the seer said nothing more, just smiled at her.

She shook her head, chuckling. "So how do we stop them?" she asked, glancing at Funanya. Philyre ran over the layout of the City between the west gate and the Heart Hall in her mind. The streets were convoluted and could allow multiple ambushes, but the one choke point, assuming the Berintan attackers already had the gate, was the Heart Hall itself. It was built as a fortress with one entrance. Once sealed, the doors could hold back an army.

She remembered the Heart Hall from the original invasion, and how Yarr had prevented the officials of the City from sealing it. It seemed appropriate that the shifter be held off there this time.

"So the steps of the Heart Hall. We can harass them along the route, but once…"

"Not in the open," Funanya interrupted. "You are no match for Farai and his warriors in the open."

"But how…" Before Philyre could finish, Erosan arrived. Confusing him, Erosan sat down to peel off soaking wet boots. Something else moved on the edge of Philyre's vision on the right, but her mind was too tired to pay attention to it.

Dana and Funanya stared at Erosan until he noticed them and said, "Done."

Dana nodded, profoundly pleased.

"The way is clear?" Funanya demanded, less willing to accept such a vague response.

Erosan's face darkened, and he stubbornly stared back at the Berintan. Philyre felt like she was watching a hound demon stalking; it was as if Erosan were raising hackles of his own.

Funanya stared down the Ennead with confidence, her hand tightening on her spear in readiness.

"I said I was done," Erosan groused, shaking his feet off. "Yes, the walkways are cleared."

Philyre had to think about it for a moment but realized Erosan was referring to the aquifer. From any of the dozen entrances, there were routes under the City through those tunnels and waterways. They had all explored that region of the deep underground. Philyre had lost Enneads down there before, fallen from the uneven, broken stones around the overflowing aquifer.

"And you know the way?" Funanya insisted.

"You doubt me? You are the invader here!" Erosan rose to his feet as he spoke, openly reaching for a weapon. Funanya's grip shifted, the spear tip point falling into readiness.

"We all know," Philyre interrupted, stepping between the two opponents and surprising herself by putting her back to Funanya to face Erosan. She had only known the Berintan for a short while, but she felt the greatest threat was Erosan, not Funanya, although she could not say why. "We all know the way, Funanya. Erosan, stand down. Get warmed up. Take food. Rest."

She thought she saw something change in Erosan's angry stare and found herself reaching over her shoulder, groping at air, for the spear that usually lived there. She had never, in all her life, considered the other Ennead a threat, yet the hostility was thick from Erosan tonight.

"We have a problem," a new voice said.

Tearing her eyes from Erosan, Philyre located the speaker standing to the side. She slowly connected the shadow to the movement moving beyond the fire, but there her coherent thoughts ended.

She took a step back, reaching for her spear, this time frantically, and finding it absent. With one hand, she pushed the seer away, placing herself between the newcomer and Dana defensively. Her heart leaped into her throat.

Red eyes, those of a demon, looked back at her, but the speaker's face was calm. Still, Philyre felt like a tauran scenting a keim beast on the prowl.

"Oh relax," Funanya said. "Worry about what he said, not who said it."

Hearing her calm, Philyre slowly released her posture and tried to understand what she was looking at.

The Ennead male was taller than any of them and more muscled than even Erosan. He wore a simple shendyt and had paired kukris on his belt, one of which she recognized as the "spare" Dana had given her before she went into the desert. He looked Ennead enough, and his skin was a particularly dark shade, but his eyes were red as Ero's light at high noon. The sight of them set off a feral terror in Philyre, and she struggled against it as she slowly recognized the Ennead's tattoo.

She had known this shifter in the days before the Berintan invasion. This was Askaran.

"I take it my eyes haven't changed," Askaran groused. His words seemed to be directed at the Berintan.

"Nope," Funanya brightly reported. "Now, what do you mean by a problem?"

Askaran turned his red glare on Erosan, who stiffened under it but did not seem to share Philyre's fear. Instead, Erosan tensed in anger.

"Let me guess," the shifter said as he advanced to stand directly before Erosan. "You were wounded by a demon."

Erosan flinched but quickly squared himself. He set his expression and said nothing.

"Sixteen days ago. It was the day Maurn left. It has healed well," Philyre reported in Erosan's silence.

Askaran glanced over his shoulder, which Philyre could see had been stitched. In Philyre's memories, Askaran the shifter was taller, better. This Ennead looked … not worn out, but distilled. Like Philyre, the shifter had lost any sophistication of Ennead society. They were one small step from being feral themselves.

"So you *do* have a shifter watching over you," Askaran said. "He's due back soon, isn't he?"

"He's late. Usually, it's fifteen days. We were expecting him yesterday," Philyre confirmed.

Askaran turned back to Erosan and looked him up and down. He snorted. "Come on, pup. You and me, now, outside the walls."

To Philyre's surprise, Erosan snarled back. "Why should I listen to you? The shifters have done nothing for us since—"

Askaran scooped up the Ennead by the throat and pressed him against the crumbling wall behind him. Dana stepped forward as if to Erosan's aid, but Funanya put out a hand and delayed her.

"Now," Askaran said. "You come, or I drag you." He dropped Erosan, turned away, and walked through the camp toward the nearest gate.

Erosan contemplated the command for another moment, but Philyre was careful not to show her thoughts on the matter. She wasn't sure if Erosan would want her to overrule the newcomer, or if seeing Philyre's approval might make Erosan all the more determined to disobey.

The seer stared after them, not looking away even after Erosan had vanished down the streets, following the shifter. Her brow remained furled.

"He's doing his job. Protecting you," Funanya said, drawing the seer out of her pensiveness.

Dana cocked her head, squinting into the distance, no doubt seeing something, but her expression remained confused. "I can't see—"

"Course not," Funanya said. "Askaran is … different. His demon's riding close, and so he'll be hidden."

"I can't see Erosan," Dana corrected.

The words sent a chill down Philyre's back.

"Course not," Funanya repeated, her eternal calm unfazed. "You told me once that black blood was poison to Enneads. I didn't realize what that meant until now, but…" she trailed off, reading the expressions of the Enneads surrounding her, including the seer. "Apparently, neither did any of you."

"I don't understand," Philyre said, her voice choked.

Funanya shrugged. "It's going to kill Erosan, right? To be poisoned by demon blood? Don't worry about it. Sing, dance, pray … do whatever it is Enneads do before battle. Askaran will take care of this. Get some food, Philyre. Tomorrow, we'll be taking on a tusked demon. You'll need your strength."

She wanted to scream at her in frustration. She was desperate to know what she was talking about and why she was avoiding explaining. She knew Funanya wouldn't answer, not in front of the others, but she wanted to try. She had once been the leader of the party.

She was meant to guide the others. How could she lead when she did not know where they were going?

She was following a seer once more. That required trusting her.

Her stomach rumbled.

"Got something more to eat? If I'm going to kill a tusked demon, I'll need more than just a bite of fish."

Dana laughed, and Philyre's spirits lifted. Funanya released her grip on the spear, turning it back into a resting position. Retrieving something from a nearby seat, she presented Philyre with a length of white ruin fish meat. Knowing what it was, she raised an eyebrow at her.

"Not for eating," she told him. "But tusked demons don't have any weaknesses I know of. I'm going to show you how to poison a weapon. From what I've heard, even Yarr will go down hard if we can poison him. So will any of Farai's warriors. You've got white ruin fish. How is that on a weapon?"

Philyre glanced at the fish, then at the desert seer. "I don't know."

"Effective," the seer said. The cold tone of the word made her flinch.

Pushing aside her unease, Philyre retrieved a spear of her own and sat down to learn from the Berintan. She tried to stop thinking about Erosan but knew, deep down, that she had been right. Erosan was lost.

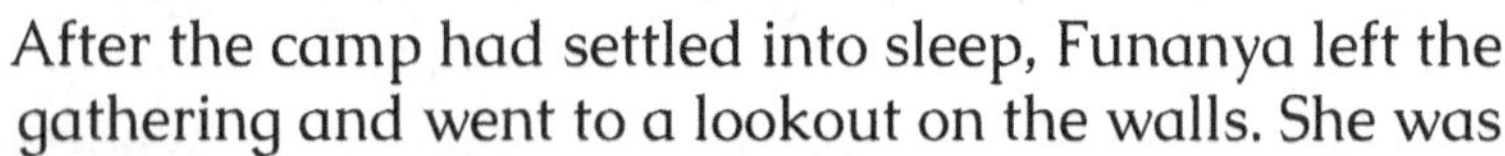

After the camp had settled into sleep, Funanya left the gathering and went to a lookout on the walls. She was not surprised when Askaran appeared, stalking her. He did not speak, not when the demon was so close to the surface. His lust was feral once more, making her suspect he was not merely choosing not to speak, but could not.

She invited him into an abandoned bed.

It was not until his passion had finished that he left her for the balcony. She joined him there, feeling the tension leave him.

His eyes were still red, but Funanya was unafraid. If the demon took him over, he would shift. Until then, he was her Ennead, and she was happy with that.

"I don't envy you," she said, curling up under his arm. "I've killed, but it's different for you, isn't it? Doing that."

He growled, but the sound was light. "You understand it better than any non-shifter I have ever met. I didn't even tell you. Did they all figure it out?"

Funanya shrugged, knowing he would see it despite the pale light. "Maybe. It's not hard, not now." She let the pause linger for a dozen heartbeats before asking, "Is that where all the demons are from? Black blood finding its way into Enneads?"

Askaran sighed. "I think so, once, long ago. My mother talked about it, about our homeland. It was overrun by demons, spreading black blood among us, changing us. In coming here, we created the shifters, those who could come back from that change."

Demons had not always been native in Nanterac, that much she knew, and neither had the Enneads. If the Enneads had come, so had the demons. "Why didn't you leave them in your homeland? Why bring them here with you?"

At last, he turned to face her and smiled, but it was fleeting. "The shifters weren't meant to be. The plan had been to send the demons away, to here. The original thirteen drove them into the Alightening Hall and banished the demons through space to this planet. But one of thirteen had fled his duties and returned to the City. And in doing so, he bound it to the magic, banishing the City as well. As the thirteen were pulled through, they became the first shifters. Only those of their blood can become shifters, although keying a new shifter is never a certain thing."

His gaze was sad when he looked down at her. "We have fought since to prevent what happened on Terac from happening here."

"But never told the population," Funanya said.

Askaran looked back to the stars and moons above. "To avoid panic, the seers and shifters hid it from the people of Terac. They killed any who witnessed a demon being created. They killed those who had been wounded by demons, just in case. They tried to contain it."

"Like a plague."

"Yes, like a plague. But once we came here, we had shifters, and they could fight demons safely. So our purpose became protecting the population from the demons and from the panic. No one could walk the desert without us."

"To protect them," Funanya said.

"And if we failed to do so, to stop any contamination from reaching the City."

She read his expression in the shadows. "Maurn was doing that?" she guessed. "If any of the Enneads here were injured, he was killing them. The others talk about how few survive out here, but it's not just demons killing them. The shifters will do it."

"To protect the population," Askaran said in agreement.

"So Erosan…"

"…is dead," Askaran finished. "I could have arranged it better, had him fall in battle, but he was too close to a change. There was no time. They know black blood is poison. I will tell them I did it to save him from a painful death. That is all they need to know."

"For the best," Funanya agreed, thinking of the way the serpent demon had once chased Askaran, ignoring the Berintan around it. "Be bad if he shifted tomorrow and decided to kill his friends instead of the enemy."

Another growl rumbled from Askaran's throat, this one of pleasure. "You understand."

His posture had changed, no more than tightened muscles but still obvious to Funanya. She put her hand on his arm.

"You're resisting," she said. "Have I not satisfied you enough tonight?"

Askaran grimaced, but he pressed his body against hers as he answered. "I am making up for lost time," he said. "You know me far too well, Berintan."

Hearing the jest, Funanya grinned. "And you, Shifter, need some manners."

Sitting apart in the small house, Dana watched the Enneads adjust to the strange arrival of the shifter among them and the loss of Erosan. She knew they did not understand it, not fully. Only Philyre, the cleverest of them, suspected it was any more than releasing Erosan from the poison that would have killed him anyway.

They all agreed Erosan had been more unsettled of late, and Philyre convinced them the man had been hiding his pain for their sakes, trying to finish his duty. She set up the damned fool as a hero for them to emulate.

Nothing was required of Dana as a result. She understood now more than she had before. All the pieces of history, things that had been shrouded in the haze of distant past, now came to her. Sitting among the ancient stones of her fallen City, the seer saw so much it made her cry.

In her mind, she lay beside Askaran and Funanya. She heard Askaran speaking through Funanya's ears and knew she would never be able to see Askaran with her visions again. But she could see where he passed, what he said, or what he did through the imprints left behind on others. So she listened to Askaran talk of the older world he, himself, had never known and of the secret the seers had kept from the Enneads.

She cried but left the two lovers when Funanya's lust rose and words were left behind.

During her time in the jungle, Dana had spent days alone, hunting or playing in the trees and greenery of the new home. She was used to solitude, but this solitude felt uneasy. Then, she had been free to wander and ponder, never worrying about taking too long to consider something, or even if she reached a conclusion at all. Once done thinking, she could go back to seeking food, or building a new tool, or go for a swim, or any other number of distractions.

Now her mind was not still. She could not ponder without knowing more and more.

She sat in the corner of the house, her eyes tearless for the moment but wearing dried salt on her face. As she winked open her eyes, layers applied themselves over the little house, revealing to her the family who had lived here at the time of the invasion. She knew their fates instantly. The father had been slain when the Berintans had come to the City. The mother had escaped with the baby, who was now six and becoming skilled at weaving, like his mother. The child played with others in the far north, among rocky hollows and under tree-capped shelters. He was lean, for this new home was sparse. His younger sister, born three years ago, had died of fever a few weeks prior. The mother now watched her elder son, terrified of losing him as well. The young Ennead knew of her dread, but carried on, trying to ignore their uncertainty and hiding it from each other.

As she sat, Dana saw the next layer on the home, the grandparents. They had done well. Neither had lived to the invasion.

Before them had been another weaving family, but before that, a baker's. And before that, a carpenter and his twelve children, only one of which had continued the trade. Wood had been common back then and the furnishings elaborate. They had carven perfect forests into the legs of chairs and waterfalls into the surface of tables. They had made everyday door posts into detailed family histories and decorated the eves with monkeys and parrots.

The carpenter had lost ten children to the demon's blood. Upon the tenth, he had walked into the jungle, seeking death himself. He had found it.

Bile rising in her throat, Dana pushed back the vision. In a jolt, she was back in her empty house. She had gone over four hundred years back to the time before the City's arrival on Nanterac, but all that remained now was the dusty shadows of the empty house.

She felt a hand on her shoulder, and she pulled sharply away, scrambling for her blade and brandishing it. There were fresh tears on her face. Her vision was clouded.

Blinking away the tears, she finally recognized Philyre. She carried no light but stood in the starlight of the window, her hand still out cautiously, awaiting recognition.

"A desert seer with a knife," Philyre said, her voice soft as a sigh. "A runner with a spear. A shifter with red eyes. An enemy as a friend…" Her silhouette shrugged. "The world will be upside down when I wake, I fear."

Dana straightened slowly out of the fighting stance Askaran had taught her. She slowly put away the kukri and wiped her face.

"I heard you," Philyre said, approaching with her hand out now that danger was done. She did not say what she had heard, Dana realized. A whimper? Or was that below the stature of a desert seer? A sob? Or perhaps she had screamed when she had seen the carpenter's throat slashed by the demon's claw, a claw that had once been a loving hand.

Desert seers were meant to lead the people with calm and knowing. They were the center of planning, strategy, cunning. She was supposed to be a beacon of hope. She was meant to understand every Ennead of the City, know their names, their dreams, their purpose in life. She was meant to be more than a weeping child.

"I need rest," Dana said, turning away from where the starlight would show her tears. She could not lead these Enneads if she was unable to control her own emotions. "I will sit, trance." She folded her legs under her, not caring that she was in the center of the room. Askaran had taught her this calm, the rest of the shifters. She clung to it, wishing it would give her more comfort now than it had in the past. It had never worked, not like it could for Askaran, but it was the best she could do.

With her eyes shut, trying to hide the layers of knowing that chased her, Dana did not see Philyre sit beside her, but she felt her. The air moved when she sat down, dust tickling their legs. She sat so close, the heat of her warmed Dana's side, even though their skin did not touch. She had removed the spears but still wore her running skirts, like the one she had worn the day of the invasion. She had kept a piece of that tattered cloth, and it was still hooked over her belt on her right side, behind where the kukri could sit.

Behind her eyes, Dana saw Philyre's life, from the first day of memory to this decision to come to her now. It had been a whimper, she knew. Philyre had heard Dana's trembling whine in the darkness and gone to seek her. Her heart was filled with pain upon seeing her in the house, her wide eyes tracking things she could not understand, tears on her face. She hurt knowing Dana was suffering with her gift, and she wished, with all her might, that somehow she could provide some relief.

Then Dana felt it, a warmth beyond any she had known before. Her mind was filled with beauty and awe so pure it made her gasp. Beside her sat an Ennead unlike any other. This Ennead had known battle enough to give her calluses on her heart to match those on her palms from holding spears, yet she was filled with joy. Not the joy of killing—that had been Erosan's joy, or rather the joy of Erosan's demon—but the simple joy of company, of companionship.

In seeing into Philyre's mind, Dana was filled with love.

The layers of the world faded into the background, the whole of her attention now on the Ennead beside her. She leaned to the right, allowing skin contact, and the presence of Philyre's emotions made her senses tingle. A haze, like the warm coverings of a desert wrap against the harsh wind, came over her mind, and there was, blessedly, peace.

Philyre said not a word as Dana laid her head on the runner's shoulder. At the back of her mind, Dana knew Philyre had fallen into a pile of broken walls as a child, scratching scars into the shoulder and neck, but the fact was simple, not steeped in history. She could linger there, with Philyre, without falling down the path into her ancestors or the history of the walls that had scarred her. It was peace.

The tension in Dana's chest eased with a single sigh. She placed a hand on Philyre's knee, filling her mind with the shared joy from the contact. Through Philyre, Dana felt every emotion swelling, from confusion to ecstasy. The moment, shared with Philyre, sealed her from the outside torrent of knowing, and her tears dried instantly.

She felt a kiss on her cheek as she finally let go of the chaos of her mind and, flooded with love, slept.

Farai listened to the seer's muttering words every night. Every night, they were all the same.

Stones and glass. Broken walls. The floor a gaping hole, filling with water...

For the last four nights, the seer had been talking in her sleep more, the sentences clearer and more detailed. *Stone and glass. Broken Walls. The floor a gaping hole, filling with water. Crushing death. Doom and darkness...*

He had tried, after the second night, to trick her into discussing her dreams, but she had refused the chapman. Even when he went to drug her food, she refused to eat. On the third day, he had shoved the drug down her throat, but she had fallen into a stupor. No new mutterings had come of it.

Stone and glass. Broken Walls. Crushing death. Doom and darkness...

On the final night, they camped beyond the walls of the city, Farai felt a hot wind rush over them. Although it had happened only once before, when the army had been camped a day from the city six years before, he recognized it.

A stone formed in his stomach as a sweat broke over his skin. Clenching his teeth, Farai sat up in his bed to listen.

The voice of the Grand Archon came to him, grizzly and sour.

"The gates are open, but the entrance to the Heart Hall is sealed," the voice said.

Farai lowered his voice. None of the other Berintan around him seemed to notice the intrusion of the Grand Archon's will, but he did not want them to think him mad. "We will retrieve the portal as you asked," he answered, "even if it means breaking down the doors of the Heart Hall."

"It is not there, not now," the voice said. "It lies below, in the aquifer. The Heart Hall is unnecessary for you. Send Yarr in, then go to the aquifer."

"We will seek it below, as you say," Farai said, the sweat itching on his skin from the incessant heat.

"Good," Grand Archon Amadi replied. "Be swift. I want my prize. Now listen…"

As the cold words carried in, the impossible heat went on, Farai learned exactly where to find the portal under the city. The aquifer, initially a mystery they had not fully explored on their last visit, would not remain safe this time.

Once the instructions were given, the heat swept away. By comparison, the night felt cool.

Farai again checked the others, but none of the warriors were awake and the sentries were too far away to have overheard. As he settled back into the sheet, Farai glanced at Yarr, who lay with a rock as a pillow and a single sheet over him to keep the glowmoths off. He suspected they would meet a shifter or two within the city. They already knew there were Enneads within, and a guardian shifter was expected. He would have to set Yarr against them.

But he needed Yarr away. The shifter should not be allowed into the aquifer, now that Farai knew where the portal truly lay. The Heart Hall would provide the solution.

Then he needed Funanya dead. The atra poison he layered onto his blades would do that well enough.

CHAPTER 22

Yarr watched from a distance as Farai dragged the Eldest Seer into the City behind the warriors. There were no defenders, disappointing them all. Yarr had expected Farai to use the seer against her people, but no Enneads came out to challenge them. He smelled them in the air and saw evidence of their passage everywhere, but none approached them.

Instead, Farai, dressed in his armor and carrying the blade of his rank, met up with his warriors at the steps of the Heart Hall.

The doors were shut.

In all his time, Yarr had never seen the doors closed. Upon the invasion, he had ensured they remained open at the seer's request. Now on the wrong side of them, the mosaic on the door was confusing. It looked like a spiral of a tropical storm but with trees and water-falls in each arm. The center, which was complete when both enormous doors were closed, showed a city surrounded by sand.

New writing crossed over the door, written in a charcoal black against the sandstone. *For the shifter within*, it read.

From what he recalled of the City, the portal stone was within, or at least it had been until the floor had collapsed. But if that had been false, perhaps it was just within, sitting on a pedestal for the taking.

He could take it and shift to cross the desert. Within three days, he could be handing the portal to Grand Archon Amadi and reaping his rewards.

"What does it say?" Farai asked.

Yarr shrugged. "Something about a shifter." He eyed the door. "I will open it and find out. We will see if the portal is indeed where it was meant to be."

Farai gave him a nod.

Yarr kicked off his sandals. Having already walked shirtless through the shaded streets, he had only to remove the sokoto to be nude. His small bag was left in the lee of a building as he made the change into the monster.

The tusked demon lumbered up the polished glass steps of the Heart Hall and paused for a moment at the entrance. Adjusting his weight back, Yarr squared his shoulder, aimed his enormous horned head, and smashed it into the doors.

Behind him, the seer started laughing, a hysterical cackle Yarr had only heard before when she was drunk.

Yarr leaped back and was peppered with the farthest-flung stones. His scales easily resisted the colored glass shards, although he heard one of the warriors cry out when a stray shard struck his shoulder, cutting him deeply.

The door was smashed wide.

Once the debris settled, Yarr was shocked to see an Ennead standing within the first corridor. Not just an

Ennead, he slowly recognized, but a shifter. In fact, a shifter so close to its demon, the eyes were already red.

And he recognized him.

The seer was still laughing, her mirth reduced to chuckles, but her face tear-streaked from her hysteria.

Farai grabbed her arm and pulled her aside. "Deal with this!" Farai shouted. "We will go around."

Yarr wondered briefly how the Berintans knew where to go from here but decided it did not matter. As impossible as it seemed, Askaran again stood before him. It was time to finish the old shifter off.

The Eldest Seer's protests fell off as she was dragged away. Before the sound of her voice had faded into the distance, the Ennead before Yarr changed.

Although he had defeated the shifter once before, Yarr felt uncertainty for the first time in his life. Askaran had always hidden his demon, worked against it, shifting only when it became absolutely necessary. Yet here, he had held his red eyes even when not shifted. For the first time, Askaran moved like a demon, not an Ennead in a strange body.

But his demon within raged, and Yarr knew better than to try to control it. He became the best of both, a mind of an Ennead with the strength of a monster.

The demon had no fear but charged into the building with horns lowered.

Dana felt the ground shake above and knew the shifters had come to blows. The Heart Hall would hold their battle until one of them was finished. It had been

Askaran's insistence, and she had agreed with keeping them out of the waters.

Down in the aquifer, Funanya and the others were ready, their spears hidden on the walkways, laced with white ruin poison. Funanya knowingly took the position farthest from the entrance. She would be the one to call the attack.

Looking over the aquifer, which stretched for several hundred paces into the distance, Dana surveyed the battleground. Stairs led down from the Hall, but the base of them had been chipped by water and were worn slick. The water covered many of the carvings of the aquifer, leaving the tops of the images visible in the dim torchlight. Swamp plants, none of which were native to Nanterac, clung to the brows and noses of the Enneads depicted on the walls. Even the obsidian eyes were cloudy with algae.

Dana blinked, and the image changed subtly. Now the image was that she had had as a child, a vision brought to her by another desert seer on the night she had fled the City with Askaran. The Eldest Seer had built that vision, planting it into the mind of everyone who came to the Heart Hall. With his final breath, he locked it into place, making it linger even beyond his death. The floor above was caved in, but the lighting was softer in the evening. The water level had been different—lower—and the plants were absent. But the pedestal that had stood in the Heart Hall, trickling water into the great cavern below, had been blasted apart, giving Archon Farai and his misguided desert seer a lie to take home to their master.

In reality, Dana saw now, they had stood but strides from the portal itself, unable to see it through the vision the previous Eldest Seer had placed in their minds. The floor had been intact, unbroken. They could have reached out their hands to touch the portal stone itself, but they had been unable to see it.

A noise echoed down a nearby corridor, and Dana caught a vision of the approaching Berintan party. Had the other seer been left behind, or had she suppressed her protection? Dana was not even sure such a thing was possible. But she saw her enemies approach now with clarity.

Funanya glanced over from the waters, showing she had heard it as well. They waited in the cold water, as ready for Farai and his warriors as they could be, their poisoned spears waiting.

Dana placed her hand on her travel bag, the same one she had carried across the desert. The bottom of it was dripping now, the linen soaked by the blue orb tucked in its depths.

Now that she had her prize, she had to keep it.

Farai walked the path, following the Grand Archon's instructions. The aqueducts all led into the aquifer under the Heart Hall. He moved south along the water's edge until he found another connecting branch, then turned, and approached the main aquifer.

They paused as they entered the cavern itself, but there were too few of them to bother with songs or war cries. Strangely silent, the entire group stood in the entrance, staring. The aquifer chamber was immense. Weak torches set along walkways reflected in the expanse of water. The distant pillars were lit enough to show the vast water that lay between them, but he could not see the far side of the cavern. They had to be here; who else would have lit the torches?

"How, in a desert, is there this much water?" Farai asked.

None of his warriors answered.

Seeing the Eldest Seer lean away, keeping herself in the corridor, Farai drew his first sword. Pulling the gag from her mouth, the archon lowered his khopesh at her throat.

"This is the work of the portal orb," he said. "I know it now. It's not destroyed. Tell me where to find it."

The seer stared up at him, her expression not defiant as it had been of late, but thoughtful. She analyzed his face and then carefully said, "In … a … bag."

Farai's mouth, open for a harsh reprimand, closed slowly. Collecting himself, he said, "We will seek those who carry it. I see evidence of recent passage here. They are expecting us." He took measure of his warriors and found them unusually quiet. Berintans were not accustomed to battles in small numbers. This was no single match and no pitched battle. It was a strange mix of the two, and it left them confused.

But he still saw eagerness in them as he instructed, "Funanya is mine. If any others defend her, cut them down. This is our final battle before the road home, into the glory and praise of the Grand Archon." He lifted his sword, keeping the poisoned edge away from the pooling water. "I will lead the way."

They moved into the cavern, watching the pillars as possible ambushes, and were disappointed until they reached a central crossroads. North would lead to the stairs up to the Heart Hall. Undecided, Farai paused.

Behind him, a warrior gave a cry and stabbed into the water. and Farai glanced back to see an Ennead appearing from the water, spear leading in the attack. Dark skin and the black waters had provided perfect concealment. Splashes sounded around them as more warriors rose from the waters, but all Farai cared about was the golden-skinned warrior he had hunted across the desert who climbed out to confront him.

Farai drew his second sword, certain his back was protected by his finest warriors, and faced Funanya.

"At last," he said.

"Indeed," Funanya replied, her white teeth bright in the torchlight as she smiled. "This ends today."

CHAPTER 23

The Heart Hall their battleground, the shifters fought like giants, forgetting the world below them. The walls and pillars were crushed beneath the muscle of the demons now brought into their strength. Yarr and his demon were as one, the demon dictating the strength and power while Yarr controlled the strategy. Against such a large opponent, it had to be this way.

But Askaran was not a mindless demon to be fooled by quick maneuvers and misdirection. Every time Yarr went to strike, Askaran blocked him. The claws were vicious, and the scales hard as stone. Twice Yarr wounded his enemy, but neither scratch slowed the colossus demon.

Askaran attacked with greater ferocity, and he cut through Yarr's scales. When Yarr swung his tail club in, Askaran bit down on it, trapping him. Using his claws, Askaran hauled Yarr in for a killing bite.

But as they became entangled, the ground buckled. Before the teeth closed over Yarr's throat, they were both falling, stones raining around them.

They landed in water.

Yarr reoriented himself over several moments. They had fallen into the aquifer, causing a cave-in. Not far, Enneads and Berintans were enmeshed in a skirmish, although the dead bodies were mostly Berintan. He spotted the white robes of the Youngest Seer on a separate walkway.

As he made to advance on the seer, he heard a roar. Behind him, Askaran rose from the waters. The debris was thickest here, piles of it forming islands where once only water had lain. Pillars were strewn across like bridges, albeit unsteady ones. Yarr's demon answered the thought, *more like logs over a river, in a place where once that had been a common sight.*

He could not match this shifter, Yarr recognized. Askaran was no longer battling his demon, but using it.

But there was one final trick to be used; Yarr shifted back to Ennead.

The smaller shape slipped through the colossus demon's claws, scratched but no longer held. Confused by the strategy, the colossus demon was awkward in chasing after Yarr. He expected to have a reprieve as Askaran's mind battled with the insane bloodlust of a demon chasing an Ennead. Capitalizing on the disorganized attacks, Yarr ran for the seer.

Before Yarr could reach the young seer, the sounds behind him changed. Glancing over his shoulder, he saw Askaran land, as an Ennead, on the walkway behind him. He was, having regained shape, naked and unarmed. His eyes remained as red as a demon's form.

Unarmed, he could beat him. Yarr did not need the seer at all.

"You are an idiot to challenge me like this," Yarr taunted, turning. "Couldn't keep your demon in check when an Ennead is the target?" He waited as Askaran approached.

Once he was within reach, Yarr struck.

Askaran moved faster than Yarr had ever seen. The muscles of the Ennead were thicker as if the demon were still lingering in the body. Before Yarr could finish the strike, he felt the crunch of a fist in his ribs at the sternum. He slid on the smooth surface of the walkway, falling back a dozen paces.

The demon in him answered. If Askaran could harness a demon's strength even in Ennead form, so could Yarr. He had been balancing with his demon for more years than Askaran, who had spent centuries denying his beast. If anyone could bring Ennead and demon together in one form, it would be Yarr, not Askaran.

Despite being winded, Yarr was on his feet before Askaran was atop him. He led with a punch and caught Askaran in the chest before he could dodge or block. Fast as Askaran was, Yarr matched him in speed, but Askaran's strength was greater, forcing Yarr to deflect blows instead of blocking them directly. But Yarr was a veteran who preferred to be without weapons. He knew how to best aim his strikes.

Askaran stumbled to one knee when Yarr kicked out, pulling him over. Seizing the opportunity, Yarr moved in, lashing down at the other shifter with enough strength to crack an Ennead's skull.

With sudden speed, proving he had led Yarr on, Askaran caught Yarr's fist. Yarr realized he had put his weight entirely into the strike and could not pull away.

In the next instant, Askaran's other fist slammed into Yarr's chin. The bones shattered, splinteringing into soft tissue deep enough to steal all coherent thought.

Yarr knew he was falling back but never felt the landing.

Once the hiding places were given away, the main body of Enneads attacked the invading Berintans. No longer subdued villagers accustomed to shifters doing their work, these were hardened warriors of the desert. Funanya was pleased to see them challenge the Berintan warriors who had come with Farai, even strike a few down by surprise and toss them into the water. The poisons were quickly in the blood of those who had been caught unaware. Those would soon fall, leaving only a handful for Philyre and her Enneads to confront.

Funanya herself had one target, the archon. So long as Farai lived, the competition for the portal would remain, and the city would never rest. Askaran had his hands full with Yarr now. Farai was too dangerous to leave for the youngers. He was Funanya's alone.

Funanya squared herself before the man who had once been her commander. Her spear and hunting knife faced off with his fine armor and his swords, one obsidian and one stolen Ennead metal khopesh.

Seeing her, Farai released his armor ties, ready in case he fell into the water. They were all fine swimmers, but no one swam well weighted by leathers. Even the Enneads had forgone any protection for their attack, knowing anything that impinged their movement could spell death in the deep water.

He dropped his armor, his expression a snarling smirk as his eyes fixed on her.

Funanya leveled her spear at him in readiness. The clumsy spear had not been designed for throwing but for long thrusts. She had shortened it to make faster attacks possible but limiting its reach. Against Farai's swords, it had seemed a good trade-off.

"Indeed. This ends today."

Teasing, she made a short jab at his side, but he swept the khopesh across and knocked it wide. The scythe-shaped weapon was clumsy in blocking, reminding Funanya that he had had little experience with it during the six quiet years since the conquest. Keeping her spear central, Funanya repeated the poke, but at the other side. He knocked it aside again. The shaft of the spear—taken from the shifters's stronghold in the Valley of Vaseil—had been all but petrified by time and was too strong to be damaged by the sword's edge. It had dulled two saw blades when they had gone to shorten it and showed no danger of being injured by Farai's metal blade.

Farai answered the second tap with a swing from his Ennead khopesh, knocking the spear wide, then slashing at her shoulder with his Berintan blade, edged with obsidian but made of wood. While it lacked the strength of the metal, it was sharpened to a fine edge, allowing it to cut even with the barest touch.

Funanya swung the spear around ahead of the sword, rotating it to block the obsidian edge. She used both ends of the spear, the blade facing the obsidian and the haft facing the khopesh. Her hands stayed centered on the shaft, requiring only tiny motions to pivot it into Farai's next attack.

He moved in closer, resorting to tight jabs of the swords that relied on their edge and less on his speed or strength. The khopesh had been poorly maintained, Funanya recognized. She had seen how Askaran had oiled his kukris. The metal was strong, but it blunted easily and rusted if allowed to dry out.

She could see rust on Farai's blade. In his ignorance, would he know how to sharpen a metal sword? The edge was already irregular, chipped. Where a chip on an obsidian edge revealed new sharpness, a chip in the metal would weaken this blade, particularly if he was not using momentum and strength to cut deeply.

But it did not have to cut deeply. Dana had warned he had lined the weapon with atra poison. One cut would be the end.

The walkways limited their movement. Funanya drove him back until he was beside the pillar. Using the pillar itself as a wall, she skipped over his shoulder. She landed and lunged, completely changing her weight and striking with the haft of the spear. She wished it could be the blade end, where she had placed the white ruin poison, but did not have time to rotate the weapon sufficiently.

The butt of the spear slammed into his left shoulder with enough force to break bone.

He cried out and turned, lashing at her with both blades faster than she could match. She kept the blades from touching her skin but could do little else. She accepted being driven back.

The frenzy began to slow as the strength went out of his left arm, the deep bruising, or even possible break, weakening him. The khopesh moved with less precision.

Funanya dropped low on the edge of the walkway. Farai swung his strongest arm in, and Funanya knocked it aside with her spear. She pivoted the spear and drove the tip for his abdomen, but he blocked it with the khopesh, the metal of the blade still strong enough to keep her spear from his belly. His sword and her spear tip, thrown wide, went into the water briefly, splashing both Funanya and the walkway with cold water.

Funanya stood, slamming Farai back a step with her shoulder now that both blades were set too wide to cut at her.

He stumbled back but slipped in the blood and water that had pooled behind him. Sliding, Farai went down onto one knee to catch himself.

Vaguely, Funanya heard a loud crash far above her, but she ignored it as irrelevant.

One hand on the spear, Funanya stabbed for Farai's throat before he could rise.

Farai slapped the spear aside with his khopesh, and the edge caught in the wood of the shaft. When she rotated her spear back to guard her center, she pulled the blade from Farai's weakened grip. It flipped away from them, clattered off the pillar, and fell into the water.

As she moved to stab down in finality, an ear-splitting crack shot through the cavern. Reflexively, she looked up to see the roof break, split, and fall in.

She did not fear the cave-in; it was far enough from the battles to be harmless to her allies. No, what caused her terror was the sight of two entwined monsters falling through the floor of the Heart Hall and crashing into the water on the far end of the walkways she stood on.

Turning her attention quickly back to Farai, she was too late to stop him from knocking her spear aside. Farai's next slash caught on the clothing, then the skin of her arm. She stumbled away quickly, trying to gather herself.

She felt her skin burn where the sword left its teeth marks in her right forearm, but she paid no attention to it. The sword had been in the water. The atra poison would have washed off. She had to hope so.

By the time she again lifted her spear, the Berintan was gone from the walkway.

She searched but saw no sign of him except a wet puddle of blood and water at the walkway's edge.

A roar interrupted her search. The shifters at the far side of the cavern crashed into each other once more. The entire cavern shook.

The rest of Farai's warriors had fallen, either into the water or along the walkways. Philyre walked among them, only three of her Ennead fighters with her. They had found another survivor and were tending him, their leader keeping a wary eye on the rampaging shifters not far from their position.

As she went to join Philyre, Funanya approached with her spear lowered to the edges of the walkway in readiness. She doubted Farai would have the strength to swim with his wounded shoulder, but she would not be caught unprepared if he surprised her.

"Philyre!" another voice called before Funanya could identify herself to the Ennead on the walkway. All eyes turned to the speaker, Dana, who was on another walkway a dozen paces distant. "Black blood! Stay out of the water!"

Funanya remembered the water in the hides in the Valley of Vaseil and how careful the shifter had been to keep the seer from that water after the demon had been slain in the room. The blood would dilute, but how much?

The Youngest Seer herself was soaking wet. Like the Enneads and Funanya had before the battle, Dana had been hiding in the water. She had disappeared as they had waited, citing a need somewhere else. Now, she stood alone on a walkway behind them, her bag held tightly to her side, shouting a warning.

"Head back to—" Philyre shouted back, her voice catching when she, like Funanya, saw something move behind Dana.

"Dana! Look out!" Funanya shouted.

Farai had risen from the water behind her, still carrying his obsidian and wood sword. The seer failed to turn fast enough. He slashed the blade across her back.

Philyre rushed forward but stopped at the edge of the walkway. She could swim—Funanya had seen all the Enneads do so as they set their ambush—but now the warning from Dana stopped her. She saw Philyre grit her teeth, then sprint off down the walkway, seeking a way across.

Funanya had no such trepidation. She dove into the water, her spear in hand and an Ennead blade tucked into her belt.

Funanya caught only glimpses as she swam to Dana's aid. The seer had reacted with warrior's strength and stood with her weapons in hand opposite Farai. But her bag had been cut at the strap, and Farai had it in hand as he positioned himself across from Dana, his sword leveled to keep her back. He wore a sick grin for a moment and attacked, seeming surprised when the seer responded with her own blades. She turned his strike and cut at his chest. He had to dodge back. He tried twice more but with similar results. One of her attacks even shallowly slit his thigh.

Funanya spotted Askaran approaching from the far side, running to Dana's aid. She felt triumphant. So long as Dana could hold him off, Funanya would soon be behind Farai and Askaran before him. His end was at hand.

But Farai glanced to the side. To her surprise, he pulled a knife, throwing it at Askaran as the shifter began to charge him in earnest. Ignoring the seer, Farai fled down the walkway, vanishing into the corridors and the shadows there.

Although the knife had not hit her, Dana collapsed in his wake.

Funanya pulled herself out of the water, checking on Dana first. The girl had a thin line of blood down her back where Farai had sliced at her but otherwise was hale. With having been in the water, all poison would be off the blades, and the cut itself was minor, but Dana's face was a mask of pure abject horror as she watched him flee, bag in his hand.

"What's wrong?" Funanya demanded, taking Dana by the shoulders and shaking her gently. The wide, dark eyes of the seer remained vacant, but her mouth moved slowly.

"The orb…"

Funanya tried to follow the gaze of the seer, but she was staring into darkness, looking down the corridor where Farai had vanished. The girl dropped her weapons. One clattered at her feet, but the other slipped from the edge and vanished into the deep dark of the water.

"What…" As the realization struck her, Philyre arrived. She wrapped her arms around the seer protectively, and Funanya was too shocked to even comment about the closeness.

"The portal orb," Dana whispered. "I had it."

"In the bag," Funanya finished when the seer let her words trail off. "So? Let's go get—" She meant to call for Askaran to join them, certain the knife had been too minor for it to stop the mighty shifter.

She stopped, her chest tightening. Dana's tear-filled eyes narrowed, the whites flickering as they tracked invisible things.

She knew the Ennead was seeing visions and knew that, by her terrified expression, they were unpleasant, but Funanya still jumped back when Dana spun around, facing back where the shifters had finished their battle, and screamed.

Askaran kneeled on the walkway a dozen paces away. He clutched his side, teetering. The word he choked out stopped Funanya's heart in her chest.

"Atra."

Then he too fell.

Funanya's head spun as she rushed to Askaran's side. He had a single open wound across the shoulder where the knife had grazed him, and the flesh around it was white-tinged, like skin soaked in water for too long. But he gasped as he fell, his eyes rolling back.

Farai poisoning his blades had been expected, but had the knife had enough remaining after the swim to kill? It had been sheathed…

Atra poison would make a grown man or woman collapse when given in water, as Funanya had. But in a wound, it was far more dangerous. The effects were swift and profound. It would stop his heart in a matter of moments.

Farai would have an antidote. Any warrior dealing with the poison risked being his own killer when handling it without that. But Askaran did not have time for her to chase Farai down. With every breath, his face blanched further, his lips taking on a blue tinge. His mouth was now open in the empty effort for air that would never fill his lungs, not with the poison strangling him.

She remembered that feeling and knew his was faster, worse. She kneeled beside him, her fingers finding his pulse on his throat as it slowed. Beyond them, Dana was crouched, sobbing as Philyre comforted her uselessly.

Askaran's voice came to her, a memory from a lifetime before when they had been unexpected enemies, meeting in the desert. Then, he had shown her the white ruin fish, warning her, "Your heart will speed before you have even taken your second bite, and it will stop by the third."

If atra would slow his heart, could white ruin poison do the opposite?

Having been in the water, Funanya rushed to Philyre. "Your knife! Give me your knife!"

The Ennead gave it over without question, but the sobs from the seer seemed to soften after she did.

Running back to Askaran, Funanya grit her teeth and, wincing, cut Askaran across his thick shoulder, right across the demon tattoo.

He gave a gasp of shock, allowing her to take solace in hearing him breathe.

"Watch Askaran," she commanded the approaching survivors as she scooped up her spear. She let out a long, stabilizing breath, her eyes on the passageway where Farai had vanished. "And get out of my way."

She would take the antidote from Farai's corpse if required, but she would have it.

Bolting down the walkways, Funanya rushed through the dark passages, the only light the reflections from the main aquifer. "Farai!" she called, knowing he would hear her in the echoes. "Farai! You coward!"

After two corridors, she caught sight of the obsidian blade coming down at her as she rounded a corner.

Dodging, Funanya fell from the walkway, but the water nearest the exit, which she could see at the end of this corridor, was shallow. When she rose to her feet, holding her shortened spear, the water reached her ankles. She had already forgone footwear and found the smooth tile easy on her bare soles despite the fast current pulling on her. The cave-in had cracked the wall and floor closer to the exit, drawing the water steadily, like a river, down into a dark opening near the stairs out.

Farai followed his strike with a throw; a second knife sailed after her. Instinctually, Funanya swung her spear across the path and knocked it wide. The knife clattered into the stone wall and shattered, littering the water with obsidian shards.

Lowering himself from his hiding place in a florid alcove, Farai's expression was savage. The face paint of his ark had been washed away by the swim, and he was already bruised from their earlier fight. The sword was in his right hand, while he held his left tighter against his body to shield it. He wore the seer's bag over one shoulder. Funanya caught sight of an empty vial in the alcove and thought she could see the thin white fluid it had once contained on the edge of the obsidian sword he now pointed at her.

But in that pouch on his belt, she would find the antidote, she was certain.

She lowered herself, ready and balanced. Something pricked against her feet, and she realized the missed throw had filled the water around her with obsidian, each piece able to slice her bare skin should she step on it.

Sliding her feet, Funanya met Farai as he dropped into the water from the walkway, his feet protected by sandals.

"Should have stayed with your new friends," he taunted, the familiar obsidian blade glittering in his hand.

Funanya rotated her grip, testing the purchase of the wet shaft. Content, she replied, "I will return to them shortly."

They had closed, and Funanya stabbed the spear in. Farai pushed the spear toward his feet with his sword, counting on the spear being too short to strike him. He stepped in, ready to use his sword to cut into Funanya's core.

But she stepped forward as well, too close for the swing of a blade. Mirroring Askaran's style, she slammed her knee into his chest. He bent forward but held his weapon, stabbing into the tight space. She dared not take even a light wound. There could be poison in it.

Would they die together?

"Funanya!" someone shouted, and Farai's attention turned to the speaker. Standing in the light seeping down the corridor from the exit, Funanya saw Philyre.

Philyre threw her spear.

The throw promised to impale Farai, and the archon pivoted to avoid it. He was stronger than Funanya and dragged her with him, trying to put her into the path of the attack.

Funanya pulled down, slipping under his arm. The shards of obsidian in the water cut into her left arm and side. The water flowed red.

Philyre's spear sank into Farai's gut. He doubled up, howling.

Seeing him drop his sword, Funanya snatched it up and raked it across the inside of the archon's leg from where she crouched before his bent body.

The howl was cut short. The man gasped, realization striking in a blink. The water at their feet was now crimson, despite the ongoing flow of fresh water washing across their ankles.

"I brought my friends with me," she told him, using the blade to cut his belt—a familiar action even after the years—and grabbed his pouch.

He staggered a step, then collapsed. As he struggled to hold himself upright a moment more, Philyre sliced his throat with a kukri. With a final gurgling protest, the Berintan fell face-first into the shallow water.

"The bag!" Dana shouted from the passageway.

Funanya was already turning, ready to run back to Askaran, but paused when she saw Dana standing where she had recently seen Philyre. The seer was pointing at Farai.

The seer's bag lay beside the dead archon. Teased open by the flow, the bag released its contents. In the swift running water, a blue orb of glass rolled quickly away, heading for the cleft in the stone and the abyss beyond it.

Philyre scrambled after it, but Funanya knew she could not catch it. It bounced and slipped over the tiles, right into the opening, to fall into the impossible depths below.

And there it paused, trapped right where the drop began. While the water flowed around it, the orb stayed suspended in the gap, waiting until Philyre retrieved it.

Funanya saw the flicker of light on a thin fishing line that had formed a net to catch the wayward portal orb. From the top of the stairs leading out, a voice said, "Done."

The Eldest Seer sat on the stairs, her frown prominent and self-important. "Good," she added, narrowing her eyes on Funanya. "Do you have what you need?"

Made aware of the pouch in her hand, and the life that may yet be fading, Funanya ripped open the mouth of the pouch and found the vials. For each one of poison, one was an antidote.

Grabbing one, she sped back along the walkways, desperate to reach Askaran before he breathed his last. Behind her, she heard Dana say, "But we cannot see demons."

"Dear child," the Eldest Seer answered in a voice that carried deep into the aquifer, "I do not know why this Berintan seeks what she seeks, but I know what it is. And I know she helped me, so I will help her. Even I cannot say if it will be in time."

CHAPTER 24

When Dana finally felt the sun on her face again, she became aware of the tears that were drying on her cheeks. Behind her, Askaran followed, supported on one side by Funanya. Philyre had come with them, while three other survivors fished out Archon Farai's body and disposed of it in the desert for the scavengers. They had already dragged out the bodies of the Berintans that could be easily reached without touching the water. Shifters would have to fetch the others.

It was over. They were safe.

Maurn arrived three days later, having been caught in a sandstorm. He and Askaran spoke at length before going into the aquifer and doing the deed with Funanya's help. Dana noted that Maurn kept staring at the Berintan warrior. It was not affection, not like the look Funanya and Askaran shared, but rather a profound respect.

The Eldest Seer taught Dana what she could about the gift they shared. Dana knew, although she could not see it, that their conversations would be few. The Eldest Seer was already letting go. The day Maurn left, she walked into the desert like a shifter and was not seen again.

The Enneads would return once Maurn told them of the City's renewal. By then, the poison of the black blood would be washed from the waters, and the City could be rebuilt.

And once they returned, Dana would turn her attention to the Berintans. She would not have the attack come again. Grand Archon Amadi had already tried to claim the portal twice, and Dana suspected he would do so again once it became clear his agents had failed. They would have to act first to address this threat.

But for all her chasing of visions, she could not see this Grand Archon. She wanted to believe it was because he was too distant, but Dana knew in her heart it was not so.

The implications of that woke her at night and would, she knew, until she went back across the desert, and found the monster himself.

The End

CHAPTER 1

Cloaked from cowl to ankle in shour cloth, Amadi paced the mirror hall, the unnatural fabric making no sound as he moved. In each polished glass, stolen from the Last City of the Ennead, his form was as indistinct as a shadow, blurred by the weave of the cloth.

He paused at one mirror and glared into the sand-etched surface. The images of a prophecy flashed through the frame, distorted by the irregular glass. His visions were stronger in the mirrored surface; what he saw within his mind was given clearer form. While others had stolen weapons and metals from the ransacked city, Amadi had found only one treasure worthwhile, mirrors. Far better than the still waters or polished metal surfaces he had utilized in the past, the mirrors brought his visions into focus.

Within the glass, a drop of water slid out of a blue glass stone, dripping down the stone pillar on which the stone rested. The carvings of the stone were vines never grown on Nanterac. The drop joined the blue-lit waters deep in a cavern.

He knew the stone, the portal stone of the Last City. He had once believed it destroyed, but the powers of the Seer who had created that illusion were fading. The stone had been there, mounted over the underground cistern of the Last City. Above, the city itself was mostly empty, the Enneads scattered by battles and driven north by Amadi's Berintan army years ago.

A woman moved in the shadows along the walkways in the vision, her skin the muted gold of a Berintan. She wore no face painting of rank or clan, an outcast despite her formidable skills. Once, she had presided over her own clan as an archon sworn to Amadi. Now, Funanya was a source of endless frustration for him.

In the vision, he saw her battle Archon Farai, her spear a match for Farai's obsidian sword. Farai was beaten into retreat and fled down a corridor. Water splashed, enormous demons wrestling in the waters nearby.

Amadi pulled his visions away. These things had happened already; he could do nothing with this information. Farai was slain. Funanya's friends resided in the city now, although the outcast herself had made a home at a nearby oasis instead.

The Ennead city no longer interested Amadi. Only the portal stone mattered.

Straining at the magic, he brought his attention back to the stone's current whereabouts. It fought against him, like swimming against a current, and Amadi gritted his teeth against its pull. The stone was his way home. He would have it.

The image in the mirror tracked through dou-ble-sunset-lit skies, dove through the cloud of a dust devil on the reg desert, then rose over the sweeping red sand dunes. The light of the suns went blue as Ero, the red sun, set, leaving the desert in a cerulean glow. The rare flicker of plants flashed below his sights as he approached his target.

But as he spotted the Last City's walls, the vision blinked out, and he was left staring at his own twisted reflection in the mirror. His face was shrouded entirely, a column of dark cloth with a small slit for vision.

Biting back on his frustration, Amadi closed his eyes. His rage swelled, then subsided, as he drew a long breath. *Smashing the mirror will accomplish nothing,* he warned himself.

It would make me feel better.

Physical power was not needed, not yet. The powers of the mind—his hekau—were all he required.

Ignoring the disagreement within him, Amadi checked the mirror hall. Once he was certain he was still alone, he pulled out the golden case from the folds of his shour cloak.

The black leaves of the shaben tree, dried and crum-bled, filled the palm-sized box. The smell of it was like a crushed beetle in the mud, musty yet sour. If they were soaked in spirits for five days, the fibers could be woven into shour that was safe to wear, but, without that preparation, the leaves and bark of the black tree were considered poison.

It has killed many, the voice within pointed out. *Just not in the manner they anticipated.* Amadi selected a small spiral of leaves with gloved fingers. He closed the box and stowed it once more. Then, ready, he stared into the mirror and willed the power of his hekau back on its quest.

He passed over mountains in his vision this time, through the crumbling foothills and into the sands of the deserts once more. An oasis flashed below him as the light intensified in blue sunset. He felt the wind at his back, pushing him like he was a predator bird soaring toward prey.

The wind seemed to turn in the next blink. Like a storm front, the pressure rose against him, fighting to push him back from his goal. The force rose until his travels over the desert came to a halt, leaving him suspended in the dimming light of a cloudless sky.

Unclenching his teeth, Amadi delicately placed a small shard of shaben leaf into his mouth.

The visions accelerated, blasting through resistance and launching his mind forward through time. The mirror's surface appeared to crack, a dozen different manifestations of the future occupying the spaces between the fissures. As soon as he brought his attention to one, the others changed to match, following the next thought to the next prediction.

At times, he felt resistance, but the hekau blasted through the obstacles. Nothing could hide from him now.

He put the scenes to memory as fast as they appeared, guiding the amplified powers to the single goal, the portal orb.

In a moment of clarity, all the visions coalesced.

A white-robed Ennead woman—no, she looked to be a girl still—stood atop a dune. The wind could not move her braided tangle of black hair as she looked back to the city. She adjusted the travel bag on her shoulder and moved away, the hem of her sand-cloak newly mended. She had wrapped her legs well against the blowing sands; only her face showed its dark skin.

A haze covered her features like heat rising through the double sun's intensity, but that in itself identified her. She was a seer, the last on Nanterac. Without the shaben leaf, he would not have even been able to get this close to her in visions.

But with the enhancing hekau of the toxic plant, he could do more than just observe. He would have it.

Determination seeped through, and he willed his own vision to form, a false vision much like the one that had hidden the portal orb from him for years. Into that vision, he poured the unbridled strength begotten from the shaben leaf, lending it exquisite detail and authenticity. Then, his concentration failing, he gifted the vision to the girl he had seen.

Amadi awoke slumped against the far wall, facing the now-cracked mirror. His head throbbed, the taste of dirt still on his tongue. The red haze over his vision slowly cleared, allowing him to recognize the shadows of evening.

Foolish risk, he heard in his ear.

Amadi came to his feet and checked himself over; the shour had not slipped. Even if an attendant had come through, they would not have seen anything but the black cloth. And the Berintan people knew better than to disturb their Grand Archon, even if they did not understand what he was doing.

"It worked," he muttered to himself, standing tall. His hand ached, and he glanced down to see black blood oozing through the dark cloth. "You punched the mirror."

Had to, the voice within answered. *Foolish risk.*

"It will get us home," he replied. There were other mirrors should he need the power of the shaben leaf again. But for now, his muscles felt as if they had been stretched. He would have to retreat to a trance and rejuvenate. Stitching his hand would be best, but he had no one to perform that task. It would not do for the Berinta to see their god bleed.

Home, the beast within grumbled. *Freedom.*

"Perhaps," was all Amadi could offer. He did not know what lay beyond the portal now—it had been hundreds of years since the Enneads had come to this world—but it had to be better than the hellhole that was Nanterac.

Leaving the mirror hall, Amadi walked the marble halls of his Grand House and into the cavern below. Surrounded by the drip of water running down the cracks of the cave, he settled down into a trance.

It was only a matter of time. If you enjoyed this book, hop over to your favorite platform and leave a review!

Book Club Questions

1. Enneads insist that all jobs have equal value, that a shifter is no more valuable than a cobbler. Why would a society such as that struggle? Where would it excel?

2. Berintans believe only your skill matters, having no concept of birthright. Where would that society struggle? Where would it excel?

3. How did the environment control the tension and struggles in the story?

4. What did you think of Funanya's change of loyalty? Did it feel logical or contrived?

5. Many fantasy novels focus on the hero's journey or young protagonists entering the world. How did "To Walk into the Sands" deviate from that?

6. The demons' origins are revealed near the end of the book. Did you suspect it? What instances of foreshadowing were there? Was it well balanced or too obvious for you?

7. If you had to choose a color for each character (Dana, Funanya, and Asakaran) which would you choose and why?

8. Dana sees many futures and must choose the correct one to be right about what will happen. What experiences with fortune-telling have you had? Were they accurate or not?

9. What impact would knowing futures, even possible ones, have on the human mind? How would it change our society?

10. What would have happened if Funanya had been unable to call Askaran back from the colossus demon form? How would his absence change the ending?

Follow the author at dlambertauthor.com.
Get special updates and deals by signing up
to the Newsletter! Start with a FREE EXCLUSIVE
short story series of four books of Espar,
including the short "To Dream"!

Author Bio

At a young age, Deborah's rampant imagination kept her up, lending great detail to all the terrible things lurking in the night. In desperation, her mother suggested she invent her own stories to distract her brain. She has been doing that since, channeling her ideas into sword-and-sorcery-style fantasy novels and shorts.

In her other life, Deborah is a veterinarian. She lives in Sooke with her husband of 15+ years, their two sons, and three demanding felines.

Discover more at
4HorsemenPublications.com

10% off using HORSEMEN10

www.ingramcontent.com/pod-product-compliance
Lightning Source LLC
Chambersburg PA
CBHW020328010826
48973CB00005B/1175